TALE OF THE STEADFAST BROTHERHOOD

K.C. NORTON

RILEY ROOKHOUSE

Cover illustration by Hannah Elizabeth, HannahElizabeth.ca

Cover lettering by James T. Egan, BookflyDesign.com

Managing editor: Diane Callahan, QuotidianWriter.com

Copy editor: Angela Traficante, LambdaEditing.com

Sign up for notifications of upcoming releases by Riley Rookhouse at RileyRookhouse.com

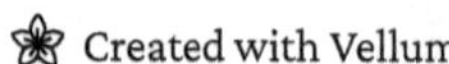 Created with Vellum

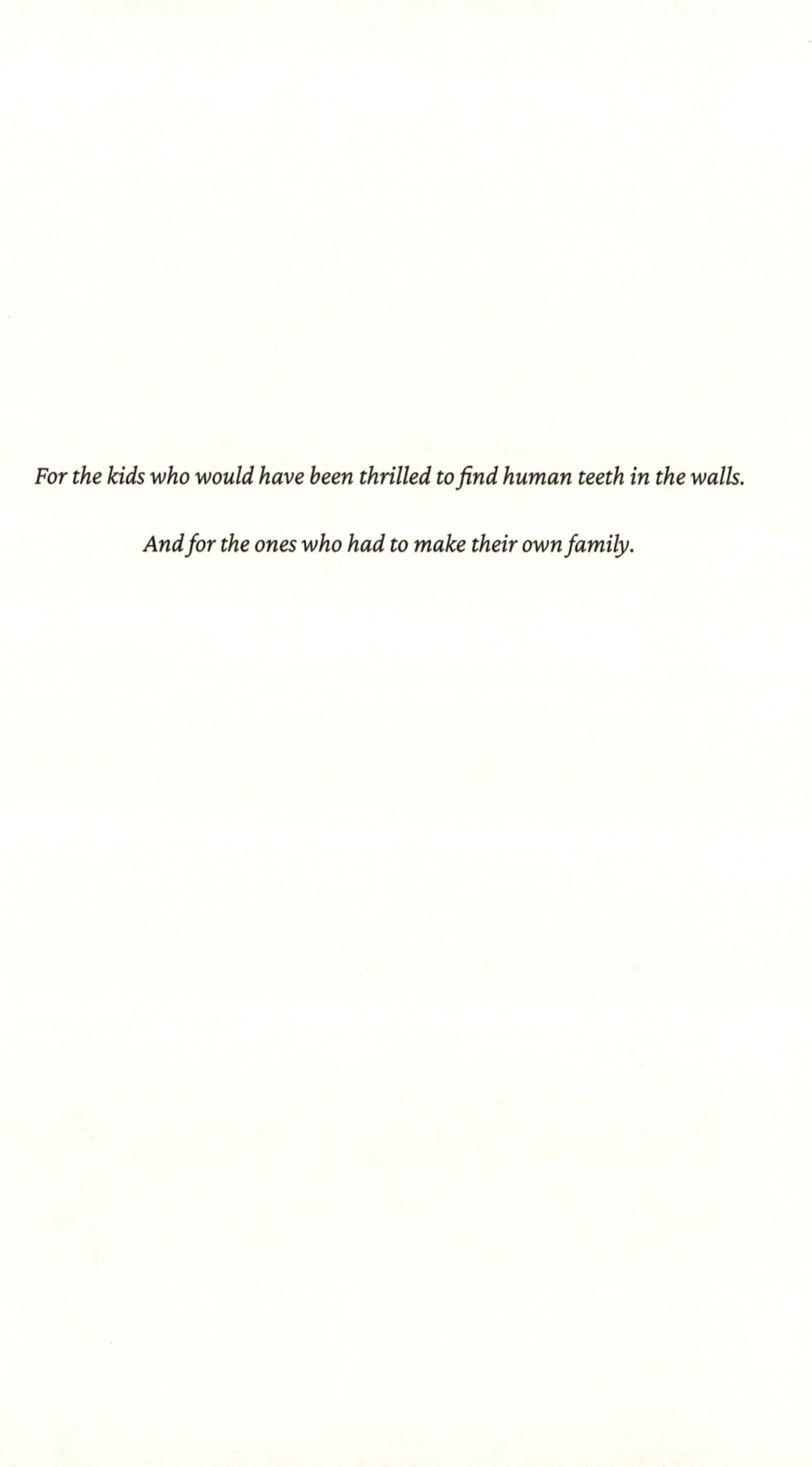

For the kids who would have been thrilled to find human teeth in the walls.

And for the ones who had to make their own family.

CHAPTER

ONE

I had only been alive for seven months or so—and only conscious for one of those—when I first laid eyes on mainland Dregandresal. I had spent my whole life, up to that point, following my irritable creator throughout the gray, damp confines of Kovin Isle. My disappointment upon viewing the mainland could not be overstated, for it was just as monochrome and windswept as the island we had so recently left behind.

"You don't suppose that the ship got turned around halfway across the Split Seas, do you?" I asked as I examined the buildings.

They could easily have fit in at the port in Upper Bound, although Hudson of Hardwick Home was notably absent. The rest might as well have been a copy of the port city we had left behind nearly two weeks before, with a large population of broad-winged skipgulls making their homes along the rocky embankment to the east and west of the main harbor. The only difference I could see from where I stood was that there was no great hall like Fenguard Keep watching over the city from a vantage point above.

"Nope," Emerald grunted. "This is Kinmore, all right. I remember the smell well enough."

I itched to lay my hand on one of his arms and slip into his senses, just for a moment. Judging by the way he wrinkled his broad, upturned nose, the smell was an unpleasant one, but I wouldn't have cared. As a creature made of little more than light and magic, I could not touch, taste, or smell anything in my current state. The only time I had ever been capable of doing so was when I inhabited Emerald's body.

At the time, given the circumstances, I had not been able to enjoy the experience. The only opportunity I had to experience such things on my own were within the confines of my mind-cottage, and I could not be sure that what I experienced there matched the real world, or whether it was entirely fabricated from my own imagination.

Emerald leaned against the railing of our ship, a three-masted frigate known as the *Harbinger*, and stared out over the rainy sea. He did not look like a man who was coming home. Debatably, he did not look like a man at all. There were those who believed that his half-jotunn heritage made him something else entirely: a monster at worst and a beast at best. He was taller than any human I'd ever met by a long way, and the shorn-off nubs of his tusks stretched his mouth wider than most people's. His gray-green skin set him apart, as did the squareness of both his figure and his features.

When he had created me, Emerald had designed me not as his mirror, but as his antithesis. Regardless of whether I appeared as Simon—as I had during our voyage—or as Simone, I was lean and fine boned, and would never have been mistaken as anything but human. With practice, I was learning to not only alter my mode of dress, but also the small details about my person, although I was never able to stray *too* far from his original design. I could not change the color of my scarlet hair, although I had managed to give myself freckles once. Emerald had never been able to satisfactorily explain how I came to be more than a magic spell, but whatever the case, his will still held sway over me in forms both large and small.

It was easy to work out why my looks mattered so much to my friend. I was painfully aware that he despised his appearance after a lifetime of abuses, and he wished that he could be other than he was. I did not feel the same. If I had been the one to conjure *him* from thin air, I would not have desired to change a single aspect of his person.

Well, aside from his fashion sense. And possibly his feeling of self-worth, although I was increasingly convinced that the two were inexorably intertwined.

When I failed to reply to his observation, he cast me a sidelong glance. *[What are you plotting over there, Crim?]* he asked through our mental link.

[To say that I'm plotting would be an overstatement, I'm sure.] I hastily averted my eyes, determined not to reveal the least hint of jealousy that he could interact with the world in ways that were denied to me. Sometimes I was able to appreciate the irony of how much each of us longed to possess traits the other took for granted; today was not one of those days. *[I'm simply wondering what we'll find at... 'home.']*

Emerald grunted in disgust. *[Kinmore isn't home, any more than the members of the Brotherhood are family. Other than Brother Harmony, there's no one there who will be happy to see me. The followers of Guise don't look kindly on the Aidea. I have no doubt that even Harmony will be disappointed to learn that I have embraced my talent for lightweaving in the years since I left.]*

That revelation gave me pause. All through our interminable boat passage to the mainland, I had given my attention to monitoring the well-being of my surly companion. It was far more important to me that he refrain from falling back into his cups, and to that end, I had done my best not to pry into delicate subjects. There was, I felt quite certain, no subject more delicate than his childhood—the little hints he had given me made that quite clear. All the same, we were bound for Kinmore with the express intent of delving into his past, shrouded in mystery though it remained to me.

Perhaps the time for prying had come at last.

[If Harmony is your friend,] I asked, *[then why would he ask you to limit yourself by not taking advantage of your natural skills?]*

Emerald sighed and ran his fingers through his black hair. He had allowed it to grow out on our voyage, along with the stubble on his chin and jaw. "You'll see," he muttered aloud.

Usually when Emerald cut short our internal conversations, it meant that he was afraid that I would read too deeply into his thoughts. Sometimes, his wishes were enough to deter me, but in this instance, I would not be rebuffed.

"You'll need to reveal the truth before long," I whispered, granting him the privacy of speaking aloud. Our means of communication had become more fraught of late, after everything that had happened in Upper Bound. "I know you aren't looking forward to it, but..."

Emerald groaned and shook his head, then reached one arm toward me, resting his hand on the railing of the ship in front of me. At first, I thought that he was gesturing for me to be quiet, but even as he cut his eyes away from me toward our wake at the stern, he rotated his hand so that it sat palm up against the wood.

[Go on, then,] he thought.

I hesitated, not sure if I had interpreted his request correctly. It was not the first time that he had given me access to his memories intentionally. While we could communicate in words even at the very limits of the magical tether that bound me to him, direct contact between us allowed me more insight into his consciousness than he generally preferred.

[Come on, Crimson, don't make me say it.] He wiggled his fingers limply.

I needed no further encouragement. I laid my hand over his, taking care not to overlap *too* much. The other passengers were avoiding the rain, and the crew of the *Harbinger* was preoccupied with docking, but no doubt someone would notice if I allowed my hand to disappear through his.

I couldn't touch Emerald any more than I could touch the railing beneath his hand. What I *could* feel, however, were his thoughts and memories. Usually, they were quite vivid, but today was different. A mass of smoky, half-formed faces swirled together, wreathed in shadows that obscured most of the details entirely. A few small figures were sharp enough to identify, but I gleaned very little about them from his mind, not even their names. Only one figure loomed above the others: a man who looked a great deal like Emerald, with a kindly smile that gave away his identity at once. This was Brother

Harmony, Emerald's mentor. He wore plain, shapeless robes, and he stood with his back bent slightly and his arms extended, as if stooping to greet a small child with a warm embrace. There was sorrow woven in those memories.

Before I pulled away, I pushed back with a single sharp recollection of my own: Tincrown stepping out of the door of his home the very first time we'd met him.

Emerald left out a soft, longing sigh as his hand clenched around empty air. *[You didn't need to do that. I'm fine, Crimson. All this nonsense with Guise is well in the past.]*

[Just like the scent of Kinmore?] I asked wryly.

My companion glared down at the docks. *[Point taken.]*

The sailors around us were in the midst of final preparations, tossing lines to their dockworkers below. For the most part, the sailors ignored us, as they had the rest of the trip. From what I could tell, the Trader's Guild was used to seeing jotunn and half-jotunn aboard their ships. Whether their indifference was born of familiarity or contempt, I could not say, but none of them had paid us much attention since we boarded, and they were equally nonplussed by our pending departure.

[Why are your memories of the Brotherhood so obscured?] I asked. *[They're murkier than anything you've shown me before, even when…]* I almost said, *Even when you were drinking,* but stopped myself short. Neither of us needed the reminder of those miserable days in Fenguard Keep. *[…when I looked without asking.]*

[Dunno. Because they're old memories, I guess? Or maybe because I do my best not to dwell on them?] Emerald stood upright again and rolled his shoulders. *[It's not as if I think back fondly on that time, Crim. They're just as murky to me as they are to you.]*

"Oy." One of the crewmembers stopped behind us and tried to tap my shoulder. I jumped back just as his finger passed through the collar of my handsome, double-breasted wool coat.

The soldier stared at his finger in astonishment, then he lifted his eyes to mine. In return, I stared down my nose at him and pretended to flick a speck of imaginary dust off of my lapel. "Can I help you, sir?"

The sailor squinted at me. I had gone to the trouble of making myself appear damp from the steady drizzle, and fortunately, I cast a shadow of my own, but I was painfully aware of my other tells. I wondered if the sailor was seeing the same things that the dock master, Hudson, had noticed during our ill-fated confrontation: my lack of breathing, the fact that the breeze only stirred my hair when I remembered to *pretend* that it did, and that the deck beneath where I stood was wet, unlike the place where my companion had lingered and blocked the drops from striking the wood.

The sailor licked his lips and seemed to decide better of asking further questions. "I only wanted to tell you that we're puttin' down the gangplank. You oughta gather your things." He shuffled backward over the salt-stained boards, still watching me intently.

Technically speaking, it wouldn't matter if the sailor realized that I was an illusion. Emerald was licensed to cast me, so if the matter came before a Conjury official, my existence could be explained. My relative autonomy, however, could not, and *that* was one secret that we didn't want anyone to work out. There was no telling what the Conjury would do to me, or to Emerald, if my actual nature was discovered. Every time someone recognized what I was, I ran the risk of being uncovered.

"We've got our things," Emerald said coolly. I neither had nor needed any physical possessions, and everything Emerald carried with him was stored in the leather pack he wore, a parting gift from his adoring doctor who waited an ocean away.

"Right." The sailor slowly lowered his finger. "Well. Then as soon as the plank's down, you can be on your way."

Emerald shook his head once the sailor turned his back on us. *[When we're in the presence of the local Conjury representative, you'll need to be more careful.]* He strolled toward the gangplank, weaving between the men and women gathered there. The other passengers were starting to emerge from below, making their own plans for departure.

[It's not as if I can stop people from touching me, Em. What am I supposed to do?]

He mounted the gangplank and ventured down. With each step,

the wood plank flexed and creaked, while I walked behind him, silent as a cat. When I glanced back toward the ship, I found the sailor who had tried to touch me watching us with narrowed eyes.

[I know that you can't control them, but what you can do is be a bit less obvious about your independence, at least for this meeting. Just be quiet. Observe, rather than speaking. Be... subtle. You do know the meaning of the word, don't you?]

Without waiting to make sure that I was following, he strode off along the dock, leaving me at the base of the gangplank that protruded from the *Harbinger's* deck. I pursed my lips and as I hurried after him, leaving no bootprints in the mud-smeared cobbles of the city's streets.

He was one to complain. If he'd wanted a quiet, meek companion, he shouldn't have made me as I was. Emerald had no one to blame for my behavior but himself.

It didn't take me long to realize that Kinmore was, in fact, quite different from Upper Bound. Both cities sat at the confluence of an inland river and the ocean, but that was where the similarities ended. Upper Bound had been relatively well-to-do, but Kinmore was more clearly divided into bitterly poor neighborhoods and extravagantly wealthy ones. I had only ever met one proper street urchin, a salty dwarven girl named Tala whose mettle suggested that she'd learned to fend for herself early in life. Dozens of such children wandered the lower streets of Kinmore, sad eyed and soaked to the bone, some with animals trailing after them. They were narrower than Tala, gaunt and ashen, and they watched us with hungry eyes.

[Are they homeless?] I asked, following close on Emerald's heels.

[I'm sure some are.] My companion hunched his shoulders but belied no concern. His apparent indifference shocked me.

[But why? I thought the Brotherhood of Guise ran an orphanage.]

[The Brotherhood can't take in every unfortunate child on the continent, Crimson. Besides, I'm sure lots of them have families.] He gestured to the small apartments that lined the narrow streets

like two close-set honeycombs. *[People all over Dregandresal live in places like this. And just because a child doesn't have a home doesn't mean that they're alone in the world. When the rent can't be paid, whole families wind up fending for themselves on the streets.]*

[And the Conjury allows that?] I shook my head in disgust. *[I would have thought that an organization with such sway would be able to ensure that everyone in the cities it controlled was at least properly fed and safely housed.]*

Emerald stopped in his tracks and turned to stare at me in disbelief. *[You really think that the Conjury gives two shits about people like this? All they care about is policing the use of Aidea and collecting taxes. Aster's sake, Crimson, I know you're naive, but you've met Dirkus. You think Dirkus cares about hungry children, or rats living in the walls of flophouses? You think Benedite does?]*

I balled my hands into fists. *[You work for the Conjury, too, Em. Why would you support an infrastructure that cares so little for its citizens?]*

Emerald swallowed hard and let his eyes drift toward a window above us, where a thin-faced woman scowled down at us through a grimy windowpane. The moment Emerald's gaze met hers, she darted back.

[Because if I didn't work for them, I'd be here,] he thought dismally.

I had been wrong before. Emerald was not indifferent. He was resigned.

None of it sat well with me, and as he led me into the nicer districts, I only grew more annoyed. Why should the denizens of the wealthier areas live in such comfort, while people within the walls of their city were forced to scavenge for scraps? I had nothing against simplicity—life in Dyrne had been simple enough, but nobody went without.

Emerald turned sharply and mounted the steps of a tidy, marble-fronted building. As he did so, I found myself eying his relatively plain clothes. I had spent my whole life badgering him about his appearance, but for the first time, I considered that his manner of dress might have less to do with modesty than allegiance. He might never blend in with a crowd, but he would fit in better in the lower reaches of the city than he would here.

Perhaps that was more deliberate than I had given him credit for.

He laid one hand on the door and stopped. *[Remember, the Conjury expects you to be an ordinary illusion, bound to my bidding. Subtlety is key, all right?]*

[I can manage subtlety,] I agreed, although I was less than thrilled about the prospect of keeping my head down and pretending to be empty-headed. Only when Emerald held the door open for me did I realize that this was a reversal of our natural roles. Usually, it would have been my job to do the talking and draw attention from him. I doubted that this shift in our dynamic would suit either of us.

The Conjury's headquarters in Kinmore was not particularly grand. It could not compare with the Fenguards' high hall, although there was an air of formality to the decorations: carved recesses in the vaulted ceilings, busts of important figures placed on plinths about the edges of the room, and unsmiling paintings of heroes and politicians covering the walls. I paused at the first of these, which depicted a woman who reminded me a bit of the augur Amaya. A plaque at the bottom of the gold frame read, *Henda.* No prominence title, no place-name, nothing. Only Henda.

[Keep up, Crimson,] Emerald reminded me, and I hurried on, keeping my eyes downcast so that I would not accidentally take interest in anything else unfamiliar.

At the end of the entry hall stood a heavy wooden desk guarded with wards and sigils. A bored-looking young man in purple silks glanced up from a ledger as we approached.

"Do you have an appointment?" he asked. His Osmarian was crisper than the accents I had grown used to on Kovin Isle, with sharp consonants and truncated vowels.

"Not exactly." Emerald reached into one of the secret pockets inside his coat and produced a letter. It was well-worn by now, tattered at the edges, with creases that had been folded and refolded so many times that they let the light through the seams. I had watched Emerald fiddle with that letter anxiously throughout our voyage. He might not remember his childhood in the Brotherhood clearly, but he was certainly in no hurry to return.

The secretary plucked the letter out of his hand, scanned it for a few seconds, then bent over a bouquet of covered brass tubes that protruded from one side of his desk. He flipped one open and said, in that same brusque tone, "Commander? I have the Emerald Flame here."

A woman's voice from within the tube let out an aggrieved sigh. "*Took him long enough. Send him back at once.*"

The secretary flipped the cap closed and gestured toward the door to his right. "Commander Finch will see you."

Emerald didn't thank the lad before striding toward the door. My mouth was already open to cover for his rudeness when I remembered my role. Fortunately, the youth was already engrossed in his ledger once again and paid me no mind whatsoever.

Emerald held the door again as we stepped into a well-appointed office. It reminded me a bit of the room in Fenguard Keep where Edur had first welcomed us, with its military portraits framed in gold and its heavy einwood furniture.

The woman who sat behind the desk was one of the most interesting individuals I had yet laid eyes on. Most of the people I had met on Kovin Isle shared comparable features, with a few noteworthy exceptions such as Burp, Errol, and Yoyoh. One of those commonalities was *skin*, residents of Dyrne notwithstanding. Commander Finch, however, boasted a fine pelt of golden-brown and eyes the color of autumn honey. Her features were an uncanny mixture of humanoid and feline, from the shape of her eyes to the set of her flat nose to the structure of her lean figure beneath her purple-and-gold Conjury uniform. She sat on the far side of the venerable desk, with her clawed fingers interlaced and her mouth turned down in a disapproving frown.

"Emerald Flame," she said coolly, "you are late."

Emerald didn't bat an eye as he dropped heavily into the chair across from her. "I came as soon as I got your letter."

Finch's eyes narrowed to glittering slits. "You did not respond to any of the babblebirds we sent." Unlike the secretary, her vowels were rounded and smooth as riverstones. "Why is this?"

"I didn't receive them." Emerald slouched in his chair and crossed his legs, making himself at home. "I would have come sooner if I knew that I was wanted."

"You're evidently a difficult man to track down," Finch replied. "We've been trying to reach you for months."

Emerald inclined his head. "I apologize for the inconvenience. I spent half a year in the backcountry of Kovin Isle, investigating the suspicious deaths of several of our scouts."

As far as I could tell, Finch hadn't blinked since we entered the room. She had barely twitched a muscle. The overall effect was quite disconcerting. "Knowing your reputation, I can only assume that you solved the mystery?"

"A local laird was to blame. We traced the evidence back to him, but he escaped before we could bring him in. I have reason to think that he perished in the Cronemire." The half-truth slid easily from Emerald's tongue. This was the official story, the one which Dirkus and Benedite had reported to their superiors. It was a lie that served our purposes twofold, since it protected both the people of Dyrne and the secrets of the Cronemire itself.

"Hm." Commander Finch's whiskers twitched. She didn't move a muscle as her eyes flicked upward to my face. "Your illusion is staring at me."

I kept my eyes fixed on her and my expression vapid as she examined me. I had been so intent on her words that I had forgotten to act *empty*.

Emerald waved a dismissive hand in my direction without turning his head. "I didn't see the point in pretending, since you know what he is. Would you feel more comfortable if I kept up the pretense?"

Finch's eyes seemed to bore into me, but I stood stiff as a corpse beneath her scrutiny.

"No," she said at last, "you needn't bother. There's no point in taxing yourself unnecessarily, and what I would prefer is to have your complete attention. The matter I wish to discuss with you is...

delicate. I assume I don't have to tell you that nothing I say today is meant to leave this room?"

"I understand protocol, Commander," Emerald said.

"Good. I'm glad you came, inspector, even if you *are* late. I require the assistance of someone who knows the Brotherhood of Guise. Someone they trust... and someone *we* can trust. Are you such a person, Emerald Flame?"

Emerald smiled wryly. "The Conjury has given me everything I have, Commander. It has *made* me. I know exactly where I stand, and to whom I owe my loyalty."

I, too, knew where Emerald's loyalty lay, and it was neither with the Brotherhood nor his employers. He had done his best to distance himself from the former, and he had actively deceived the latter. I agreed with his choices wholeheartedly, but all the same, I recognized that he was playing a dangerous game, one that could cost us both everything if he lost.

Fortunately, Finch knew nothing about this at all. She finally moved, relaxing back into her chair and letting out a little sigh of exhaustion. "I'm glad to hear it. You won't believe the rumors about the Brotherhood these days."

Emerald leaned forward, and I had to fight to keep myself from following suit. "What rumors?" he asked. His tone belied little more than curiosity, but even without touching him, I could sense the swirl of alarm and intrigue and uncertainty radiating off of him like steam.

Commander Finch lowered her voice and licked her pale lips. "They say," she rumbled, "that a member of their order can speak directly with Lord Guise himself."

Emerald scoffed. "Impossible."

Finch nodded. "That's exactly what I would have said if I hadn't seen the results for myself. But there's more to it than that. This follower of Guise? They say that with a single touch, she can shatter a person's mastery of the *Aidea*."

Emerald's shoulders pulled taught. "What do you need *my* help with?"

"I want you to visit the Brotherhood," Commander Finch said. "And I want you to find out what's really going on."

[I hate to be the one to say this,] I thought, *[but if she's right, wouldn't getting involved with this investigation pose a potential threat to my health and well-being? Sister Aster seems to think that one of the gods helped make me, and I don't fancy the idea of getting unmade by a different one.]*

Emerald's attention was still fixed on Commander Finch. *[But what if she's right? There might be a connection between whatever's going on here and what happened with the Crone back in the bog. If that's the case, we should find out everything we can.]* Aloud, he said, "Tell me everything, Commander."

It seemed that I would get no say in the matter, although I couldn't argue with his logic. Once again, Emerald and I had wandered into the midst of a situation far more complicated than we'd anticipated.

I could only hope that this adventure would have a happier end than the last.

Commander Finch dragged one clawed finger between her speckled brows. "I'll tell you what I can. I should warn you, however, that it is difficult to separate fact from fiction in this particular case. The Conjury has had an amiable relationship with the Brotherhood since well before I was posted here."

"How long ago was that?" Emerald asked. "I beg your pardon, Commander, but I've never met a leonhite in person. I didn't know that any of you worked for the Conjury."

Finch let out a derisive sneeze that was distinctly feline in nature. "How many half-jotunn Castcadesmen have you encountered? I'm not the only rarity in this room."

"I'm not a Castcadesman anymore," Emerald retorted. I wasn't entirely sure what a Castcadesman was, but I held my tongue and kept my peace. Emerald didn't need any more distractions.

"No. You're something even more unusual." Finch's eyes flashed. "You're independent. Which is precisely what makes you so valuable to me. As for how long the Conjury has collaborated with the Brotherhood? You must know that it reaches back to well before your time, given your own experience."

Emerald chuckled darkly. It did not escape my attention, as it had surely not escaped his, that Finch hadn't answered his question.

"As I was saying," Commander Finch went on, neatly sidestepping any meaningful response, "the Brotherhood is usually compliant with Conjury law. Every so often, they send us a batch of new recruits, as you know from personal experience."

[Batch,] Emerald thought bitterly. *[As though they're being manufactured for your personal use.]* I wasn't sure whether he meant for me to hear, or if he was simply so disgusted with Finch's word choice that it bubbled over into my own head.

Ah, yes. Good to know that he departed from the Brotherhood was so long ago that he can't possibly be emotionally invested in this case. I kept my face blank and my thoughts to myself.

Finch was still talking. "Local rumors have indicated that the Brotherhood has found a new way to encourage conformity among its members. As you surely recall, Guise encourages... adherence to a common average." Finch smiled wryly.

"Not exactly," Emerald corrected her. "According to the scriptures, Guise adores nothing more or less than absolute mediocrity."

Finch's smile widened to reveal an abundance of teeth. "Your words, or theirs?"

Emerald's smile was just as bitter. *"The blade of grass that grows the highest is the first to be cut."*

"Oh, you *do* know your texts." Finch let out a yelp of laughter that startled me so badly that I almost recoiled.

You are on stage, Crimson. You are completely still. Be a tree. Be a stone. Be something that doesn't react when the scary lady makes an alarming noise.

"I had ample opportunity to memorize them all." Emerald sat back in his chair and bit his lip, staring down at his boots.

The leonhite drummed her claws on the desk. "Oh, I reckon you did. And also figure that you're the tallest blade of grass wherever you go."

Emerald lifted his head sharply, and I fought the urge to narrow my eyes.

Finch's smile widened, and she pressed the pad of one palm to her own chest. "Don't mistake my words for an insult, Emerald Flame. I pride myself on many things, but mediocrity is not among them. I suspect that you are no more ordinary than you appear to be. People like us are not grass at all. We are more like *wildesprigge*. Some people view us as weeds who've spoiled the appearance of the lawn, but we are awfully hardy. Difficult to root out." Her glistening black lips twitched with the ghost of a smile.

Emerald searched her face and did not reply. I could not quite decide if I liked Commander Finch or not. One thing was clear, however: we could not *trust* her. I might be predisposed to making friends with society's outcasts, but I was well aware that no one who wore the Conjury's violet silks could be trusted. Not by us, at any rate. There was too much to lose.

Finch sniffed and pressed on. "At any rate, between the rumors and the lack of new recruits, I took it upon myself to investigate."

"I expect that you didn't get far." Emerald's hands were clasped together so tightly that his knuckles had gone pale gray. "The Brotherhood of Guise doesn't open its doors to outsiders, not even the Conjury. I expect that hasn't changed much since I left, or you wouldn't have been so eager to bring me back. So what exactly did you see, Commander?"

Finch wrinkled her nose. "You're right about the doors. But one thing *has* changed. Ever since this acolyte claimed to speak to Guise himself, the Brotherhood has been hosting events. Garden parties, if you will." Her eyes flicked toward my face briefly, then back to Emerald's. "They want to share Guise's gifts with the public. I saw someone lose their *Aidea*."

Emerald sat up a little straighter. "Meaning?"

Finch took a long, slow breath, choosing her words carefully. She was canny, no doubt about that. I wonder what she made of us.

I wondered if she'd picked up on some evidence that suggested we were not what we seemed. I had the distinct impression that she was testing us. Not just Emerald, but me, too.

"You are a Lightweaver," she said at length. "You know that things are not always what they seem. I *believe* that I saw a Kineticist approach this acolyte and offer up his gift to Guise. I believe that the acolyte laid hands on him and removed his ability to channel energy. I believe that he walked into that tent with a gods-given talent, and he emerged as an ordinary man. Or, how did you put it? Mediocre?" Her sardonic smile made another brief appearance.

Emerald brought one thumb to his lips and bit down on the pad, stifling a private thought that he did not care to share with me. His bright-green eyes unfocused, as though he was looking inward rather than outward. "You believe that you saw this. But you aren't sure."

"It could be many things." Finch spread her hands wide. "It could have been a performance. It could have been staged. Perhaps the temple managed to acquire a large enough chunk of stone from the Aidea Nulda, and the loss of power was only temporary. I can't say for sure, but imagine, Emerald Flame. Just imagine what the Conjury could do with someone who had the ability to remove people's powers with the touch of a hand."

I very nearly shivered. Yes, imagine what they could do, this collective of powerful men and women who collected taxes from their citizens and then left them to scrounge for scraps in the streets. Imagine what they could do if they could take away people's gifts on a whim. I had seen a few portraits of Conjury members, and while their features varied, in my mind, they were all Dirkuses and Benedites, more intent on lining their pockets and crawling to the top of the heap than in doing anything worthwhile.

If pressed to choose one evil over another, I would rather set Edur Fenguard up as a figurehead than watch the likes of Dirkus rise above the rest. At least Fenguard had been a man of unflinching conviction, even if his actions bordered on the monstrous.

To my surprise, Commander Finch didn't appear particularly excited by the idea of such power falling into the Conjury's hands. How many people were like Emerald, working for a power they secretly despised, using it as nothing more than a means to an end?

"That would certainly be something," Emerald agreed softly. "I'm sure the folks at Venta Bulgarum would be interested in, ah... *employing* a cast-off with that particular ability."

[Cast-offs, Castcadesmen... I hope you're going to explain all of

this.] As the conversation wound on, it was becoming increasingly difficult to hold my tongue.

Emerald rolled one shoulder and turned his head very slightly, but he didn't face me. *[Castcadesmen are **Aidea-users who work for the Conjury. Cast-offs are, hm... outliers. People with unusual skills that don't fit neatly into the known categories of magic users.]***

People like Aindreas. People like Nechtan.

No wonder Emerald was getting tetchy as the conversation unfolded.

Finch nodded. "The trouble is, I'm not sure that there *is* a cast-off involved. I can think of a dozen reasons someone might want to pretend that they were blessed."

Emerald's eyebrows rose. "Hold on. Do you really believe that a *god* is involved?"

Commander Finch's features pinched with worry, and she averted her eyes, focusing on the desk rather than either of us. She sighed heavily. "I don't *want* to think so. And to be perfectly frank, if any of the gods *were* to make an appearance in Kinmore, I'd rather it not be Guise. Speaking as the *wildesprigge* among the short grass, you see."

Emerald let out a grunt of begrudging laughter. "Have you reported this incident to your superiors?"

Finch licked her lips with a rough, pink tongue. "There is not enough to report yet. I'd rather wait until I have all the facts. And the only way that I'll be able to do that is if I *have* all the facts." Her golden eyes rose to Emerald's face again. "Which is why I need a seasoned investigator who can enter the Brotherhood and tell me everything they learn. We have one contact inside already, but they haven't been able to get me the information I need, and I could desperately use someone with experience. Someone who the Brotherhood will trust. And it would help if that person had a good reason not to play turncoat." She nodded toward me.

For one terrible moment, I thought that she was implying that she *knew.* About me, and what I was. But her gaze found Em's again, and I realized that she only meant that Emerald had a talent that the

Brotherhood would rather suppress than nurture. If he returned to the fold, he would lose his ability to summon me.

All my short life, I had told myself that I had little to fear when it came to my own safety. Emerald could be harmed, which would harm me in turn, but there was nothing that could touch me directly. Knives and arrows, fists or poisons, Aindreas's grasping hands and the Fenguard's penchant for drowning were of no immediate concern to me. I thought myself an unassailable fortress, too tricky to catch and too powerful to be contained.

No doubt Edur Fenguard had felt the same, before he met his end.

It was not so hard to play deaf and mute through the rest of the meeting. Commander Finch's words washed over me in waves, but nothing stuck.

When Emerald got to his feet and shook the commander's clawed hand, I kept my eyes on the spot where our new Conjury liaison had been sitting. It was not until Emerald whistled and snapped his fingers that I turned to follow him through the door. I could feel Finch's eyes on my back as we made our way back down the long hall, past the secretary who did not so much as raise his head from his work as we took our leave.

When at last we stepped out into the open air, Emerald took a deep breath, as if he'd been holding it all the while.

"Gods," he groaned, rolling his shoulders and letting his head roll back until the bones in his spine cracked loudly. "That was something else, wasn't it?"

I stared down at the jet-black buttons on my tall boots. Our conversation with the Commander had given me plenty of mull over, but one question plagued me above all others.

Emerald paused on the bottom step and turned to face me. "You can talk again. I'm sure it pains you to have held your tongue for more than half an hour, Crim. Come on, let me hear what's rattling around that head of yours."

"Do you think it's possible?" I asked.

Emerald's brow wrinkled. "What do you mean?"

"That a god has come to Kinmore." I examined the city in a new light, even as the sun dipped behind the tall buildings, casting misshapen shadows over the streets and turning the sky above us shades of sienna and rust.

"That's absurd, Crimson. I'm sure there's a rational explanation. The gods don't walk among us. They don't give a rip about ordinary people." Emerald gestured to the city, where the poorer boroughs lay below the wealthy ones, sloping down toward the slate waves and their foamy whitecaps. It was a grim palate. "And if they did, you think they would come here?" He laughed bitterly, turning up his collar against the breeze that rolled in off the sea. "If I were a god, I wouldn't."

[How can you say that?]

He set off down the street, following a memory rather than any current map. *[The gods forgot Kinmore a long time ago, Crim.]*

That wasn't what I meant. In the short time I'd been alive, I'd seen little signs that suggested that the gods cared very much indeed. I thought of Aster, the wild forest goddess Emerald followed now; the Middling Godlet, who may have had a hand in my creation; and most of all, the Crone, who I was certain had helped us defeat the Fenguards in the Black Hollow. Or perhaps I had helped *her*. At any rate, it seemed foolish to dismiss the presence of a higher power just because Emerald hadn't seen proof with his own eyes.

If the gods had indeed returned to the continent of Dregandresal, I agreed with Commander Finch. I would not want to cross paths with Guise the Unifier, god of conformity. Emerald had peppered me with insults both teasing and sincere throughout our travels, but even he had never implied that I was anything less than extraordinary.

And neither was he.

THREE

Emerald's chosen path led us out of the upper city, then out of Kinmore proper altogether. We passed through a guarded set of gates, and Emerald produced his papers for review once again. This time, I was so lost in my thoughts that I had no trouble pretending to be a simpleminded illusion.

Beyond the outer walls, Kinmore's environs expanded to give the residents a bit more room. Instead of being crowded cheek by jowl, these houses boasted small garden plots between them. Some even had pigs and chickens penned in the back yards. It reminded me a little of Dyrne, although we didn't pass a single goat. The houses were more angular than the sod-roofed huts of the highlands, reminiscent of the luxurious stone buildings in the wealthy portion of the neighboring city.

Emerald chuckled to himself as we approached a three-story building. "Still here," he said. "Who would have believed it?"

[You know this place?] It was growing dark, but the lamplight spilling through the windows illuminated the sign hanging from a beam out front: *The Lute & Goose.*

[All too well. It's where I heard Coirpre play for the first time.]

That stopped me in my tracks, but Emerald was still making his way up the paved walk, and I had little choice but to follow. It was, however, mighty tempting to ask if he would show me that memory.

The very first night of my life, I had stepped into a tavern much like this one. McLachlan's place had been bristling with life, full of adventurers armed to the teeth, merchants dressed in bright fabrics, and half a dozen lambkins, never mind the now-familiar figure of a green-clad bard. This establishment was more reminiscent of Cait's little inn in Dyrne. They fell silent as we stepped through the door into the yellowed light, treading on floorboards that looked as if they'd been laid half a century before, and had spent the intervening years absorbing spills and stains.

Its tables were populated by grubby farmers and carpenters with calloused hands, many of whom swung toward us as we entered. A few of them whispered to one another as they eyed us over.

[Are these people all followers of Guise?] I asked anxiously.

[No.] Emerald sounded weary, even inside my head. *[But most people are wary of jotunn all the same.]*

A man behind the bar stared at us with wide eyes, a bottle held in one hand and glass in the other. His mouth fell open.

"*Steadfast?*" he cried.

Emerald lifted one hand in greeting.

The man let out a whoop of surprise and scurried out from behind the bar, leaving both the bottle and the glass behind. He flung his arms wide and embraced Emerald in a mighty hug, thumping him on the back a few times.

"The great Emerald Flame returns!" he crowed.

I stared at my friend in consternation. *[Who is this? I didn't realize you had admirers.]*

[Nor did I. I wasn't exactly popular when I left.] Emerald appeared just as puzzled as I was. *[And he used my old Brotherhood name first, so he must be associated with them somehow...]* The link between us prickled with his discomfort as he extracted himself from the other man's unexpected welcome. "How did you hear that title, um...?" he asked the barman.

"Yerik," the man said. "It's Yerik now. And of course I know your title. You're a folk hero, aren't you?" Yerik placed his hands on his hips and grinned up at my companion. "We heard stories about you for years. You're one of the biggest celebrities to ever pass through here."

I covered my mouth with one hand to hide my smile and widened my eyes as far as they could go. "Why, Emerald, I didn't realize you were a *celebrity*."

My friend's eye twitched. "M'not."

"Oh, don't be modest. We've been following your adventures ever since you left." Yerik pivoted toward me. "And I know who you are. Crimson Smoke. You look *just* as I imagined. I can't believe I get to meet you in the flesh!"

"Er," I said, wondering how to respond to that. I'd never had flesh and doubted that I ever would.

Evidently, Yerik did not need my input. He pointed to the wall behind the bar. "In fact, I just heard the new one about your exploits in Upper Bound. Thank *goodness* he was there to save you."

"The new one?" I echoed.

At my side, Emerald covered his face with his hands and choked back a groan.

It took me a moment to realize what Yerik was pointing to, and when I did, I let out a sputter of laughter. A portrait, easily twice as large as life, presided over the faded wood and collection of dusty bottles. A blue-eyed, golden-haired man grinned down from the canvas. He was young, eighteen at the oldest, with a wickedly clever grin and a handsome lute settled in his lap. His fashion sense, as always, was impeccable, and the artist had captured his careless demeanor in every detail. At his feet, inexplicably, sat a fat white goose, which gazed up at him with uncharacteristic admiration.

"Coirpre?" I coughed once. "Coirpre was here recently? When?"

Yerik was staring at the portrait with the same vapid adoration that the goose portrayed therein. "Only for the night. He played us his new song. It was a bit fantastical to be believed, but he has such a way with words that I could almost picture that I was there at his side, defeating the Lady of the Bog as his squire."

"Bards don't have squires," Emerald mumbled into his hands. *[I can't believe he wrote that damned song.]*

[Yes, you can. He told you he would. Frankly, I'd have been surprised if he didn't.] The sheer size of the portrait beggared belief, but it was a captivating likeness. "We should have one commissioned for you," I suggested.

"Oh, could we?" Yerik clapped his hands to the side of his face. "A matched set would be *marvelous.*"

"Enough jaw-wagging," the man seated at the bar called out. "Am I to have my drink, or not?"

"Come join us," Yerik suggested. "Anything you like is on the house." He didn't wait for Emerald's reply before trotting back to his duties.

As we followed, I examined Yerik more carefully. I had never quite worked out how old my companion was, but I thought Yerik might be a few years younger, though it couldn't be by much. His curly, jet-black hair was pulled back in a voluminous queue, and his rounded cheeks and single dimple made his smile altogether charming and boyish despite the graying stubble that dusted his chin. His complexion was darker than Tincrown's, and his broader features suggested that he hailed from some other part of the continent, but I had met so few people outside of Kovin Isle that I could not glean anything useful from this observation.

The rest of the patrons watched Emerald with slitted eyes, and their attitudes suggested that they did not view my friend in the same favorable light that the barman did.

[Is Yerik a... friend?] I wasn't sure how to phrase my question. Everything Emerald had told me led me to believe that he didn't have many of those. I wasn't sure what lay between them, but there was a strain of what might have been fondness that Emerald felt for the man. Nothing like desire, certainly, but something bittersweet and sorrowful.

[No. Not really. He was in the Brotherhood for a while, but we only spoke a handful of times. The children without Aidea live alongside those who have it, but their lives are... separate.]

[Ah, but you have some shared history.] That explained the sadness. Yerik had found someplace that he belonged, and Emerald never had.

Or, at least, no place that he could stay for very long.

[It's complicated. Our experiences at the Brotherhood were very different. Those of us with a knack for the Aidea are treated—well, you'll see.] Emerald dropped down onto a stool and rested his elbows against the hardwood.

[Do you know why he was taken in?] I asked. *[I thought you said that not every errant child found a home with the Brotherhood.]*

Emerald lip curled into a knowing smirk. *[Look again.]*

While Yerik pulled a beer, I studied his profile. He was thickset, with broad shoulders. He reminded me of someone I'd met before.

[Oh! He isn't human, is he?] Now that I saw it, I wondered how I failed to miss the resemblance to the other dwarves I'd met.

[Half-human,] Emerald corrected. *[Most of us at the Brotherhood had mixed parentage.]*

I puzzled over that revelation. Emerald and Tincrown had been drawn together like magnets, but now that I thought about it, I hadn't encountered any other romantic partnerships like theirs, or offspring of similar unions—at least to my knowledge. I'd never thought to question it. I had only questioned the mechanics of procreation once or twice, and Emerald had been in no hurry to explain them.

I watched Yerik work for another minute or two, wondering what his parentage meant to him. Emerald made no secret of the fact that he despised himself, and he'd been repulsed by the jotunn we'd encountered in Upper Bound. Did Yerik feel the same way about himself?

I hoped not. But judging by what Emerald had told me about the tenets of the Brotherhood, I wouldn't be surprised to learn that he did.

I wondered, too, if Emerald resented the fact that people might not notice that Yerik was anything other than human, when that was the first thing people observed about *him*.

When his other customers were satisfied, Yerik returned to us, mirroring Emerald's pose across the counter. "What can I get for you? Anything you like, just say the word."

"I need—" Emerald's eyes strayed toward the array of bottles beneath Coirpre's portrait, and I bit my tongue. He swallowed hard. "A room. Two beds, just for the night." He wanted a drink, badly. I could feel it so deeply that it almost felt like *my* desire, but he resisted temptation, to my great relief.

"Oh? Are you passing through?" Yerik beamed at us. "Following Coirpre on your way to another great adventure? You know, I've found it inspiring, to think that one of us could amount to something. I mean, *really* amount to something, not just pouring drinks or tanning hides. Imagine, one of us undesirables, with a *prominence title.*" He shivered in delight, and his eyes glimmered. "I bet you're headed to Venta Bulgarum, aren't you? Or off to the Infested Mountains to do another favor for the king?"

[Another *favor?*] I wrinkled my nose. **[How come he knows things about you that even I've never heard?]**

Emerald ignored me. "Nope. I'm going home."

Yerik's smile faltered. "Home? You mean…"

"I've heard the rumors," Emerald said. "Reckon I ought to see for myself."

The two of them stared at each other for a long moment. Then the barman straightened up and took a steadying breath. "Let me see about that room," he said.

In the end, Yerik settled us in the Lute and Goose's finest room. It was homey enough, well-worn but tidy, and featured a large canvas depicting the two objects that the establishment was named for.

"Too bad there isn't another picture of Coirpre in here," I mused as I sat down at the end of what was, ostensibly, my bed. "The one over the bar is really something."

"Can't argue with that," Emerald muttered as he flung off his embroidered pack. He sniffed himself, then he wrinkled his nose in disgust. "Good gods, I smell like Kinmore Harbor, or worse. I need a bath. And a haircut. And…" He squeezed his eyes shut, and I felt the knot of tension building in his stomach.

"And dinner?" I prompted.

"I don't know if I can eat right now." He shucked off his overcoat and hung it on a peg by the door.

I dangled my feet over the edge of the bed. I had long since worked out how to make it look as though I was sitting on a piece of furniture, even though I wasn't actually touching it. If Yerik had flung open the door in that moment, the scene before him would have appeared perfectly ordinary.

But it wasn't, and my lack of material body wasn't the most unusual thing. Emerald was not prone to confiding in me, not out loud. Except in the most dire circumstances, I was usually forced to read between the lines of his grunts and grumblings. Speaking about his emotions, aloud no less, was new territory for both of us.

"Are you nervous?" I asked.

"Mm." He raked his square-knuckled hands through his mop of black hair. "I... am."

"Would you like to talk about it?"

"No," he snapped, balancing on one leg to remove first one boot, then the other. "In a perfect world, I'd push all my inconvenient emotions way, *way* down and flee to the far end of Dregandresal—or across the seas, if I could. But since that isn't an option, I'll have to settle for talking, won't I?"

I didn't laugh. Instead, I turned to face him, crossing my legs and pretending to lean back on my palms. "What part are you worried about?"

He let out a bitter laugh and began to pace the room. Judging by the pale track worn in the hardwood, he wasn't the first to do so. "All of it. I mean, gods above and below, how do I even express it? I wish there was a way that I could just show you that didn't make it feel like I had to live the whole thing over again." He stopped moving and frowned down at his palm. "I suppose I could, but it's awful, some-times. Expedient, though."

An idea occurred to me, and I bent forward, resting my elbows on my knees and intertwining my fingers. "You know, there could be another way. One that might not feel so intrusive. You remember me telling you about meditations I did with Sister Aster, back in the Cronemire?"

Emerald nodded. "You mentioned it."

"She said that the process is different for me than most people. That it's a bit more, hm, *metaphysical.* But I'm sort of you, aren't I? In a roundabout way. So maybe I can take you there."

My friend arched one bristly eyebrow. "You want to take me to a place that only exists in your head?"

I thought of the blue ceiling with its golden stars, and how the same motif had been drawn in the book Aster showed me, in conjunction with the Middling Godlet. Maybe that place didn't really exist, but Coirpre had warped and bent the walls the one time he managed to summon me. Besides, I wasn't real either, not in the traditional way.

"I want to try," I said at last.

Emerald considered me for a moment, then sat down on the edge of his bed so that we faced one another. "All right," he said. "Where do we start?"

"Good question." I pondered the possibilities, then held out my hands to him. "We've been able to enter each other's heads before. You can control me, and I—" *I can control your body even when you can't.* Our recollection of the day when I'd taken possession of his body lingered between us, weighted down by the memory of little stones.

Emerald picked up where I'd left off, glossing over the awkward pause as neatly as Commander Finch had bypassed the question about her arrival in Kinmore. "So you think that we might be able to go to this other place if we travel together?"

"Just hold out your hands," I said. "If I end up possessing you accidentally, I'll back off."

"Same." Emerald extended both hands to me, and I overlaid my palms with his.

It was always easier to read his mind when we were in direct contact with one another. I had stumbled into other people's heads a few times, but the thoughts I gathered from them were never clear unless they were offered willingly. The only time I'd managed to get a whole story from someone other than Em was when the Cronemire had shown me the Fenguards' history. The Black Hollow had been a hub of power, and all of my senses and abilities had been heightened within that locus.

Stepping through Emerald's mind was less organized than that experience had been. His memories did not play out in front of me like a private performance. They came and went in snatches, just as my own did when I was not bent upon remembering a particular incident.

This time, instead of rifling through them the way a dandy might dig through his wardrobe, I tried to imagine that I was taking Emerald's hand and leading him somewhere. One of the things that was so unusual about the mind-cottage Aster had helped me build was that I was real there. Tangible. I could touch things, and feel things, and interact with them, just as everyone navigated the ordinary world.

"I don't think it's working," Emerald hissed.

I kept my eyes closed, frowning in concentration. "I know it isn't. Take my hand, Em."

"You know that I can't..."

"Just try."

Emerald huffed, and his palm clenched beneath mine. "I'm telling you, this isn't—"

I mirrored his movement, and my fingers tightened on warm skin, closing over his wrist. I could even make out the individual ridges of old scars, the straight lines cut into Emerald's skin by his own hand. The sensation was so alarming that my eyes flew open in surprise.

Emerald and I sat across from each other. He was perched on a stone, while I sat cross-legged on another. The place around us was dimly lit, with only the skeletons of trees grasping at the twilight sky above us. I took a deep breath, reveling in the fact that I could smell. There was salt on the breeze, just as there had been when I briefly occupied Emerald's body in Upper Bound. A slight breeze stirred the bare branches, and the rich smells of earth and decay permeated the air. Birds startled in the trees above us, and I felt the updraft of their wings when they took flight.

I knew exactly where we were. We sat in the woods of Lower

Bound, just as it had been in the first moments of my consciousness, the night when Emerald summoned me into being and I became myself for the first time.

The night after his failed attempt to take his own life.

Emerald let out a guttural cry and rolled away from me. The second he broke my grip, he vanished, and I was left alone in the woods.

"Hello?" I asked into the silence. I was not expecting Emerald to reply, but as the breeze stirred my hair, I held out hope that I would receive some answer. Some sign.

Had we been alone in the woods that night? Or had something else been present? I rose, reveling in the sharp crack of sticks and old leaves beneath my boots, and cast my eyes about, but there was no one but me in that empty place. No god of confluence. No spectral figure. Even when I tried to imagine an otherworldly presence, none appeared.

With a sigh, I let myself reappear in the room of the Lute and Goose.

Emerald lay on the floor, one arm braced against the wood, gawking at me. "How?" he demanded, struggling to sit up, but he trembled so badly that he fell back again.

"I've never been there before," I admitted. "Not in the mind-cottage, I mean." I curled one lock of scarlet hair around my finger, remembering how the breeze had felt cool against my skin. It was jarring to hop back and forth between that place and this one, where I was once again only real to myself.

Emerald gave up trying to stand and settled for bracing his back against the side of his bed. He stared down at his wrist.

"I could *feel* you," he said uncertainly.

"You could?" I sat down across from him. "I thought... Well, I *wondered* if I had imagined it."

Emerald shook his head, pressing the fingers of his other hand to the same place mine had grasped. "That shouldn't be possible. You're a lightweaving, Crim."

"I do *lots* of things that shouldn't be possible," I reminded him.

My blithe tone of voice did nothing to smooth the wrinkle

between his eyebrows. "No, you don't. You do things I can't explain. Things that don't make sense *to me*. But this? This goes against the natural order. Against the rules of energy *Aidea*. It doesn't make sense *at all*." He sounded almost annoyed, but when I studied his face more carefully, I realized what he was trying to hide.

Emerald was afraid.

"I'm sorry," I began, although I wasn't sure what I was apologizing for.

At the same moment, Emerald spoke over me, thrusting both hands in my direction. "Do it again."

It was easier the second time, and within a few seconds of reaching for him, I had pulled Emerald back into my mindscape. This time, we appeared in the room of my own creation, the one where I had been trapped until Coirpre summoned me.

"Hm." Emerald let go of me, but he didn't disappear this time. Instead, he got to his feet, squinting at the dummy in the middle of the room. "What is that?"

I coughed into my fist as I surveyed the misshapen green sackcloth propped up on its pole. It bore only a passing likeness to my friend, although I had spent a good portion of my last visit bruising my knuckles on it in frustration.

"It's nothing important," I said quickly.

Emerald peered into the dummy's lopsided smiling face, then at me. "Hmm." He moved to adjust its collar, but when he did, his hand passed through the material as if it did not exist.

Or as if *he* did not.

"Well," he said, holding his fingers up for inspection.

I sidled past him and reached for the dummy, popping its tattered collar a bit more upright. After a moment's consideration, I whirled and pressed my hand through Emerald's intangible chest.

"What am I thinking?" I demanded.

"How should I know?" Emerald sidled out of reach. "And stop that, it's uncanny."

"That's so strange. I could touch you only a moment ago." I huffed in annoyance.

Emerald rearranged his own coat, running his hands over the

dark cloth. "Let us assume, for the moment, that our roles here are reversed. I wonder if I...?" He held out one hand before him, clasping his gold and emerald pendant with the other. His fingers moved in an intricate pattern, one that I had only seen a few times. A moment later, the dummy burst into flames.

"Stop that!" I yelped as the canvas blackened.

Emerald snapped his fingers, and the fire went out. "Fascinating. So I can cast a secondary illusion here without dispelling you, and it becomes real."

"The one time you intentionally dispelled me, I was able to hide out here." I scowled at the ceiling, where a soot stain marred the field of golden stars. "And I'll thank you not to set my house on fire again."

Emerald stood in silence for a moment, pondering the implications of this new discovery. "This certainly warrants further study. However, we already have one case before us, and you were asking questions about the Brotherhood. What did you hope to accomplish here?"

"My original idea had been that we might be able to visit those memories together. When I was training with Sister Aster, I could walk through rooms I'd already visited in search of clues that I'd missed the first time around. I thought that we might be able to do the same thing here, but it seems that this is *my* realm." I prodded the still-smoking wreckage of the Emerald-dummy with the toe of my boot.

Even before this new complication, I hadn't entirely understood how I was able to come and go from this place. I hadn't always chosen which rooms to revisit, any more than I had chosen to take Emerald to the woods where we'd, in essence, met. My subconscious had guided me.

"I wonder if we can make a door into your memories," I murmured. I had managed to trick myself into casting a small flame once. Did those rules apply to this place?

Emerald arched a brow. "That doesn't make any sense, Crimson."

"It makes sense *to me*," I retorted. "Perhaps that will be enough to make it work." I turned to one of the blank walls, the one that

Coirpre had once pulled me through. It was smooth and blank again, utterly undamaged by his magical influence.

I squinted at the wall, walking through my logic. "When I first visited Sister Aster, she told me to imagine a place where I felt safe. She made it sound as if anyone could do it. And if this place only exists in my mind, and I was created from *your* mind, wouldn't it make sense that we'd be neighbors?"

Emerald groaned. "You're talking in circles, Crim. Let's just go back to our room and—" His mouth snapped abruptly shut.

A door had appeared in the middle of the otherwise blank wall. It was made of dark wood, with a curved top and simple emblem burned into the wood of a circle with a line through the middle, like the sun setting over the water, sinking into its own reflection.

"How did you do that?" he demanded. "I didn't see you casting an illusion, and *I* certainly didn't do it."

"I'm not sure that the *Aidea* is needed here," I said. "This place follows my rules."

Emerald sucked in a breath. "What in every hell *are* you, Crimson?"

"As you've already pointed out, that is a mystery for another time." I waved him toward the door. "Now, come along. If I'm right about this, you'll be able to show me everything I need to know."

Emerald hung back as I padded to the door. The iron handle was smooth and cool to the touch. The door swung open on creaking hinges; it was heavier than it looked, and I had to lean against it to force it wide. Darkness lay beyond, and I waved Emerald forward.

"You first, neighbor," I told him.

He did not smile. Instead, he lifted his chin, rolled his shoulders back, and strode toward the new room, shaping its contents even as he went. The moment he crossed over, my friend vanished. I started as the broad-shouldered man that I had grown accustomed to morphed into a gangly boy who barely reached my shoulder. His clothes changed with the rest of him, bearing more resemblance to the sackcloth dummy than to the traveling coat he'd worn only a moment before.

He sighed and hunched his bony shoulders toward his ears,

which seemed more prominent than ever. For all that he'd changed, there was no mistaking the fact that this was the Emerald Flame, albeit much younger than I'd ever seen him. He was pimply and sullen-faced, and his greasy hair fell in a limp mop over his brow. When he spoke, his voice was higher than it had been before, and it cracked when he asked me, "Well, are you coming or not?"

With that, I followed him into his memories of the past.

FOUR

"What is this place?" I asked Emerald as I examined the long shelves that spanned from floor to ceiling. The room we entered was a spacious one, but the furniture did not suit it at all. The wooden desk that stood between the door and the window was made of some dark, heavy hardwood that sucked all the light out of the place. An ornate, high-backed chair stood on the far side, facing inward, while two smaller chairs stood alongside us. A single large book bound in unadorned leather sat on the corner of the desk. The place was both unwelcoming and grandiose.

I didn't care for it at all.

"This is the Brother Modest's office." The boy Emerald dropped into one of the chairs. His feet did not quite reach the ground. "I'm about to be told off."

I studied him, hovering behind the second of the smaller chairs. "What for?"

Emerald sucked his bottom lip, watching the door intently. "You'll see."

I was startled by the heavy tread of boots outside. I turned just as a man stepped through the door, which had only moments ago connected Emerald's mindscape to my own. Now, it opened into a corridor lined with stone and brittle plaster walls.

In the mindscape, Emerald's memory was warped and exaggerated. The man who stepped through the door was almost impossibly tall, and for a moment, I thought he might be jotunn himself, or else a giant of some ten feet in height. It took me a long moment to realize that this was not the case at all, that he was simply a man whose importance had made him seem immense and overbearing. His face reminded me a bit of Edur Fenguard's, but the version of the deposed laird that occupied his most unflattering portraits. His dark blond hair was cut short, and his robes were dull and brown, remarkably like the sackcloth skin of my Emerald-dummy.

"Brother Steadfast," he said, using the same name that Yerik had used when we first entered the Lute and Goose. "I have just come from speaking to Brother Harmony." The newcomer breezed through me; apparently I was only real in my *own* mindscape. Which made a certain amount of sense, I supposed, especially if this was Emerald's memory.

Young Emerald kept his head down and stared at the toes of his worn boots. His own clothes were more pedestrian than the man's robes, though they were shabby and secondhand and did not fit him well. He tugged at a loose thread on one sleeve, revealing a bit of his arm.

I sucked in a breath when I saw the raised, dark lines upon his arm revealed in the shift of cloth. "Already?" I asked aloud, not thinking.

Teenage Emerald cast me a sulky glance and tugged his sleeve back into place.

The man did not appear to notice that I had spoken, and he settled down behind the desk, arranging himself tidily and sitting up tall. His smile was disingenuous when he clasped his hand before him and bent across the table toward the child version of my friend.

"You know why you are here, of course," he said.

Emerald nodded, not lifting his head.

The man cleared his throat significantly. "Do you know why you are here?" he asked again, making each word crisp and clear, as if he thought Emerald might be too stupid to understand.

My friend's anger flowed into me, but he kept his voice even as he said, "Yes, Brother Modest. I know."

The man sat back. "We have warned you time and again about using the *Aidea,* Steadfast. It is displeasing to Guise, and your branch more than any other is an abomination to him. You craft beautiful lies." I could tell that *beautiful,* in his mouth, was more of an insult than a compliment.

I made a rude gesture at the man, since he couldn't see me.

"They'll want me to use it," Emerald mumbled. "In the Conjury, when I'm sent away. Shouldn't I at least practice?"

Brother Modest sniffed. "You will have ample opportunity to do so, but not here. Not where your magic might taint the other children. Guise frowns upon you threefold, Brother Steadfast. He loves that which is ordinary. That which is simple. That which is neither pleasing nor displeasing to look up. I understand that it is tempting to compensate for your appearance by using your *Aidea* to—"

Emerald's hand clenched to a fist in his lap, and a low growl emitted from his throat. Brother Modest disappeared, leaving his chair empty and the room silent. There was nothing across the desk from us but the chair itself, and spinning motes of sunlight falling warm and golden through the window.

I shuddered. "Who was *that?*"

"The head of our order." Young Emerald thumped his thigh with his fist, as if he were pummeling Brother Modest's face. "He was awful. I hated him. He didn't have any connection to the *Aidea,* and he acted as if it was a personal blessing."

"Ugh." I wrinkled my nose at the high-backed chair. "What a comprehensively unpleasant person."

Emerald let out a shaking breath and finally lifted his eyes to my face. "You see why I didn't want to come back?"

A soft knocking sound behind us startled us both, and we turned back to the doorway. Another man stood in the entrance, wearing the same robes as Brother Modest—but that was where the resemblance ended. This man's skin was an ashen gray-brown, like parched earth, and his long black hair was pulled back in a knot. Ground-down tusks jutted upward from his lower jaw, and he smiled almost fondly at Emerald.

"Here you are, Brother Steadfast. I wondered where you'd run off to. Come, let's take a walk."

I knew who this was, because there was only one person from Emerald's past that I had ever heard him name before today: his mentor, Brother Harmony.

Emerald made a soft sound, and when I glanced back at him, the gangly youth had shrunk to a small boy, perhaps five or six at the oldest. There was no mistaking those bright-green eyes or that mop of black hair, but it was difficult to reconcile the smiling, plump-cheeked child before me with the countenance of my surly and tormented companion.

He didn't look at me, only jumped off of his chair and hurried over to Brother Harmony, slipping his small hand into the man's much larger one. They stepped out the door together.

"I'm told that you have discovered how to use the *Aidea*," Brother Harmony said. "Impressive, little brother. Very impressive."

"I'm not in trouble?" Emerald asked. His voice was sweet and soft.

This boy is the same person who cast himself into the Bounder out of self-loathing, I thought, and I had to look away for a moment.

"Of course not," Brother Harmony said. "Your *Aidea* will be a great service to society one day. Guise only chooses his strongest followers to bear such a burden. You will never be his chosen, but important work lies ahead of you."

Young Emerald's mouth puckered into a frown as he trotted down the corridor, hurrying his steps in order to keep up with Brother Harmony's deliberately slowed but much longer stride. "Is Guise mad at me?"

"Guise is testing you, little brother. But you are strong, aren't you? That's why I chose this name for you. You may be a Light-weaver, but when the world tempts you to use your power for your own benefit, you will be strong enough to defy it."

The two of them turned abruptly, stepping through a door that led to a courtyard outside. The day was just as beautiful as it had seemed through the window, despite the fact that these memories took place years apart. Why did Emerald remember a place that had treated him so poorly as being filled with warmth and sunlight?

Perhaps because it was the closest thing to a home he'd known growing up.

What a depressing thought.

The courtyard itself was nothing remarkable: a few trees, several benches scattered across grass so green that I was not sure I trusted Em's memory of the color, and a stately marble fountain that sent a plume of clear water spouting high into the air. Brother Harmony and Emerald were the only two people in the courtyard. Was the Brotherhood really this quiet, or had he simply erased everyone else from his recollection?

"Is that why my parents didn't want me?" Emerald asked. "Because of what I can do?" The worried expression on his face was heartbreaking.

Brother Harmony sat down on the edge of the fountain and trailed his fingers through the water. "I don't think so, little brother. They couldn't have known."

"Oh." Emerald folded his hands behind his back and scuffed one toe in the dirt. "Then why? Was that a test, too?"

"I won't explain that now," Brother Harmony said softly. "You are too young. I will only say that your mother's reasoning was sound. You and I are not like other people, not only because of what we can *do*, but because of what we *are*. We can never be what Guise most wants us to be, but if we try hard enough—if we are good enough, and live quiet lives, and do not give in to passion or pride, if we are unobjectionable enough, then we will earn Guise's approval in the end. Do you understand?"

I balled my hands into fists, too stunned by these words to speak. This was the man Emerald looked up to? The one person who he had thought of as a father figure?

Beside the fountain, baby Emerald nodded. "Yes, Brother Harmony. I will do my best."

Brother Harmony ruffled Emerald's short mop of hair. "Good boy," he said, his voice as warm as the sunlight, thick with approval.

There was nothing I could say to change the course of things. Emerald had been so young then, and he must know by now that Harmony had misled him. Didn't he?

Or was his failure to become *unobjectionable* one of the things that had driven him to punish himself again and again, even until today?

I stood a little way off the fountain, listening to the two of them talk. I tried to follow along, but I soon lost the thread of their conversation. It was easy to hate Brother Modest after only a few moments, but there was something even more terrible about watching these two together, seeing the gentle way that Brother Harmony guided this much younger version of my own mentor.

You think you are helping him, but you are not. I wanted to grab Brother Harmony by the front of his robes and shake him, if only I had that power here. *You are not doing him a kindness. You are telling this boy the same words he will repeat back to me on the bank of a river that nearly claimed his life. He trusts you, while you might as well be slipping the stones into his pockets that he will carry for the rest of his life.*

And yet, for all that it angered me, I could not blame the man himself. He was clearly acting out of love, telling Emerald the same stories that he had been told when he was a boy. His advice was well-intended poison, and he was feeding it in little doses to a child who trusted him.

I turned away, and as I did so, I moved. Not in the mindscape, but in the real world. I was aware of the pressure of Emerald's skin against mine only for a second as we slid back into place, on the floor of our rented room in the Lute and Goose.

Emerald—*my* Emerald—fell back against the side of his bed, blinking slowly as if he had just emerged from a stupor. His green eyes took a moment to focus, and when they did, he leaned toward me again.

"Crimson?" he asked gently. "What's wrong?"

I lifted my hand to my face, where tears spilled across my cheeks. "I'm sorry," I told him.

He cocked his head, his thick brows pinching in puzzlement. "Sorry for what?"

"For—" *For the fact that the only person you trusted in childhood didn't deserve it. For the way people have spoken to and about you all your life. For leaving you to face that life alone.*

For not being there when you needed me.

Emerald was still waiting, and I could not make myself say the words. I would only end up crying harder, and he would end up comforting me even though he was the one who'd been hurt.

"For making you go back there," I said at last.

Emerald chuckled mirthlessly and ran one hand through his hair. He closed his eyes and took a steady breath. "We're already here, Crim. You didn't make me come back, the Conjury did." He got to his feet. "I'm going to take a bath and get some dinner. And then we're going to try that again. I want you to teach me how to do it. We'll see if I can get there without touching you. If so, it would be a pretty clever trick."

I smiled to myself as he headed into the washroom and began to wrestle with the old and evidently cantankerous spigot for the washtub. Leave it to Emerald to seek mastery over something magical which he couldn't understand. I had no doubt that before the night was out, he'd have developed a formula for how to use the mindscape to our greatest advantage.

Maybe it would come in useful for our time in the Brotherhood. While the pipes creaked to life, I contemplated our reasons for coming to Kinmore, recalling what both Brother Modest and Brother Harmony had said about Guise's view of the world. Part of me hoped that Guise really *had* come to Kinmore, speaking through a mortal mouthpiece, dwelling among his acolytes.

After the way his followers had treated my friend in his youth, I wanted a word with him, god or not.

CHAPTER

FIVE

"Did you sleep well?" Yerik asked over breakfast the following morning.

"Mm." The dark shadows under Emerald's eyes should have answered that question, but either Yerik was oblivious to my companion's exhaustion, or he was being polite.

I turned the full brilliance of my smile on the younger man. "It was a lovely room. Thank you *so* much for your hospitality. That portrait of the goose was impeccable."

[You're overdoing it,] Emerald thought as he laid a wafer-thin slice of cured pork onto a piece of freshly-baked bread. I wondered what it would taste like, and tried not to be jealous of the fact that I would never know.

Yerik didn't seem to think that I was laying it on too thick, however. "Thank you very much, Master Crimson," he said, bowing his head slightly. A proud smile lit up his features. "I painted it myself."

"And the one behind the bar, as well?" I nodded toward the massive portrait of Coirpre, with the sloe-eyed goose gazing longingly up at him.

"It's the biggest canvas I've ever attempted." Yerik drew himself up to his full height, being with pride. "Is it a good likeness?"

"It's as if he were here in the room with us," I said. "Only twice as large as normal."

[You're making fun of him.] Emerald took a bite of his meal.

[I am not,] I thought back, still smiling at Yerik. *[Name one thing I've said that isn't true.]*

"Thank you very much, sir. I'm quite proud of it." Yerik rocked back and forth, toe to heel, heel to toe. He seemed to be waiting for something. After a few seconds of nervous movement, he cleared his throat.

Emerald lifted his eyes to Yerik's face.

"I just wanted to say good luck, Steadfast. I know you'll solve whatever's going on at the Brotherhood. You were always good at putting things right." The tips of Yerik's ears flushed a bit darker, and he bowed once. "I hope to see you again before you depart Kinmore." He hurried away, leaving Emerald staring after him, still chewing and more than a little bemused.

[I think he likes you,] I thought.

Emerald choked on his bread.

[But maybe not as much as he likes Coirpre,] I amended. *[As far as we know, he hasn't painted you in the company of any variety of waterfowl.]*

"Damnit," Emerald rasped out between hacking coughs. *[Where do you get that impression? We were classmates. That's all. I hardly remember him from the Brotherhood. I can't even remember the name he went by back then.]*

[You weren't friends?]

[I wasn't friends with anyone, not really.] He finally managed to get his breathing back to normal and returned to his meal. "We should discuss the plan for approaching the Brotherhood," he said aloud, a clear signal that the prior topic of conversation was no longer viable.

I pretended to lean one elbow on the table. "Are you asking my opinion?"

[No.] Emerald took our conversation private again. *[I'm*

preparing to deliver the bad news. It isn't safe for you to accompany me.]

I shuddered, recalling the last time that Emerald had banished me. It had been in the middle of an argument, very much against my will, and while I had mostly forgiven him for the incident, I wasn't looking forward to repeating the experience.

"No. You are *not* putting me..." *[You are not putting me back there while you solve a mystery on your own. I won't allow it.]* I wasn't sure how I would enforce this assertion, but I was determined.

[Calm down, Crimson. I'm not talking about sending you away. You can still be around. You can follow me. But the risk of being found out in this instance is...] He stopped midway through layering a piece of cheese and another slice of pork onto a fresh cut of bread. *[If the Conjury finds out that you've become independent, we could be taken in. You're an anomaly, and they don't take kindly to people doing things with the Aidea they don't understand. And the Brotherhood... Well, you saw what I remember. We don't know what we're walking into, but between Commander Finch breathing down our necks and the Brotherhood's hatred of the Aidea, it's too risky.]*

[It's not as if Finch will be there,] I thought sulkily.

[She has another agent inside already, remember? Someone else who's reporting to her. We can't take the risk.]

He was right, although I resented it. Solving a mystery was difficult enough without all the limitations that my identity created. I would always be pretending to be something I was not. *[I wish I could have a real body,]* I thought, burying my frown in my palm.

[Let me just conjure one up for you, then.] Emerald lifted one thick eyebrow as he finished off his breakfast, before reaching for mine. *[In the meantime, you can find other ways to investigate. Be a bird. Or an alley cat. The elasticity of your current form has its uses.]*

Oh, what a relief, to know that I can be useful to the great Emerald Flame, even when I can't touch, taste, or smell anything in the real world. I kept my thoughts to myself, in part because I really did enjoy our work. We had made a mess of things in Upper Bound, but we had also saved lives. We'd stopped a pair of centuries-old murderers. We'd found a way to protect Dyrne, at least for the time being. Wasn't that worthwhile?

All the same, I wished that I could be more than an instrument. Emerald had enjoyed six months of peace and quiet in Dyrne without me, but I had no life outside of Emerald's proximity, nothing that I enjoyed for its own sake. The only mark I would ever leave on the world was a legacy of furthering justice inasmuch as I was able, and even that would be Emerald's, at least in the eyes of the Conjury, who thought I was a husk.

A useful husk.

How irritating.

[Don't sulk,] Emerald said, polishing off the last of the breakfast Yerik had provided me, which I was incapable of enjoying. *[I'm not looking forward to this, either.]*

At least we would be unhappy together. Petty though it may have made me, I found some small comfort in that.

WE BID Yerik farewell before setting out for the Brotherhood. The enthusiasm of his farewell only reinforced my belief that Yerik knew Emerald better than my companion let on. Then again, it would not be the first time that my friend was oblivious to someone's attention. He'd seemed surprised by the fact that Coirpre was willing to give him the time of day, much less assist in saving his life.

"So what's your plan?" I asked peevishly as Emerald led me through the streets of the little burg. Kinmore had shrunk behind us now, its regal buildings and dilapidated rowhouses blending into one another in the distance. "Are you just going to stroll up to the compound and tell them you're home?"

Emerald didn't answer, and when his silence dragged on a beat too long, I turned to face him. "Please tell me that's not your plan."

"I'm one of them—"

"You are *not!*" I retorted.

"I *was* one of them, back when I didn't have a choice." He ran his hand absently through his hair, focusing his attention on the green fields and rolling slopes around us. Sheep dotted the hills like little clouds come down to earth. They reminded me of Errol, with his fluffy coat and neat black hooves.

"I got very good at hiding what I felt," Emerald continued. "Even if Brother Modest is still there, he won't know that I've turned my back on Guise."

[Or rebelled against the Conjury.]

His spine stiffened, and he swiveled his head around to glower at me. **[He can never know that. Nobody can.]**

Yes, I thought, *it's a secret that no one can know... apart from Amaya and Tincrown and Errol, and the dwarves from the Deepvein Mine, and all the inhabitants of Dyrne.* Did a secret that a hundred other people were in on really count as a secret anymore?

There was no point in arguing that topic, so I returned to the subject of our main discussion. "How are you going to convince them to let you inside? If Yerik has been able to keep track of your reputation from afar, surely your work for the Conjury is common knowledge?"

"I'll tell them I quit," Emerald said, as if it could possibly be that simple.

I raised a skeptical eyebrow and turned my gaze sidelong toward a particularly attentive cluster of sheep, who had come over to investigate us. They stared at us with vapid, unblinking eyes, still chewing mouthfuls of dewy grass. Sheep, I decided, were pretty much like goats, only stupider.

"Why would they believe that?" I asked.

"I think I can convince them."

I rolled my eyes. "Forgive me, Em, if I'm not entirely sold on your acting abilities. If Modest asks *why* you've come, what are you going to do? Grunt at him? You should have a story worked out in advance, at the very least."

"Fine." Emerald stopped short, rolling his heavy shoulders forward, tucking in his chin, and turning his eyes to the hard-packed ground beneath our feet. "You were right, Brother Modest. I thought that I could distinguish myself in the Conjury's service, but they will never see me as anything other than... *this.*" He waved one hand to indicate his person, his mouth bowed in a mournful frown. "You tried to warn me that the world will never accept anyone who looks like me, and I was too stubborn to understand that you were protecting me. I should never have fooled myself into thinking that I was an exception."

I stared at him for a moment, marveling at his contrition, which did not contain a single hint of irony. As his words sunk in, I dragged my hand over my face, letting my stubble prick against my palm. "Gods," I muttered. "Are you even acting, or do you really believe that?"

Emerald straightened up again and smirked at me. "Of course I don't believe it. But Brother Modest will, because I'll be telling him exactly what he always thought to be true. That I won't fit anywhere. That I'm a disgrace to everything the Brotherhood stands for."

I nibbled my bottom lip, trying to work out the right words to express my feelings. "Em, after what happened in the Bounder..."

What happened. As if it was a mere accident, and not something that my mentor had done of his own free will. As if a breeze had carried him over the side of the bridge, and not his own momentum.

Emerald's uneven smile widened, although there was no mirth in it. "Are you asking me if I'm serious about hiding away in the Brotherhood for the rest of my life?"

"I don't know." I curled one lock of my scarlet hair around my finger, wishing for all the world that I was better at discussing such things. We'd only danced around the subject of his self-loathing and the way it had manifested during our tenure on Kovin Isle. "Maybe."

Em let out a huff of laughter so unexpected that it scared the sheep, who balked and spun before scrambling away across their field.

"Believe me when I tell you this," he said, adjusting his grip on the embroidered pack that Tincrown had made him over the summer. "There is no power in Dregandresal that could convince me to spend the rest of my days in that place. I'd heave myself into the Bounder again rather than give Brother Modest that satisfaction."

I didn't find that assertion as comforting as he seemed to think I would.

When Emerald stopped again, we were still in the middle of nowhere. The road had followed a gradual and winding incline, skirting vernal ponds and rocky outcroppings and hand-built stone walls that were likely older than the thoroughfare itself. Although the slope upon which we found ourselves could not compare to the rugged natural beauty of the Mooncrest Highlands, it still provided us with a view of Kinmore and the glittering sea to the south. The weather had relented, and little patches of sunlight spilled through the clouds, gilding both the air and the land below them in a shower of golden light. From our position, I could even make out the sloping roof of the Lute and Goose.

"I like it better out here," I said, lifting one hand to shade my eyes as I admired the view.

"Because you can't see the slums," Emerald said, ever the pessimist.

"Perhaps you're right."

"I know I am," he said. "Because that's why *I* like it better. I'd rather sleep rough in a place like this than be trapped in the city where people can't stop gawking, and where all the things I hate about civilization are jammed cheek by jowl into one place."

Just because Emerald preferred one thing over another didn't mean I felt the same way. I liked being seen, because that was what I was *for*, but it was more peaceful out here. I didn't have to worry about someone working out what I was. Besides, the quality of light was different in the wild places. The interplay of shade and sunlight skimming over the high grass made me feel that I was, somehow, among friends.

"Why did we stop?" I asked. "Surely not for the view?"

"Because we're almost there." Emerald hooked a thumb up the slope. "I don't want anyone at the compound to see you changing, or you'll sabotage my cover story."

"Right." My shoulders drooped. "What should I be, then? A bird, or...?"

"Whatever you like," Emerald said.

"How generous." I crossed my arms, trying to think. I had been a bird once before, and while it had been helpful to be able to fly around and follow the huntsman Oidche from afar, it had its limitations. A bird flying through a wall would attract attention. Perhaps I should try something else. Something smaller and less conspicuous.

Changing my appearance wasn't difficult when I was altering my clothes, or sliding between the poles of Simon and Simone. Turning myself into something else required a bit more effort and had left me disoriented the first time I tried it. I'd had more experience with such things, though, after all the time I'd spent in my mind-cottage.

I shifted into a new form for the very first time, and Emerald jumped. "Crimson?" he asked, letting his eyes skim over the path in an ever-widening search. "Oh, Aster's sake, please tell me I didn't accidentally dispel you..."

[I'm here,] I told him, looking up at him from my new vantage point. *[And I must say, I never realized how large your nostrils are until this very moment.]*

"Did you turn yourself invisible?" he asked, ignoring the dig. "I thought that was impossible, since you can't be *nothing*..."

[I'm right **here.***]* I fluttered up to his eye level, perching on his nose. Technically, I didn't need to move my wings to fly, but acting the part always made it easier to trick my body into doing impossible things. *[I thought I should be something small. Unobtrusive.]*

Emerald lifted his finger to his nose, and I trundled across to rest on the tip. I was slightly smaller than the joint upon which I stood. My waggling black antennae kept fluttering at the upper end of my field of vision, and when I opened my wings again, the glossy red of my chiton came into view.

Subtlety wasn't my forte, even when I was the size of a thumb-pad.

"A beetle?" Emerald asked, examining me. "That's, hm, that's different. But I suppose it makes sense. Because you're a pest."

I did my best to scowl at him and discovered that beetle anatomy was not particularly compatible with facial expressions.

"I like this," he added. "You can't talk back." Before I could point out that I was still capable of conversation with him, *thank you very much,* he lifted me to his shoulder, waited for me to climb into his collar, and resumed his trek up the slope.

So far, the land had been lovely and green, the seasons on this part of the mainland lagging a few weeks behind what we had experienced on Kovin Isle.

As we crested the hill, however, the green and gold of the countryside fell away. The plain below us was brown and weathered, populated with once-white tents that were now splattered with mud. These temporary dwellings circled a weathered stone wall, within which stood the compound that I had briefly experienced through Emerald's memories.

[I didn't realize it would be this... muddy.]

"It usually isn't," Emerald murmured. "I wonder, though. If people have gotten word that an emissary of Guise lives here, maybe they're coming here to see if it's true."

[This many people outside of the Brotherhood follow Guise?] From our vantage point, I could make out some of the figures meandering back and forth through the muck.

"What did you think?" Emerald asked as he began the descent toward the front gates. "That only members of the Brotherhood cared about him?"

[That's how it worked for the Sisterhood of the Crone.]

"If that were true, who would call the sisters in to say rites over the dead? You saw the deference with which McLachlan treated them. Even Edur Fenguard wouldn't interfere with them."

[That's different. Fenguard** knew **that the Crone was real.]

"If you asked Brother Modest, he would tell you that he knows Guise is real." With each step, Emerald's shoulders rose higher toward his ears. I couldn't feel the muscles tensing beneath my feet, but his nervous energy thrummed through me, loud and unmistakable as a drumbeat. "That's how faith works, Crim."

I wasn't so sure about that. I had believed in the Crone, at least to some extent, long before I set foot in the Black Hollow. How could I have stepped into the Sisterhood and told any of them, to their faces, that I did not believe their goddess? The sisters were kind. They were sincere. The way in which their order moved through the world made life that much better for the people around them. What was the purpose of faith whose leaders only used their status to condemn and malign the people they held power over?

I had long since made up my mind about Guise. I didn't *want* him to exist, because as far as I knew, he was of no benefit to anybody.

We were halfway between the brow of the hill and the front gate of the compound when one of the tent-dwellers spotted us.

"Hello, there!" She lifted her arm in greeting, beaming at Emerald as if he was a long-lost friend.

[You know her?] I asked.

Emerald shook his head. *[Don't think so.]*

The woman hurried toward us, her hands outstretched. As far as I could tell, she was human, with pale skin and nut-brown hair and a smattering of either mud or freckles across her nose. Her hair was cut to chin length, although it looked as if it had been hacked off with a knife, and—

[Gods above and below, what is she wearing?] I understood that not everyone could afford to be discerning about their clothes, but she appeared to be wearing a linen pillowcase.

Emerald had no time to answer before the women reached him, taking his hands in hers.

"Welcome, Brother!" she exclaimed. "Have you come to seek the wisdom of Guise?"

"Erm," Emerald said, too alarmed to be eloquent.

She released one of his hands and stood on her toes to caress his cheek. "Guise has truly blessed you, Brother. One cannot be too proud when one has nothing to be proud of."

Emerald reeled away from her as if she'd slapped him across the jaw. I wished desperately that I could have spoken, either to distract the woman or to reassure him. I wished that I could shove her away. I wished that I could bite her. I wished that I could tell her what exactly I thought of her.

Instead, I crawled up Emerald's shoulder and into his collar until my tiny feet sank ever so slightly into his skin. I sent a little frisson of comfort through him at the same time that I said, *[She's wrong, and you know it.]*

"Thank you," Emerald said aloud, and I was certain that he was speaking to me even though it was directed at this unhelpful, small-minded stranger. "I have indeed come to serve Guise. I grew up here."

The woman's smile somehow became even brighter. "You did? Of course you did. I should have guessed that. Truly, Brother, you are an inspiration. What are you called?"

Emerald started to answer, choked, and then corrected himself. "Steadfast," he said.

"Steadfast," the woman repeated, savoring the name. "A wandering lamb, returned to the flock at last. Have you heard the good news, Brother? Guise speaks through his mouthpiece in the presence of everyone. I've seen it myself!"

"I look forward to... communing with the mouthpiece of the Unifier." Emerald's eye twitched.

The woman bowed her head and released his other hand at last.

He didn't ask her name before turning away from her, tucking up the collar of his greatcoat and stomping away across the muddy lawn toward the gate. Several of the people we passed called out, "Hello, Brother!" in greeting, as if he were an old friend.

[This is worse than being insulted outright,] he thought. *[Why couldn't Finch have found someone else to come here?]*

[You could have refused her, couldn't you?] I asked. *[Told her that you were too close to this investigation to be objective? Made some excuse?]*

[Maybe.] Emerald's eyes flicked toward the high walls of the compound. *[And it might not have been a lie. But I'll be honest, Crim... if Guise really is trying to assert more control on the world, I want to be involved.]*

[Why?] I asked, but I felt the answer before he said it, his anger radiating off of him like heat.

[Because of what we learned in Upper Bound,] he told me. *[Because of what Edur Fenguard did to the Crone. Because we now know for certain, Crim, that it's possible to kill a god.]*

CHAPTER

SIX

In Emerald's memory, Guise's compound had been solitary and welcoming. Brother Modest had been terrible, of course, and Harmony's advice had been insidious, but the compound was still the closest thing he'd known to a home.

Either Emerald's memory was faulty, or the intervening years had not been kind to the place. The grass was brown, and it crackled under Emerald's boots as he followed a stranger into the monastery's beating heart.

The inner halls of the compound were no better. The plaster was flaking, and the bricks in the floor were cracked and chipped, the mortar between them slowly turning back to dust.

[I assume the dilapidation is intentional,] I noted. *[You can't be too proud when you have nothing to be proud of.]*

Emerald snorted. *[Truly, this shoddy brickwork was the will of Guise himself.]*

The man who had met us at the gate did not offer his name. When Emerald asked to speak to Brother Modest, he'd simply told my friend to follow him before flitting away down the corridor.

I recognized the door where our guide stopped to knock: it was the same one that had appeared in my mind-cottage when Emerald

53

took the lead. Emerald cracked his knuckles in anticipation while I peeked out of his collar.

"Come in!" called a voice. I'd only heard it once before, but there was no mistaking it as anything but that of the tall, onerous man I'd met in Emerald's memory.

My friend suppressed a shudder as our guide opened the door.

Brother Modest himself had changed in the intervening years. His hair was now streaked with silver, and the lines around his mouth and eyes had deepened, but when he looked up to see who it was, the curl of his lip was entirely too familiar. He'd been studying a large tome, but as Emerald ducked through the doorway, he closed the cover and pushed it away.

"Brother Steadfast," he said, his voice dripping with an intent akin to cruelty. "My, how you've grown. I thought you'd moved on to bigger and *better* things. Made a name for yourself, have you?"

"You know him, Brother?" asked the man standing in the doorway.

"Of course. This is one of our foundlings." Brother Modest rose to his feet and approached Emerald. Time had altered their relative proportions: there was easily twice as much of Emerald as there was of the older man, but even so, it was clear which of them had power over the other. "What brings you back here, Steadfast?"

[Look around,] Emerald told me. *[See if you can find anything noteworthy in here. We're unlikely to get a better opportunity.]* Aloud, he was already repeating the same speech he'd given me on the road. To my surprise, he seemed less disturbed by Brother Modest's snide remarks than he had been by the woman we met outside.

Because he knew it was coming, I realized. *Because he was braced for this man to be an ass.*

The man who'd brought us there shut the door in our wake. I waited until Modest turned away from Emerald to take flight.

I flitted off across the room and landed on the bookshelf. There were a few more objects in the room than there had been in Emerald's memory, but not many. The covers of the books were dull, and the spines gave no indication of their contents.

I wasn't sure what I'd hoped for. A magical charm? Some sort of obviously enchanted artifact? A letter, penned in a godly hand, reading *Dear Modest, I'm just going to pop in for a quick visit before lunch?*

Unlikely. Still, I had expected some sign of Guise's presence. If the god was speaking through one of his disciples, Brother Modest was a likely candidate. I had already begun to imagine Guise as Modest's twin, with his sneering mouth and receding hairline, but perhaps with an otherworldly glow and an additional foot or two of height.

Finding nothing on the bookshelf, I climbed to the ceiling, hoping for a better vantage point. If Guise *wasn't* truly present, how would Modest fool people into believing he was? The *Aidea*, perhaps?

What was to stop someone like *me* from impersonating a god?

As I scanned the room, my eyes were drawn to the heavy tome Brother Modest had been reading when we arrived. Unlike the books on the shelf, it lay in such a way that I could see the cover, which said, in block lettering, *REGISTRY OF UNDESIRABLES.*

Undesirables. That was the word Emerald had used to refer to the children who were raised by the Brotherhood.

I was silently stewing about this thoughtless phrasing when I heard Emerald say, "I have decided to forgo life outside the walls. I want to return to the Brotherhood, to do for other children what you did for me."

[Now, hold on…] I waggled my antenna.

"I'm not sure that I follow." Below me, Brother Modest steepled his long, slim fingers and leaned forward on the desk. "You wish to serve Guise as… what? A mentor to the undesirables?"

"I would be able to advise children to avoid the same mistakes I've made," Emerald said. "I thought… I thought Brother Harmony could train me." His voice cracked as he said his old mentor's name.

[Oh, Em…] Hearing his voice give like that made my heart break a little.

[Settle down,] he thought peevishly. *[I can act, you know. Where did you think you learned it from?]*

[I assumed it was all from Coirpre,] I admitted.

Emerald coughed and tilted his head to one side so that he could glare up at me.

"Brother Harmony," Modest repeated, as if this was the piece of the puzzle he'd been missing. "Of course, of course. Like calls to like. I shouldn't be surprised that you would miss him."

"He was like a father to me," Emerald said, and gods above and below, *that* line was not an act. The truth of it reverberated through Emerald's core and into mine.

"I assume that the timing of your arrival is not a coincidence," Brother Modest said. "You are aware of everything that's been going on?"

Emerald nodded slowly.

"I have not forgotten you, Brother Steadfast. You were never a true believer. You were proud. Spirited. *Stubborn.*" On Modest's lips, each of these words was an indictment. "Are you certain that you don't wish to see proof of Guise's presence before you ask to return? As I recall, you were obsessed with finding proof for everything."

[Of course you were,] I thought, puffing up a bit with pride. **[Even back then, I bet you were methodical.]**

Emerald rapped his knuckles on the arm of his chair and nodded again. "I was, Brother. I always wanted everything to be fair. But I think I've given up on trying to remake the world to match the version of it in my head. I'm only one man."

"If indeed you can be called a man," Modest said. "I see that you've grown wiser in your time away. Perhaps you *would* be a good influence. It would help the children see that pride will only end in folly. As you know, Steadfast, the blade of grass that grows the highest is the first to be cut."

I'd heard those words before, in Finch's office, rolling off of Emerald's tongue like scripture.

"I've never forgotten that," Emerald murmured. "How could I?"

Brother Modest nodded serenely. "Wise words stay with us."

Emerald took a deep breath. "In answer to your earlier question, no, Brother Modest, I don't need proof. I have seen evidence of Guise's presence everywhere I go in the world."

"You have been brought low." Brother Modest's facial expression was composed, almost benevolent, but his tone belied his glee at seeing his old student bow and scrape before him.

It was a good thing I was an insect at the moment, because if I'd been a person, I would not have been able to still my tongue. Come to think of it, my anatomy was imaginary, and therefore presented no true limitation. If I wanted to scream curses at Modest from the ceiling, I could probably find a way.

I smothered the urge, but only out of respect for my friend's plan.

"I have considered your request, Brother Steadfast." Modest crossed his legs at the knee and leaned back in his heavy wooden chair. "I will allow you to stay here on the condition that you assist Brother Modest with his duties. If you prove yourself useful, I will permit you to stay on. And in the meantime, you'll get more proof than ever." He got to his feet and strode past Emerald, throwing open the door. "Brother Lightfoot, are you here?"

The man who'd led us into the compound appeared as if by magic, although I thought it more likely that he'd been lingering in the hall and listening in on the conversation.

"Yes, Brother?" Lightfoot dipped his head.

"Steadfast will be staying with us for the time being. We will need to find quarters for him. Has anyone taken over Sister Subtle's old room? No? Then that will do. And bring him some clothes, too."

Lightfoot waved for Emerald to follow, and I took flight from the ceiling, landing atop my friend's head.

[Did you find anything useful in there?]

[Nothing,] I told him. *[Although I hardly expected him to be keeping a god behind the desk. If we're going to figure out what's going on here, I expect we'll have to look a bit harder than that.]*

THE ROOM where Brother Lightfoot led us was somehow even more depressing than the rest of the compound. Emerald had to duck to squeeze through the door, behind which lay only a bed that was much too small for his frame, and a desk and chair clearly made for someone half his size.

"The afternoon meal has already been served," Lightfoot said.

His eyes swept over Emerald. "Although I expect you won't suffer much for that, big lad like you. Dinner will be served at six, and the necessary—"

"I remember," Emerald said gruffly. "I don't imagine much has changed since I was here. Guise smiles upon consistency."

"Of course." Lightfoot's simpering smile made me simmer with quiet rage which, for some inexplicable reason, was not echoed in Emerald. Why didn't he hate this man as much as I did?

Because he expects people to be petty and ignorant, I reminded myself. Whereas it came as a surprise to me every time.

"I'll try to find clothes that will better suit you." Lightfoot backed away a pace. "Welcome back, Brother Steadfast." He turned and hurried down the hall, living up to his name.

[I hate him,] I said at once. If I'd had the ability to speak aloud, I would have happily done so before he was out of hearing. *[Did you know him from before, too?]*

[No.] Emerald passed his hand over his eyes and sighed deeply. *[He must have arrived after I left. It's been, what, twenty years since I was here? No, more than that. Although I do seem to remember that Sister Subtle was a lambkin. No wonder this place is cramped.]*

[I didn't realize that the Brotherhood allowed women to join,] I mused.

Emerald sat down on the edge of the little bed, which groaned beneath his weight. *[Most orders aren't like the Sisterhood, you know. Of course, they had their reasons for only allowing women to serve the Crone, given the nature of their calling. Other gods and goddesses aren't so circumspect.]*

[Speaking of a calling... explain the names. I can see where Lightfoot got his, but Modest?] I fluttered out of Emerald's collar and alit on the wall behind him. *[He seems the exact opposite.]*

He turned to face me, as if talking to a beetle via a mental link wasn't the least bit out of the ordinary.

[The names we're given when we arrive are based on the qualities we should strive for to better serve Guise, and to remind us of

our faults,] Emerald explained. *[For example, as I recall, Sister Subtle had a habit of speaking a bit too bluntly—]*

Someone's fist knocked against the door, sending a shower of plaster dust spinning through the air.

"Come in," Emerald said, turning his back on me.

The door opened, and the accompanying emotions that flooded through Emerald were so vivid and intense that, for a moment, I lost my sense of both place and time. The man who stood on the far side was known to me, although his once-black hair was now more salt than pepper, and the laugh lines around his mouth revealed his age. His eyes, however, hadn't changed in the slightest, and when they fixed on Emerald, there was such immense affection in them that I had to look away.

"Brother Harmony." Emerald got to his feet. This time, when his voice cracked and wavered, it was not a performance.

Harmony set the bundle in his arms upon the desk and pulled Emerald into a crushing hug. In the years since the events my friend had shown me, he'd grown taller than his old mentor by nearly a head, but in Harmony's company, he still seemed like a boy.

"Look at you, Steadfast." Harmony held my friend out at arm's length. "You've grown up. I wasn't sure—you stopped writing, and I heard you changed your name."

"You knew about that?" Emerald pressed his palm to his face, scrubbing at something. Aster's sake, was he *crying?* I'd never seen him cry while sober.

"I live in a monastery, not under a rock. Of course I've kept up with you, Steady. You strayed from the path I set you on, but you did well. Very well, all things considered. I resigned myself to the idea that you'd forgotten me."

Emerald let out a little hiccup somewhere between a laugh and a sob. "Of course not."

In the course of my short life, I had seen my friend in all sorts of vulnerable situations. He had fallen in love, and subsequently left the object of his affections behind. He had flirted with disaster on the bank of the Bounder. He had condemned and berated and despised himself on more occasions than I could count.

In the end, though, this show of emotion was the one thing I could not bear. My experience with fathers was limited, and Emerald was the closest I came to having one of my own. Harmony might be a surrogate who claimed to offer paternal affection, but I could not in good faith call their relationship loving.

Yet how could I express this, when doing so would mean calling Emerald's oldest meaningful relationship into question? What purpose would it serve?

Out of respect for his feelings, I tucked myself into my mind-cottage to give the two of them a moment of privacy. Once there, I let myself shift back into one of my usual forms as Simone, although I donned the glossy red-and-gold battle armor I had worn during Burp's combat for his kingship.

Alone in my own mindscape, I approached the dummy-Emerald that I had bruised my knuckles on only a few weeks before. I straightened him up, smoothing the wrinkles in his greatcoat, and made him a promise.

"When you were little, you had to face this place alone," I told him. "That will never be the case again. I'll find a way to protect you this time."

CHAPTER
SEVEN

[*Crimson?]* Emerald asked.

I wasn't sure how long I had spent puttering about in the mind-cottage. I had been reluctant to reemerge before I was summoned, and I'd spent the intervening time arranging and rearranging the space, adding decorations and taking them away again.

The moment he called for me, however, I popped back into the world beside him.

"Oh, goodness, I wasn't thinking." I glanced down at myself, flicking at my armor as if in an attempt to remove an imaginary speck of dust. "Thank goodness we're in your room and not a common area—" I lifted my eyes to my friend and stopped short, drawing away from him. "Em, are you being *punished?*"

My friend rolled his eyes in annoyance and plucked at the dull brown cloth of his new garments. "Surely you've worked out by now that this is how the brothers tend to dress."

"Well, yes, but..." I swallowed down the first, second, and third retorts that came to mind. The fourth, however, would not be silenced. "Only, we *just* got you that new coat, and the shirt really did suit you..."

"I don't mind the outfit," Emerald said, making a sharp gesture with one hand to indicate that the conversation was over. "Where have you been? Did you learn anything useful?"

"I..." I fumbled for a lie, but could not produce one in time for it to be believable. "I was hiding, if you must know."

Emerald narrowed his eyes. "You wasted all that time?"

"Where were you? Did *you* learn anything?" I shot back.

Emerald coughed and turned his eyes to the floor. "I was busy."

"Busy transforming into an absolute scruffmuffin," I muttered under my breath. I raised my voice a little before continuing. "I don't know much about this place, so I'm not sure what's out of the ordinary yet."

"I have the morning to get myself settled," Emerald said. "Apparently, Guise will be making an appearance tonight, whatever that means. If we're lucky, maybe we can figure out what's happening and get this all settled as soon as possible. We could be back on the road by tomorrow."

I held my tongue. That would certainly be my preferred outcome, but our luck was a slippery thing.

"But just in case," Emerald went on, "we can take a tour of the compound. If you don't mind...?" He gestured toward me. "I doubt that stepping out of my room with a redheaded stranger dressed in plate mail will win me any support from the Brotherhood."

I returned to my beetle form and resumed my place at his collar. The fall of his hood offered me plenty of opportunity to hide amid the folds, where even my scarlet shell would not be seen. Once I was situated, Emerald stepped out into the hall.

[I didn't get a chance to ask many questions last night,] he told me. *[I spent the whole evening catching up with Brother Harmony. He was being cagey about the situation with Guise, but I think he believes that it's real.]*

[Did he at least mention who the mouthpiece is? You know, Guise's emissary. Is it Modest?] Perhaps it was irrational of me, but I didn't want to call the man "brother." He was certainly no kinsman of *mine*.

[He made it sound as if it's someone I know,] Emerald said.

[Which could be anyone, I suppose. I recognize a fair few of the other brothers and sisters by sight. I mostly stayed with Harmony, since he's one of the few who had any grasp of the Aidea, and those of us with talents were assigned to him.]

The halls of the compound all looked the same to me, but Emerald navigated them as though it was second nature. Twenty-and-some-odd years was not long enough to strip the Brotherhood from his muscle memory. We passed a few other brothers and sisters of Emerald's age and standing, most of whom looked at him askance once his back was to them.

[You don't suppose that Brother Harmony could be the one....?] I asked.

Emerald's reply was immediate. *[No. He would have told me. He suggested that one of my peers was somehow involved, but I spent a lot of time alone back then. I could pass most of my old classmates in the street and not know them from a stranger.]*

He turned right when he reached an outer door, and we emerged into a courtyard. The massive once-white marble fountain had turned pale yellow, its flow reduced to a trickle, and the reservoir at its base filled only halfway with an algae-clogged pool.

So far, I had been dismissive of the compound, but there was something about the courtyard that gave me pause. *[Do you feel anything here, Em?]* I asked.

[Feel? Feel how?] Emerald's confusion was understandable, given my limited senses. He stopped short beside the fountain, scanning the courtyard for evidence of anything amiss. A handful of morose children were huddled by one wall, ignoring us as they played a game that appeared to consist of poking something on the ground with a stick.

I struggled to find the right words. *[There's something unsettling about this place. The way the shadows fall a little too dark. Have you noticed that?]*

[It only seems that way because the place is so bleak,] Emerald assured me.

I wasn't convinced. There was something about the play of light, the way night seemed to linger in the hollows even in daylight, that left me leery.

[Gods, it really has been ages,] Emerald mused, indifferent to the subtle oddities that stood out like warnings to my eye. How could a Lightweaver fail to notice what was so clear to me? *[It's so much smaller than it seemed. Although, honestly, I can't believe I'm saying that. I always felt cramped here. Squeezed. But it was the only point of reference I had for what life could be. Now I know how much more is out there, and how damn pitiful this place is by comparison.]*

His meandering path brought us back inside. Here, too, the shadows stretched a shade too long, but it wasn't as noticeable as it had been in direct sunlight.

[Kitchen and dining area's through there.] Emerald gestured one hand vaguely to the left as we passed. *[I had dinner with Harmony last night, and it was excruciating. Not on account of anything he did, but because of everyone else. Good to know that hasn't changed. And the prayer room is in there, which...]* He managed to make a noise of utter derision in his mind.

As we passed the room he'd just indicated, I caught sight of a massive, faceless statue standing erect in the middle of the room, flanked by backless benches. I wondered if all gods were depicted like that, without defined features, before I recalled the image of the Crone displayed in the entry room of the Sisterhood back on Kovin Isle. Their goddess had a face. Perhaps Guise's visage was blank because his followers wanted to see themselves in him.

Or maybe the small-minded artisan merely lacked the talent and imagination to bring the stone rendering to life.

[...children's housing is that way, you already saw Modest's office, and then there's just the library. Oh, and the catacombs.]

[I beg your pardon?] I asked. *[We're wondering where these people might be hiding a god, and you didn't think to mention there were catacombs?]*

Emerald shrugged one shoulder. *[No one ever goes down there.]*

[Which is precisely why we should?]

Emerald hesitated briefly. *[No. Let's go to the library.]*

[What do you mean, no? Every mystery we've ever solved has required consulting the dead for evidence!]

He snorted and kept moving, passing row after row of children's rooms. *[That's hardly true.]*

[It's true of every mystery I've helped solve, then. Think of Throop in Dyrne. Think of the bodies in the Cronemire!]

[We were solving murders then, Crim. It's different.]

[Just a peek...?]

[Library first.] I felt as if a door had been closed inside his head, but not the one that had shut me out of his thoughts when he was at his lowest. It was a strange sensation, as if he was cutting something off before it could be examined too closely, but not from me. From himself.

Before I could explore the nature of his aversion to the catacombs, Emerald was already striding down the hall. I wished that my miniature mandibles could clamp onto his skin and give him a real start, but alas, I could not impact his physical form in any meaningful way. Short of flying away to conduct my own investigation, I was stuck with him. Given his state of agitation, I thought it best not to leave him alone.

He turned through a door into a room lined with shelves of books on one side and writing desks on the other. The desk at the farthest end was occupied by a lone figure, dressed in the manner of the rest of the Brotherhood, painstakingly copying out the text of one manuscript onto loose folio pages.

Emerald stepped toward the shelves, studying the spines of the books. *[If they really have made contact with Guise, they must have learned some new way of doing so. It's been a long time since I read any of Guise's texts, and I didn't believe in gods back then, not really. Now, of course, I feel differently.]*

[Because of what happened in Upper Bound, with the Crone?] I asked.

[That, and my experience with Aster.]

Those words brought my antennae to attention. *[Hold on, you never told me—]*

"Steadfast?" We both froze at the sound of Emerald's old Brotherhood name. The woman who had been seated at the desk now stood behind us, her hands clasped in front of her and a soft smile tugging at her lips.

Emerald's bemusement radiated through our connection as he stared at her, searching through his memories in an attempt to connect her face with a name. It was a pleasant face, with high, prominent cheekbones, a broad nose, and impossibly large eyes that sparkled with amusement. Her curly black hair was cut short, held back from her face by a plain brown stretch of cloth.

Every aspect of her attire was of the same shapeless cut as the clothes worn by the rest of the adults, but there was something radiant in her features that made the whole dreary room just a little less bleak. I had been in her presence for less than a minute, and already I could have picked her out of a crowd of thousands, not only because her features were so distinct, but because of the energy that flowed around her. It reminded me of the inescapable pull I'd felt in Yoyoh's presence.

It reminded me, too, of how I'd been drawn into the consciousness of the Crone when the Black Hollow came alive.

I had not yet made up my mind about whether I should panic or be entranced when Emerald let out the breath he'd been holding. "Al?"

The woman laughed and opened her arms, and to my astonishment, Emerald leaned forward to meet her. She barely reached his shoulder, and even when she stood on her toes, Emerald had to bend his knees in order for her to kiss his cheek. It was the warmest welcome I had even seen him give... well, anyone. Even in Tincrown's company, he had acted as though the doctor was a particularly delicate piece of fine porcelain that might crack if he wasn't careful. With this woman, however, he went so far as to lift her off of her feet, causing her to squeal with surprise and amusement.

"Put me down, Steady!" she exclaimed, and Emerald did as she asked. She fell back a pace but did not go far, and she kept one hand on his arm even after he'd let go. The blood was high in her cheeks, highlighting the coral tones of her umber complexion.

"My apologies, Sister Allure." Emerald tried and failed to force the smile off of his face. "I'm certain that Guise would be displeased by my impertinence."

My confusion redoubled, not only on account of my friend's sudden good humor, but because of Allure's answering chuckle. They were not mere acquaintances. They were... *friends?* Even that did not seem right.

Allure took Emerald's hand and beamed up at him, pulling him toward the table beside the one where she'd been working only moments before. "You might be surprised to learn that the Brotherhood has gotten a few things wrong about our god."

Our god. Of course it would be reasonable for her to think that Emerald still believed in Guise, or at least that he'd returned to doing so. That was, after all, the story he'd told in order to gain access to the building, but it seemed a shame that he would have to hide the truth from someone who'd greeted him so warmly. Unless it was all an act, but I was not convinced of that. His happiness upon recognizing her had been bone deep and irrefutable. I felt a little more alive having experienced it for myself.

It was not enough, however, to alleviate my misgivings about the corona of power that swirled around her. Perhaps Emerald had noticed it, too.

For whatever reason, Emerald did not correct her. He merely slid onto the stool across from her and leaned one elbow on the writing table. "Is that so? I'm surprised you feel comfortable saying so where anyone can hear you."

Allure laughed, then she hastily lifted one hand to cover her mouth. In her mirth, she'd revealed her teeth, and in doing so had confirmed something I had already suspected. In addition to one chipped eyetooth and a crooked canine, she had two much larger teeth in her lower jaw, both of which had been filed down to nubs.

Like Emerald, she had jotunn ancestry.

I wondered what else she was, and immediately felt sick. *What else?* Hell after hell, I sounded like Dirkus. Knowing the details of Allure's parentage wouldn't tell me any more about her than Emerald's complicated genealogy told me about him. If anything, the knowledge of how most people viewed jotunn was more enlightening, because it suggested how Allure had most likely been treated by her peers and mentors, especially in a place like the Brotherhood.

I was so lost in my own circular thinking that I only half heard the next words Allure spoke. "It would be quite hypocritical, Steadfast, for one of them to scold me for speaking *about* Guise, given that I now speak *for* him."

Emerald sat back so abruptly that he nearly toppled off of his stool. "You're the mouthpiece?"

Allure laughed again. "I prefer to think of myself as his ambassador. His emissary. After all, he has blessed me and cursed me in equal measure. He gave me the face of one who can have no cause for pride, then burdened me with his greatest gift. I cannot be saved, but I can be the savior of those who choose to dedicate their lives to him. So, yes, when I speak on the true nature of Guise, those who dwell beneath this roof listen. It is in their best interest."

Sister Allure spoke with confidence, but there was no pride in her speech, or malice, either. I could easily imagine how Brother Modest would have delivered this little speech, and the undercurrent of self-importance he would have leaned on.

[Well, that's convenient,] I thought. *[You're friends with the very person we're here to see. Which is funny, since I distinctly recall you telling me that you didn't have any friends growing up...]*

Emerald jumped, as if he'd forgotten that I was there. *[Crimson, you absolute fool, be quiet. If she really is the one we're here to see, that means she's the most dangerous person in this building.]*

I had already suspected that, given the ripple of power that constantly ebbed and flowed around her, but I fell silent all the same.

"I am so happy to see you again," Allure said. She reached for his hand, and although Emerald flinched this time, he did not pull away. Instead, he held still, like a rabbit in the presence of a wolf.

This time, Allure cradled Emerald's hand palm up in one of her own, and used the other to push back the sleeves of his robes. He shivered when her fingers brushed against his wrist and turned his face away.

"Oh, Steady." Allure traced her fingers over the raised marks on his arms. "I hoped that you'd found peace outside of the order."

"I did," Emerald blurted.

Allure shook her head, as if she did not believe him, then she held her own arm up to his. She pulled her sleeve back to reveal a beaded bangle circling her forearm. "Some things never change. You are still restless, Brother, but there is peace to be found here. We don't have to forget the past. We can make peace with it, I promise you."

The way she spoke that word, *brother*, was more of an endearment than a title. Surely Emerald hadn't been hiding a sibling from me all this time? But the way Allure looked at him wasn't entirely familial, although I wasn't sure how else to categorize it.

She loved him, there was no doubt in my mind about that. But love, as I'd already learned in my brief life, came in many different forms, and this variety was new to me.

"You're shaking." Allure pulled her sleeve back into place then covered Emerald's arm as well. "Are you afraid of me, Steady? You have no reason to be. I can take care of your problem for you, but I would never do so without your permission."

Emerald cleared his throat, but his voice still came out in a rasp. "My problem?"

"Your power. It is a burden you need not bear, but you will decide that for yourself in your own time."

"My *Aidea*," Emerald said.

"Of course." Allure's eyes swept over him. "That's why you're here, isn't it? Because you heard that I could take away your pain?"

I bristled at the implication that Emerald's status as Lightweaver was the source of his mental turmoil. I was one of the best things that had ever happened to him, if I did say so myself. How would taking away something that was such a large part of his identity make him *better*?

"No," Emerald said. He pulled his arms back to his chest, crossing them in an obvious gesture of self-defense. "That's not why."

Allure nodded, but it was obvious from her expression that she didn't believe him. "It doesn't matter, I suppose. I was sad when you left, but I'm glad that you've returned, regardless of the reason. Sister

Humble has returned as well. The only one missing is Reticent, and if he comes back, our family will be reunited again. Wouldn't that be lovely, Steady?" She traced her finger over the letters on the page of her copied manuscript. "It would make everything worth it to have you all here with me. That's what I've prayed for, you know. I have done as Guise commands, and in return, he is giving me the one thing I most earnestly desired." She closed her eyes, and a beatific smile stole across her features.

I was at a loss for words, which was probably for the best. I had no idea what to make of Allure's presence, or her confessions. When he'd spoken of the Brotherhood, Emerald had recalled Harmony clearly. He'd seen his old mentor as a father figure, but he had never once mentioned anyone else in the compound.

Even more baffling, his confusion at this reunion was as deep seated as my own. I could *feel* the depth of his affection for Allure, undercut with his wariness toward her claims related to her power. Beneath all that, however, lay an unvoiced anxiety so profound that it made even *my* stomach pinch, despite the fact that I did not really have one.

"It's good to see you again," Emerald told her.

Allure chuckled. "You still doubt what I can do. Of course you do, you always needed proof. Is *that* why you're here? To see if the stories are true?"

There was no reason to lie this time, so Emerald answered honestly. "Yes."

"You shall have it tonight." Allure lifted her pen and dipped it into her inkwell. "I should finish this page, but rest assured, our god will walk among us. You will see the proof with your own eyes. We will speak again when you're ready to believe me. Until then, be well, my brother. I am so glad to have you home."

With that, she effectively dismissed us, and Emerald retreated from the library. The moment he was out of her sight, he collapsed against the wall outside with one hand pressed to his chest and the other braced against the wall behind him.

[Emerald?] I thought urgently. *[Are you all right? Who is Allure?*

And Reticent, and Humble? How did she know about the marks? Who is she to you?]

He did not answer right away, choosing to focus on his breathing and the gradual slowing of his heart rate. He trembled like a small branch in a high wind.

[She was my sister,] he said. *[She was my sister. And I don't understand how I forgot.]*

CHAPTER

EIGHT

Emerald's nervous demeanor lasted through the rest of the morning, and precluded any visit to the catacombs. My earlier desire to consult the dead now seemed quite pointless, given that we'd found what we were looking for in the person of Sister Allure.

[What else can you tell me about her?] I asked as he wandered the courtyard in an aimless sort of way. The children were no longer engrossed in their stick-poking game, having been called away to lessons inside.

[We grew up together.] Emerald dropped down onto the stones alongside the sorry excuse for a fountain. He was still shaking from the earlier encounter, although I could not fully grasp why. Once again, I wished that Tincrown could be here with us to help unravel the tangle of emotions that bound my companion up in their knots. *[She was one of the most important people in my life, Crimson. And I haven't thought about her for years. How can that be? Forgetting her would be like forgetting...]*

He stopped short as his befuddlement was replaced by something like real fear.

[It would be like forgetting Tincrown,] he finally finished.

72

To say that Emerald was, in my experience, always levelheaded and rational would have been a lie. I had watched him sink into the depths of utmost despair, had felt his self-loathing as if it were my own, had seen him enraged and intoxicated and hopelessly in love. Throughout all of that, however, he had not been prone to forgetfulness.

[Maybe it has something to do with her connection to Guise,] I thought.

[Maybe.] It was obvious that my suggestion had not entirely alleviated my friend's worries, but it was equally clear to me that no other answers would be forthcoming at this time. We would have to wait until evening and see what the Brotherhood, and Sister Allure in particular, had planned.

"Steadfast?" Brother Harmony emerged from one of the halls and raised his hand in greeting. "There you are. I was wondering where you'd run off to. The children have just come inside for their lessons. Would you like to meet my current charges?"

"I..." Emerald ran his hand over his robes as he got to his feet. He seemed lost, but Brother Harmony's presence gave him something to move toward, and he went willingly.

Privately, I had my own concerns, although I was too wary of Emerald's well-being to give them voice. Nevertheless, the question remained.

If Emerald could not trust his own faculties, which of mine could *I* trust?

THE ROOM to which Harmony led us contained three students, all of whom were deeply engrossed in reading from primers.

They could not have been more different from one another. One, a rather pudgy girl, had wild red hair bound back from her pale face; beside her sat a dark-skinned boy so skinny he seemed to be mostly knees and elbows; and at the end of the row, next to an empty desk, sat a brown-furred lambkin.

I had, until that moment, only made the acquaintance of two varieties of lambkin. The most common were like our friend Errol, with white wool and no horns at all. The shepherdess superior of the Convent of the Crone was another type altogether, with deep brown wool, floppy ears, and curling horns. This lad was another sort entirely, somewhere in between the two. On top of it all, he wore a pair of unusual glasses that were held in place by a strap that went around the back of his head.

All three of the children looked up as Emerald stepped into the room. The scrawny boy lifted a hand in mute greeting, while the girl shrank away.

"Hello!" the lambkin said brightly. "Oh, you must be Brother Steadfast. I heard about you. I think I've got your old bed in the dormitory, you know, it's got your name carved into the bedpost and everything. Do you like mushrooms? Because I think I found your notes in one of the library books as well…"

"That's enough, Quell." Harmony's voice was kind but firm. "You will have plenty of chances to discuss your personal interests with Brother Steadfast if he chooses to remain with us after tonight."

"Ooh." Quell's eyes, magnified behind his thick glasses, widened further still. "You're here to see Sister Allure, then?"

Emerald nodded. The moment he'd walked in the door, he'd resumed his usual hunched posture, and I wouldn't have put it past him to slink over to the empty desk and mash himself into the child-sized chair.

Harmony gave my friend's arm a reassuring pat. "Please introduce yourself to Brother Steadfast," he said, nodding to the girl first.

She took her pen in both hands, apparently failing to realize that she was staining her fingers with ink in the process. As she spoke, she kept her eyes down rather than make eye contact of any sort.

"I'm Sister Svelte," she said. "And my burden is to be an Arctician."

"Very good," Brother Harmony said kindly.

The skinny boy bit his lip and made a series of complicated motions with his hands. At first, I thought he might be attempting some sort of *Aidea*, since I had seen both Emerald and Coirpre use hand signals as part of their Lightweaving, but nothing magical resulted from the motions.

"Brother Blare can't talk," Quell said. "He's—"

Harmony held up a soothing hand, and Quell fell silent. "I am perfectly capable of translating, Quell." He directed his attention to Emerald. "Brother Blare is nonverbal, but we have devised a means of communication."

"I'm familiar," Emerald said. As he spoke, he made gestures with his hands just as Blare had done. "You've borrowed the custom from the people of Danilas Freehold, I think?"

Blare's face blossomed into a shy smile, and he nodded eagerly, responding to Emerald's question. His hands moved quickly, but now that I knew what I was looking for, I found the movements easy enough to interpret, especially given Emerald's existing knowledge of the silent language.

Yes, Blare signed. *From Danilas. Brother Harmony brought me a book, and we all learned.*

Emerald spoke to Harmony, but kept signing as he did so, presumably to make things easier for Blare. "Why don't you sign every time you speak to each other, then?"

Brother Harmony folded his hands behind his back. "He needs to learn how to function in the real world, Emerald. Outside of these walls, people are not so understanding. If accommodations are made for him here, he will grow complacent. Besides, he hears well enough to get by."

Blare's smile vanished, but when Emerald glanced at him again, he tapped his chest, closed his eyes, and bowed his head. *My burden is...* He made another gesture, but this one I did not recognize.

"Blare is a Stonefeather," Harmony clarified.

I had never met a Stonefeather before, and it seemed that Emerald hadn't either, judging by his curiosity.

"I'm Quell," the lambkin butted in. "And I'm a Sonicist, which means I deal in sound. Brother Harmony says that's why I talk so much, but..."

Harmony raised his finger to his lips.

"But I just like talking, and I don't think it's the same thing at all," Quell finished. He lifted his chin in a small act of defiance. It did not escape my notice that, of the three, he was the only one who had not declared his gifts to be a burden.

Harmony chuckled. "Well, be that as it may, I think we can all agree that there is rarely a moment's peace to be had here. Brother Steadfast, will you introduce yourself?"

"Uh." Emerald blinked at him. "You already did?" His words lilted up at the end.

"I have not told them your burden," Harmony pointed out.

Would that I could have given him a piece of my mind at that moment. It was quite tempting to do so, and I gave serious consideration to the notion of leaping off of Emerald's shoulder, transforming into my usual self, and telling Harmony where he could stuff all his talk of burdens and "the real world."

I held my tongue for the sake of our investigation, while Emerald forced a smile. "My burden," he said, "is Lightweaving."

"Ooh." Quell kicked his hooves back and forth.

"I've never seen real Lightweaving before," Svelte added, in the tone of one who couldn't decide if they wanted to try something new or not.

"Nor will you," Harmony told her. "Brother Steadfast's presence is proof that fostering the *Aidea* goes against Guise's will. He left us, and he has returned, forsaking his ties to the unnatural arts. Now, who has finished the reading?"

Emerald withdrew to one corner of the room to watch the duration of the lesson. The children, for their part, answered Harmony's questions while sneaking occasional curious glances at the silent figure in the corner. Quell, in particular, was obviously bursting with questions he couldn't ask in Harmony's presence without facing his mentor's disapproval.

[What's on your mind?] I asked my companion.

Emerald kept swiping the pad of his thumb across his lower lip again and again and again. *[That it wouldn't be difficult to accommodate Blare. It wouldn't cost them anything at all.]* After a weighty pause he added, *[I'm thinking how strange it is that I remember sitting in these lessons, but I can't recall what burdens my classmates carried. I can barely recall their faces. And I'm wondering what kind of* **Aidea** *allows you to rewrite someone's memories—or erase them entirely.]*

He did not ask me what was on my mind, but if he had, I would have been forced to obfuscate. It was evident to me that I could not spend this whole investigation as a fly on the wall or a beetle on the neck, but I had not been made with subtlety in mind. I needed to find a way to be more useful, but I was not yet sure how I might go about that.

That question, too, would have to wait until we knew more about what we were up against when it came to the matter of Guise.

The children's lessons dragged on until dinner, at which point we all filed into a crowded hall. While I envied Emerald the ability to experience food and drink, I found that I was not quite so jealous when it came to that communal meal. Emerald shoveled down his rations without complaint despite their dubious consistency.

By the time the sun began to set, a nervous buzzing filled the corridors of the Brotherhood, like a hive of bees stirred to action by the presence of a new queen.

Allure did not make an appearance in the dining hall, and when the mentors began to herd their students toward the entrance of the compound, there was no sign of either her or of Brother Modest. Emerald trailed after Harmony, who had no trouble keeping track of his three wards.

[Stay on the lookout for anything suspicious,] he warned. *[I know that you're quick to believe stories about the gods, but I still think that whatever's going on here has a less-than-divine explanation. I've seen cast-offs manage all sorts of strange and unlikely things, and the followers of Guise are perfect targets for any sort of scam involving the* **Aidea.** *They fear it, so they don't understand it.]*

I was inclined to agree, but I did have one question. *[Do you really think your friend is capable of that sort of deception? You were so pleased to see her when she first spoke to you.]*

The crowd spilled through the gates, merging with the congregants who had taken up residence in the tent city beyond the walls. As the crowd swelled, Emerald grew more nervous and moved closer to Brother Harmony. *[I don't know what to think, Crim. All I'm asking is that you keep your eyes open tonight. You can go anywhere, watch anyone. Just make sure to keep out of sight.]*

Given the sheer number of people who were crowding toward the largest of the tents, I didn't think it would be difficult to move about unnoticed. The sun was setting without fanfare, with overcast sky giving way to the bruised blackness of night, absent any radiance that might be considered lovely. I found that unnerving. Sunsets were, in my experience, quite lovely, but I found myself wondering if Guise—who, according to his followers, detested loveliness in all its myriad forms—had manipulated the very heavens into banality.

The tent toward which we were bound was enormous, but even so, I doubted its ability to fit all of us. Between the Brotherhood and its hangers-on, there must have been some two thousand souls making their way across the plain. Two thousand souls, plus me. I did not count myself among their number, because I was still not sure what precisely I *was*.

The walls of the tent were made with canvas so heavy that only a little light was visible from the outside. When we passed through the flaps at last, we were greeted by a blazing fire at the center of the tent, the smoke from which rose upward through an opening at the peak. Several members of the Brotherhood had been assigned the task of telling people where to go so that they did not draw too close to the fire, and that pathways would be left between the various sections. Rows of seats had been constructed by some hasty hand, climbing higher and higher as they reached the walls. I was not entirely convinced of their stability, but the faithful climbed into them without a second thought. There were not enough seats for everyone, and those who could not find a place to perch crowded the aisles or lingered by the tent walls in hopes of catching a glimpse of some supposed miracle.

By virtue of our affiliation with the Brotherhood, we were allowed a spot near the front, with only the wards of the orphanage seated below us.

As Emerald slid into his seat, one of the men behind us grumbled. "I knew it was too good to be true. Best seat I've gotten yet, and we're stuck behind a pair of *them*. I'll be lucky if I can see anything."

Emerald turned his head slightly, but before he could comment, the man's fellow elbowed him.

"Guise speaks through a half-jotunn, you idiot. Hold your tongue."

[Well,] Emerald thought, **[*that's a new one. Never been compared to the hostess of a god before. Don't think I like it.*]**

[*It could be worse,*] I pointed out. **[*He could be Dirkus.*]**

Emerald bit back a grunt of laughter. When Harmony lifted his eyebrows, my friend pretended to cough into his fist.

The commotion was building to a crescendo when, quite abruptly, the tent fell silent. The stillness moved over the crowd in a ripple, beginning by the entrance and spreading until it reached us.

I took that silence as my cue and lifted off from Emerald's shoulder, sailing high enough above the crowd that no one paid me any mind. Quite frankly, even if I'd taken the form of a rampaging dragon, I don't think people would have looked twice. Every eye in the tent was fixed on the white-clad figure that had just entered, and on the object she held in her hand.

Emerald might be inclined to categorize people in terms of beauty or ugliness, but I reserved such judgments for clothes. I could, without the slightest misgivings, label burlap a most displeasing fabric, and I would happily commit my love of silk and velvet into verse, but people were different.

Whatever else people might say about Allure's appearance, she was arresting. She had traded in her brown robes for a white linen mantle and bound her hair between a headwrap made of the same material. Even without the *Aidea*, the upright way she carried herself hinted at her confidence, and the thrum of magic around her only added to her presence. Open-mouthed congregants bent toward her like moths drawn to the fullness of a summer moon, and a few even reached out their hands to grasp at her garments. In the firelight, the coral undertones of her skin were burnished to a high copper, and her dark eyes magnified the flame.

"Welcome, good people," Allure said. Her voice had been soft in the library, but in the tent it carried without augmentation of any kind. The audience was as silent as an aspen grove, with only the occasional whisper of shifting fabric or the groan of wood when someone adjusted their posture and tested the strength of those makeshift stands.

Allure carried something in her arms, and I dipped lower to examine it.

[Where are you, Crimson?] Emerald asked. Like the rest of the audience, he was transfixed, but he was clearly not prepared to believe in Guise's presence just yet.

[I'm here, but I can't tell what she's got. It looks like a book made of... metal?] I circled closer. *[Or maybe it's a box?]*

Allure lifted her arms above her head, holding the object aloft. "Brothers and sisters, you know the teachings of our god. *He who stands closest to the fire...*"

"*Is the first to burn,*" the crowd finished for her. Some of them were already weeping, while others bared their teeth in anticipation of whatever was to come.

[I think I've seen that before.] Emerald shifted in his seat. *[No, maybe not... it looks quite plain for a sacred object, but I suppose I shouldn't be surprised.]*

[Another failing of your memory?] I asked, hoping that my anxiety on the subject wouldn't be too obvious.

[More likely the result of my unwillingness to pay attention in class,] Emerald admitted. *[The study of Guise's theology never did hold my attention.]*

I could understand why, but I was starting to wish that he'd been a bit more alert during those old lessons. As Allure laid the box at her feet alongside the bonfire, the shadows around her shifted subtly. Her power was palpable, sharper than before, honed to a fine point. She could wield it like a weapon.

"Who among you will be purified in the eyes of Guise?" Allure's smile was welcoming, but the object at her feet told another story. It twisted the play of firelight, swallowing it whole.

I did not trust it. I did not, in fact, like it at all.

"Come, now." Allure held out her arms. "Don't be afraid, brothers and sisters. I know that some of you are burdened by the *Aidea*. I know how it eats at you. It makes you feel special, but like all power, it comes with a price. Kineticists' bones break apart under the strain of their efforts. Those who harness energy are often struck down by lightning. Those with the burden of Cosmic sight go mad when they gaze into the wild scope of the universe. Sonicists go deaf." She sought out Emerald's face in the crowd. "Lightweavers, blind."

[Is that true?] I asked.

[Yes.] Emerald had his hand pressed to the middle of his chest, and I was certain that he had done so out of instinct, in order to protect the pendant that he used to summon and maintain me. *[Very slowly, though, especially when you stick to small illusions. Lightweaving is like staring at the sun. You can't do it too often or for too long without suffering the consequences.]*

[You can't?] That was news to me, as I'd stared directly into the sun on more than one occasion, but I supposed that made sense. Light and shadow generally affected me differently than they did other people.

I had never considered what creating me would cost Emerald. Prior to my becoming sentient, he had only summoned me when necessary. Was the pleasure of my constant company worth the cost of his future sight? How come he'd never mentioned it?

Because he didn't think he had *a future,* I realized dismally. Why would a man who had tried to end his own life worry overmuch about how his magic would harm him in old age? He could do much worse merely by letting himself stray too deeply into his own thoughts.

"The *Aidea* has no love for you." Allure rotated on the spot. "It subverts order and defies divine law. Those who believe they control it are only its tool, a hammer to be used until you are discarded. Let me free you from its grasp. Let me liberate you. Do not be afraid. It will not hurt."

"She saved my son!" a woman cried from somewhere along the tent wall.

I whirled and fluttered closer to her. It would be quite damning if this woman was a plant of some kind, or if her son had conveniently vanished after being, as Allure had put it, *liberated*.

But no, the woman stood with her hand on the shoulder of a young man. The fellow looked… stretched. Narrow. Then again, he was wearing a sack for a robe and didn't appear to have bathed in days at least. *Most* of the people in that tent had a lean and hungry air about them.

A round of applause from the far side of the tent drew me away from the wan youth. A girl, perhaps fifteen years old, had risen to her feet and was stumbling down the steps toward Sister Allure.

"Welcome." Allure held out her arms, beckoning for the young woman to approach her. "What is your name, little sister?"

"B-Brigane," the girl stuttered. "Of Kinmore."

Allure laid her hands on the girl's shoulders. "Welcome, Brigane, child of Guise. What is your burden?"

Brigane glanced back at her family, who nodded their approval. "I'm a Magnetist."

"No." Allure lifted one hand to the girl's chin, turning Brigane's head so that their eyes met. "You are not defined by your burden, little sister. Are you ready to be free? To live in your own power, and not the shadow of your magic?"

"Yes, Sister Allure." Brigane's voice was soft, but she only had to speak over the crackle of the fire in order to be heard. The audience was silent and still, giving the unsettling impression that the tent was inhabited only by ghosts.

"Then show me." Allure's thumb stroked the girl's cheek. "Show me what you can do."

Brigane's eyes widened. "But Guise—"

"Guise will take what is willingly given, and no more. This will be the last time, child. I swear it."

Brigane licked her lips and closed her eyes. Everything about the exchange sat wrong with me. The idea that magic was a curse was laughable. I was magic, after all, and I had seen people do terrible things even without the help of the *Aidea*. I was quite sure that Allure had gotten the whole thing backward. Magic was a tool for people to use, like a knife or a bowless or an axe, and not the other way 'round.

The way in which it was used depended entirely on the nature of the person who could wield it.

But what about Dyrne? I wondered. *What about the people who sought to live simple lives, and who had to hide from the outside world because an accident of their birth rendered them invisible? What would the likes of Nechtan and Kristine give up if it meant that their burden could be lifted, and they might live as anyone else does?*

What about the sailors who were offered up as sacrifices to the Black Hollow in exchange for the Fenguards' longevity?

I didn't think that Allure was right about the burden of the *Aidea*, but I wasn't sure that she was entirely wrong, either.

"Have no fear, Brigane," Allure said. She let her head roll back. "Show me what you can do. Show me the weight you have carried."

[This is creepy.] I fluttered back toward Emerald. *[What should I be looking for now? What's she going to do? Surely she wouldn't harm the girl in front of a roomful of people?]* There were, of course, different types of harm one person could do to another, as the Brotherhood alone had proven.

[I don't know.] Emerald was perched on the utmost edge of his seat. *[If Allure really has the sort of Dominition that would allow her to make people forget things, she couldn't just take away someone's memory of the Aidea. It doesn't work like that.]*

[Unless she's a... what did you call them, a cast-off? The ones whose magic doesn't follow the known rules?]

Emerald didn't have an answer for that. His gaze was fixed on Allure and Brigane. The girl's mouth had fallen open, and her whole body tensed in concentration.

Her power wasn't as great as Allure's, so even when she flexed it, I couldn't feel what she was doing. In fact, I wasn't entirely convinced that she was doing anything at all, until the first of the coins hit the ground and began to roll through the mud toward her.

They came in a trickle first, pulled from the pockets and pouches of the faithful, drawn toward her from every direction like lines of ants. The coins were joined by rings and keys, pendants and emblems, buttons and hairpins and rivets. People cried out as their belongings were pulled away from them, first clinging desperately to their possessions and then, when Brigane's *Aidea* called too strongly to the items, hastening to unclasp necklaces or remove earrings before they could tear themselves free.

I landed on Emerald's shoulder and saw that his jaw was tensed tight, his hand still pressed to his chest. The gold chain that held his emerald pendant in place was trying to slither toward Brigane. If he released it, the gem that he used to summon me would be yanked away, and I would be, at the very least, dispelled. Who was to say what would become of me if the necklace was drawn into the midst of Allure's ritual? What if he could not recover it—or he did, only to find its power drained away for good?

[Emerald...?] I asked.

A muscle in his jaw jumped. *[I won't let it go, Crimson. I promise.]*

That was easier said than done. The trickle of metal objects drawn toward the center of the room had become a swiftly-flowing steam. The more metal that reached Brigane, the louder she seemed to call to the rest. The objects clung to her skin, climbing her arms and legs to make a mismatched sort of armor of gold and silver and copper and iron, lapping across her bare arms like scales. Brigane was panting, and her brow glistened with sweat even as the metal made its way to her.

"She's powerful," Emerald said aloud through gritted teeth. The gold chain bit into his skin until it drew blood. *[Maybe this is part of the plan? To rob people and turn their riches over to the Brotherhood? What a waste of talent, if that's the case.]*

At the center of the room, backlit by the flames, Allure and Brigane loomed large. The fire flared brighter for a moment, sending impossible shadows climbing the tent walls. Brigane swayed on her feet as the exertion of her power and the weight of her new armor dragged her to her knees, but Allure only grew. It was a trick of the light, but a monstrous one that warped and contorted her silhouette almost beyond recognition.

"Guise!" she cried. "Grant your daughter a respite from her burdens. She is faithful, Unifier! She is your willing servant."

The earlier silence of the tent had been replaced by the muffled hubbub of fear and consternation brought on by unexpected chaos. Emerald squeezed his eyes shut and gritted his teeth, but he never let the pendant go.

Because of this, he did not see what happened next, but I did. Even if I'd wanted to, I could not have looked away.

Allure's eyes rolled back, and her lips turned up in a satisfied smile. Her power swirled around her like smoke, channeled through her hands and into Brigane. A moment later, a shockwave radiated outward from the pair of them, sending the objects that Brigane had collected scattering in every direction. The metal rained back to earth, and Emerald let out an enormous sigh of relief as his necklace stopped fighting him.

The fire was reduced to embers, and Brigane collapsed to all fours, letting out a long and wordless wail so shrill that it made the congregants around us cover their ears. Brigane gripped the handfuls of coins and buttons lying pell-mell all around her, lifting them in her fists and letting them stream through her fingers like sand through an hourglass.

"I can't feel them," she cried. "I can't *feel* them. They've always called to me, I could sense them even without seeing them, and now..." Tears streamed down her face, and she sat back on her heels, turning her blotchy face to meet Sister Allure's. "Now, it is quiet. Peaceful. You've freed me. Bless you. Bless you!" She grabbed at the hem of Allure's robe and prostrated herself in the mud.

Allure knelt to run her hands over the girl's hair. She looked drawn and weary, as if the effort of removing Brigane's *Aidea* had drained her own to its limit, but her gentleness never flagged. "I am but an instrument of the divine," she said.

Brigane slumped to the ground, and Allure scooped up the object that she had carried into the tent with her.

"Reclaim your belongings," she told the crowd.

"Stay!" someone cried, and others quickly joined in.

"My son is an Alchemist. Please, help him!"

"I am a Kineticist. Sister, my bones! I'm in such pain! Please, have mercy!"

Allure shook her head. "Another time. I will help you when I can." She swept out of the tent as the grasping hands of the crowd reached after her, tugging at her pale linen robes. In her wake, those who had not been helped were quick to gather up the loose bits of metal, regardless of who they had belonged to.

[Was it a trick, Em?] I asked. *[Can you see how she did it? What branch of the* Aidea *was she using? What sort of magic would you call that?]*

My friend's only answer was to stare slack jawed at the young woman by the fireside. Her friends and family had gathered round her, weeping with relief and hugging one another as if a miracle had taken place and a death sentence had been pardoned. Brother Harmony was already herding the children toward the exit, but Emerald didn't budge. Blood dripped down the back of his neck to stain the collar of his simple robe. His heart was hollow, numb with horror.

A few paces away, the two men who'd sat behind us squabbled over who would get to keep the trio of mismatched gold buttons they'd retrieved from the tent's beaten-earth floor.

CHAPTER

NINE

Emerald found Brother Harmony and walked after him in silence. Quell chattered animatedly the whole way, describing what we'd all seen in the tent as though he alone had been there.

"I can't imagine what she must feel like, can you? I mean, I don't know about metal, but I know how *sound* feels, and it's always there, just always, there's never *not* sound. Even when it's dead quiet, that's still something. What do you think it would be like to have your powers taken away like that? I bet you'd feel empty and lonely, and it would be so boring in your head you could hardly stand it. I bet it'd drive you mad. Not that I *hope* she goes mad or anything, I guess if she didn't like it, she wouldn't have offered her *Aidea* up, but still…"

Svelte wrapped her arms around her middle and stared at the ground as she walked. Her freckled nose was wrinkled in concentration, but I couldn't gauge what she was thinking. I longed to ask her —my passive role in our current investigation was beginning to take its toll on me.

As we returned through the front gates of the compound, Blare tapped her on the shoulder to get her attention and made a single gesture toward his temple, followed by a tilt of his head.

87

Svelte nodded and nudged him with her shoulder as a sort of reassurance.

In the courtyard, Emerald peeled off from the group. Harmony glanced back, and the expression of fond recognition that stole over his features sickened me. It was a look that said, *He has always been difficult, but he will come around.*

I wished that we could leave then and never look back. Whatever Allure had done to Brigane was horrible, but the girl had wanted it. She had been grateful. Let the Brotherhood have their rituals. Someone else could intercede. It was no business of ours.

The layout of the compound was still so confusing to me that I didn't understand where we were going until we got there. Emerald shoved open the door of the unlit library and slammed it shut behind him, collapsing against the woodwork.

"What," he panted, "in every cursed or hallowed hell did we just see?"

I could barely contain myself. I leapt forward from his shoulder, expanding back into my usual form as I did so. I had not stopped to think whether I would appear as Simone or Simon, and for once, I had given no thought to my wardrobe.

"Are you certain that it wasn't a trick?" I asked, spinning toward him. "Maybe the two of them were in on it together. Could Allure have used some sort of charm or sigil to dampen the girl's gifts?"

Emerald leaned his full weight back against the door. "I don't know, Crim. It wasn't just what happened to Brigane. There were all sorts of *Aidea* in play. The way the fire reacted, the way the shadows came alive, none of that was natural."

I folded my hands behind my back and began to pace the floor of the library, crossing and re-crossing the gap between the writing desks and the shelves. Allure's unfinished manuscript still lay on the table, although she'd managed to write out another page's worth since we'd visited that morning. Appearing in the open in the midst of her private domain felt like an act of madness, but if I had to skulk around in silence for another moment, I was going to do something very ill-considered indeed.

"So there were multiple *Aidea*-users involved. Laird and Lady

Fenguard worked together to complete their rituals. What's to say that the Brotherhood isn't doing the same?"

Emerald shook his head. "I might believe that, if I couldn't tell how powerful Allure is all on her own."

"Then perhaps she can control more than one branch of the *Aidea*," I suggested.

"It's... possible, I suppose." Emerald pushed himself upright and retrieved one of the writing desks, dragging it in front of the door so that nobody would be able to force it open—at least, not without creating a terrible fuss and giving me time to rearrange myself. "At least you're aware of how dire the situation is."

"What does that mean?" I demanded.

He glanced over his shoulder and waved one hand at me. "Well, just look at you. I can't imagine a clothes-dragon like you doing *that* on purpose."

I glanced down at myself and nearly shrieked in dismay. "Oh, Aster's ankles, what am I *wearing?*" To my horror, I discovered that I had somehow robed myself entirely in a foul shade of violent yellow, with the sole exception being a corset that, for some unholy reason, rode on the *outside* of the whole ensemble. I looked rather like a daisy that couldn't decide whether to dress in trousers or a smock and decided that choosing one was ultimately unnecessary.

"I blame you for this," I said, hastily rearranging my accouterments into a less lurid and fashion-blind ensemble. "You've been all over the place today. I can't help it if I'm a little absent-minded as a result."

Emerald sank down onto the stool he'd occupied during our first visit to the library. "I know. It was just so *strange* to see her. You can't understand what it's like."

"What?" I asked archly. "To have someone else be responsible for my memories?"

He shook his head and rapped his knuckles against the table with the steady repetition of a clock. "To lose track of time like that. Sometimes I feel like I never left this place, and in others, it feels like I've lived a whole lifetime on the outside. You've only been around half a year. You haven't had a chance to forget anything like that."

His sadness softened me, and I hopped up to perch on the stool beside him, the one that Allure had used when she was working. I didn't admit how much it meant to me that he'd acknowledged my independence from him, however conditional it may be. I wondered when he'd come to think of me as my own person, and not merely an extension of himself.

Regardless, I was pleased that he had.

"Do you think that you've really forgotten things?" I asked. "Or have you simply buried them?"

Emerald raised one heavy eyebrow. "What's the difference?" Before I could answer, he let out a little huff of understanding. "Ah, the mind-cottage. You think it's possible to revisit what I know about Allure."

I picked at the hem of my black velvet blouse. "I think it would be helpful to know what sort of *Aidea* she has. I'm not sure I'd believe her reply if we walked up and asked her out outright, but maybe the answers are buried in there. You'd have studied together, wouldn't you?"

Emerald nodded glumly, and I knew that we were both thinking of the three students we'd encountered earlier in the day. "We can try. I'm not opposed to it." He settled in and closed his eyes for a moment.

Nothing happened.

"Did you forget how to do it already?" I asked.

Emerald grunted and opened one bright-green eye, narrowing it at me. "No. I'm just not sure where to go. When we practiced at the inn, I didn't get to see what I remembered. It was more like... I recalled the *feel* of my memories, but not the details. That won't help us at all."

He had a point, and I had no immediate solution. It gave me some comfort to know that we were in uncharted territory here. Still, I had a vague notion that there must be a way to do what we intended. The mind-cottage was my realm, and I was its monarch, at least in my little corner of the metaphysical plane.

"Let me try something." I reached over to take Emerald's hand. Unlike Allure, however, I hesitated before touching him, giving him every chance to pull away. He sighed his agreement, and I settled my hand over his palm, so that we barely overlapped.

His memories weren't usually such a jumble, but as he'd said, these were very old and half-forgotten. It made sense, I supposed, given how long ago they'd taken place. I latched onto the first one that had any real shape to it.

I meant to drag it with me to the mind-cottage and unpack it there, but instead, the inverse happened. Rather than bending this bit of Emerald's memory to my will, I was dragged into it and swept away.

THE LIBRARY LOOKED MUCH as it still did, although the scattered sheaves of loose vellum that had littered the desk were absent. I was nowhere to be found; nor was Emerald, at least not my version of him. Instead, the oil lamps burning on the desks illuminated two small faces. One was a girl of perhaps ten years old, who could never have been mistaken for anyone but a younger version of Sister Allure. Her curly hair was cut short and ragged, as though whoever had wielded the scissors had been more invested in haste than in the result.

The other figure, I decided, I would refer to as Steadfast. He was no Emerald yet, and so much life experience separated him from my companion that I could not bring myself to think of them as the same person.

The two of them sat side by side at the desks. Steadfast had a book open in front of him. Judging by the late hour and the fact that the library door was closed and latched, I suspected that they were not meant to be there anymore than Emerald and I were in the present day.

"Try again," Steadfast suggested in the high, clear voice of his younger days. "There's no rush." He nudged the book closer.

Allure puffed up her cheeks. "We already tried..."

"And we'll try again," Steadfast finished. "Come on, now, little sister. You can do it."

The girl inched her stool closer and peered down at the pages between them. I couldn't feel anything Steadfast experienced, and Emerald was somewhere out of reach, but I didn't need my other senses to understand the strength of the connection between the two of them. Allure's skinny shoulder bumped Steadfast's, and he didn't flinch away. The two of them hunched over the pages of the text, their heads nearly knocking together.

It was a far cozier scene than I would have envisioned could unfold in that solemn place.

"Say it aloud," Steadfast coaxed.

"I can't. I'm so stupid, Steady!" Allure's face crumpled, and she collapsed forward on the desk, cradling her head in her arms. "Brother Modest is right about me!"

Steadfast patted her shoulder. "Come on, Al, you're not stupid."

"Then why are the words all jumbled up?" she wailed.

"I don't know." Steadfast's brow wrinkled as he contemplated his answer, but when there was none to be found, he simply pointed at the page. "What's this word?"

"I don't—!"

He cut her off, but he spoke with patience and kindness. "You do. You know this word. Just this one word, out of all of them. Ignore the rest."

Allure sniffed and brushed her hair out of her eyes. She followed the angle of Steadfast's finger. "The," she said. "But that one's easy. Even a baby would know it."

"If you say so." Steadfast glanced at her sidelong and moved his finger a fraction of an inch along the page. "And this one?"

Allure squinted at it for a moment. "...Blade."

"And this one?"

"Of."

"And this?"

"Grass... Oh, but it'll take forever to read it this way!" Allure flung her hands in the air, scattering loose pages in the process.

"How long," Steadfast asked sensibly, "does it take to write a book? Seems to me you have to write it one word at a time. And you read it the same way, too. Isn't that right?"

Allure's despair had been replaced by frustration. "Maybe, but I'll be a hundred years old before I finish the book at this rate."

"So?" Steadfast tilted his head to one side. "Do you have someplace better to be?"

"You've read every book in the library." Allure crossed her arms and glared at him. "Every single book, and don't pretend you haven't."

"Mm. Wanna know how I did that?"

Allure nodded eagerly.

Steadfast made a great show of looking one way, then the other. Once it was clear that they were alone, he waved her closer, lowering his voice as if sharing a secret of the utmost importance. She scooted her chair closer still, her eyes opening wide. Her cheeks darkened a shade, and her eyes dropped to his mouth.

"How?" she whispered.

"One word," Steadfast whispered back, "at a time."

She let out a snort of laughter and swatted at his shoulder. "Guise frowns on the clever!"

"And yet the brothers give you grief for being slow to the finish." Steadfast sat back, looking mightily pleased with himself. "What's wrong with doing things a bit more deliberately, anyway? You'll still get there in the end, if you're patient enough."

Allure waved to the shelves around them. "You really think that I'll be able to read all of these books at my snail's pace? Please, Steady."

The confident smile on Steadfast's face never wavered. "Who are you going to believe, Al? Modest? Or me? Because I think you can do it, and I'm usually right about things."

Allure pressed her lips into a thin line. Without answering him, she got to her feet and padded over to the nearest shelf, letting her small fingers trail over the leatherbound spines. She seemed to be considering the possibilities, pondering all the places those books could take her—if only she could unlock their mysteries.

EMERALD PULLED AWAY FROM ME, and I blinked a few times in my attempt to reorient myself.

"Did you see that?" he asked gruffly.

"That depends." I glanced down at myself, relieved to find that I was back in my body, such as it was. Twice before, my consciousness had been separated from my appearance. This time was not nearly as traumatic or unpleasant as either of those had been, but it was still disconcerting. "I saw you teaching Allure to read."

"Mm." Emerald placed his palm on the desk where the book had been in his memory. "I'd forgotten that entirely. How can I have buried so much of myself, Crim?"

"We still didn't figure out what sort of *Aidea* Allure has," I pointed out. "Perhaps we could try again?"

"Not tonight." Emerald got to his feet. "I'm tired. I'm sorry, Crimson."

I hadn't realized how weary my friend had grown. Stepping into that memory had done something to him. In the future, I would have to make more of an effort to remind myself that this was no ordinary investigation, and that it cost my friend dearly to go digging through the past.

"Don't worry," I said, keeping my voice as breezy and indifferent as I could manage. "It will keep. We haven't seen evidence that anyone is being harmed, after all." I didn't like what had happened to Brigane, but she'd chosen it for herself. I couldn't begrudge her that, or despise Allure for providing a service that people seemed to *want*. The Conjury had waited months for answers. Surely they could wait a little longer.

"I'm going to bed." Emerald shifted the third desk away from the door and returned it to its usual position. "Would you mind if I had a bit of privacy tonight?"

"Not at all." I slipped back to the floor. "I'll find some way to occupy myself."

Emerald nodded and yanked open the library door without so much as a backward glance. His emotions were so close to the surface that they bled through our connection, even though I was making an active effort to give him space.

In truth, I was glad that he'd asked to be alone. It was obvious to me that I couldn't let the entire burden of our investigation fall upon Emerald's shoulders, given that he had other burdens to bear already. In the past, he'd had to face the world alone, but not now. He had me, and I was going to be useful, one way or another. The beginnings of an idea had taken root earlier in the day, and if

Emerald knew what I was planning, I was certain that he would put a stop to it.

Which was why I hadn't asked, of course.

As I prepared to rearrange myself, I happened to glance down at the loose pages Allure had left out. The last line she had copied was the same one she and the audience had chanted during the ritual only a few hours before.

He who stands closest to the fire is the first to burn.

CHAPTER

TEN

When the sun rose on the Brotherhood the next morning, I set my plan into motion. I was sitting on the edge of the fountain when the first resident of the compound emerged into the watery sunlight. He was rubbing his eyes with one knuckle and yawning, but when he saw me, he stopped in his tracks.

"Hello!" I said cheerfully, waving to him.

For a long moment, he gawked at me, before turning on his heels and fleeing back into the building.

I stayed where I was, twiddling my thumbs. I was fairly certain that I'd thought my whole plan through. It helped that the followers of Guise weren't experts in matters of magic, and I was counting on their fear and dislike of the *Aidea* to provide a certain amount of protection. If their ignorance proved too great, I had an escape plan.

I was still sitting there when the stranger I'd encountered returned with Brother Modest in tow. The expression of utter distaste on his face annoyed me, but I forced myself to smile. After all, he had no idea who I was, and he had no reason to suspect that I knew him by anything other than reputation.

"Thank you for fetching me, Brother Cumbersome," he told the other man, before turning his full attention upon me.

In his haste to retrieve the head of the order, Brother Cumbersome hadn't been subtle. Modest must have been at breakfast in the dining hall, because we were soon joined by a steady trickle of other brothers and sisters in their dull brown robes, some of whom had brought bowls of porridge or half-eaten apples along with them. Emerald and Harmony were among them, and when he saw me, my friend let out a wordless growl of frustration.

[What in the name of every hagmouth in the Cronemire are you doing?] he demanded.

[Relax,] I assured him. *[I have a plan.]*

He did not seem comforted.

Brother Harmony strode toward me, folding his arms before him and letting his lip curl to one side. "Who are you, child, and how did you get in?"

I slipped off the edge of the fountain and landed on my feet. I was not used to being half the size of most people, but my association with Emerald meant that I was used to looking up to meet my friend's eyes.

It was only natural for Harmony to assume that I was a child, because I had gone to great lengths to look like one. I had dressed myself in a child-sized silk shirt and gold-threaded jacket, and arranged my body to have the proportions and ratios I'd observed in the other children in the Brotherhood. It had taken a great deal of effort, since previously in human form, I had only been able to become Simon or Simone. And while I could make modifications to my appearance, I could not become someone else. The one time Emerald had tried to give me an entirely different humanoid appearance, it had backfired spectacularly.

I spent the whole night reasoning with the magic that made me, however. When I was Simon, I was simply a male version of myself. My female appearance, Simone, did not exist *in spite* of Simon, or in opposition to him. They were both *me*. I didn't have to fundamentally alter any aspect of myself in order to become one or the other.

Once I had realized that, it made sense that I could change form in other ways. When I became a bird, I did not become any old bird —I became the bird version of myself. Likewise when I became a beetle, or any other sort of beast.

So it had followed quite naturally that, if I was going to become a child, I would simply need to arrange myself into a younger version of myself. Which was more easily said than done, because unlike Emerald, I'd never had the chance to be one. I could not regress. I had to invent myself as a younger person.

Once I'd realized that, it hadn't been hard at all.

I rocked back on my heels and lifted my chin a jot further than necessary, just so that Modest would know that he didn't intimidate me in the least. "I got in," I told him, using the higher voice I'd been practicing ever since I managed to transform my body, "with magic."

The assembled brothers and sisters gasped, and Emerald's eye twitched. *[Crimson...]*

I had been made for theatrics, so I resorted to them. "Oh, kind sir, it is a sorry tale." I clasped my hands beneath my chin and let my lower lip wobble most piteously. "I never knew my mother, and my father was a cruel man. Please don't make me go back! I've heard that this is the only place a child burdened by the *Aidea* might find a safe haven."

"You have the *Aidea?*" Modest arched an eyebrow. "What kind?"

"Better that I should show you," I said, and proceeded to walk through the side stone walls of the fountain.

Modest's eyes widened, and for a moment, even he seemed taken aback by my abilities. "That is quite irregular, child."

"I know." I faked a shuddering breath. "It marks me as a cast-off, doesn't it? That's what my father said. He threatened to hand me over to the Conjury, but I'm not even sure I want this power." I sniffed and rubbed my palm against my cheek, wiping away the illusion of a tear.

Modest considered me for a moment. The cruelty in his expression had faded, replaced with something more like indifference. It was the closest I'd ever seen him come to evincing empathy. "You have heard that our god walks among us?" he asked.

I nodded and stepped back out of the fountain, still sniffling.

"Then you must also know that only those who believe in Guise receive absolution," he continued. "If you wish to stay here, you must follow our rules. Those cursed with the *Aidea* cannot be allowed to contaminate the other students, and disobedience will not be tolerated."

"Yes, sir," I said meekly.

"Very well." Modest clapped his hands once and turned to Brother Harmony. "It seems you have a new student to fill out your class. You know what to do. In the meantime, don't the rest of you have somewhere to be?"

The rest of our audience exchanged sheepish glances as they departed, and Brother Modest strode back into the building, leaving only Emerald and Harmony with me.

[That wasn't terrible,] I observed. *[He was much worse to you when you were little. Is it because I'm new?]*

[It's because you look human,] Emerald replied bluntly.

Brother Harmony approached me and dropped to one knee so that we might be of a similar height. "Hello, child," he said. The word that had been unkind on Modest's tongue was kind on his. "I'm sorry that you've been made to feel unwelcome, but you are not alone anymore." His eyes swept over me, and a new wrinkle appeared between his brows.

Does he suspect me? I wondered. Turning into a beetle and flying away was still an option, but if anyone was going to make the connection between what I was and what Emerald could do, it would be this man. If he did, the whole investigation would be put in jeopardy.

To my relief, he said nothing of Lightweaving. There was something else on his mind.

"Are you a boy?" he asked me. "Or a girl?"

I blinked at him, blindsided by the question. I had just come to terms with the fact that I was both and neither in order to make the magic work properly. "Yes," I told him, and offered no more insight.

A smile played over Harmony's lips. "Very well. I do not know what name you have gone by in the outside world, but here, we are given names that remind us to put our faults aside." He twisted around to look at Emerald. "Do you have any idea about what to name our new sibling, Steadfast?"

Emerald blinked once. "Vagabond," he said. "Judging by their attire, they would do well to adopt some humility when it comes to appearance."

[How dare you?] I demanded.

[You said it first,] he reminded me.

"Sibling Vagabond?" Harmony repeated. He was clearly dubious of my friend's choice, but having extended the offer, he could hardly retract it now. "I suppose that will do, at least for the time being. Come... Vagabond, let's get you settled in." He got to his feet and gestured for me to follow as he led me toward the corridor.

[I don't know what you're thinking, Crimson,] Emerald thought, *[but this is foolish. And dangerous. What if Modest takes you at your word and asks Allure to 'ease your burdens?' We could be found out, or you could be erased.]*

[I'm in no more danger than I was yesterday when you let Allure take your hand,] I told him as I trotted after Harmony. *[Besides, if there really is a god involved, do you think there's any chance of hiding just because the brothers don't know me? The sooner we solve this, the safer we'll be.]*

[I don't like when you go rogue,] he complained as he stomped after us.

I wasn't particularly worried whether he liked it or not. I was far more preoccupied with the way the magical pressure within that tent the night before had risen to a crescendo just before dying away entirely.

Emerald was a talented Lightweaver, and he had more brains inside that thick skull of his than anyone else I knew. Even so, there would be no way for him to defend himself if Allure turned on him. She could ruin him if she wanted.

We would have to use everything at our disposal to avoid that scenario, and that included me.

. . .

I HAD BEEN PREPARED to explain myself to Modest and Harmony, but I had *not* anticipated how I would be greeted by my peers. Blare, Svelte, and Quell had returned to their shared room by the time I was escorted to my new quarters.

Emerald had pretended to bring me some clothes more suited to my new position in life, then stood guard outside the door while I "changed." My short, vibrant red hair refused to be tamed, standing upright at the back so much that I looked like my head was wreathed in flame. It was a good disguise, but it had resisted my attempts to control it, and I was rather peeved with Emerald's magic for obeying my orders sometimes and ignoring me at others. I didn't *want* to look like such a scruffmuffin while meeting my new classmates, but my fate had already been decided.

Emerald shooed me forward, and I shuffled my feet as I approached, not quite capable of bringing myself to look at any of them.

Harmony folded his hands before him. "Sibling Vagabond, this is Sister Svelte, Brother Blare, and Brother Quell. Vagabond, this part of the room will be yours." He gestured to a small bed in one corner of the room, alongside a little desk and a three-drawered nightstand.

I nodded. "Thank you, Brother," I mumbled. I wasn't faking my nerves, although I couldn't explain them. I was quite sure that if my new classmates made fun of me, I would drop dead on the spot, riddled with shame. The notion was preposterous, given that I had been tangled up inside a god nearly a month before. Why should I care what these children thought of me?

The obvious answer was that I shouldn't care in the slightest.

And yet I did.

"Children, I hope that you will be welcoming." Harmony gave them a stern look. "We will be leaving you here for the moment, as we have some things to discuss with Brother Modest, but I trust that you will treat your new sibling with *kindness* and *empathy*." He put special emphasis on those last words, which suggested to me that there had been times in the past where his advice was ignored.

I hadn't expected to be thrown to the wolves quite so readily, but Harmony was already ushering Emerald through the door.

[Don't leave me here!] I thought desperately.

Emerald stepped into the hall, ignoring my plea. *[Good luck, Vagabond. This was your idea, and there's not much I can do about it now.]*

The door closed behind them, and I stared at the wood in consternation. Emerald was right, of course, but that didn't mean I had to like it.

With deep misgivings, I rotated to face my new classmates, all three of whom were staring at me with curious expressions. Blare sat on his bed, Svelte hovered next to her desk, and Quell sat in his chair, watching me through his thick glass lenses.

"Hello," I squeaked.

"Vagabond?" Quell asked without preamble. He adjusted his glasses as if hoping to get a better look at me. "That's a funny sort of name. Usually they name us after things we don't like about ourselves, or rather things *they* don't like." He nodded toward Svelte. "Like her. They call her Svelte to make her feel bad about how she looks so that she'll be so self-conscious that she doesn't argue any time someone's awful to her."

"Quell!" Svelte's voice had a hard edge to it. "You might be a chatterbox, but you don't get to speak for me." She rounded on me. "You don't have to answer him, he just says whatever comes into his head and doesn't worry about how it will make people feel."

"Well, it's true," Quell shot back. "But I still don't understand why they'd name someone Vagabond, because if you *are* a vagabond, I don't think you'd want to keep being one, and if you're not, I don't know why they'd want you to become one."

This back and forth hadn't left me any opportunity to respond, which was something of a relief. That sensation was short lived when Svelte rolled her eyes at the lambkin and spoke to me instead. "How old are you?" she asked.

I had tried to make myself look about the right age to be lumped in with them, but in truth, I had no idea how old that was. "How old are you?" I retorted.

"I'm twelve," Svelte told me. "And so is Blare."

She gestured to the other boy, who lifted one hand in silent greeting.

"Oh." I studied Blare, comparing our relative builds. "You're a year older than me," I decided.

"I'm only two and a half," Quell said proudly, "but that's because lambkins grow up fast. What are you?"

"Um." I held up my hands. "I don't know. A cast-off, I think?"

Quell rolled his eyes and swung his legs above the floor. "That's not what I meant. I mean, what *are* you? A human? You look human, but you can never tell with people here."

"Oh." That was another question I didn't have a ready answer to, but since I'd been modeled after Coirpre, I supposed I was *meant* to be human. "Yes."

Quell sniffed. "Well, I hope you're not going to be a prig about it."

"*Quell,*" Svelte said again, with the sort of put-upon air that Emerald used with me when he found me tedious. "He's new. Be nice."

Blare made a sharp motion in Svelte's direction.

"Sorry," she said, turning back to me. "*They?* Is that better? Harmony called you *sibling.* Does that mean you're not a boy or a girl?"

I shrugged one shoulder. "It's a bit of both, really."

She smiled. It was the first time I'd seen her looking anything other than annoyed or shy. "Sorry for getting that wrong. I'm used to living with *only* boys. Nice to know that there are one-and-a-half of us now. I know a bit about being a little bit of both, even if it's not quite the same. My mother was a dwarf, and my father was an elf. Being in between can be lonely, but there are a lot of us here."

Blare patted his chest and made a few gestures of his own.

"He says—" Quell began.

"He says he's human, but he won't be a prig about it, either," I said. My connection to Emerald was still good for something, even if we were focused on different things.

Blare laughed, and Quell looked me over again with new respect. "He did," the lambkin agreed.

"And you?" I lifted my chin to Quell. "Are you half-lambkin, or...?"

Quell wrinkled his nose. "Don't be disgusting. Don't you know that lambkins can only have children with other lambkin?"

I tried to tread lightly, in case I'd offended him. "You don't look like the other lambkins I know," I told him.

Quell pushed his glasses farther up and spoke in a professorial tone. "You've probably met prairie lambkins before. They're white all over and don't have horns at all. There are also forest lambkin, but I'm the third kind." He puffed up his chest and jabbed his thumb into the middle. "I'm one of the mountain varieties. We're the best kind to be, because we adapt so much better to all sorts of terrain."

Svelte leaned over and whispered to me out of the side of her mouth. "People say mountain lambkins are bad luck."

Quell glowered at her.

"I'm not saying *you* are!" Svelte lifted her hands in self-defense. "I'm just saying, you still are a bit like the rest of us, even if you aren't half-and-half."

The parts of Quell's face that weren't hidden by his wool flushed to an angry brown. "I never said I was better than anybody, Svelte. They *asked*."

Blare hastily cut in. *No making fun of one another. We've been through enough.* He gestured toward me, then patted his chest again. *I may be a full human, but I can't talk. My parents tried to help me at first, but eventually they gave up.*

I rocked back on my heels and signed in return as I spoke to him. "Just because you couldn't speak? That's awful!"

I couldn't sign then, either, Blare replied. *Brother Harmony taught me that. Now my hearing is getting worse. And I'm sick a lot. People aren't...* He paused, hands frozen in midair as he considered his next signs. *Patient. They don't like what they don't understand. I know that interacting with me is work, and most people aren't interested. No one else wanted me, so here I am.*

Svelte had been following along, and she jumped in where Blare had left off. Her signing was clumsier than ours, and she got a few of the gestures wrong, but it was better than Harmony's refusal to participate at all. "So it's not all bad, being here. Quell is bad luck, *supposedly...*" She used an unfamiliar sign to indicate her friend's name. "I'm not welcome with either side of my family since my parents split up, Blare can't talk, and you're a cast-off. At least the Brotherhood gave us a home. And maybe someday, they'll make us normal."

"We'll never be normal," Quell spat, making a single violent sign. *Freak.*

We could be closer, Blare pointed out.

I stared around at my three classmates. My earlier shyness had disappeared, replaced by a sense of kinship that was not entirely familiar to me. "Would you really give up your *Aidea* for Guise?" I asked.

Quell puffed up his chest. "Never! I'm going to stick around until I get big enough to head out on my own, and then I'll get work as a Castcadesman. Or maybe I'll go live on my own, like Henda!"

I'd heard that name before, although it took me a moment to place it. I'd seen a bust of her in the Conjury's lobby when we first arrived in Kinmore.

There's no point in giving it up, Blare signed. *My Aidea isn't what makes me different. Even if I didn't have it, I'd still be an outcast. At least with a skill, it's possible that I'll be able to find work or a community when I'm grown and gone. I doubt the Conjury will hire someone like me, but you never know.*

Svelte bit her lip and stared down at the toes of her tatty leather boots. "I'm not sure," she said. "I think about it sometimes, but I'm not sure what it would fix. I don't like my magic much, but it's no worse than being fat or a half-breed."

"Don't call yourself that!" Quell snapped.

"Why not?" Svelte lifted her chin. "They're both facts."

Quell crossed his arms and glared at her. "There's a reason people use that phrasing, Svelte. Call yourself fat if you want, but you're not livestock any more than I am."

Svelte's lips twitched.

"Don't say it!" Quell cried.

"I would never call you livestock, Quell," she replied.

Blare interrupted their conversation to sign to me. *What about you, Vagabond? Would you give up your* Aidea *if you could?*

"That's a good point." Quell turned to me. "You could live a normal life without your magic, couldn't you?" There was genuine envy writ large on all three of their faces. None of them knew that they had something I, too, longed for: bodies. *Autonomy.* They were free in ways I might never be.

I couldn't tell them that, though, so instead, I merely shook my head. "Without the *Aidea*, I don't know what I would be. I'd rather stay as I am and learn to be content with that than try to please the likes of Brother Modest."

All three of them tittered at my expression.

"He's awful, isn't he?" Svelte whispered.

The worst, Blare agreed. *But Harmony is nice. We're like a little family here.*

"We're certainly the closest I've ever had," Quell agreed.

Their sentiments echoed Allure's when she spoke of her child-hood, but Blare's assertion didn't leave me reassured. Emerald had felt some connection to his peers back in the day, and yet he'd grown into a man who loathed himself more than he loved himself. Two decades from now, any of these children could be doing as he had done, standing on the edge of a bridge above a river and making a choice that they couldn't take back.

Emerald was the closest thing I had to a biological family, and I had my figurative hands full minding him. If I was going to insert myself into this little found family, too, how in the names of Aster and Ardus would I have any hope of looking after them all?

CHAPTER

ELEVEN

By the time Emerald and Harmony returned, the four of us were seated on the floor in a circle. The other children were taking turns explaining the nuances of their favorite games, including Stick-Poke—an endeavor that seemed to begin and end with the practice of poking unfamiliar objects, flora, and fauna with anything besides one's fingers—and Find the Bones.

"Do you go to the catacombs?" I asked dubiously.

Blare shuddered. *Never. They're off limits.*

"And they're creepy," Svelte added.

"We don't go looking for *human* bones," Quell explained. "But the Brotherhood is really old. There are all sorts of little nooks and crannies where things have gone to die. Mice, mostly. Stuff like that."

Svelte huffed. "I don't think they died on accident. I think someone put them there. I've found owl pellets and raptor castings in all sorts of funny places."

I found teeth once, Blare signed with a grin.

"Ew." I shivered at the deliciously unsettling promise of finding small trophies hidden around the compound. "What kind of teeth?"

Baby teeth, I think. They fell apart when I touched them.

"Human baby teeth?" Svelte squealed.

Blare shrugged. *Human, dwarf, elf, who can tell? But they definitely didn't belong to mice!*

The door swung open, and we all turned to look up at our mentors as they entered. Emerald's expression was perfectly neutral, which suggested that he was in a foul mood and didn't want anyone to know what he was thinking. Harmony, however, seemed perfectly at ease.

"It looks as though you're all getting along," he said, smiling down at us. "I'm glad to see it. It's time for lunch, and then we'll be walking Emerald and Vagabond through our lessons. How fortuitous that we should have two new arrivals so close together."

Emerald flinched, probably bracing for Harmony to put two and two together, but Harmony seemed blithely ignorant of the fact that our combined presence might be anything more than coincidence.

Our little group got up, and we all made our way to the dining hall. I hadn't given much thought to this element of my existence, since I so rarely gave thought to things like food and drink and other ancillary matters unless I was immediately faced with them.

[Any suggestions for how to handle this?] I asked.

Emerald glanced at me. *[Oh, so you're asking for my help now?]*

I fell into step behind Quell. *[Don't taunt me, or I won't tell you what I've learned, and that includes the rules of Stick-Poke.]*

[I beg your pardon?]

I ignored him and stared up at the ceiling.

He huffed. *[Fine. Pretend to grab a tray, and I'll figure out the rest.]*

I gathered the illusions of a meal as Emerald watched sidelong, filling my imaginary tray with the appearance of food. None of it looked particularly appetizing, which didn't seem fair. If I was going to pretend to eat, couldn't I at least pretend that it would be food that was worth enjoying?

I slid onto a bench beside Svelte, who was already talking to Quell about something they'd reviewed in an earlier class. Our little group had found a table in one corner of the room, and the other children gave us all a wide berth, although I drew plenty of curious glances.

Emerald and Brother Harmony sat down together at the far end of the table.

"I was thinking about the section we read from the book the other day," Svelte said. "You know, the one where the bird with all the bright plumage gets killed and stuffed for a lady's hat? And I wondered—"

"Svelte," Harmony interrupted gently, "I see you've taken extra helpings. *Again.*"

Svelte froze with her mouth hanging open, a spoonful of porridge halfway to her lips. She slowly lowered her hand, returning her spoon to the bowl. "Sorry," she murmured.

"I'm not scolding you," Harmony said in that same, honey-sweet voice. "I'm just reminding you that Guise favors those who exercise moderation."

A ghastly silence fell over our little group as Svelte pushed her tray away. "Sorry, Brother," she said again.

Quell and Blare exchanged a dark look, and Quell mouthed the words, *I told you so.*

The way she curled into herself to try and appear smaller seemed almost like a direct mirror of my friend, who still had barely touched his own meal. His reluctance to eat might have been on account of the unappetizing offerings, but I wondered if there was more to it. If, perhaps, a younger Emerald had received a similar scolding from his mentor in this very room all those years ago.

Rather than eating, Emerald was squinting at Brother Harmony, as if seeing him more clearly. The older half-jotunn had tucked in as if nothing untoward had happened, and I wondered why my friend didn't say something. *Anything.* How could he sit in silence before a man who was so comfortable killing others with kindness?

Everyone at the table jumped when Brother Lightfoot sat down next to Emerald.

"Steadfast," he said in his wheedling, venomous voice, "isn't it lovely to be among old friends again?"

Emerald raised an eyebrow. "Seeing Allure was certainly—" He cut himself off as another person sat down across from him, next to Brother Harmony.

The newcomer was about Allure's age, which I supposed made her close to Emerald's age as well, although—with no disrespect intended to my dearest friend—she wore it better than he did. Her sleek blonde hair was pulled up in a high ponytail, and her large, upturned eyes were a crystalline blue. The grace of her movements and the high cut of her cheekbones suggested elven heritage, and her pointed ears confirmed it. My first thought was that she could have been Coirpre's elven counterpart, but only when the bard maintained his illusion of youth.

"Hello, Steadfast," she said.

Emerald tilted his chin down. "Humble. It's been a long time."

[Humble?] I repeated. *[Your... other sister?]*

[Allure might think of her as a sister, but I certainly don't.] Emerald's nostrils flared subtly at the mere suggestion.

"What brings you back to Kinmore?" Humble asked. Her tone was still polite, but her smile was predatory. "Here to see what's become of our old friend?"

"She restored my admittedly shaky faith in the Unifier," Emerald said through an unfriendly smile of his own. "It felt like a sign."

"I know exactly what you mean." Humble bowed her head. "I was working in Venta Bulgarum, but when I heard the news, I felt called to return."

Quell squeaked. "You work for the Conjury?" he asked. "Are you like us, then?"

"Burdened?" Humble's smile showed too many teeth. "Yes, little brother. But just like Brother Steadfast, I knew that my connection to our dear sister was a sign. I was meant to come home. I had strayed too far from the path Guise set me on."

Emerald pursed his lips. *[Well, now we know who the Conjury sent in my absence,]* he thought. *[Just what we needed: another complication.]*

[I understand that you don't like her,] I observed, *[but isn't she on our side? In the sense of trying to sort out everything that's going on with Allure and Guise, I mean.]*

Emerald's eyes flicked toward me. *[Sure. And what happens when she writes to Finch about you?]*

It was indeed a precarious situation. The Brotherhood wasn't supposed to know that I was an illusion; the Conjury wasn't supposed to know that I was anything but.

"Surely the lifestyle of the Brotherhood is a step down from what you're used to?" Emerald asked.

Humble pressed one hand to her heart and let her eyes flutter shut. "That's true," she admitted. "But the brothers gave me my name for a reason, Steadfast. If I valued the creature comforts of the city above the uncomfortable but abiding truths of Guise, I would be no better than a nonbeliever."

Brother Lightfoot smiled unpleasantly to himself. "All our little lost lambs came hurrying back home the moment the truth reached their ears. Isn't it sad, Brother Harmony, how fickle their faith can be, even after everything our god has given them?"

Brother Harmony scraped the last of his porridge out of his bowl. "You judge them too harshly, Lightfoot. All of Guise's children walk their own path, and they arrive where they are meant to when the time is right." He glanced sideways at Svelte's untouched tray, where her porridge was forming a thick film across its congealing surface. "Svelte, my dear, if you're going to take so much, don't *waste* it."

Svelte's pale cheeks darkened as she reached for her bowl. "Sorry, Brother," she whispered, so low that I doubted Harmony could hear her this time. The other children had finished eating, but in my fascination with Humble and disgust with Harmony, I'd forgotten to pretend to join in. I mimicked eating alongside Svelte, who barely raised her eyes from the table as she choked down the remains of her lunch.

I'd only been her friend for a few hours, but I was already cataloging all the things I'd say in her defense next time.

I could not abide a bully, even if he *had* been Emerald's mentor.

THE AFTERNOON CONSISTED of a series of dull lessons, in which Harmony droned on about the will of Guise, the burden of *Aidea,* and a meandering parable about two brothers, one of whom embraced Guise and lived a simple but prosperous life and died at a very old age, and the other of whom tried to become a hero and ended up dying an early, grisly, and ignominious death.

I stared intently at Harmony and did my best to pretend that I was following along, but in truth, I was paying more attention to the older children. Sometimes when Harmony spoke, he turned his back on the class so that he could make notes in chalk on a sheet of slate at the front of the room. How was Blare supposed to keep track of the lesson when he could neither hear Harmony clearly, nor read his lips?

Then again, perhaps Blare could do without these particular lessons. I found them mostly depressing. When it became clear that my participation was not required, I allowed myself to think back to the night before in the tent. Emerald's memory hadn't revealed anything about Allure's natural gift for the *Aidea,* but perhaps we could try again.

Dinner passed without further incident, although I noticed that Svelte took much smaller portions, even smaller than Quell's, despite the fact that he was half a head shorter and nowhere near as broad. Svelte had a dwarf's build; no matter what she did, she would never look like Humble any more than Emerald would. As I watched her poke halfheartedly at her tiny bowl of stew, I fought down a flare of anger. Unless Emerald was able to give me a body of some kind one day, I would never have the pleasure of eating. Why should Svelte be denied something that was within easy grasp?

"Hey," Quell said, pointing at my tray, where Emerald had earlier conjured the illusion of a hunk of fresh bread. "Are you going to eat that?"

I was about to tell him no when I realized that he wanted it. As far as anyone in the compound knew, I was a regular person who had the ability to walk through solid objects. If Quell tried to touch my bread and found nothing but empty air, we would have to answer a lot of inconvenient questions.

"I was saving it for last!" I blurted and snatched it off the tray, stuffing the whole thing into my mouth in one go. It tasted like nothing, but it filled my mouth as I struggled to chew.

"Moderation, Sibling Vagabond," Brother Harmony reminded me. "There's no need to be greedy."

"Mmph hmmph," I replied, doing my best to bow my head respectfully while talking around a mouthful of magical not-bread.

Harmony pursed his lips in displeasure, but to my right, Svelte was giggling instead of looking sad. On balance, I thought it a fair trade.

CHAPTER

TWELVE

Getting into bed that night required a bit of creativity. I had to wait until no one was looking before darting under the illusion of a blanket, carefully layering it over the reality of the one beneath me.

"Good night, Vagabond," Quell said.

"Are you scared?" Svelte drew her knees up to her chest and hugged herself. "I know the first night in a new place can be creepy, but you're safe here."

We've got your back, Blare signed. *Don't be afraid. You've got a family now, one that won't throw you out for being different.*

Thank you, I signed back. *I'm not afraid, just tired. Thank you.*

Harmony and Emerald returned to make sure that we were all in bed before dousing the lamps.

[Harmony wants to talk to me after this,] Emerald told me as he put out the light on my bedside table. *[I'll let you know when I'm back in my room, and we can meet in the mind-cottage.]*

[All right,] I said, faking a yawn for the benefit of my bunkmates. *[See you there.]*

"Rest well," Harmony told the children. And then, because he could never miss an opportunity to preach the gospel of his god, he

114

added, "An unquiet mind is a troubled one, but an unburdened one finds peace easily."

Fortunately, I was facing the wall, so he didn't catch me rolling my eyes.

The two men withdrew, leaving us alone in the darkness. I was no stranger to lying awake while other people settled down to rest, so I rolled onto my back and folded my hands over my chest, staring up at the ceiling. There was a crack in the plaster above me, just visible in the moonslight spilling through the windowpane. I wondered how long it had been there, and why no one had bothered to repair it.

Blare's breathing deepened, and Quell eventually broke out into a snuffling little snore. He'd removed his glasses before lying down, and he looked incredibly vulnerable lying there, curled up in a tight little ball beneath the threadbare sheets.

It took Svelte longer to fall asleep, and her sleep was nowhere near as deep as the boys' was. She kept twitching and spasming for a while, until at last she went still and lapsed into a deeper slumber.

I awaited Emerald's summons, returning my attention to the ceiling above. In truth, I wasn't particularly interested in the crack above my bed. It was merely something to look at while I considered everything I'd learned. It was difficult to know what might be a clue. On our last two cases, I'd known what was happening. People were turning up dead, and we were meant to figure out who was responsible. This time, I knew that Allure was up to *something*, but I wasn't sure what. Emerald and I hadn't even been called in to investigate a crime, per se. This was an entirely different sort of puzzle than what I was used to, and I hadn't yet worked out how to set about solving it.

Perhaps I should find a way to spy on Allure directly... but only if I could do so without arousing suspicion. Could she sense the *Aidea* that made me, just as I sensed her power? And if Guise truly was speaking through his mouthpiece, would he be able to sense my—

The crack in the plaster moved.

Every thought scattered from my head in an instant. I froze, forgetting to feign either blinking or breathing as I watched the black furrow shift every-so-subtly.

Fear did not come naturally to me. After all, I had encountered very few things in the world that could harm me directly. Yes, I had been frightened on behalf of my friends, and I had known horror in the Black Hollow when I melded with the Crone, but the subtle shiver in that one crooked strip of shadow ignited a deep-seated terror such as I had never known. It seemed to me that the plaster warped and bowed before my very eyes, collapsing toward me as if under a great weight. The crack widened to a gap behind which a shapeless, hungry thing pressed its unseen eye to the opening.

Don't let it come through, I prayed, although to what god, I didn't know. *Whatever it is, don't let it in.* The distant scrape of claws against stone wafted down through the fissure, and its breath was desperate and hungry in my ear. It knew that I was there. It knew what I was, I was quite certain of that. I wanted to scream, but I was simultaneously afraid that if I did, it would pounce. There was nothing to do but hold perfectly still and keep my eyes open. If I closed them, something terrible would happen.

If I blinked, it would get me.

The thing behind the crack remained unmoving, watching me intently. Its shifting made a faint but terrible noise. A whisper of bone on bone. The memory of flesh turned to ash and ground into the gaps between pavers.

Who are you? What *are you?* I wanted to ask, but I did not want the answer. My lips parted as I steeled myself to speak.

[Crimson?]

Emerald's thought had me rocketing upright in bed, one hand pressed to my chest. It was as if a spell had broken. The soft breathing of my schoolmates was the only sound in the room, and when I looked up at the ceiling, the crack had shrunk back to its former, benign proportions.

[Crimson?] Emerald called again. **[*I'm going to the mind-cottage now.*]**

I lay back down, but for a few seconds I continued to stare upward. Whatever I'd experienced before had ended as swiftly as it began. Only when I was satisfied that I was not in imminent danger of being pounced upon did I allow myself to close my eyes and retreat to the mind-cottage.

Emerald was already there, standing in front of the dummy I'd made of him weeks ago.

"Well," he said, before running his hands through his hair letting out an exhausted sigh. "That was tedious."

"Hm?" I was still shaken from my encounter, and since my body more or less existed in the mind-cottage, I was also *shaking*. My heart fluttered against my ribcage, and my knees could barely hold me upright. If this was what fear felt like, maybe I shouldn't be so quick to wish myself into a body after all.

Emerald didn't notice my distress, since he was still frowning at his likeness. "I think Harmony suspected something. If I had to guess, he wanted to leave you alone with the children this morning to see if you'd disappear or become disrupted somehow when I left the room. Which you didn't, so I suppose congratulations are in order. You took a gamble that appears to have paid off." He turned to me and crossed his arms. "So now we're both on the inside. I hope you're happy."

"Mm," I agreed. My tongue cleaved to the roof of my mouth, and I forced myself to breathe—not because I needed air, but because the tightness in my chest threatened to crush me.

"Crimson?" Emerald took a step closer. "Are you all right?"

"I just had a..." I licked my lips as I tried to marshal the right words for what I'd just experienced. "I think I had... a dream? Is that possible?"

Emerald shrugged. "I wish I knew. You have a habit of breaking the rules. I thought you couldn't become anyone but Simone or Simon, but here you are."

"I can't become anyone but *Crimson*," I said, gesturing to my diminutive form. "Which I still am, thank you very much." Talking made me feel a bit more like myself, and with every passing second, my fear seemed more absurd. Nothing had happened, not really. Besides, Emerald was right. I was rewriting rules all the time. Why couldn't I dream if I wanted? And if a creature made of light *were* to have a nightmare, didn't it make a certain amount of sense that I'd envision a beast made of shadow?

"Let me know if it happens again," Emerald said, and just like that, we put the matter behind us. "In the meantime, I'm exhausted, but I want to try entering my memory again. Being back in our old bedroom reminded me of something, and I think it has to do with the *Aidea*, but I only remember bursts and snatches of it."

I gestured toward the blank wall. "Lead the way."

Emerald narrowed his eyes in concentration, and when I glanced toward the wall again, a door had appeared. I recognized it as the weathered wooden door of the bedroom that I now called home.

Emerald reached for the handle, but I hung back.

"Aren't you coming?" he asked.

I don't want to go. What if it's still in there? I eyed the door suspiciously, curling my hands against my chest. I wasn't sure that I wanted to see whatever lay beyond.

But it was only a memory, and I knew that I was acting like the child I appeared to be. I had resolved to help my friend, and more than anything else, he needed a line of defense between himself and his past. In returning to the Brotherhood, he had faced more than his fair share of shades and shadows, and it was only right that I do the same.

I shuffled forward, despite my vague misgivings, and followed him through the door.

Steadfast sat in his room, a book open on his lap. He was reading a text about mushrooms, lost in a detailed explanation of their taxonomy and uses in both medicine and poison, when the door of the dormitory flew open and Allure came tumbling in. She was six years old; Steadfast had only just turned eight.

"What's the matter, Al?" he asked, slipping a bookmark between the pages and setting the encyclopedia of mycology aside.

Allure collapsed next to Steadfast's bed and began to sob. "They took it. They took it! I tried to get it back—"

"Oh, stop being such a baby." The blonde girl on the far side of the

room rolled her eyes at the pair of them. Her pointed ears and upturned eyes suggested a hint of elvish ancestry. It was Humble, unless I was very much mistaken. "I'm trying to work." She couldn't have been much older than Steadfast, but she had the air of a woman in her thirties who had spent her whole life being inconvenienced by the people around her. In that regard, she hadn't changed much, at least according to Emerald's memory.

There was space for a fourth child in the room, but the bed was empty. The sheets had been turned down with military precision, but whoever slept there was absent. The layout of the room hadn't changed. Quell had been right when he speculated that he had ended up in Emerald's old bed. Humble was sitting in Svelte's corner. The empty bed was the one to which I had been assigned.

Steadfast glared at the back of Humble's head, then he returned his attention to Allure. "What did they take, Al?"

"My bracelet." Allure choked on the word and held up her slender arm as evidence of what she'd lost. "The one Mom gave me. It's all I had from her..."

"No one cares about your swamper elf mother," Humble snapped.

Steadfast bent over to rub Allure's back. "Shut up, Humble. You're just jealous that her mother loved her enough to give her anything."

Humble leapt to her feet so fast that her chair rocked back on its legs. She clenched her hands into fists and glared at the pair of them with the color high in her cheeks. "And you're jealous that I'm not as ugly as either of you!" she cried. "I hope whoever took that stupid bangle throws it in the latrines and you never get it back." She stomped toward the door and out into the hall, slamming it behind her.

Allure sat back on her heels, scrubbing one little fist against her eye. "That wasn't nice, Steady."

"She isn't nice," the boy replied. "Don't worry about her. I'm sure she'll find Reticent, and the two of them can conspire against us like they always do. Now, who took your bracelet?"

"Brother Benevolent," Allure said. She wrapped her small hand around her wrist where the bracelet should have been. "Subtle and Considerate held me down, but everyone else was out in the yard, just watching." She let out another sob.

"You know better than to go out there with them," Steadfast said kindly. "Nobody looks out for us but us, remember?"

Allure nodded through her tears. "I shouldn't have done it, it's my fault..."

"No, it's not. It's their fault for being awful, but don't worry. I won't let them get away with it." Steadfast got to his feet and padded toward the door. "Stay here, and if anyone asks where I went, tell them I got sick at breakfast, all right?"

"All right," Allure agreed. She sat on the floor beside his bed and hugged her knees into her chest, much as Svelte had done before lights-out. It must be fairly common for the children of that miserable place to find ways to comfort themselves, since they had no one else to do so.

Steadfast left through the door. I worried that when I followed him, I would be spat back into the mind-cottage, but I passed through the door without issue and followed him down the hall. He seemed to know exactly where he was going.

Rather than heading to the courtyard, he stopped at one of the other doors and pushed it open. There were more beds inside, although the room was roughly the same size. I hadn't realized that there was any advantage to having the Aidea, but evidently Modest's desire to avoid "contaminating" the other students meant that those who could control magic had a bit more space to themselves.

Rather than go poking around the room, Steadfast rotated on the spot, nodded to himself, and sat down on the floor.

He waited there for a while, fiddling with something in his pocket and murmuring to himself, until the door of the dorm flew open. Four children tumbled through: a human, a lambkin, and two with at least a bit of dwarven heritage. The smallest of them was flailing his fists almost at random, while the other three laughed and taunted him, each shoving him in turn so that he could never find his feet.

"What's the matter, Brother Assertive?" the largest boy taunted. "Are you scared that there's no one here to save you?"

"Stop!" the boy wailed, trying to escape their torment. "Let me go, I've got nothing worth taking!"

I had not recognized Brother Assertive until he spoke. He was a scrawny child, and like Allure, his curly hair had been cut short by someone who had no interest in maintaining it. When he spun to face the ringleader, however, I realized that I knew him. It was Yerik, our friend from the Lute and Goose.

"Don't talk back to me, new boy." The largest lad, who I presumed must be the inaccurately named Brother Benevolent, caught Assertive by his shirtfront. "I'm in charge, and if you even think of tattling on me, I'll—"

"Boss?" The lambkin cleared her throat, then she nodded to where Steadfast sat, watching the scene before him unfold.

Benevolent shoved Assertive away, and the half-dwarven boy collapsed against the end of a nearby bed.

"What do you want, freak?" Benevolent snarled, advancing on my young friend. Steadfast was big for his age, but Benevolent was older and taller, and he had two friends in his corner, besides.

"I want you to stop picking on Allure," Steadfast said. He didn't bother to get up from where he sat. "Guise despises those who covet that which is not theirs."

Benevolent snorted. "I didn't touch your little girlfriend."

"No?" Steadfast blinked innocently and held up a hand. In his already-broad palm lay the charm bracelet that Allure had showed him in the library.

Considerate let out a cry of anger, and Benevolent's cheeks flushed dark.

"Don't touch my stuff, freak!" he snapped. "How did you even get that?"

Steadfast scrambled back, still holding the bracelet. "I didn't touch anything of yours."

"Yes, you did." Benevolent thrust his hand into his pocket and removed a bracelet, the perfect twin of the one in Steadfast's palm. For a moment, he gawked at it.

A smile broke over Steadfast's face as he wriggled his fingers, and the bracelet in his own hand vanished.

For a few seconds, no one moved, and then every hell broke loose. Steadfast lunged at Benevolent, who feinted away, clutching the real stolen bangle. Brother Considerate tackled Steadfast, while Sister Subtle lunged for his knees.

"Leave him alone!" cried Assertive, but Subtle turned on him and drove her horned head into his gut, sending him sprawling.

In a matter of mere seconds, Steadfast was curled on the floor in a ball, nursing a split lip. Benevolent and Considerate loomed over him, and the latter smacked his fist into his palm a few times, making his intentions painfully clear.

"How are you going to get out of this, freak?" Benevolent sneered.

Someone in the doorway sighed and leaned against the doorframe. "Well," the newcomer drawled, "isn't this charming? We've got a thief in our midst."

Every eye in the room turned toward the new boy. He had black hair that framed his pale, narrow face in loose waves, and eyes so pale that the iris was almost indistinguishable from the white. He was lean and tall, and although he was no older than Emerald, he gave off a strange ripple of power, even in the memory. When he smiled at Benevolent, the other boy shuddered and backed away.

I knew without having to be told that this was the fourth member of Emerald's childhood family, Brother Reticent.

He pointed a slim finger at Considerate, revealing that his nails were painted black. "Let him up," Reticent said.

"Or what?" Considerate demanded, crossing his arms. "Are you going to tell on me?"

"Shut up," Benevolent hissed.

"Tell on you?" Reticent chuckled. He stepped forward, and I realized that he had not come alone. Humble blocked the doorway, her hands held out to either side and a smug smile etched on her pretty face. "I don't think you know who I am."

"You're a freak, like him." Considerate jabbed Steadfast with his toe.

"That's right," Reticent agreed, striding forward. "We're little monsters, aren't we? And do you know why people are afraid of monsters?"

Assertive whimpered, and Subtle elbowed him in the gut to shut him up.

"Because we're always there." Reticent tapped his finger against Considerate's chest. "Because even when you're sleeping, we know exactly where to find you. And because of what we can do."

He backed up abruptly, but Considerate was still staring at him in slack-jawed wonder, hypnotized by whatever he saw in Reticent's eyes.

"Steadfast," Reticent said, "get up."

Steadfast scrambled to his feet and hurried to the door. Humble glared at him as he scurried behind her.

"Get out of here," he told Assertive. The young half-dwarf did as he was told, pelting away down the hall as fast as his short legs would carry him.

Reticent turned on his heel and strode back toward the door. He stopped just before reaching Humble and glanced back over his shoulder. "Bother any of us again," he warned, "and you'll have to come through me."

With that, the three of them swept into the hall.

The instant they were out of sight, Humble smothered the fire she was holding and grabbed Steadfast by the ear, twisting hard. "What were you thinking?" she demanded. "Starting a fight, using your Aidea... If Modest found out what you'd done, we could all get in trouble. Again."

"Ow! Let go!" Steadfast wriggled against her grip like a fish on a line.

Humble flung him through the door, and he staggered toward his bed, one hand pressed to his bleeding lip and the other folded over his stomach. Humble followed, and Reticent shut the door behind them.

"Steady?" Allure leapt to her feet and hurried to his side. "What happened?"

"He started a fight with those idiots, thanks to you," Humble complained. She stalked to her desk and dropped back into the chair. "I bet you anything Modest will hear all about this."

"I don't think so," Reticent said. He perched on the edge of his bed, regal as a small king holding court. "They'd have to admit that they were the ones bullying Allure and Assertive, and I don't think they will. Besides, if they do, I'll teach them a lesson."

Humble shivered, but the way she looked at Reticent was more awed than alarmed. "Would you really?"

"Of course." Reticent tilted his head slightly and caught Steadfast's gaze. "Nobody looks out for us but us."

Steadfast nodded his agreement.

"Whatever." Humble reached for the book she'd been reading earlier. "Can I get back to my studies now?"

Steadfast sat down heavily, and Allure snuggled up beside him, wrapping her skinny arms around his waist. "I'm sorry you got hurt, Steady. I'm glad you tried to get the bracelet back for me."

Steadfast winked and held out the hand that had been clutching his middle. In his palm sat the bracelet Benevolent had taken. The real one.

"Oh!" Allure pounced on it and cradled it in both hands. "But how?"

"I was wondering that, too," Reticent admitted.

Steadfast reached into his pocket and produced a large, green marble. He held it up so that the light spilling through the warped windowpane refracted through it.

"I figured I'd need proof of what Benevolent had done," he explained, and he wiggled his fingers again. An instant later, a second bracelet appeared in his hand. An illusion, cast by a budding Lightweaver with only a cheap ball of glass as a focus. "So I made it."

WHEN WE RETURNED to the mind-cottage from the memory, Emerald was quiet. He reached for a chair, and even though none had been there a moment before, it sprang into being at his moment of need. He slid down into it and folded in on himself, bracing his elbows on his knees.

"Was that your first mystery?" I asked.

"Hm?" Emerald shook himself. "Oh, yes, I suppose it was."

I knelt beside him. "Where do you go, when we step into the memories?"

He frowned, as if the question itself puzzled him. "I'm... *me.* Why wouldn't I be?"

"Is that why you're upset right now?"

"Not exactly." He twisted his fingers together and frowned down at his hands. "That wasn't too bad, honestly, until Reticent showed up. You know, I didn't think about Allure until I saw her again in the library, and the same with Humble, but Reticent..." He trailed off and leaned back in his chair.

When he didn't elaborate, I tried to coax him along. "Did you like him? The way you like Tincrown, I mean?"

Emerald choked on a laugh. "No. Gods, no, he was my brother in every way that mattered. It was *never* like that. I just never think about him. We reached a certain age, the rest of us got sent off to train as Castcadesmen, and Allure decided she'd stay. I haven't seen them since. Which is natural, I suppose. Children grow up." He seemed skeptical, though, and I got the impression that he was trying to convince himself as much as me.

"What could Reticent do?" I asked.

Emerald rapped his knuckles against his forehead in frustration. "I don't know. I don't *remember.*"

I opened my mouth to ask something else, but before I could formulate a full question, I paused.

I could make the mind-cottage look however I pleased. In the past, it had looked like rooms I had already visited, or scenes that I wanted to reexamine for evidence. It could take any form I chose, but when left to its own devices, it became a simple one-room dwelling with whitewashed walls and a pale blue ceiling scattered with painted gold stars. Tonight, it looked just the same as it always did, except for a noticeable flaw in the middle of the plaster.

There was a crack in the starry ceiling of my mind-cottage the exact size and shape as the one above Reticent's old bed.

CHAPTER

THIRTEEN

"Aren't we going out into the courtyard?" I asked my new siblings after breakfast the next morning. Svelte was already leading us back to the room, but I was in no rush to spend my morning beneath the crack in the plaster that had invaded my subconscious.

Blare shook his head. *We usually don't. The other kids don't like to get close to us, and even when they do, the Brothers don't like it.*

"They don't want us to *contaminate* them," Quell added, putting a bitter emphasis on the penultimate word. "Which is stupid, because it's not like *Aidea* is catching. It's not *monkrot!*"

"That's not why they want us to stay inside," Svelte murmured. "They want to keep the other children safe."

Quell huffed. "From magic?"

"No." Svelte tugged on a loose curl of her hair. "From us."

I made no further protest as we retreated to the room. The way I saw it, ordinary children were just as dangerous as those with *Aidea.* Emerald's memory should have been sufficient proof of that.

"So what do we do all morning, if we don't go outside?" I asked when we reached the room.

Svelte sat down on the floor beside Blare's bed. "It depends. We

126

do go outside, sometimes, but only when the Brothers are there to watch us. One time I tried to play Stick-Poke with some of the other kids in the winter, and a boy got his finger stuck to the metal pole he was using. He blamed me, even though I had only been watching."

I perched on the edge of my desk and crossed my legs underneath me. "What happened?"

Svelte shrugged. "The other kids took his side. It was all of them against me. Harmony was *so* disappointed."

I pulled on my hair, aching with the unfairness of it all. "Even Harmony didn't believe you?"

Svelte leaned back against the side of Blare's bed. "Oh, he did. But he told me that he was disappointed in me for putting myself in that situation. He said it would teach me a valuable lesson about keeping out of people's way."

I shot an incredulous look at Quell. I had wondered why Emerald insisted on being solitary, and why he'd had such a hard time opening up to the people who cared about him. Now, I was beginning to see why.

Blare sat behind Svelte and ran his fingers through her hair, separating it into individual locks and deftly weaving in small braids.

"So we just... sit here?" I asked.

"Sometimes Quell reads to us," Svelte said.

Blare finished the first braid and signed, *We could visit the library.*

"No, thanks," Svelte told him. "Allure's there a lot of the time, and she gives me the heebie-jeebies."

"We could play Find the Bones," Quell suggested.

Svelte wrinkled her nose. "*You* can."

Blare drummed his fingers on his knees before suggesting, *We could show Vagabond...* He stopped before signing whatever it was he meant.

"Ooh." Svelte sat up. "Yeah, we could. What do you think, Quell?"

The lambkin shook his head. "They're new, Svelte. We don't know if we can trust them."

"Trust me with what?" I leaned forward. If I'd been subject to the laws of gravity, I would most likely have toppled off the edge of the desk. "I'm extremely trustworthy. What are we talking about?"

"It's a secret." Quell lifted his chin in an effort to look taller than he was. I'd done the same thing myself when facing down Emerald on a few occasions. "A secret for the orphans of the Brotherhood, and I'm sorry, Vagabond, but you're new. Maybe when you've been here longer."

My curiosity was piqued, but Quell had made up his mind. He reached for his book, flipping open to his bookmark, where he began reading. It was a history of Dregandresal, told from the perspective of Guise's followers, and centered heavily around a bloodthirsty god-king named Bendasha, who did all sorts of terrible things.

I couldn't focus on what he was saying any more than I could pay attention in Harmony's tiresome lessons, so I let my mind wander.

Inevitably, my eyes strayed to the crack in the ceiling. In the daylight, I could easily make out the wood beams and crumbling straw insulation inside.

Frankly, it was embarrassing that anything so mundane had driven me to such distraction. In the future, I would marshal my emotions more rigorously.

By early afternoon, I was convinced that I was about to die of boredom. Emerald had spent years in these lessons, but a day and a half was more than I could take. No doubt there was some measure of peace to be had from a quiet life, but the prospect of spending a decade or more dressed like a street urchin while listening to the tedious drone of Harmony's voice left me aching for any scrap of adventure, however small.

Halfway through his aimless musings on the subject of yet another Augur or Vulcanist who had met their demise as a result of their use of the *Aidea*, I decided that I could stand it no longer, and raised my hand.

Harmony stuttered to a stop. "Yes, Vagabond?" he asked. "Do you have a question?"

"I do." I offered him my most winning smile and folded my hands in front of me again. "Why does Guise dislike the *Aidea* so much?"

Harmony tapped one finger against the slate. "That's what I've been trying to tell you, child."

"You've told us that he *does* hate it, and that everyone who embraces their gifts dies horribly, or ends up banished to the *Aidea* Nulda, or gets struck by lightning, or goes blind. You haven't said why. Why give people magic if they're not supposed to use it?"

Harmony's smile was ripe with condescension. "Guise is not all-powerful, child. Besides, you might as well ask why he makes some of us fat." He gestured to Svelte. "Or mute." He indicated Blare. "Or..." He waved one hand toward Quell, but couldn't seem to settle on the appropriate adjective. "We all have burdens, even those who do not have the *Aidea*."

Svelte slid lower in her chair in an attempt to appear smaller.

"But what makes them *burdens?*" I pressed. "Why do you have to make it sound as if there's something wrong with people for being who they are. Why can't Guise love us as we are? Because it seems to me that if a god doesn't like anything about what makes us individuals, he's probably not the sort of god I want anything to do with."

Harmony's brows pulled low. "Sibling Vagabond, if you have no love for our god, then why have you come here? Perhaps you should seek out another residence more suited to—"

Emerald cleared his throat. "If I may, Brother?"

Harmony breathed in through his nose, folded his hands behind his back, and stepped aside. "Very well, Steadfast, let's see if you can answer this one."

Emerald plodded up to the slate board and began to speak. As he did so, he signed along for Blare's benefit. "As you know," he said, "my faith has not always been... resilient. I have only recently returned to the Brotherhood. I'm certain that Harmony is more knowledgeable when it comes to doctrine, but I'm more than capable of speaking to the history of the Brotherhood. Who knows why the Conjury was started?"

Quell's hand immediately shot into the air. When Emerald nodded to him, he blurted, "Henda started the Conjury because all sorts of people were running around doing terrible damage with their magic. Even when people made laws, there was nobody to enforce them. Those with *Aidea* could do whatever they wanted, whenever they wanted. Ordinary people were dying all the time just because powerful magic users were fighting for the upper hand. It was one war after another for hundreds and hundreds of years. The Conjury was founded to help establish peace."

"Exactly so," Emerald agreed.

"Really?" I asked. I hadn't meant to interrupt, but I was startled by this insight. My experience of the Conjury was hardly that of a beneficent council focused on defending the people. They were the one I had to hide from to keep from being interrogated—or even destroyed. They were the people all of Dyrne feared. In my mind, the Conjury was made up of snobs, bigots, and power-hungry barons. Since when were they the good guys?

Emerald smiled wryly at me. "Why do you think the people tolerate them? Why do you think the ruling classes of almost every nation-state across Dregandresal work with them?" When I didn't immediately reply, he answered for me. "Because no matter how powerful a king and his army might be, they can't stand against a man who can pull meteors out of the sky using only his will, or wash away a hundred miles of shoreline with a single wave."

I gawked at him. "And *that's* what the Brotherhood stands against?" I asked.

Brother Harmony nodded. "I know that each of you have small amounts of magic, and that all of you believe that you can use it for good. And perhaps you would... at first. History books are littered with those who sought to use their power to protect those they loved, or to fight for what they believed in. When they came to rely on that power, however, it corrupted them. They started making selfish choices."

Like hiding a village from prying eyes to protect the man you love. I wasn't convinced that Emerald had misused his power when he used an illusion to hide Dyrne. I believed in his moral code. But I had also seen the Fenguards use *Aidea* to "do the right thing," and commit atrocities in the name of the greater good. And Aindreas hadn't used the *Aidea* to kill the Conjury scouts, but his magic had certainly helped.

Still, I wasn't convinced that ignoring one's ability to do magic would solve the problem. "Even without magic, people would still have advantages over one another."

Harmony nodded, and that knowing smile that I was coming to hate played across his lips. "Like wit?" He gestured to Emerald. "Like strength? Anything that can be used to dominate or oppress our fellows is frowned upon. Guise asks us to think of ourselves as the equals to our neighbors, no more, no less. Some of us will never fit in, but if we can do our best to conform and make ourselves useful to our brothers and sisters—" He caught himself, then nodded to me. "To *all* of our siblings, then we will find our place in the world."

I fell silent, puzzling over all of this new information. I had never heard the principles of the Brotherhood laid out so clearly and coherently before, and now that I understood the reasoning, I found it difficult to debate. People in the past had suffered because of magic... but people in the present were suffering because of the Conjury, and I could see for myself the toll Guise's teachings had on the people around me. There must be another solution to the problems caused by misuse of the *Aidea*.

Even beyond the suffering I had witnessed in my friends, I could not believe that everything I was, and everything that went into the making of me, was rotten at its core.

I WAS LOST in my own thoughts for the rest of the night, and only when it came time to get ready for bed did I remember the other thing that had troubled me. As the sun sank toward the horizon, the shadows throughout the compound deepened, and I was reminded of the fissure in the plaster above my waiting bed.

It was possible, of course, that the crack in the ceiling of the mind-cottage was the result of my own fixation. It would not have been the first time that the mindscape offered me a clue to the mystery I was trying to solve. I told myself that I had put it there.

The other option—that the thing in my room had followed me into my own head—was too terrible to contemplate.

While Harmony made sure that we were all safely ensconced in our beds, Emerald spoke to me while pretending to tidy the room. *[Are we going to try to explore another memory tonight?]*

I lay back, hovering just over the pillow, snug beneath the illusion of my blanket. *[Not tonight. There's something I need to investigate on my own.]*

[Oh?] He glanced at me out of the corner of his eye. *[Any chance you're going to tell me what it is?]*

I folded my hands over my chest and did my best impression of a child drifting off to sleep. *[I will if I learn anything.]*

[It's for the best. Last night was...] He trailed off, but the bruises beneath his eyes told the story well enough. He was exhausted. Poking around in his long-suppressed memories left him weary and defeated.

[Get some sleep tonight. You know I don't need it. I'll follow up on my lead, and I'll tell you how it went in the morning.]

[I hate leaving you alone,] he thought as Harmony opened the door of the children's room. *[I did too much of that in Upper Bound.]*

[It's not the same thing at all,] I reminded him. *[Even great investigators deserve rest.]*

He smiled to himself. *[You know where to find me.]* With that, he followed Harmony into the hall.

A few seconds after they were gone, Quell sat up in his bed. "Vagabond?" he hissed.

I sat up as well. Moonslight illuminated his silhouette, and although I could not make out his expression, I could see that the set of his small shoulders was defensive. "What's wrong?"

He hugged his knees. "All that stuff you were asking in class today... do you believe what they said?"

"I don't think—" I almost said Emerald's real name, but caught myself just in time. "*Brother Steadfast* was lying, if that's what you mean?"

Quell shook his head. "I don't, either. The facts are the same in everything I've read, but the way they said it made me wonder if... if they're right, about our *Aidea*. If it makes us dangerous."

I had no idea who might overhear us from the hall, and I was already in the midst of questioning everything I'd believed. I didn't have a ready answer for him.

In many ways, I had advantages over Quell. I had only been myself for half a year, but I had all of Emerald's knowledge and intellect to draw on, whereas Quell had less than three years to build his worldview. In that sense, I was far worldlier than he was.

But everything I knew came from Emerald, and Emerald's mind had been shaped by the Brotherhood. If Emerald was wrong about things, wouldn't I be wrong by extension? I knew better than anyone else how fallible Emerald could be when it came to himself, and that included his relationship to the *Aidea*.

"I think it might," I told Quell. "But I also think that what you do with your power depends mostly on who you are as a person. I think a better use of Brother Harmony's time would be to teach us how to be good people, and make decisions rooted in kindness and love rather than greed."

He exhaled in obvious relief. "I agree. My *Aidea* is part of me. I don't want to hurt anyone with it, but I don't want to hurt myself by ignoring it. Does that make sense?"

"Perfect sense," I agreed.

Svelte had been quiet, but at this point she piped up from her bed. "That's easy for you to say, Quell. Your magic is, at worst, annoying."

"Hey!"

"Not like mine," she went on. "And not like that girl in the tent. What could she do with a power like that to benefit anyone?"

"She could use it to make a shield for herself if she was attacked," I said.

Quell nodded. "Or learn how to focus on specific metals, and use it to figure out where miners should dig!"

"Maybe she could learn to use it to make incredible jewelry," I pointed out, because even as a penniless orphan, I was still obsessed with the finer things in life.

"Or crush an army of soldiers inside their armor," Svelte muttered.

Quell flopped back into his bed and squirmed around, trying to get comfortable. "You're such a pessimist, Svelte."

She only laughed in response.

Blare had been quiet all the while, and I wondered if he was only listening, or if his hearing was bad enough that he couldn't make out the words. I had seen people use enchanted items to channel *Aidea* through common objects—take, for example, the gloves Tincrown had worn to help him determine cause of death, and the goggles that Dawyd had commissioned so that he could see the invisible townsfolk. Couldn't the *Aidea* be used to make his life easier? Magic couldn't solve every problem in the world, but if people would stop being afraid of it, surely we could put it to better use.

"Night," Svelte said.

"Good night," Quell replied.

In his bed, Blare made a soft sound.

I lay back again, and my eyes fixed once more on the aperture in the plaster. If nothing else, it served as a reminder that Emerald had been right about some things. The *Aidea* could be frightening, especially when we didn't understand it.

CHAPTER

FOURTEEN

Gradually, the other children dropped off to sleep, and the moons rose higher, changing the angle of light until the white ceiling faded to deep gray, almost indistinguishable from the flaw that marred its surface. The crack looked quite innocent so far, but I was not fooled. Like Quell, I had questions, but I was certain that the thing in the ceiling was better suited than I was when it came to supplying answers.

I stared at the crack and waited. *Come on, you wretched thing, show your face. Let me see you. Let me get a good, long look at you. We have matters to discuss.*

The seconds passed in silence, and the crack never moved. Perhaps I *had* dreamed it the night before. The Brotherhood was playing tricks on Emerald's mind, and his mind was what gave me life.

As if he could sense my distress, Emerald reached out. *[Any luck with whatever you're up to?]*

I squinted at the crack. *[No. And if you knew what I was doing right now, you'd probably think I'm being silly.]*

[I usually do.]

I smiled in spite of myself. *[Rude. Aren't you supposed to be asleep?]*

[I'm trying. It's harder than it should be.]

Recalling the tiny bed in the room he'd been assigned, I asked, *[Trouble getting comfortable?]*

[Trouble settling my mind.]

[Mm. And you know what Guise has to say about an unquiet mind.]

I couldn't hear his soft bark of laughter, but I felt it through our connection. I was happy to bring him even a little mirth in a place that had put him through so much heartache.

I shifted around like Quell had done earlier, although of course no change of posture would make me more or less comfortable than I already was. My anxiety was internal, but I had no way to dispel it. *[Emerald, when you were younger, did you ever... see anything strange here?]*

[One could argue that the whole experience was strange. Are you asking about something in particular?]

I lay on my back, staring upward, and I had the sensation that Emerald was doing the same thing. It was reassuring to imagine him a few rooms away, lying in his too-small bed, my anchor point to this world. The last time that we'd been apart like this had been in Upper Bound. I was used to being at his side, and although he wasn't far removed, I was lonely without him. The other children were nice, but they didn't know who or what I was, and I was tired of having to always pretend.

[Last night, I thought I saw—]

A soft cry from the other side of the room roused me, and I sat up, letting the illusion of my blanket fall away.

Svelte was fast asleep with her mouth wide open, and Quell was snuffling to himself with his face pressed to the pillow. In between them lay an incongruous sea of darkness through which the moonslight could not pierce. It was gathered around Blare's bed, swirling about the bedpost in black eddies. Within that burgeoning cloud, a long-limbed figure stooped above Blare, its many-jointed fingers curled like talons. It was too tall to be a human, too narrow to be a jotunn, too translucent to be anything alive.

It was made of *Aidea,* nothing more or less. I looked at it, and I knew.

The creature was like me.

[Crimson?] Emerald asked. ***[What did you see?]***

I had not made a single sound, but the creature's head whipped toward me. From the midst of that inky blackness, two eyes like dying stars peered out at me. It bared its teeth in a silent snarl, revealing its long, narrow muzzle.

I had been so preoccupied with the silent interloper that I had failed to realize what had alerted me in the first place. Blare lay on his back, but unlike our roommates, his spine was bowed and his limbs were flung wide. He arched on the bed, making incoherent sounds of pain. To my horror, white foam bubbled from his lips, and his teeth chattered so violently that I was afraid they would shatter in his jaw. His mewling cries faded, and he began to choke.

And even then, I could not bring myself to move.

[Crimson, what's happening?] Emerald's voice became more frantic.

The creature moved away from Blare's bed toward mine, and I thought, *It can hear me. It can hear everything we think.*

It moved toward me, falling onto all fours as it stalked across the knotted boards between us. Everywhere it stepped, it left pools of shadow in its wake. The miasma of unnatural darkness hovering over Blare's bed remained, spreading toward me.

I shook my head and drew back against the headboard, curling into a ball. I could not leave Blare, but I could not let that thing touch me. I wasn't sure what would happen if it did, but I knew that it would be something terrible and irrevocable, and that I would never be the same afterward. The shadow-beast was everything that I was not, except that we were born of the same source.

The shadow-beast lifted itself up onto the edge of the bed and tilted its head to one side, then it kept turning. If it had a spine, it would have surely broken. It opened its awful mouth again.

I did the only thing I could think to do, the one thing that would ensure I wouldn't have to hear whatever that monster made of the void had to say.

I screamed as loud and long and high as I could manage.

I was still screaming when the door flew open, and Emerald burst through, a lantern held high over his head. The shadow-beast lifted one clawed hand to shield its face from the glow, and an instant later, it vanished.

Emerald plunged directly through the spot where it had been standing, hurrying to Blare's side. His small frame was still contorted in a rictus of pain, and the foam on his lips was now tinged pink with his own blood.

My screams had roused the other two children. Svelte reached Blare's side even before Emerald did and immediately rolled him onto his side.

"Has this happened before?" Emerald asked her.

Svelte nodded. Even with her usual pallor, she was paler than usual, especially when it was bathed in moonlight. "Brother Harmony calls it a seizure. He's always had them, even before he came to the compound. It was part of the reason his family—" She cut herself off and rubbed Blare's back.

The boy was already relaxing, and he was breathing again, too. Quell hung back, wringing his little hands.

My cries had roused those in the nearby rooms, and Harmony entered a few moments later, bearing his own lamp. He shooed Emerald aside and checked Blare's pulse.

"Poor child," he murmured. "You're safe now. I'll take him to the infirmary. Steadfast, please make sure the others are all right."

He lifted Blare up in his arms as though the child weighed nothing and retreated through the door. A cluster of fretful onlookers clutched the collars of their dressing gowns as they tried to sneak a glimpse of whatever had happened.

"Out of the way," Harmony said in that gentle, irresistible voice of his. "Return to your rooms, there is nothing to see."

Emerald shut the door behind him, and the four of us were left alone in the half-lit room.

"That was good thinking, Svelte," he said.

The girl sat back down on her bed, playing idly with one of the braids Blare had woven into her hair—was it only that morning? It felt a lifetime ago. "After the first time it happened, Quell found a book about it. We wanted to know what to do. The worst time was when it happened at dinner and he almost choked." She shivered. "It's never happened at night, though. If we hadn't woken up in time, he might have—"

She trailed off, staring at Blare's empty bed.

"Vagabond woke us up," Quell blurted.

They all turned to face me, and I recoiled from their collective gaze. There was kindness in their expressions. Gratitude, even. My guilt threatened to crush me beneath its weight. I had been so afraid of the shadow-beast that I had almost let Blare die.

"Thank you," Svelte told me, redoubling my self-loathing. "You saved him."

I shook my head. "I just yelled."

"And you got him help," Quell insisted.

[It's not as though you could have rolled him over,] Emerald pointed out. *[Even if you had known what to do, you wouldn't have been able to it. There's no shame in that.]*

I met his gaze. *[Are you serious? Didn't you see the thing that did it?]*

The lines around his mouth deepened. *[What thing?]*

[The monster. There was a shadow-monster in this room, and it tried to kill Blare!]

Emerald hesitated for a moment before shaking his head. *[I didn't see anything, Crimson.]*

That was impossible. He'd looked right at it. He'd walked exactly where it stepped. I was sure that I'd seen the surprise on his face just before his light dispelled it.

But perhaps he'd only been looking at Blare.

When I didn't elaborate, Emerald got to his feet. "It's been a long night for everyone," he told us. "Try and get some rest. I'm going to see if Brother Harmony needs anything. There are ways to treat Blare to reduce the likelihood of that happening again."

He waited until the other children had climbed back into bed.

[Aren't you going to ask what I saw?] I demanded as he reached for the door handle.

[It was probably just a dream, Crimson. A night terror. They happen sometimes.]

[Not to me,] I reminded him.

He shook his head, and once again, I had the impression that he had opened a doorway in his own mind, glanced inside, and then decided to close it again without investigating. That wasn't like him at all. The Emerald I knew wanted answers and would go to great lengths to obtain them. Why was he so quick to dismiss something that I had seen with my own eyes?

Maybe for the same reason that he'd forgotten so much of his childhood.

He left the room, returning to his own quarters. Harmony's abandoned lamp was still burning on Blare's side table, but none of us got up to put it out. I found the light a relief, even though it illuminated the damp pillowcase where Blare's head had lain during his seizure.

Above me, the crack in the plaster yawned like a leering mouth.

I WAS NOT sure how much time passed before Svelte began to cry. She did so quietly, smothering her tears in her pillow, but her misery was unmistakable.

Quell slipped out of his bed and tiptoed over to her. His little hooves struck sharp against the floorboards until he reached her and pulled himself up into her bed. He curled against her and rested his cheek on her arm.

"Do you want me to sing?" he whispered.

She nodded, and Quell drew a deep breath before breaking into a sweet song in another tongue. It was a lullaby. From the moment the first notes reached my ears, I began to relax, my worries washed away.

I had met a Sonicist before, although I hadn't known the name for her gifts. Dionara Fenguard had used the same branch of the *Aidea* to coax the truth out of anyone who heard her play, whether they wanted to spill their secrets or not. Quell's song was as different from hers as the shadow-beast was from me.

Svelte's sobs were soon replaced by heavy breathing, but Quell didn't stop singing. I wondered if his song was as soothing to him as it was to our friend. Could people be affected by their own *Aidea?* I had never thought to ask. There was so much I didn't know about the world.

As the last notes of Quell's song died out, however, something I'd said earlier occurred to me. When speaking to Emerald, I'd called the shadow-beast a monster. I had heard someone else use that term recently—although, in all fairness, they'd *spoken* the word years ago.

Do you know why people are afraid of monsters? Reticent had asked the children who stole Allure's bracelet. *Because we're always there.*

Because even when you're sleeping, we know exactly where to find you.

FIFTEEN

When Emerald awoke before dawn from a fitful sleep, I was standing in the middle of his room. He let out a yelp of alarm and tumbled sideways out of his too-small bed, only to hit the floor with an echoing thump. A moment later, a green flame flared to life in his palm, illuminating us both.

"Gods above, Crimson," he grumbled, struggling to his feet. "What is wrong with you?"

"I was letting you sleep," I retorted.

He waved one hand at me. "You're standing in my room, in the dark, dressed like an undertaker!"

It was true. In the night, my nerves had gotten the better of me, and I had rearranged myself into Simone, dressed myself in black, and wandered the halls of the Brotherhood like a ghost. I had felt too vulnerable as little Vagabond. As I walked, I watched for shadows, just in case any more should come to life. I had even visited Blare in his sickbed, just in case the beast returned for him. Like Emerald, the boy had slept fitfully but without incident.

"I have had to be careful," I said, crossing the room in three strides and turning on my heel. The walls of the Brotherhood were beginning to feel like a cage, and I like a tiger trapped inside them.

The trouble was, I could leave anytime I wanted... but only if I was willing to abandon my friend and our investigation. *Friends,* now that the other children were involved. "I wanted to see the shadow-beast before it saw me."

Emerald blinked at me in bemusement. "Shadow-beast?"

"The thing I saw last night," I snapped, still pacing. "The thing that attacked Blare."

Emerald's brow wrinkled, and he shook his head. "Blare had a seizure. Svelte said it's happened before."

"I know very well what Svelte said." I stopped in front of him, folded my arms, and glared. My black skirts billowed around me, as if stirred by the wind. "What about what *I* said?"

Emerald only blinked at me.

"I told you that I saw something attack Blare. You looked right at it, and you didn't see it. You told me that it was a night terror!"

My friend licked his lips. "Last night?"

"Yes!"

Emerald got up, too, and gestured sharply with both hands. "And you are absolutely *sure* I heard you?"

"You replied!" I exclaimed, throwing my hands in the air in dismay. "Are you calling me a liar?"

Quite abruptly, Emerald's face lit up with a broad grin. "I knew it." He spun away toward his lamp, abandoning the tiny green flame that had danced between us until that moment. "I knew it!"

He was delighted, but I was even more lost than I had been a few moments before. "What do you know, exactly?"

"You're telling me that I experienced one, perhaps even two things in the last day alone that I do not currently remember." Emerald was practically writhing with excitement. "Last night, I stepped into a memory that I had almost entirely suppressed, even though it had to do with three of the most important people in my life. Until a few days ago, I had completely forgotten Al. What does that tell you?"

"That you spent the last few years of your life repressing a terrible childhood?" I asked.

Emerald opened his mouth to argue, hesitated, then waved me

away. "Perhaps. But what it tells *me* is that someone is indeed capable of altering memories."

"Oh." I pressed my hand to my mouth, thinking back over the things that had confused me about the Brotherhood. He'd remembered the building as being more imposing, Harmony as being more fatherly, and forgotten his fellow children entirely. "*Oh.* But then how come you didn't forget everything?"

"Mentalism is a tricky practice, and everyone's talent is different. People can be permanently damaged by the careless alteration of memories, but someone with real skill could pluck out a single part of your life. It would make your memory related to that subject... tricky. *Faulty.* If they wanted you to forget a place, you might remember traveling there, but not the route you took, and you might be unable to answer as to whether you'd ever arrived. There's one cast-off—Mattvik, who the Conjury's been after for years—who could move people's memories around from one mind to another! It's a fascinating branch." He paused. "Although I find it less fascinating when it's affecting *me.*"

I bit my bottom lip, worrying it between my teeth. If I'd had a real body, I suspect I would have bitten hard enough to draw blood.

Emerald leaned back against the little desk beside his bed. It groaned beneath his weight, but did not collapse. It was made of sturdier stuff than it seemed. "You've thought of something," he observed.

"What if you weren't supposed to forget a *place?*" I asked. "What if someone wanted you to forget a person?"

He crossed his arms in thought. "That would be a valuable skill, certainly. It would also make it damned difficult to figure out who was responsible. You wouldn't remember who to look for."

"Maybe not," I said. "But we might be able to use process of elimination."

Emerald beamed at me, the way a teacher might regard a favorite student. "Might we indeed?"

"When you were growing up, there were four of you in that room. Now that the Conjury is investigating the Brotherhood, they've sent two spies to investigate... you, and Humble. Sister Allure is the mouthpiece of Guise, the axis around which our investigation spins. Who are we missing?"

My friend's eyes unfocused slightly. "You think Reticent is involved?"

I wasn't sure how to explain the connection I'd made between the shadow-beast and the boy from Emerald's memory. Reticent's threats toward the other children had been vague at best. All I had was instinct and a particular turn of phrase that snagged in my memory, and I knew how easy it would be to derail our investigation by following my instincts rather than the facts. All the same, I wasn't ready to discount them entirely. In the end, I only said, "I think it's possible. And I think we ought to consider it. Do you remember what he could do? With his *Aidea*, I mean?"

Emerald bit his thumbnail and stared into the corner of the room for a long moment before slowly shaking his head. "I can't. I *should* know. We *must* have discussed it. It should be right there, but..." He lifted one hand to grope at the air, as if the memory might be hovering just outside of his head, waiting for him to catch it. "Gods, that's *frustrating*."

Another thought slammed into me. "Emerald, could a Mentalist make you forget that you had *Aidea*?"

"Hmm." Emerald scratched the stubble on his jaw. "I don't think so. I mean, maybe they could make you forget what you'd learned, but... I mean, you'd still *have* it. Mentalists can blur things. Confuse them. Even obscure them. They might be able to make you forget your own name, but they couldn't make you forget that you *existed*."

"Not even a cast-off?" I asked.

Emerald puffed his cheeks out and bobbed his head from side to side. "Cast-offs complicate things, but you'd have to be exceptionally powerful. To *totally* erase something from a person's memory, however, you'd have to erase everything to do with it. Otherwise, when something reminds them of the subject, the work you'd done to hide it would unravel, at least temporarily. At the very least, they would know that something was missing."

"So you might have forgotten Reticent until seeing Allure, and Allure's bracelet, reminded you?"

Emerald chuckled before throwing my own words back at me. "I think it's possible. And I think we ought to consider it."

"Well, we know one thing for sure." I ran my hand over my skirts to smooth them down, although they already lay perfectly. "Your memory is affected, but mine is not. I remember the shadow-beast plainly, so whatever was done to you doesn't extend to me."

Emerald paused and blinked a few times. "Shadow-beast? We were talking about Reticent. What do shadows have to do with anything?"

Well, if there'd been any doubt that someone was messing with my friend's mind, that settled it.

I was debating whether I ought to try and explain again when someone knocked three times on the door.

"Brother Steadfast?" Harmony's voice was muffled by the wood. "Are you ready?"

Much to my chagrin, I had given no thought to the time. It hadn't occurred to me how things would look if the other children woke up and found me missing.

[I'll explain later,] I said, even as I shrank down to the size of a beetle and flitted away through the wall. I passed close to the ceiling, over Brother Harmony's head, and through the hall where a few people were already up and moving. I flew faster than any ordinary beetle could have dreamed until I reached the door of the room I shared with the children.

Svelte was still snoring, but just as I began to rearrange myself, Quell sat up and glanced toward me. "Vagabond?" he asked in alarm.

Well, that's it, I thought dismally, sitting up in my bed. *There's no way he'll have missed that, and he'll start asking all kinds of difficult questions.*

Quell fumbled on his bedside table for his glasses and held them up; the strap fell limp below the lenses, not yet affixed to his horns. He looked me over and breathed a little sigh of relief.

"I thought something had happened to you, too," he said. "My vision's as bad as Blare's—" He caught himself and set about securing his glasses in place instead. When he spoke again, his voice was barely a whisper. "I hope he's all right."

"I'm sure he will be." Svelte sat up and yawned. "It's happened before."

Has it? I wondered. *Or do they only believe it has? What if whoever made the shadow-beast is messing with people's minds in an attempt to cover their tracks?* Now that I know it was possible to compromise people's memories, whose statements could I trust?

No one's.

Perhaps not even my own.

AFTER BREAKFAST, instead of returning to the courtyard or their rooms, all the children who lived in the compound were funneled into the prayer hall to sit before the statue of Guise.

Prior to that point, I had only glimpsed the room in passing. The statue itself was the room's most obvious feature, surrounded by enough stone benches to accommodate everyone's seating needs. I thought the room quite plain until I turned my face upward to the carved wooden corbels that supported the elaborate ceiling. At first, I thought that the corbels were decorated with some sort of sickly rosette motif, until I realized that they were not flowers at all. Dozens of einwood faces glowered down at us, their mouths twisted in unique but similar disappointment. Higher still, the square coffers of the paneled ceiling housed still more scowling effigies.

"Those are ghastly," I muttered.

Svelte tipped her head back and leaned so far that she nearly overbalanced. "I hate them," she whispered. "Harmony says they're all likenesses of previous brothers and sisters, you know. Every one of them was a real person. They all died in service of Guise."

"They don't look particularly thrilled about it," I whispered back.

People were still settling in, and I took the opportunity to study the rest of the assembly. Without the swarms of faithful that gathered outside, this group was much smaller than the crowd that had gathered in the tent to watch Allure work her... well, to work her magic, ironic though that was. The hundred or so children ranged in age from infants to young teenagers, although it was obvious that they were separated into smaller groups based on their age.

"Are we really the only ones here with *Aidea?*" I asked.

"For right now," Quell whispered from my other side. "But only because the older class already gave up their burdens. They did it right at the beginning... none of them wanted to be sent to work for the Conjury before they got the chance, you see."

"Did you all study together?" I asked softly.

Quell shook his head. "Nope. They were all Sister Allure's students, since she's the only member of the Brotherhood who has any *Aidea*. And she used hers to take theirs away!"

Svelte nodded. "She doesn't have to teach now."

While they were talking, another cluster of students had caught my eye. They sat together, some in mobile chairs like the one Shepherdess Superior Lindsee used, others holding canes, and others still with asymmetrical features. When one of the girls met my gaze, she sneered through a cleft palate and made a rude gesture. I smiled in response and lifted my hand slightly in greeting.

"Blare would have ended up with them," Svelte told me, tipping her chin to the other group, "if he wasn't a Stonefeather."

The last three people to file into the hall were Brother Modest, Blare, and Allure. The mouthpiece of Guise was wearing her plain brown robes again, but even so, the gravity of her presence was undeniable.

When he saw his friend, Quell squeaked. "He's all right!"

Modest stopped at the feet of the immense state of the faceless god and bowed low. Funny, I thought, to have a statue without a face under a constellation of such detailed portraits.

"My brothers and sisters," Modest intoned, "Guise is good. Last night, one of our brothers suffered the effects of an illness beyond healing and passed close to death. Thanks to swift action and our fervent prayers, he was granted a reprieve."

[Prayers?] I thought. *[I thought he needed medical treatment.]*

[He's a holy man,] Emerald replied. *[He doesn't understand the first thing about medicine, but he'll prostrate himself before Guise ten thousand times before he acknowledges that any of us know more about the subject than he does.]*

"Praise be to Guise!" Modest raised his hands above his head and held them there, crying out toward the heavens—and toward the scowling faces of his dissatisfied forebears.

"Praise be to Guise," the children and their mentors replied with varying degrees of enthusiasm.

Allure placed one hand on Blare's back and signed to him with the other. *Take your seat, child.*

With his head down so that he wouldn't have to look at anyone in the assembly, Blare scurried away from her. He had to wend his way between the rows of other students, and he nearly tripped twice. Not out of haste, either. I didn't see the first culprit, but I registered the second one, and how he stuck out his foot just as Blare passed by.

If I'd had access to a militant branch of the *Aidea*, I would have been a destructive force then, indeed.

When he finally plopped down next to Quell, Svelte leaned around me to sign, *How are you?*

Blare made two signs so sharp they were almost violent. *I'm fine.*

"Focus, children," Brother Harmony said. "Brother Modest is speaking."

In the center of the room, Sister Allure tipped her head forward and folded her hands in front of her. As Modest carried on, I watched her eyes subtly scan the crowd. When she found Emerald, seated on Harmony's far side, her lips curved up in a soft smile.

"I know that this gathering is unusual," Harmony told us. "And I do not wish to draw undue attention to one of our students, but I do want to remind you that Guise cares most for the least among us. Take Sister Allure." He gestured behind him, to where she stood with her head down. "A half-jotunn, born of a swamper elf, who has struggled at every turn to find her place. Cursed with *Aidea*, and yet…"

"And yet Guise speaks to me, and not to you," Allure said. She did not raise her voice, but still it carried through the room. Modest flashed a scowl over his shoulder, but Allure kept her head down, the picture of abject humility.

[*I'm afraid I like her,*] I admitted. **[She has style. He can't argue with facts, can he?]**

[Interesting to know that they don't see eye to eye.] Emerald dragged his thumb over his bottom lip.

[Well, he is horrible to her...]

[I can see why she wouldn't like him,] Emerald agreed. *[But you'd think they'd want to put on a unified front of the faithful if they were working together to stage a fake religious revival, wouldn't you?]*

He had me there.

"Precisely," Modest said through gritted teeth. "All of which reminds me of the parable of the lost lambkin." He folded his hands behind his back and returned his attention to the audience.

"Not this one," Quell muttered, curling in on himself. "I *hate* this one."

[Oh, dear,] I thought. *[This can't be good.]*

"Once," Modest said, in the lilting tone of someone recounting a story he knows by heart, "there was a little village, where therein lived a hundred lambkins. They lived peacefully, sharing the labor equally among them. They raised crops, tended mushroom colonies on the outskirts of the forest, and lived simply and happily."

I narrowed my eyes at him. That didn't sound so bad. I must be missing something.

Modest began to stroll around the base of the statue, gesturing idly with one hand as he recited his tale. "One of them was called Fable. She was taller than the other lambkins, and cleverer, too. By the time she was only five years old—an adult, by lambkin standards —she had begun inventing mechanical wonders to make the lives of her fellow villagers easier. She invented a device to help them draw water from the well. Unlike the rest, she also had biological *Aidea*, and was able to use magic to help the village thrive. With her help, their gardens grew more luxurious and more bountiful than ever before. The village flourished, and every one of them said that Fable was the one to thank for their increasing good fortune."

[Why do I get the feeling that something horrible is going to happen to Fable?] I asked Emerald.

Emerald snuck a glance my way. *[Doesn't take a genius to work that out, Crim.]*

"One day, Fable went into the forest to scout the area and see if the village could be expanded. Night fell, but she did not return. So what did the villagers do?" Modest chuckled to himself. "Remember, they had thrived before Fable was born, but their lives had become easier with her help. They had grown fat and lazy and accustomed to letting Fable do their work. They decided that they could not live without her efforts. So when morning came, and she had not returned, they formed search parties and went out to look for her. Some went to the north, some to the south, looking high and low and calling her name. Fable. Fable!" Modest pantomimed the lambkins' search, placing one hand over his eyes and looking all around. A few members of the audience giggled, although there was cruelty in the older children's faces.

I glanced toward the girl whose gaze I had caught earlier. None of the children in her part of the room was laughing, and my friends had all sunk into a sullen, miserable silence.

"Did they find her, children?" Modest shook his head and sighed theatrically. "I'm afraid we will never know. Because one by one, their search parties were picked off by weirlings that roamed the woods. More groups were sent out to look for their family members, then more, until only a handful of women and children remained. Then the weirlings fell upon the village, and with only the weakest of their number left, they could not defend themselves. Every last one of them was eaten alive, and their houses and gardens were burned to the ground."

I wrinkled my nose. *[By weirlings? Are they known for lighting fires?]*

Emerald scratched his nose, hiding his sudden smile behind his palm. *[I dare you to raise your hand and ask that question. It sounds like Brother Modest has the same disdain for facts as some bards I could name.]*

[At least Coirpre's stories are entertaining.]

[Of course they are. Half of them are about me.]

"Do you see their fatal error?" Modest asked. "The lambkins should have closed ranks, should have accepted that their lives would return to their old rhythm... but no. They cared so much about what one individual could offer them that they allowed themselves to be divided. It is not that way in the Brotherhood. One lost lambkin will not doom the whole faith... no matter how special that individual might believe herself to be."

He did not acknowledge Allure, but it was perfectly obvious who he meant. For her part, she stood there, silent and unmoving as the statue itself.

"As the village should have done, we will gather close and care for those who know their place. Pray for Brother Blare that he does not fall ill again, and that Guise will watch over each of us equally. The blade of grass that grows the highest..."

"*Is the first to be cut,*" the children echoed.

"Precisely." Modest dipped his head in agreement. "Your studies will resume as normal after the noon meal." With that, he turned and strode out of the room.

Even before he reached the door, a frisson of whispered gossip passed through the room.

At my side, Quell let out a breath he'd been holding for a long time. "I hate that stupid story," he said. "It's one of Brother Modest's favorites, and I swear he looks right at me every time he tells it!"

At least he didn't show you off like a trick pony, Blare signed. *It's not like I chose to have a seizure... why did he have to march me in here in front of everyone?*

"We should not question Brother Modest's judgment," Harmony cut in. "And the parable of the lost lambkin is one of the oldest stories in our order. I assure you, Brother Quell, it has nothing to do with *you.* The message is for everyone, lambkin or not."

Quell huffed and crossed his arms. "If you say so."

"I do."

We did not speak again as we joined the line of people filing out of the room. Emerald's assertion that there was tension in the order was evidently true, but I wasn't sure what that meant for our investigation.

As we moved toward the hall, a flash of blond hair caught my eye. Sister Humble was standing next to Brother Lightfoot, nodding as he spoke to her. I couldn't make out their words, but the sight of her ignited a new thought in me.

Emerald didn't remember much about Reticent, or anything about the shadow-beast. Had whoever modified his memory gotten to her as well? If she really was the other person Finch had sent to investigate the order, perhaps she had uncovered something useful.

Unless she's in on whatever's happening. If Emerald was to approach her directly, she might not trust him. She had no reason to suspect me, however. Besides, Emerald might not remember to ask her about the shadow-beast, or Brother Reticent.

I needed to find a way to talk to her on my own.

My mind wandered throughout the afternoon's lessons, for many reasons. Harmony had decided that it would be worthwhile to spend the whole session dissecting the symbolism of the awful parable that Modest had told during the meeting, and I had already decided that it was utter nonsense. My time was better spent trying to tease out the threads before me.

I had seen the shadow-best twice now, and yet I was the only one. Something about its presence had been deeply familiar, but I wasn't sure *how.* It was more than the fact that the play of light and shadow always called to me, although it was my nature to be drawn to color and illumination. I was made of light, after all. Shadow was my antithesis. My inverse.

But the creature wasn't just any shadow, and I had never encountered anything that could hear the mental connection I shared with my best friend and creator. There was not a doubt in my mind that it had reacted to our thoughts the night before, but that shouldn't be possible.

Although, how could I prove that? In theory, *I* shouldn't be able to exist, and yet there I sat, lost in thoughts that I should not be able to generate or sustain without the conscious effort of my would-be master.

At dinner, I watched for signs of Humble, but her work in the kitchen kept her busy, and I had no opportunity to sneak off and pester her with a surprise interrogation. I needed an excuse to get close to her... without alerting her to my true nature, lest she report me back to Finch and I be deemed an aberration.

By the time we settled in for the night, I was in a foul mood. The crack yawned above me, one more thing that I would be forced to confront on my own.

"Good night, Vagabond," Harmony said.

"Night," I grumbled, though I would rather have spit in his eye than bid him good evening. The myriad limitations before me had left me sullen and despondent.

[We should try another memory this evening,] Emerald suggested as he and Harmony withdrew. *[Maybe we can learn more about Reticent.]*

I blinked up at the ceiling. *[You remember that we suspect Reticent?]*

[Obviously, or I wouldn't have suggested it.]

[What about the shadow-beast?]

[...the what?]

I groaned aloud and threw my arm across my face. *[I'll explain later. After the children fall asleep, I'll come to your room and we can talk more freely.]*

I had expected that the children would be unsettled by the events of the previous night and might take longer than usual to fall asleep, or that they might want to talk about Blare's attack.

I was not, however, expecting Blare to pop out of bed only seconds after the door closed in Emerald and Harmony's wake. He relit his lamp, and Svelte did the same.

"What's happening?" I asked, sitting up in bed.

Quell mashed his glasses back onto his face. "Do you want to talk about what happened, Blare?"

The boy nodded. He slid to the end of his bed, crossed his legs, and stared directly at me. *I know you saw it,* he signed.

My jaw dropped. *You remember it?*

"Remember what?" Svelte asked.

Not what. Who. Blare's hands trembled as he signed. *Vagabond saw the shadow man.*

CHAPTER

SIXTEEN

"The shadow man was here?" Svelte screeched.

"*Shh!*" Quell pressed a finger to his lips.

"Don't you shush me!" Svelte shot back in a stage whisper. "The shadow man was here last night during Blare's attack?" She swiveled her head toward me. "Why didn't you say anything?"

My mouth moved, but no sound emerged.

They didn't think we'd believe them, Blare signed for me. *Just like you didn't believe me the first time.*

Svelte huffed and leaned back against her headboard. "Fine."

"But you *did* see him?" Quell asked me.

I hesitated before answering. When I did, I signed while I spoke. It must be harder than usual to read lips by lamplight. "I wouldn't call it a shadow man. It was more like a beast."

It was different last night, Blare said. *It wasn't just a shadow. It was standing over me... like it was in the room with us.*

Svelte gasped and placed a hand to her mouth. "What?"

He showed up a few seconds before my seizure started. I thought I might be seeing things, but then Vagabond saw it too. Blare nodded toward me. *I could tell, because when Harmony came to take me away afterward, you were frightened. You kept looking at where it had been.*

Quell tilted his head. "Where was it?"

At the same instant, Blare pointed to the space beside his bed, and I pointed to the floor between them.

"It started over there," I admitted. "But then it came toward me."

"I don't understand. He wasn't just on the wall? He was moving around on the floor?" Quell shook his head. "That's a first."

It wasn't like before. He was solid.

"Oh, blood of Guise." Svelte bent forward and tucked her head between her knees. "Please tell me you're joking."

"Don't swear," Quell chastised.

"The shadow man is solid now!" Svelte moaned. "If now's not a good time to swear, then when is?"

"Hold on." I held up both hands until the others fell silent, then resumed signing. "Tell me about the shadow-beast. When have you seen it before? What was it like?"

Usually he... Blare shook his head. *It. You're right, it's definitely not a person. Usually it just sort of wanders around the walls. We see it in the dark sometimes. I saw it first, and I tried to tell them, but they thought I was making it up.*

"It used to be just a blob," Svelte added. "Dim, you know? But a couple of months ago, it got sharper. I've seen it a few times since then."

"A couple of months?" I repeated. "Around the time Sister Allure started doing the ritual in the tent?"

Svelte shook her head. "No, that's been going on a lot longer. Since the spring sometime."

I had hoped that there might be a direct link between the shadow-beast and whatever Sister Allure was doing. The realization that the two things might be entirely unrelated was daunting—but a place like the Brotherhood held many secrets. I really shouldn't be surprised.

"But this is the first time it's been able to move around the room freely?" I asked.

Blare nodded. *As far as I know.*

Svelte moaned again.

We sat in silence for a while, letting the magnitude of that realization settle in. After a long pause, Quell cleared his throat.

"I suppose," he said slowly, "that this makes Vagabond one of us. Officially."

Svelte's head popped up. "You think so?"

Quell nodded. "They saw the shadow man, and they yelled loud enough to get help *and* saved Blare in the process."

Svelte rolled onto her knees and clapped her hands, the threat of the shadow-beast set aside for the moment. "So we can show them?"

Quell lifted his chin and looked down his nose at me—a difficult proposition, since even while sitting I was markedly taller than he was. "If they promise not to tell Brother Harmony."

Without hesitation, I slapped one hand over where my heart should have been. "I swear, in Aster's name, that I won't tell Brother Harmony whatever you're about to tell me." That was an easy enough promise to make.

Aster? Blare signed. The gesture for the goddess's name consisted of spreading his fingers, like a flower in bloom. *Not Guise?* For the Unifier's name, he held up one hand and used the other to mime chopping off the tip of his middle finger, cutting the tallest of them down to size.

"Him, too," I said, knowing full well that any oath I made in Guise's name meant nothing to me.

"Perfect!" Svelte hopped out of bed and padded in her bare feet over to my bed. She crouched down between my bedframe and the wall. "Look at this."

Quell and Blare joined me on my bed, and we all peered down at Svelte as she removed one of the floorboards.

I whistled when I saw the little space between the joists. Inside was a veritable treasure trove of objects: toys, pictures, scraps of paper, even a ragdoll that looked a bit like a krub.

"What is that?" I asked, sliding off the bed to kneel on the floor beside the gap between boards.

"We found it," Svelte said. "Someone left it behind. There's all kinds of cool stuff in here."

"And bones," Quell added. "There are always bones. We found it while we were looking for some, but this is the best stash we've ever uncovered."

I wished that I could sift through them, but I couldn't touch anything. I was forced to let my eyes roam over the objects. There was a hedgepig carved from soap, an ivory statuette that looked like a piece from a board game, a miniature portrait, and...

And a green marble.

"Emerald," I murmured.

"What?" Svelte bent over the trove.

Realizing my mistake, I pointed to the marble. "It's emerald green. But I guess it's only glass, and not a *real* emerald..."

"Nothing in there's worth much," Quell said. "I think other kids hid stuff there a long time ago, and everyone forgot about it."

I suspected that Quell was perfectly correct on both counts, but I doubt he would have anticipated the thoroughness with which those long-ago children had forgotten their once prized possessions.

"Have you ever put anything in there?" I asked.

"No." Svelte slotted the board back into place. "But we promised we would before we leave. Leave something for the next batch of kids to find, and all that. You should, too, since you're one of us now."

I didn't think I'd be around long enough to contribute to the hoard, but I nodded. "Thank you, Svelte. I'll try to think of something interesting to include."

Quell rubbed his eye with one knuckle. "I'm tired," he admitted. "But between the shadow and the parable about Fable, I don't want to put out the lights."

We can leave the lamps on, Blare suggested.

Svelte got to her feet. "Will that stop it from coming after us again?"

I nodded. "When, um, Brother Steadfast brought the lamp in last night, it disappeared. I don't think it likes light. Since it's a shadow creature."

"We can try it tonight." Quell returned to his bed and removed his glasses once again. "But if anyone sees it, they scream. Promise?"

Svelte was already halfway under the covers, but she turned to

Blare and asked, "Do you think the shadow man *made* you have a seizure?"

Blare considered this, then shook his head. *I've had them before, and it didn't feel different. It was more like... like he saw what was happening to me, and wanted to get closer.*

Svelte shuddered. "I don't know if that's better or worse."

We all laid down again, and although we didn't talk, it took a long time for the other children's breathing to deepen. I waited, staring up at the crack, but nothing moved behind it.

I wondered what to make of the fact that the children could see the shadow-beast and remember it, while Emerald could not. Then again, the children had never met Reticent.

How come the answers I received only ever seemed to lead to more questions?

Emerald was waiting for me in the mind-cottage when I arrived. He was sitting in the chair he'd conjured for himself two nights previously, one leg crossed over the other, running his knuckles over his stubble again and again.

"We talked about something," he said. "Just before I left the room, you mentioned something, but I can't remember what. Do you?"

"I do," I said. I had rearranged myself again, this time into Simon. My clothes were simple, compared to my usual tastes, but comfortable.

When he saw me, Emerald started. "Why are you dressed like that?"

I held out my arms and looked down at myself, taking in the plain vest, the white shirt with the sleeves rolled up to the elbows, the loose double-breasted trousers and battered boots. "I don't know. Change of pace, perhaps?"

"You're dressed like him," Emerald grunted, pushing to his feet.

"Like who?"

"Like *him*." He turned his back to me. "Like Tincrown."

I winced and hastily altered my garments. "That's awkward. I didn't mean to. I've changed it now."

Emerald glanced over his shoulder and let out a snort of laughter. "That's worse."

I smirked at him. "You don't like the color green?"

"It's not just the green. You've copied Coirpre's style *exactly*."

"I thought it might make you laugh," I told him. "And I was right." I rearranged my clothing for a third time, keeping the cut of Coirpre's outfit, but changing the colors to red and gold. "Better?"

"Flashy and unnecessary, but yes, I suppose it's better." Emerald chuckled a bit, although it was clear that my temporary mimicry of Tincrown had bothered him more than he was letting on. "What were we talking about?"

I glanced upward, to where the crack between the stars still marred the periwinkle blue ceiling. "I was about to ask you what happened to the marble."

Emerald tilted his head. "Marble?"

"The one you used in the memory the other night, to create an illusion of Allure's bracelet. What became of it?"

Emerald's jaw worked, and his eyes unfocused. He tugged on the curling ends of his shaggy hair. "I don't remember."

"You don't remember the marble...?"

"I do," he said, "but not what happened to it. I suppose I could have used any bit of glass, couldn't I? Was the marble special?"

I shrugged one shoulder. "You tell me."

Emerald thought again, but the way his mouth twisted to one side made me quite sure that he wasn't having any luck.

I was so focused on him that I didn't register the change in the wall behind him right away. It had been blank when I arrived, but now there was a door planted smack in the center of it.

"Em?" I pointed over his shoulder.

He turned and huffed in surprise. "I guess I do know the answer. It's still in there. Looks like I just need to ask the right questions." There was a hitch in his step as he moved toward it, one hand cautiously extended. He shivered when he settled his hand upon the knob, but when he tried to turn the handle, it didn't budge.

"Is it stuck?" I asked.

"Locked, I think." He tried to thump his shoulder against it, but the physics of the mind-cottage were tricky, and even when he tried to kick it, the door was never quite in the same place as his foot.

"Here, let me." I shooed him aside.

Emerald went, but he couldn't resist a churlish jab. "I don't know what the point is, Crimson, it's *my* memory, and…"

The handle turned the instant I put pressure on it, and I opened the door with ease.

"You were saying?" I asked blithely.

"I was saying that you're a damned showoff." Emerald's throat bobbed as he stared into the darkness beyond. There was no hint of what we would find inside, but there was only one way to learn.

"Come along." I reached for his hand, and although he was a phantom in my mindscape, the gesture was enough to embolden him. Together, we approached the hole in the cottage wall and slipped into a memory that even its owner had forgotten.

"…A SECRET," *Reticent said. He was kneeling on the floor between his bed and the wall.*

Humble sat with her ankles crossed, utterly nonplussed by the whole situation. Steadfast sat in the middle, while Allure was curled up like a pill bug near Reticent's pillow, her knees clutched to her chest.

"You can't tell anyone," Reticent said. "Got it?"

"You know I won't, Ret," Humble said at once.

"Who would we tell, anyway?" Steadfast asked. "I'll keep it secret, too."

Reticent narrowed his eyes at Allure. "Al?"

"I'll keep it secret!" she squeaked. "If Steady won't tell, I won't."

The children were older than they'd been when Steadfast fought off the bullies who had taken Allure's bracelet, perhaps in their mid-teens. I thought Allure might be a bit younger than the others, and all the easy confidence she exuded as an adult was utterly lacking. She was almost as gangly as Blare.

"You don't have to do everything Steadfast does," Humble huffed. "Come on, Ret, you're scaring the baby."

"I'm not a baby," Allure grumbled.

"Then stop acting like one." Humble rolled her eyes extravagantly.

Reticent peeled back the board, taking the same delight in showing off the hidden treasure that Svelte had when showing me. I expected to see the same assortment of toys, but instead, there was only a metal box. It was the perfect size to fit between the floor joists. There were markings on the top, etched into the metal lid. It struck me as familiar, although I didn't think it was valuable. The metalwork was distinctive, but clearly not the work of a master craftsman.

Reticent flipped the lid open to reveal the same assortment of toys and trinkets I'd already observed, minus a few things.

"It's just trash," Humble said, wrinkling her button nose.

Reticent was unbothered by her disdain. He grinned up at the other children. "You have no imagination, Humble. You know all those faces in the ceiling of the prayer hall?"

Humble pretended to gag. "Unfortunately."

"They're creepy," Allure mumbled to herself. "They always feel like they're watching me."

"Well, they were all real people," Reticent said. He picked up one of the objects from the stash, the game piece I had noticed earlier. "And this is the same, except that these are mementos of the kids who stayed in this room before us. These were their most prized possessions. Here." He tossed the game piece to Steadfast. "What do you make of that?"

Steadfast caught the piece and held it; despite his young age, the little object was swallowed in his broad palm. He examined it with familiar intensity, holding it up to the light for closer study.

"Whoever this belonged to was lonely," he said.

Humble scoffed and crossed her arms. "You can't know that."

"Sure I can. If they cared about a game so much, why leave one of the pieces here? The rest of the set would be useless after that. Unless they didn't have the whole set to begin with, and they were holding on to this single piece because it had belonged to their family or something. In which case, my point stands." He tossed the item back to Reticent.

Humble rolled her eyes again. "Brilliant deduction, Steady. Someone who lived here was lonely. How did you come up with that?"

"Do another one," Allure said. Without waiting for Reticent to pick an object, she leaned over the edge of the bed and scooped the soap hedgepig out of the box. "What does this one tell you?"

Steadfast fought to keep his face straight. "That someone who used to live here liked hedgepigs more than they liked being clean."

Reticent and Allure laughed, and even Humble had to press her lips together to keep from smiling.

"See?" Reticent asked, holding up the box so that Allure could put it back without crushing its waxy spines. "Everything in here tells a story. We may not know the details, but we know that they were part of something. One of Harmony's old students told me about it right before they left to serve the Conjury... everyone who stays in this room leaves something special behind."

"I like this better than the faces in the prayer hall," Allure said. She lay on her belly with her arms crossed under her chin, kicking her feet up behind her. "It's nicer. It's like being part of something that Brother Modest doesn't know about and can't control."

Reticent nodded. "I agree. And I think we should each add something, since most of us will be leaving in a few months."

"Ugh." Allure hid her face in her arms. When she spoke again, her voice was so muffled as to be hardly distinguishable. "Why can't you stay? I don't want to be the oldest one here! What if I have to take classes all by myself?"

"You're too young to be a Castcadesman, Al." Steadfast patted her back. "I'm sure it won't be so bad without us. Look on the bright side. You won't have to put up with Humble anymore."

Humble rolled away and got up. "And I won't have to look at your ugly faces anymore. I'm going to Venta Bulgarum. I bet they won't allow jotunn in the city. It's civilized there."

Steadfast glowered at her back, but rather than respond to her, he turned to Reticent. "What do you want to hide?"

Reticent held up a small bag that looked like it had been hand-stitched out of a threadbare scrap of sheet. "What do you think?"

Allure stuck out her tongue. "More bones, Ret?"

Reticent shook his lank black hair out of his eyes. "What? It's my calling card."

"It's unsanitary," Allure insisted.

Humble poked around at her desk for a moment before striding back over to her previous spot. She was holding something between her palms, hiding it from sight.

"Are you going to contribute?" Steadfast asked, cocking his head. "I thought you were too civilized to associate with the likes of us."

"When I'm in Venta Belgarum, I will be. For now, I'm stuck with you." Humble stared down at the object and drew a deep breath before thrusting it at Reticent. "There. That's what I'll leave."

I had noticed the tiny canvas with its miniature but highly detailed portrait, but I hadn't looked closely. The subject was painted in profile: a lovely woman with pointed ears, cornflower blue eyes, and fine pale hair that the artist had highlighted with real gold flakes.

Reticent didn't take it. "Are you sure? That's your only picture of her."

"She didn't want me, so why should I hold on to her?" Humble waved the little painting at him. "She should stay here, like the rest of my past. I won't need reminders of her where I'm going."

Reluctantly, Reticent lifted his hand and accepted the painting. He tucked it in among the other little treasures, taking care not to knock the gold foil loose.

"You should leave your charm bracelet," Humble told Allure.

The younger girl gasped and clutched her wrist. "No!"

"Why hold on to the past?" Humble demanded.

"I won't... I'm not..." Allure's eyes darted frantically back and forth. "I'll leave Bab!" She launched herself out of the bed and scurried toward her own. The krub ragdoll I'd noticed earlier was lying beside her pillow, and she scooped it up. It was obvious from the way she carried it over to where Reticent knelt that she loved the toy, but when Reticent offered the box to her, she still placed the doll inside. It was by far the largest item in the box, and she took her time shifting the other objects aside to make room for Bab.

"There you go," Reticent said. He turned to Steadfast and held the box toward him. "We've each put in something. What about you?"

Steadfast considered for a moment before reaching into his pocket to *pull out the now-familiar green marble. "I might as well leave this," he said. "I'll get a better focus when I'm ready to officially train in Kinmore." The marble made a sharp* tink! *when it hit the bottom of the metal box.*

"Perfect." Reticent grinned down at the items. "Now no matter what, there will be something from each of us left in this room... something the Brotherhood couldn't take from us, something we loved for its own sake."

"You left bones," *Allure pointed out.*

"Of course I did," Reticent replied, "because, like Steady, I—"

WE WERE THROWN BACK into the mind-cottage so abruptly that it took a few seconds for me to realize what had happened.

Emerald looked as stunned as I felt. He placed one hand to his forehead and shook his head. "Bab," he said. "I forgot about *Bab*."

I blinked a few times. "Out of everything we just learned, you were focused on *Bab*?"

Emerald held up a hand. "Crimson, listen. When we were growing up, Allure adored that doll. She was fascinated with krubs. When she was feeling down, we'd play krub-on-the-hill."

I blinked again. Trying to make sense of memories that had been repressed was confusing enough, but I had no idea what he was getting at. "Can't say I know the game," I admitted.

"It's a test of strength," Emerald said. "We'd stand on a rock or hill or even the edge of the fountain and try to knock the other one off. Whoever remained standing at the end of the game won."

"Like Burp and Squelch did in the Cronemire," I said. "Although I assume you didn't drag one another off to lay eggs in the swamp afterward."

"We did not," Emerald agreed. "But we would joke about it. She thought it was hilarious. She was smaller, so I let her win a lot, and she would joke about how it was my turn to be the girl."

"And you're telling me about this now because...?"

"Because I forgot!" Emerald tapped one knuckle to his temple, as if he hoped to dislodge the memories that were stuck there. "When Burp lost the fight, I thought for sure that he was going to be killed. Even though we played that game hundreds of times!"

He began to pace the length of the room. "Why would I forget that?"

"We've already established that someone messed with your memories," I pointed out.

"Yes, but why make me forget *that,* specifically?" Emerald growled. "Whoever walled off my memory wanted to keep me from getting too close to something. In the process, they also took memories *related* to whatever I was supposed to forget. I forgot Allure until I saw her. I forgot about Reticent and Humble until I started picking at the threads. As far as I know, I buried all of this for *years*. Whoever did this to me made me forget all of them, and anything related to them. The moment I saw Bab, I remembered all the things Allure used to tell me... how her mother was a swamper elf, how she'd known krubs when she was little and she was just *fascinated* with them."

I cleared my throat. "I think you might be getting off topic, Em."

"But what if I'm not?" The length of Emerald's stride increased along with his agitation. It struck me that when I'd paced in his room earlier, it was *his* restlessness I'd been channeling. "We need to note everything I forget. *You* need to note it, because I can't keep track of what's slipping away from me. The faster and more completely I forget what we've discussed, the bigger the clue that subject is going to be."

I crossed my arms. "Like the shadow-beast."

Emerald stopped in his tracks. "Like the what?"

I shook my head. "Forget it. I mean, you will, which is the point. So, theoretically, whatever memory this person tried to bury is something that happened when you were younger."

"Yes." Emerald squeezed his eyes shut. "It would have had to be. And we don't know if this is even related to what we're here to investigate..."

"I think we can safely say that it is," I told him. "But I want to ask you to remember one more thing. That box, the one that you put your marble in. Have you seen it since then?"

Emerald twisted his face up in an attempt to remember, but after a few minutes of pondering, no door appeared. "I don't think so," he said. "Either I haven't, or I've forgotten completely. Have you?"

"I have," I replied. "And I can tell you where, but I have a feeling you won't remember this conversation long."

Emerald chuckled bitterly. "I hate this. I truly hate this. I always thought that my intellect was the one thing no one else could take from me, but here we are." He lifted his eyes to my face, and his self-deprecating smile turned gentle. "I'm lucky to have you around to keep track of me, aren't I? I couldn't do this without you."

"You really are." I preened, but for all my teasing, his words moved me. Even when I had been helpful, Emerald was slow to offer praise, and slower still to admit that my contributions were anything more than a convenience. His words left me validated and delighted. "So, shall I tell you where I've seen the box before?"

Emerald's brow wrinkled, and even before he spoke, I knew he was going to ask, "What box?"

"The one Reticent hid in the floorboards," I said. "The one where you put your marble. All the contents of that box are still there, but the box itself has been repurposed."

"Into what?" he asked.

That, to be sure, was the question that had occupied my mind ever since I realized where I'd seen it before. "I don't know. But I know who has it. It's the same one Allure carried to the tent the night she took Brigane's power."

CHAPTER

SEVENTEEN

I was not the least bit surprised that Emerald could not remember our conversation about the box the next morning, but I was also less annoyed than I had been. It was now patently obvious to me that the creature I had seen was intertwined with both Emerald's faulty memory and the claim that Guise walked among his mortal followers. All that remained was to figure out how they fit together.

Over breakfast, I pondered my list of suspects. Whoever had altered Emerald's memories had done so when he still lived here. That presented three of the most obvious possible culprits: Sister Allure, the recently returned Sister Humble, and the absentee Brother Reticent. Emerald still could not recall what branch of the *Aidea* they each used.

There were other possibilities I could not rule out, most notably Harmony and Modest.

[Do either of them have Aidea?] I asked as I stabbed my fake spoon into my fake porridge.

[Hardly. Those with Aidea would never be left in charge. Modest is a small-minded, self-righteous bastard, and Harmony leads the classes with the 'contaminated' students because he's big

enough to withstand the effects of magic gone wrong.] Emerald flicked his eyes toward Brother Lightfoot. *[Most of the other folks I recognize were my peers. They weren't in the classes with us because they didn't have the Aidea either.]*

[They might have slipped through,] I pointed out. *[Or been late bloomers?]*

[It can happen, but they were still under watch every hour of the day for years. All it would take was one slip-up, and they'd be reassigned to a different class.]

I supposed that was true for Lightweavers and Augurs, but who would know if a student accidentally used *Aidea* on someone, when that brand of magic involved tampering with someone's memory? Emerald had already admitted that he'd be at loose ends with this case if not for me, and most people weren't lucky enough to have a companion that could read their mind. For that reason, I was reluctant to dismiss Harmony and Modest, either.

I was still resolved to talk to Humble on my own, but I thought Emerald stood the best chance of talking to Allure, and I told him so as our group made its way out of the dining hall. *[We should try to track her down tonight. I'll tag along as an insect again so that I can prompt you to ask anything that would be helpful, and remember any answers you forget...]*

"Vagabond?" Harmony said, sweeping up beside me. "I'd like to talk to you in my office. Alone."

"Oh." I blinked up at him. "Now?"

"Brother Steadfast can see to the other children for a bit," Harmony told me. "We have not gotten acquainted properly, and you've had some time to settle in. Now that you have a sense of what life is like here, we should talk. Come along."

He ushered me away. As I went, I looked back over my shoulder. The other children didn't seem worried, but Emerald was watching me.

[Be careful, Crim,] he warned. *[We have no way of knowing if whoever mucked about in my head got to him, too, but he* did *know about my abilities once.]*

Of course he did. Why had it not occurred to me that the very people on my list of suspects were also the most likely to work out what *I* was? Although, to be quite frank, I was far more worried about the shadow-beast than any threat posed by Emerald's mentor.

Unless he's the one who controls the shadow-beast, I mused. The creature was made of the *Aidea*, I was quite sure of that. I'd felt it resonating through me on the night when it slunk toward my bed. Was it like most *Aidea*, doing the work of some remote master? Or was it like me?

I feared the latter, and at the same time felt a little thrill of excitement to think that I was not as much of an aberration as Emerald had made it sound.

There were no strange shadows or unexplained horrors lying in wait within Harmony's office, however. The moment he opened the door, I gasped and rushed forward, forgetting myself in my delight at the sight before me.

I had always been drawn to clutter and worldly goods, perhaps because they were so mysterious to me. I found the notion of texture and weight, of making something and engaging with it, both marvelous and impossible. Harmony evidently felt the same way, because unlike Modest's bare and soulless office, Harmony's walls were lined with shelves that groaned under the weight of his possessions.

Mugs and statues and trinkets of every kind, from the expertly made to the childish, stood side by side. Doll's dishes stood alongside a metal owl, next to a filigreed egg. A wooden carving of a dragon was sandwiched between a horse made of glass and a felted weirling cub.

It was difficult not to fall a little bit in love with the collection. I had felt the same when standing in Marsha's rooms back in Upper Bound. This assortment of objects wasn't, in and of itself, valuable. Brother Harmony had no great wealth to speak of, and he hadn't amassed these items to show them off. If they'd been worth something, they would have told me a lot less about the man. As it was, there was something about standing in front of an assortment of worthless but nevertheless cherished items that made me feel as though Brother Harmony's head had been turned inside out and put on display for any occupant of the room to see.

Among the items, I spotted a gridgen carved from soap, presumably made by the same hand that had molded the hedgepig in the children's treasure trove. I stood on my toes and squinted up at it, wondering about its provenance.

"One of my old students made that," Harmony said as he circled his desk. "In fact, almost everything on that wall has come from former classes. I haven't left the compound in years, but it's comforting to know that my students remember me and my teachings." He folded his hands before him on the desk and smiled at the display, then at me. "They have touched my life, just as I have touched theirs. And I think people your age find it comforting to know that their future does not begin and end within these walls."

"Do you know who all of them are from?" I asked.

"I do."

His enthusiasm unsettled me. Not because there was anything inherently sinister about the items themselves—gazing upon them, I certainly did not experience the same sense of foreboding that accompanied the presence of the shadow-beast. It did not give off any hint of magic. Instead, it gave me a sense of Brother Harmony's reach. All these students had come and gone. They had listened to his words, internalized his teachings, and no doubt many of them had come to the same conclusions that Emerald had.

I smothered my delight like a lantern flame and slunk over the chair that stood waiting for me. As usual, climbing into a chair that I couldn't touch or move was a rather awkward accomplishment, but I had no other choice and so made the best of it.

"Tell me, Vagabond, how are you finding your stay in the Brotherhood?" Harmony asked.

"It's... better than it was for me before I came here." I wriggled a little on the seat of the chair. "Sorry, I'm a little nervous right now. When I get anxious, I can't control my *Aidea*." I reached for the arm of the chair and let my hand pass through it, just as I had done when I first arrived. I was glad to have thought of a cover story that would explain some of my oddities—even if he *did* suspect me of being a lightweaving, he would have trouble disproving my lie.

"There's no need to be anxious," Harmony assured me. "Besides, you've only had a few days to adjust. You know, Sister Allure could help you with that little problem of yours. More than any of our other students, you have the potential to live an ordinary life."

"Because of my appearance?" I asked sharply.

I had expected him to obfuscate, or to claim that he had meant something more innocuous, but to my surprise, Harmony nodded. "I'm glad to see that you're already forming bonds, and that you're feeling protective of your friends. I assure you, I'm not trying to insult them. I'm trying to protect them." He gestured to himself. "I know how hard it can be to live forever on the outside."

I balled my hands into fists in my lap and stared at the top of his desk so that I wouldn't have to meet his eyes. I really should have been thinking of clever questions to ask, but I hadn't had time to prepare. All I could think about were the myriad ways he'd hurt my friend. My *friends.* Even among my young peers, I was the youngest of them all, and yet I was the one who saw through all the lies and bluster of the Brotherhood.

"What's on your mind, Vagabond?" Harmony asked kindly.

Without thinking through the ramifications of my next words, I told him, "I was wondering why anyone would want to be ordinary."

Harmony cocked his head, and his crooked smile remained fixed in place. "That is what Guise prizes above all else."

I resisted the urge to roll my eyes. "I know. And I've heard what you've said about the *Aidea*, and all that. But if Guise wants people to be ordinary and boring, and that you never will be, why follow him at all? Why serve a god who you believe despises you?"

Harmony had no doubt spent years smiling through the vicious verbal jabs offered by Lightfoot and Modest and others like them. The practice had served him well. His other little tells, however, revealed his mounting tension. His hands curled inward until his nails bit into his palm and his knuckles paled.

"You are a child," he said, as if my youth was tantamount to naivete. "But I can assure you, Vagabond, that I would be no more beloved in any other order, or any other line of work besides. To be ordinary is a *privilege,* Vagabond, one that we will not all experience in this lifetime."

I twined my fingers together and clenched them tight. No wonder he spent so much time teaching the children here to hate themselves. Harmony hated himself more than anyone else.

No wonder, either, that Emerald felt the same.

He did not realize, of course, that I would never be normal either, not unless we found some magic spell that would allow me to gain a body. That made my life difficult, as did having to hide my true nature from the Conjury representatives we so frequently encountered. It didn't make me want to be *more* like them. If the Brotherhood of Guise was willing to open its doors to people who had trouble finding community outside its walls, why wouldn't it choose to truly welcome them?

Harmony could tell that I was displeased with his answer, but it didn't affect his mood. "I know that this isn't what you want to hear, Vagabond. But there's no use telling people lies to make them feel better. It would only make it harder for them to transition back to the wider world once their tenure here is over."

"Because they'll be prepared for everyone to hate them?" I asked bitterly.

"Because they'll understand why others look down on them," Harmony corrected. "And they'll know that Guise loves them even when they fail to conform, so long as they keep trying."

Well, that's a load of bollocks, I thought. I had yet to meet one person here who acted out of love in Guise's name, rather than in spite of him.

"It will become clearer to you when you're older," Harmony promised. "I have seen from your questions in class that your life has been very different from the experiences of the other children. The others have felt alone all their lives, but you... I think someone has loved you in spite of yourself, Vagabond. Someone has made you feel special."

I blinked at him. He sounded almost jealous.

"Unfortunately, that can sometimes make it harder to accept Guise's message," he went on. "Don't be afraid to ask questions."

I sensed that our conversation was coming to a close, and while I had learned a great deal about Brother Harmony, none of my questions regarding his role in our current investigation had been answered. But what could I possibly ask that wouldn't give away the nature of my questioning?

Ask what a child would ask, I told myself.

"There is one thing," I blurted. "I've been having dreams. Bad dreams. I never used to, but... there's a crack in the ceiling above my bed."

"I've noticed," Harmony admitted. "Is it leaking?"

I shook my head. "It's just that sometimes, I think I see shadows."

I had tipped my face toward the floor as if in fear, but my eyes were lifted. Between my lashes, I caught the tic in Harmony's cheek and the twitch of his eye. His voice, however, gave nothing away.

"That is not uncommon," he said. "Sleeping in a new place, after an upheaval such as you've experienced, can confuse the senses. I assure you, there is nothing to fear. You are safe here. We have taken every precaution to ensure that those who seek refuge with us are protected from harm."

He knows, I thought, nearly bursting out of the chair in my excitement. *He knows about the shadow-beast. And, more importantly, he remembers!* I wished I could share this discovery with Emerald, although it would have meant nothing to him. He could not recall any mention of the shadow from one moment to the next, but Harmony could. Whoever had made Emerald forget about the shadow hadn't bothered to mess with Harmony's memory.

Unless...

My gaze slid to the bookshelf groaning with mementos of years gone by. *Unless Harmony is the one responsible for tampering with people's memories.*

I was tempted to ask a question about Reticent, but I stopped myself before I did so. If Harmony could remember things that Emerald could not, then reminding him about the past could be dangerous for me. He was the most likely to put everything together, and if he did, our investigation would be doomed.

"I will see about getting someone to plaster over the hole," Harmony said. He got to his feet and motioned toward the door. "In the meantime, try not to be afraid."

I had not anticipated his next words, but I should have, and I nearly rolled my eyes when he uttered them.

"After all, a blameless mind has nothing to fear."

I was not sure when Emerald had found time to communicate with Sister Allure, but that evening, when the children were put to bed, he called me to his side. I went instantly, taking the opportunity to rearrange myself into Simon, while simultaneously donning the most ruffly, dramatic, and out-of-fashion costume I could imagine. Emerald did a double take when I appeared.

"What's gotten into you?" he asked.

The only mirror in the room was an ancient one, the silver backing of which was beginning to tarnish. Even in its dull face, I was something to behold. I did not often favor makeup, but this time, I had powdered my face, swept my hair into an elaborate ringletted updo, and added a starched collar that stood out well past my shoulders.

"I like it," I said stubbornly.

Emerald studied me, and a deepening expression of concern twisted his features. "You do?"

"Yes." I lifted my chin. "All this talk of conforming and being ordinary is making me split at the seams. I hate it here, Emerald."

He scratched the back of his neck. "I do, too," he said.

That was all. No further mockery of my dubious fashion choices. No commentary on my presentation. He simply agreed and then turned away.

I found myself musing over the mirror. My purposes, as described by my friend, revolved around seeing and being seen. To that end, I had spent my admittedly brief life trying to control what people saw when they looked at me. On the days when I saw Simon, I tended to favor more masculine clothing and carry myself accordingly. When I was Simone, I adopted a softer touch. I had, by and large, let the needs of the case dictate my appearance and comportment.

But this case required something different from me, and it rankled. At times, I liked being Vagabond, of being neither one thing nor the other. Left to my own devices, however, I would prefer to do it *loudly*. Like this. I bent toward the mirror, tracing the sharp line of my cheekbones, admiring the way painted-on brows and green powder altered the shape of my eyes.

I'd been wrong, I realized. I had believed that I could only assume two human forms: Simon, or Simone, as needed. In truth, I was only ever *one* person, but there were so many ways to *be* that person that I might experiment endlessly and never discover all the permutations of Crimson that existed.

A physical body would be much more limiting, I realized.

I had wanted to be normal, to experience the world in the same way everyone else did, through taste and touch and smell. But Harmony's insistence on uniformity left me reeling back the other way. I might not be able to touch and taste, but I could do things other people couldn't do.

And according to Emerald, I was the only one on the continent who could do them.

"Are you quite finished admiring yourself?" Emerald demanded, with all the petulance of a child who has been ignored too long.

I straightened up and placed my hands on my hips. "Never. But for the moment, I assume we're supposed to be talking to Allure?"

"Mm," Emerald agreed. "And I don't think she'll know what to make of you if you pop in looking like that."

"Her loss," I said, and rearranged myself. My initial plan had been to return to my now-familiar state as a beetle, but when I tried, once again I was not quite what I'd expected. A plump, hairy body lay beneath me, and a lovely pair of red-and-gold dappled wings spread out to either side.

"A moth?" Emerald asked from above, lifting one skeptical eyebrow.

I twiddled my feathery antennae at him. *[It makes more sense, doesn't it, since it's well after dark?]* Besides, I'd mentally compared Allure's pull to that of a moon more than once.

"You're not small enough to go unnoticed," he pointed out.

[So I'll cling to the windowsill. Or hide among the books.] Perhaps I was being obstinate, but I didn't want to change myself into a more convenient shape just because he wanted me to.

"Suit yourself," Emerald said, and opened the door of his room.

The silent halls of the Brotherhood left me uneasy. For the second night in a row, my friends had left the lamps burning while they slept to keep the shadow-beast at bay, but who was to say that it wasn't simply lurking elsewhere, lying in wait for us?

For me?

I didn't notice anything out of the ordinary as we slipped through the halls, but the library door was open when we approached. Allure was bent over the desk in the far corner, copying the book she'd been working on the day we first encountered her, although she was several pages further along.

"I wasn't sure you'd come," she said, without looking up from her work. "How unlike you, Steady, to suggest a midnight tryst in the library."

Emerald, who was halfway through closing the door behind him, choked on a mouthful of nothing at her words. I fluttered up to the ceiling and spread my wings for balance so that I could get a moth's-eye view of the room below.

Allure laughed and dropped her pen into the inkwell. "I'm only joking, Steadfast." She lifted a pinch of sand from a little box at the corner of her desk and scattered it across the still-wet pages to help the ink dry. "I was never your type."

Emerald stayed by the door, his back pressed to it, watching Allure with the wary eyes of an animal that had wandered into a trap. "Was I... yours?"

Allure turned to him at last. She folded her hands in her lap and smiled, though there was a touch of sadness in it. "I love Guise first and best, Steady. There's no point in dwelling on something that will never matter. Although..." She swallowed and folded her hands in her lap.

I felt Emerald's worry as if it were my own. "Did something happen?" he asked. "Before I left?" It ate at him, to know that he'd forgotten important things.

Allure sucked in a breath and sat up again. She was wearing the same smile she'd offered Modest in the prayer hall, one that was entirely for show. "I've put away much of what we experienced back then. Why dwell in the past? You can't possibly have come here to discuss this."

Emerald bit his lip and lifted his eyes toward the ceiling, where I waited. "I did want to ask how you're doing," he said. I wondered what words he would have chosen to use with her, had I not been there. It was foreign to him, speaking to someone that he knew so well, and yet hardly remembered. Someone he loved, and yet could not remember loving. "That meeting the other day, with Modest..."

Allure laughed so hard that she rocked on her stool. "He is just the same as ever, isn't he? I know that he's well respected among the order, but some people never learn the lesson of their names, do they? Not like us."

"Or Humble," Emerald added, no doubt recalling how she'd acted in his memories.

Allure cocked her head. "Have you spoken to her yet? I think she might be avoiding me, which is a shame. I would have thought we'd put that all behind us."

Emerald dropped onto the stool beside her. "Put *what* behind us?"

"All her pettiness and jealousy, of course. Now that she's lived a few years serving the Conjury in Venta Bulgarum, and chosen to come back, you'd think she'd have moved on." Allure chuckled to herself. "Give her time."

Emerald stared at her in confusion for a long moment. "Humble was jealous?" he echoed. "Of *us*?"

"Of course. Between the two of us, we had everything she want-ed." Allure pulled down her sleeve to reveal the bangle at her wrist. "I had my mother's love. You had more talent than the rest of us combined. And we…" She reached for Emerald's hand. "We were closer than she was with anyone. I expect all that time in Venta Bulgarum taught her that friendship can't be bought. Why else would she come back?"

Emerald watched her hand where it lay over his, puzzling through a complex array of emotions that I could not quite parse. Perhaps they were mystifying even to him. "Maybe she heard what you can do and wanted to see it for herself."

Allure laughed again. I didn't know what to think of her, but even with my healthy levels of distrust, she had the sort of unguarded, unmusical laugh that would have made me smile instantly—if I'd had lips at that moment, rather than an inexpressive proboscis.

"No, Steady, that's *you*." She patted his hand once, then pulled it away. I felt the pang of his disappointment. He might not love her the same way he loved Tincrown, but he was starved for touch, especially from people who cared about him.

Allure got to her feet and smoothed her robes down. "I suppose you want to see it."

"See… what?" Emerald squinted up at her. She was slighter than he was, but she was still one of the tallest women I'd ever met, almost as tall as Sister Aster.

"The source of my power," Allure intoned in a deep, affected voice, before bursting into giggles. She pressed a hand to her mouth until her laughter subsided. "I'm sorry, I know I shouldn't joke about it, but it sometimes strikes me just how improbable the whole thing is. Why, out of all people, would he choose *me*?"

[She's talking about the box!] I thought.

Emerald's eyes narrowed further still. *[The what?]*

[The… Oh, never mind, just ask her.]

He didn't have to ask anything, however. Allure was already bending down to retrieve something from beneath her writing desk.

"I knew you'd want to see it," she said. "You were always looking for answers, and I can't imagine that's changed. So here it is." She set the box down on Emerald's desk with a flourish.

Emerald ran his fingers over the surface, tracing the metal inlay. "I've seen this before," he said.

"At the ceremony," Allure said.

[And under the floorboards in your room,] I added.

Emerald froze. "The toybox," he said aloud.

Allure frowned at him. "What?"

"This was in our room growing up," he said. "Reticent showed it to us."

Allure made a small noise and shook her head. "What are you talking about?"

"I thought..." Emerald trailed off, knocking one knuckle against the box. "I... never mind. I thought I'd seen it before."

Allure shook her head, and I recognized the gesture as one that Emerald had made every time I asked about something to do with a memory he'd misplaced.

Someone made her forget, too, I thought. Unless she was lying. But why lie to Emerald, if she knew that he'd forget anyway?

But if she *wasn't* lying, then what was she supposed to forget?

The memory that eluded Emerald must have taken something from both of them, but that was a confusing revelation. I was increasingly certain that the case of the shadow-beast was entwined with the investigation Finch had sent us on, and yet, once again, I couldn't work out *how.*

Emerald's thoughts had followed another track entirely. "What's inside?" he asked.

Allure nodded to the latch. "See for yourself."

Emerald's thumb found the latch, but he paused before flicking it open. "It won't do anything to me, will it?"

"Not by accident," Allure assured him. "What I do in the tent requires a great deal of concentration."

Emerald nodded and flipped the lid open. "Dust?" he asked. He trailed his fingers through the powdery substance, which clung to his fingers even after he tried to blow it away.

"Ash," Allure said. "Nothing more than ash."

Emerald rubbed his fingers together, and the dust he knocked free floated back into the box. "Huh. Why would Guise speak to you through *dust?*"

Allure fell back a pace. "You're mocking me."

"I'm not." Emerald closed the lid of the box. "I'm truly confused."

"You haven't kept up with your scripture." Allure retrieved the box and set it aside, then she flipped open her copy of Guise's holy text. "He is *always* talking about ashes. *He who stands closest to the fire...* I know you're familiar with that one. And here." She placed her finger on the page, shoving the book beneath Emerald's nose. "*The tallest tree in the forest is the first to be struck down by lightning, and its ashes shall nourish the saplings.*" She flipped a few pages back to find another verse. "*That which burns brightest shall be reduced to the finest ash...*" Her voice pitched upward as she spoke, and her movements became more frantic. "It is *written*, Steadfast, it is in Guise's holy book. Guise uses fire to cleanse that which displeases him—"

"Al." Emerald laid his hand on her forearm, and she stilled. "I'm sorry. I haven't read scripture in a long time. I'd forgotten the significance."

Allure, who had shown so much poise in her adult years, had been reduced to shambles. She was trembling uncontrollably, and her eyes welled with unshed tears. She swallowed hard and pulled away, swiping at her eyes.

"I'm sorry," she mumbled. "It's just that every time I touch the reliquary, he speaks to me. Sometimes it's a voice, sometimes it's just flashes of... *pictures.*" She returned her book to its place and hugged herself, as Svelte had hugged herself. "It's terrifying, Steady. I know I'm blessed to have been chosen, but it's so much, and when I ask why me, he shows me... terrible things, sometimes. *Terrible* things. Brother Harmony assures me that Guise loves us, but the things he shows me can be—" She choked off in a sob and crumpled inward.

"Oh, Al." Emerald didn't seem to know what to do with his arms, but when her sobbing continued unabated, he pulled her to him and rubbed one huge hand in circles across her back. "I'm sorry. I didn't understand what it meant to you. I still don't."

The instant he embraced her, Allure threw her arms around his neck and clung tight.

They stayed like that for a long time, and my discomfort grew with each passing moment. I didn't like to think that I was watching a near-stranger at her most vulnerable without her knowledge, and I decided that I ought to leave. I shuffled a few paces across the ceiling, unsure what else to do with myself.

Allure chose that moment to pull away from Emerald, and when she did, my movement must have caught her eye.

"Oh!" she cried, pointing upward. "Look at that! I've never seen one like it before."

Emerald glanced upward, too, and pulled a face at me. "I can't imagine how we missed it. It's the least subtle moth I've ever encountered."

Allure got to her feet and went to the casement, throwing open the window into the courtyard. "I hope it can figure out how to leave," she said. "You know, they batter themselves to death against the glass if you trap them in." She kept her back to Emerald, but it was obvious that she was rubbing her eyes and breathing deeply of the night air. "I'm sorry, Steady. Sometimes I get so *emotional*. It's the stress."

"No wonder, if the things Guise shows you are all that bad," Emerald observed.

"It's all right." Allure sighed up at the moons. "I manage most days. I think I'm just tired."

"I'll let you get some rest, then." Emerald got to his feet.

He wanted to say something, but he couldn't decide what. As the silence stretched thin, I unfurled my wings and dropped from the ceiling, heading directly for the window. Allure gasped in delight as I skimmed just over her head and fluttered out into the darkness, granting them a moment of solitude before they parted ways.

The velvety darkness embraced me, and I let myself rise high above the roof of the Brotherhood, until the whole compound was nothing more than glittering lights beneath me. I was in no rush to return to my bed and spend the night lying still and thinking too many thoughts. I needed a moment to myself, to exist without having to worry about anyone else's wants, fears, memories, or desires.

When the pull of my tether to Emerald tugged at my chest, I circled back, a tiny kite on the night breeze. I wished that I could find a private place where I could just be myself without having to play a part, if only for a few hours, but I didn't want to risk discovery. I would have to content myself with this little flight of fancy, so to speak.

I was on my way back to the dormitory when I spotted a figure prowling across the rooftop of the library. I circled lower to get a better view of the interloper.

When I was only a few feet above it, a long and skeletal head whipped around at an unnatural angle to fix me with its stare. The shadow-beast had changed slightly since the last time I saw it, but there was no mistaking its hunched back, its taloned claws, or the jut of its emaciated body beneath its darkened shroud.

I was not going to run this time. I dropped to the roof, rearranging myself back into Simon—vibrant clothes, powdered face, and all. My heeled shoes made no sound when they hit the shingles. I wondered what anyone would have thought to see us there, a starveling nightmare and a deliberately flamboyant dream, perched on the roof of this dour and venerable old building beneath three sister-moons.

"What are you doing here?" I hissed.

The shadow-beast moved sideways across the shingles, stalking on all fours. It bared its teeth, twisting its long neck back and forth as it rocked from side to side. When it opened its mouth, the only sound that emitted from it was a rumbling *kek-kek-kek-kek*. I shuffled back, keeping some distance between us, unconsciously mirroring its posture and movements so that even when it approached me, the same amount of distance remained between us.

"Stop that," I snapped. "I only want to talk to you."

The chattering sound from low in its throat redoubled, and recoiled. "That's awful," I said, raising my voice a little to be heard over its din.

As it walked toward me, it drove me up toward the roofline. I backed away, keeping pace with it.

For all I knew, my fear was irrational, but the shadow-beast inspired the same terror in me that it had the night it came for Blare. It snapped at me, lunging forward, letting out a little rumble each time I darted back.

"What do you want with me?" I demanded. "What did you want with Blare? What *are* you?"

It lunged once more, and this time, with nowhere to retreat, I tried to rearrange myself again. In an instant, I was the brightly-colored moth once more.

It only took a fraction of a second for me to change, but the beast was fast. It flung itself up the roof toward me, mouth open and claws extended. Its midnight talons tore through the thin tissue of my wings as I fluttered upward, and the pain that followed was tremendous.

I had never known real pain before. Even in the mind-cottage, when I'd battered myself against the walls in a vain attempt to break free, it hadn't *burned.* If I'd had a mouth, I would have screamed in agony.

It was a good thing that I didn't need my wings to move. The idea of flying helped, but even in human form, I wasn't subject to the laws of gravity. I slipped through the shadow-beast's claws and plunged through the roof of the compound, careening between rooms until I found my bed at last.

I landed beside my bed in a heap, Vagabond once more, shaking with terror. I could not bear to look at my arm; I was certain that the injury to my wing would translate into real damage to my person. And what would that mean for me? If the shadow-beast could really hurt me, who would I tell? Who would believe me?

Who would protect me?

I rolled over at last and lifted my arm. To my horror, three long and jagged gashes ran from my scrawny bicep all the way down past my elbow and across my forearm. Scarlet blood welled in the wounds. When I touched it, I couldn't feel anything, but my fingers came away red.

"How?" I whispered.

I tried to will the cut away, and after a few tries, the skin closed up. It took another effort to make the blood disappear from my fingers and robes.

When I was fully repaired, I tilted my head back toward the mattress, gazing up at the crack. Something glinted behind it: an eye that squeezed shut and vanished when it saw the lamps burning in our room.

"What are you?" I asked again, but it was gone.

It took a long time for me to gather the will to crawl back onto the bed. I was more frightened than I'd been before, but I was angry, too. I didn't like being hunted and hounded in the places I was supposed to feel safe.

The last of the moons was setting when I lurched upright in bed, finally fitting together two things that had eluded me.

I was in Reticent's old bed. Quell lay in Emerald's. The one that had been Humble's now belonged to Svelte.

And the bed where Blare lay—the one where he'd been sleeping the night that the shadow-beast stood over him in the throes of his attack—had once belonged to none other than Sister Allure.

I had followed my master to oversee his conversation with an old friend. Who was to say that the shadow-beast hadn't done the same?

CHAPTER

EIGHTEEN

The morning following my encounter with the shadow-beast, I refused to return to the room after breakfast.

"I think we should go outside," I told the other children. "To the courtyard. It's a nice day."

The three of them exchanged a flurry of nervous glances over the remains of their porridge. "Here's the thing," Quell said at last. "People here don't really like us..."

They like to mess with us, though, Blare added.

Svelte, however, glanced longingly toward the door. "It might be nice to spend some time outside..."

"We'll go outside," I decided. "If you two want to stay in, we can split up."

Quell lifted his wooly chin. "No. If you're going, we're going, right, Blare?"

Blare did not appear entirely convinced, but he nodded.

Nobody looks out for us but us, Reticent had said. Apparently, some things had always held true for the residents of the Brotherhood, even back when their predecessors had moved in.

I had yet to visit the courtyard in the company of my peers, and as we exited the building, I led the charge. I wanted to see the roof

186

where the shadow-beast and I had fought in the daylight. I wasn't sure what I hoped to find, but if nothing else, I refused to be bullied into cowering in our room, under that hateful crack in the plaster.

Unfortunately, the pitch of the roof made it difficult to see the shingles over the library, and I could only just make out the highest ridge where the shadow-beast had attacked me. From our vantage point in the yard, I could make out Allure's figure, bent over her usual table just beyond the library window, and little else.

She'd closed the window after I left last night. Had she known what I was when she ushered me outside, into the presence of the beast?

Linkage isn't proof, I reminded myself. I still hadn't found a chance to talk to Humble, but one of these days, I was going to find a way. Perhaps she could help me figure out how the missing memories and the shadow and the Unifier fit together.

"Vagabond?" Quell hissed. "That girl is looking at you, and she seems mad."

I had forgotten the presence of my small companions until he spoke, and I turned to see where he was pointing. Sure enough, a girl I barely recognized was glaring at me from across the courtyard. The moment our eyes met, she said something to her friends and began to talk toward us.

She strode right up to me, crossed her arms, and glared. "You're the one who stared at me in the prayer hall." Three of her friends gathered behind her. They were clearly there as backup in case things came to blows.

I studied the girl. There was a gap in her front lip that revealed her teeth and gums, rising all the way into her left nostril. She was older than us, perhaps sixteen or seventeen years of age. She was the one I'd waved to just before Modest delivered his little sermon about the lost lambkin.

"I saw you," I agreed.

"Well, take a good long look." The girl bent toward me, curling her split lip in disgust. "Never seen anyone like me, have you? Or like *them*, either." She jerked her thumb toward her assembled friends. One of the other girls had her hair shorn to the scalp and a puckered scar that started at her temple, sunk into the hollow of her right eye, and disappeared into the collar of her tunic. The middle girl had one arm that ended just below the elbow and stood at a pronounced angle. The final member of their little troop relied on the assistance of a cane, and her lower jaw did not align with the rest of her face.

"No," I said, although that was not quite true. At the Convent of the Crone, Lindsee had required the use of a mobile chair and two *Aidea*-operated wooden limbs to get around, and she'd lost an eye and most of one horn. Thanks to being nearly poisoned in the miasma of the Black Hollow, our friend Amaya had lost mobility in half of her face, and had some trouble moving the limbs on that side of her body.

And of course, there was Kristine, who had been born with invisible skin. Compared to that, none of these girls were particularly startling to behold.

The girl who had been speaking to me scoffed and crossed her arms. "What's your name, new... kid?"

"Vagabond," I told her.

At my side, Quell shuffled his hooves against the grass. "Let's go inside..." he whispered in a voice so small I could scarcely believe it was his.

"I'm Visage," the older girl said. She ran her tongue between the gap in her upper lip, driving the cruelty of the assigned name home. The brothers named children after what they considered to be their worst traits. Even *names* were a mockery here. With each passing day, I despised this place more.

"You think you're lucky, just because you don't look like us, huh? Well, I've got news for you, Vagabond." She took a step closer, lowering her head until her face was only inches from mine. "Bad things happen to people with *Aidea*. They might be special outside these walls, but Guise doesn't like them. He punishes people who have magic."

"Does he?" I asked.

"Yeah." Visage grinned, delighting in the rumors. "Like that kid who got burned up. He tried to do an evil spell, and got set on *fire*.

They say that the only thing left of him was ashes and an outline on the wall from where he burned alive."

"That's horrible," I said.

Visage blinked at me. "Well, yeah. That's the point."

"It's just a story," Quell muttered.

"It sounds like a Guise story, all right," I said. "I hear he's got a thing for ashes."

Visage glowered at me. "Keep doing your horrible little spells," she snapped. "He'll burn you up, too."

I was experiencing my own fair share of righteous anger, but I couldn't make sense of why she was so upset with *me*. As far as I was concerned, we were on the same side.

"Why would you want that?" I asked. "I think we're more alike than unalike, at least in the eyes of..." I flapped my hand toward the building. "*Them.*"

Visage sneered. "I've already caught you staring at me like I'm some kind of mistake." Her eyes swept over me, and she shook her head. "I know what people like you see when they look at us. They either decide to be cruel because they're scared of us, or they pity us."

"I don't!" I protested.

Visage rolled her eyes. "Come on. One look at you says every-thing. You're the kind of person who thinks being pretty is a person-ality trait. You know what people do here? Because I can tell you, new kid." She extended one finger and swiveled it around the court-yard. "They scope everyone out, and they see who looks weak. They see whose necks they can step in to get just a little bit higher. All this talk about being average goes right to their heads, because they know that all they have to do to succeed in life is grow up to be the most unremarkable version of themselves they can possibly be. The most inoffensive. They compete to see which of them will be the most riddled with mediocrity, and guess what?" Her finger stopped, pointing directly between my eyes. "They'll always be more unre-markable than you and me. And maybe that would have made us equals at one time, but that's changed. Now you can waltz into that tent with Sister Allure any night you want and become perfectly, palatably, passively *mediocre*. And we can't." She backed up a step and dropped her hand. "So we don't need to be friends, because I don't need some runty future Castcadesman keeping me around just so that they can step on *my* neck when it's convenient."

She and her friends turned away and retreated to the far side of the yard with their fellows. I stared after them, lost for words.

"She's right, you know," Svelte said. My friend tugged on the sleeve of her shapeless tunic. "We could be normal, if we wanted to be."

You could, Blare signed.

Svelte winced. "I'm sorry, B. I wasn't thinking. You're one of us, you know?"

I'm both, Blare signed. *The brothers just stuck me in the category of people they like least.* He drew his shoulders up to his ears and walked away in the opposite direction Visage had gone.

Svelte's bottom lip trembled, and she sniffed loudly. "I'm going back inside," she said, and bolted toward the door.

Quell and I were left standing by ourselves. The little lambkin adjusted his glasses.

"This," he told me, "is why we don't come outside during common hours."

"I don't even understand what I *did*!" I lifted my hands in the air, utterly dismayed. "Why are people so awful to each other? Why is Visage mad at *me,* rather than at the people who insult her just for existing? Blare *knows* that Svelte doesn't think poorly of him, so why—"

"You know why," Quell said.

I swung toward him and crossed my arms. "I really don't."

The lambkin tugged on one of his long ears. "Honestly? You can't imagine why we go after each other, instead of taking our complaints to Brother Modest? Or even Brother Harmony?"

I let my shoulders droop. Only a few hours ago, I had worried about what would happen if Emerald and I were discovered and thrown out of the Brotherhood. It would inconvenience our investigation terribly. I hadn't stopped to think about what would happen if the other children were turned away. They had nowhere to go, no one to flee to, no backup plan if the kindness of the brothers dried up.

"Exactly." Quell pointed at my face, where my expression must have laid bare my whole thought process. "We don't have much choice. We band together, or we turn on each other." He dipped his head and sighed. "We got lucky, you know. Svelte and Blare and me. And now you. We take care of each other. We're all we have. They're... they're like a family to me." He choked on that word: *family*.

I crouched down beside him. Even as Vagabond, he was a great deal shorter than I was. "I'm sorry," I told him. "I didn't mean to start a fight. I just wanted to be outside for a little while. With—" I remembered where we were, and pitched my voice lower. "With the shadow-beast prowling around, I get anxious."

"So do I," Quell admitted. He reached for my hand, then thought better of it. "Come on, let's go inside. I can show you some of our best bone finds."

"Bone finds?" I repeated as he led me to the door back into the halls.

"You know, the little caches of bones we find around the building?" Quell tried to smile, but there wasn't much joy in it. "Blare might have found teeth, but *I* found an owl skull."

"Show me," I said.

We went inside, leaving Blare sitting alone on the edge of the fountain. The kids playing in the courtyard all gave him a wide berth, and Visage kept shooting nasty looks at me as I retreated. I had no idea where Svelte had gone.

It was a miserable feeling, when your family fought. I already knew that from personal experience.

DESPITE THE FACT that Quell had shown me half a dozen little caches of left-behind bones, no doubt by Brother Reticent, my mood had not improved by lunchtime. Blare wouldn't answer when Quell and I spoke to him, and Svelte didn't make an appearance. Harmony was absent, too.

Emerald, however, was in a better mood than usual. *[We learned so much last night,]* he thought as he dug into his afternoon meal. *[I keep thinking about the reliquary. Allure was convinced that the ash has something to do with Guise's teachings, but I wonder. Don't you find it odd that the girl in the tent, Brigane, was able to drag metal from all around her, but the reliquary never moved? I wonder if it's magically inert, somehow. Maybe that ash comes from the Aidea Nulda. They use blocks of stone from the island to build prison cells for cast-offs, you know, since it renders their magic inert, but I've never heard of it* consuming someone's *Aidea...]*

[Hold on,] I thought, interrupting the flow of his tirade. *[What's this about the reliquary?]*

Emerald shot me a sidelong glance. *[The box that Allure showed me last night. Are you forgetting things now?]*

[I remember the box, but I'm surprised you do.]

Emerald sat up and let his spoon dip toward his bowl, *[Interesting. Have we discussed the box before? Perhaps in another context?]*

[We have,] I said, but I didn't bother to elaborate.

I hadn't told Emerald about my encounter on the roof, or the way the shadow-beast had managed to make me bleed. I didn't like thinking about it, and the notion of reliving the pain and fear of that experience, only for him to immediately forget again, was too much to bear. I hadn't expected him to recall the reliquary, either, but clearly I'd been wrong.

Emerald licked his lips. *[Interesting. I don't remember that at all. What I do remember is her showing me the contents. It was ash, wasn't it? Just ash?]*

I nodded glumly.

[Huh. I wonder what's different about remembering the box itself and remembering that conversation? Mentalist Aidea isn't my forte, and it's notoriously hard to study. My best guess is that whoever tampered with my memories wasn't trying to remove the box specifically. It must be tangential to whatever they wanted to remove...]

It was Brother Harmony, not me, who cut Emerald off this time.

He swept into the dining hall, stone faced and straight backed, over to where we sat.

"Brother Steadfast." His voice was barely louder than a whisper, but Quell and I both perked up to listen in, and Blare watched his lips intently. "I require your assistance. Sister Svelte is having a... difficult morning, and I'm hoping you might offer a solution to our current predicament."

"Of course." Emerald got to his feet, abandoning the remains of his meal.

As they exited the room, Blare drummed his fingers on the table. Our eyes met, and he hooked his thumb toward the door.

Without uttering a word, the three of us got to our feet. I grabbed my tray, knowing that it would arouse all sorts of suspicions if I left the illusions of a meal lying around, only to wink out of existence the moment Emerald or I forgot to maintain them. My friends did the same, hastening to clear away our mess before we scurried after our half-jotunn guardians.

Emerald and Harmony stood at the door of our dormitory. It was closed, and when Emerald reached for the handle, he sucked in a breath and yanked his hand away. Glittering frost covered the doorknob, and an icy filigree of crystals spilled out from the doorway, climbing the frame and creeping beneath the jamb. Emerald cupped his hands together and blew on them a few times.

"She's iced us out," he observed.

Harmony's movements, usually so smooth and considered, had become jerky and irritable. "That she has," he grumbled. "And judging by the chill, she's been at it for a while. I've been talking to her for the last half hour, and I'd have broken the door down myself if I wasn't worried about getting frostbite."

"What about Svelte?" I asked. "Won't *she* get too cold in there?"

Harmony sighed, and his breath formed a puffy cloud in the frigid air. I had never experienced the cold myself, but if it was that chilly in the hall, I could only imagine how much the temperature had dropped inside the room. There had been a cold hut, created by the work of an Arctician, back in Upper Bound, but it hadn't been cold enough to form *ice.*

Harmony said, "If anything, she'll be in danger of overheating. She'll have pulled all the warmth in the room into herself to make this happen."

"Harmony!" Brother Modest's voice boomed down the hall, and he came striding toward us, his face flushed with anger. Brother Lightfoot trotted behind him, wearing a smug little smile.

Harmony lifted both hands. "I'm working to resolve the matter, Brother, but this is a delicate situation…"

"I agree," Modest shot back. He stopped a few feet away from Harmony and drew himself up to his full height, which still only brought the peak of his blond head level with Harmony's nose. "One of your students is endangering the integrity of this establishment, and the lives of our other wards. I thought that between the two of you, you'd be capable of managing a single child, but clearly I was wrong."

Harmony's dark eyes flashed. "Sister Svelte is upset. She's too young to manage both her emotions and her *Aidea* at once. We need to calm her down—"

"Then sort out how to do it," Modest snapped. He jabbed the tip of one finger into Harmony's chest. "Or I will send Sister Allure in there and we can settle the matter for good."

"No!" Quell shoved past me and stamped one hoof against the floor. Beneath his fur, his face was bright red, pinched with righteous indignation. "You can't take her *Aidea* without her permission just because it makes her easy to handle! It should be her decision!"

Modest's eyes narrowed. "I think you'll find that I can do anything I like, so long as it serves the well-being of my wards."

"The boy is right," Harmony growled. "Allure is not your plaything to command. Nor is Guise. Nor, for that matter, am I. Steadfast and I will handle this."

Emerald had hung back throughout this exchange, and with this last pronouncement, a flood of pride and affection washed through him and into me. Meeting Harmony again had disappointed him; his old mentor was not the loving protector of his recollections.

In that moment, however, we both saw that Emerald's mind had not been playing tricks on him. Harmony might pick at Svelte for eating more than he approved of, or condemn the use of magic, or use kindness as a weapon against the children he cared for. He would not, however, allow them to come to harm.

He was more like Nechtan, High Priest of Dyrne, than I had realized. And he'd meant what he told me in his office the day before: that he would do whatever it took to protect us, so long as he understood that we were in danger.

Modest sputtered for a moment, glaring at the two half-jotunn who barred his way. Quell and Blare had both fallen into defensive stances. They were determined to protect their sister.

But I could do something no one else could, and I chose that moment to do it. While Harmony and Modest squabbled, I slipped through the thick wooden door of the dormitory and into the wintry room beyond.

Our little bedroom had been utterly transformed. Ice had gathered in the mullioned windows, and frost covered every inch of the room. Icicles dripped from the ceiling above. A fine dusting of snow fell in drifts across the floor.

I had never experienced winter before, and I stopped just inside the doorway, marveling at the way the autumn light refracted through the icy windowpanes. It was beautiful. I'd never seen anything quite like it.

My appreciation for this new experience was short lived. Amid all that quiet wonder, which had the added benefit of muffling the voices in the hall, there was only one thing out of place. Svelte sat in the middle of her bed with her knees drawn up to her chest, shivering uncontrollably. Her face was bright red, and she was dripping with sweat.

"Svelte?" I asked.

She jumped when I spoke. Her eyes were glassy with fever. "Vagabond?" she panted. "You shouldn't be here. You could f-f-freeze." She shuddered and wiped her hand across her brow.

"I'm perfectly fine," I assured her, padding across the floor toward her. "You're the one I'm worried about." My feet left no impressions in the snow, but Svelte was too preoccupied to notice, and I hoped that my cover of being a cast-off would help explain any anomalies regarding my interaction with the world.

"I'm f-f-fine." Svelte's teeth chattered. "It's better this way."

I pulled myself up onto the bed beside her. "Better than what?"

"Than being *wrong* all the time!" She hid her face behind her knees. "B-B-Blare was right, I f-f-f-forget what it's like for him. I'm self-f-f-centered. I only think about m-m-me..."

"Blare's all right," I assured her. "He's outside right now. Worried about you, like the rest of us are."

Svelte sniffed and lifted her head just far enough that her eyes peeked over her knees. "That's just as b-bad," she said. "I hurt his feelings, and now he's w-w-worried about me!"

"Svelte," I said, hoping that the sound of her name would calm her, and remembering too late that every name in that godawful brotherhood was a title used to put people in their place. "We're all worried." I indicated the room, still startling in its loveliness, then her. "You're hurting yourself."

Svelte shuddered. From what I could gather, she was both burning up and freezing at the same time. Her *Aidea* was taking a tremendous toll on her, and while I supposed that cleaning up all the ice and snow once it melted might take a bit of effort, I was equally certain that everyone in the hall was far more concerned with Svelte's safety than the inconvenience of a wintry room.

Well, everyone but Brother Modest. He'd made *his* priorities quite plain.

"I don't want them to send me to Sister Allure," Svelte whispered. "I don't want them to take away my *Aidea*. Then I w-w-won't have anything in common with Blare at all, and they'll send m-me away. Nobody else wants me. That girl Visage was r-r-right. My family got rid of me b-b-because I wasn't like them. If I'm not like B-Blare and Quell, th-th-they..." She sucked in a deep breath and wiped her hands across her eyes, and her next words tumbled out in a rush. "They won't want me, either."

I crossed my legs in front of me and studied Svelte. To be perfectly honest, I was tired of children suffering for the shortcomings of the adults in their lives. All the wrong people were being made to feel ashamed of all the wrong things.

"The other night, who was the first person to Blare's side?" I asked.

Svelte sniffed again. "M-me."

"That's right. You were there when he needed you." I wished I could offer her some kind of comfort as Quell had the other night, but I found that my inability to do so didn't bother me as much as it used to. I was tired of wishing to be something and someone other than myself. Doing so brought no happiness to any of the people around me, and I would far prefer to use the talents I had than to bemoan the ones I lacked. "I'm quite sure that he knows how much you care about him. He can be upset about something you've said *and* still love you."

Svelte let out a wet sob and curled in on herself, rocking from side to side. How old had she been, I wondered, when her family left her with the Brotherhood? Was she old enough to remember that day herself? Or had she relied on Harmony's descriptions of the events to shape her recollections?

"Sorry..." Svelte rubbed at her eyes. "You barely know me. You shouldn't have to comfort me like this." The intensity of her shivering had subsided, and the icicles growing over the windows began to drip.

"Oh, please." I shifted closer to her in the hopes that my proximity would make up for my intangibility. "I hear all the things the brothers say. If people get to judge you on sight just for being who you are, I think I'm entitled to love you knowing just as little, don't you think? Besides, I've known you for a few days, and *I* think you're lovely. Even if you say the wrong thing sometimes." I winked at her. "Better than being awful on purpose, isn't it?" I puffed myself up and wagged a finger at her. *"Don't eat too much. Or too little!"* I turned my attention to Quell's bed. *"Have I told you the story about a town where people cared about each other and loved their neighbors? What a bunch of fools. Guise frowns upon them!"*

Svelte let out a bank of startled laughter and covered her mouth with both hands. "You shouldn't say things like that."

"Nor should they," I retorted. "That girl in the courtyard was right. We ought to be kind to one another here. If the brothers spent half as much energy on teaching you—teaching *us* to love ourselves as they do complaining about our faults, I think we'd all be much happier for it."

I was warming to my subject when the door of the dormitory burst open and a red-faced Brother Modest staggered through. His eyes were fixed upon me, his mouth twisted into a furious little snarl.

"My office," he said. "*Now.*"

Svelte shrank away toward the headboard. "Me?" she squeaked.

Modest shook his head once, so sharply that I was sure I could hear one vertebra in his neck pop. "Brother Harmony will see to you. As for you, new... girl?" One eye twitched. "We need to have a talk."

I suppose it should have occurred to me that any insubordination might jeopardize our investigation, but I could not muster even a small show of contrition as I popped off the bed and crossed the room to where Modest stood waiting. As I went, Quell and Blare hurried to Svelte's side.

Harmony moved to block my path, placing himself between me and Modest. "Vagabond is my responsibility," he said. Once again, I was deeply aware of his physical strength, and how easy it would be for him to grind Modest under the heel of his boot if he really put his mind to it.

"See to the Arctician," Modest snapped. "I will remind you, Harmony, that you answer to *me.*" He dropped his voice an octave. "Are you really going to go against my wishes here? Now? With so many witnesses? Whose side do you think they'll take?"

Harmony's gaze drifted to the hall full of mentors and their curious, gleeful students. His shoulders dipped slightly. *He has never been the Brotherhood's favorite,* I realized. His constant injunctions to the children to keep their head down and blend in applied not only to the outside world, but to his own life within the walls of the compound.

"Go with him, Vagabond," Harmony told me at last. "I will be along shortly."

[If he tries to take you to Sister Allure, come back here,] Emerald added. Rather than argue with the brothers, he'd hastened to Svelte's side, but his anger at Modest boiled in his chest. It leaked through into me, although I had plenty of anger of my own to nurse.

[I can handle myself,] I told him.

*[Yes, well. If you **can't**, use the tether. I don't know what to look for since I can't remember everything we've learned, but your safety comes first.]*

That was one of the nicest things he'd ever said to me, but it did little to settle my nerves. Harmony shuffled aside, giving me a view of Modest's face, and it occurred to me that there were always people I disliked at least as much as the villains we uncovered in our investigations. Even if Allure was doing something duplicitous, I would still have more respect for her than I had for this man.

Modest huffed as he turned on his heel and led me down the hall. As I trotted after him, I heard Svelte say, "I'm sorry, Blare."

I glanced over my shoulder at the last moment to see Blare sign, *Vagabond was right. We're family, and real family doesn't—*

But then I passed into the hall and missed the rest of whatever he told her.

CHAPTER

NINETEEN

Slipping onto the chair across from Brother Modest's desk reminded me of the first memory Emerald had shown me, when he'd sat in the same place years and years ago. The glass window panes were a bit dirtier, the plaster more yellowed, the spines of the books on his shelf faded after years in the sun, and there were new shocks of white and silver in the man's hair. His attitude, however, was unchanged.

"So, Vagabond," he said as he dropped into his chair with a rustle of cheap cloth, "you believe yourself to be wiser than the brothers who have taken you in. Is that right?"

I would have paid good coin to give Modest a piece of my mind and then have his memory wiped clean in the aftermath, but alas, no such luxuries were available to me. I had to sit with my hands folded demurely in my lap and my eyes downcast. If I made eye contact, I was sure he would see directly into my soul and bear witness to all the frustration and disdain that festered there.

"I was only trying to make Sister Svelte feel better," I murmured.

"And you thought that mocking the sanctity of the order that took her in would lift her spirits?" Modest spat. He leaned across the desk and glowered at me. "Nobody else wants her. Nobody else wants *you*. It would be wise of you to remember just how precarious your position here is, and to act accordingly."

Those words nearly broke my resolve to keep my head down. I knew what I was, inasmuch as anyone did, and thanks to my connection to Emerald, I had far more worldly experience than my brief lifespan would suggest. Modest, however, did *not* know that. He thought he was speaking to a child under his care, and still he was willing to say these things.

What price does a Shadowweaver pay? I wondered. *Assuming that's even what they're called. If a Lightweaver makes too many illusions, they'll go blind. What happens to someone who trades in darkness and deceit?* I had begun as an idea sprung from Emerald's mind, and although I was not precisely what he imagined, my motivation still closely matched Emerald's intent for me. If that was true of the shadow-beast, whoever made it had a twisted heart indeed.

I eyed Modest with new suspicion.

"I will remember that, sir," I murmured.

"Good." Modest leaned back, relaxing his posture somewhat. "I recognize that you are new, and that your mentor's attentions are divided between looking after his students and training his assistant, but I assure you, we are not all so tolerant of poor behavior. As to your punishment..."

He paused, and I stayed perfectly still. If I had lungs, I would have held my breath.

I lifted my eyes a fraction, but rather than meeting his, my gaze landed on the book on the corner of his desk: the register of former students.

"It would serve you to remember that we are a community," Modest said at last. "For the rest of the day, you will work in the kitchens. Perhaps finding a task for those idle hands of yours will give you some appreciation for all that we do for you."

"Of course," I mumbled. My mind was already on that book. Emerald couldn't remember what skills his classmates had possessed, but they would very likely be recorded there. If only I could get him to sneak me in and open the book...

"You will report to Sister Humble at once."

I jumped and whipped my head toward him. "Sister Humble?" I squeaked.

"I'll have Brother Lightfoot show you the way." Modest got to his feet. "I hope we don't need to discuss this again, Vagabond."

"Yes, sir." I stared down at my boots, doing my best to hide a smile. I had made Svelte feel better, and I had been punished with the opportunity to sniff out two more clues. By my reckoning, it had been a very successful morning.

When I was first introduced to Sister Humble, I hadn't yet known much about her. Now that I'd seen her in Emerald's memories, however, I could see the ways she'd changed since childhood. She was still slender, and her blonde hair was pulled back in a simple chignon, although now there was silver at her temples. Her movements were precise and crisp, as was her speech when she spoke to Brother Lightfoot as I was deposited unceremoniously in her care.

"Vagabond here is reporting for duty," Lightfoot said. "This one will be helping you prepare the evening meal."

Humble looked up from the pile of potatoes laid out on the massive, scarred surface of the kitchen table. When her eyes landed on me, something shifted in her face, a slight twitch that disappeared before I could work out what it meant.

"Of course." Her mouth formed a smile, but the rest of her face remained as wooden as the carvings in the prayer hall's ceiling. "I'll put them to work." She approached me, and I hastily shuffled aside, but she was only showing Brother Lightfoot out.

The instant the kitchen door closed behind him, she locked the door and spun toward me.

"*Took you long enough, Steady!*" she hissed. "Gods' sakes, I suppose you thought you were *soooo* clever for ignoring me."

I blinked at her a few times. "I... what?"

"I thought you'd send your little poppet to talk to me after our meal the other day," she snapped, pressing her back to the door. "I'm sure you found a way to talk to Allure, but *nooooo*, not me, even though you must have worked out that Finch sent me, too. We could have been working together this whole time. But of course, Modest sticks me in the kitchen!" She threw her hands in the air and stalked back to the table, where she began to peel a potato with unnecessary viciousness. "I suppose you've worked it out already, have you? Come to gloat? I've been here for *months* and I've only learned a few things."

"You have?" This conversation wasn't going the way I'd expected, but her tone certainly piqued my interest. I shuffled closer as the potato peelings rained down onto the butcher block.

"Didn't think I'd manage, did you?" Humble asked. "And now you send Crimson to talk with me instead of coming on your own? Great. *Wonderful.* I'm so glad we could collaborate. Ooh, you *really* haven't changed, have you?"

"You know me?" I asked, momentarily surprised. I was having trouble keeping up with her line of thinking, but this was a more interesting welcome than I'd anticipated. Even better, I didn't have to pretend to peel an infinite pile of potatoes and explain why I had nothing to show for it.

Humble dropped both the paring knife and the bare potato to the table with a clatter. She braced one arm against the tabletop and glared down at me.

"I work for the Conjury, remember? Besides, there was a little while where everyone in Venta Bulgarum knew the stupid words to that *insipid* song written about your exploits in the mountains. I put two and two together. And then a couple years later, there was that *other* song about the great Crimson Smoke and his brilliance, that was sometimes *her* brilliance, and I thought: *There, he's gone and done it, Steadfast really made a name for himself.* Literally. Then you returned, and the very next day, a red-haired vagrant turns up? I'm not an idiot, even if you always acted like I was. You made this." She pointed right at me. "Well, I'm done with playing the fool, Steady. If you want to talk to me, you can address me directly."

With that, she turned back to the hill of potatoes and resumed her work.

"That's going to be a problem," I told her.

"Why?" she sneered. "Too busy making sure you get all the credit?"

I was tempted to tell her the truth, but she still worked for the Conjury. Evidently, there was little love lost between her and Emerald, and she might very well be tempted to turn me over to Finch out of spite. I wasn't entirely sure what would happen to me if the Conjury figured out what I was, but it wouldn't be good.

I would have to find some other alternative.

[Emerald?] I asked through our connection. *[I'm talking to Humble right now. She knows that I'm a lightweaving, and she thinks you're controlling me right now. What should I do?]*

It took a moment for him to respond. *[Just wait. I'm talking to Brother Harmony right now about everything with Svelte today. I'll wrap this up as quickly as I can. Just buy some time, will you?]*

That was an awfully vague order, but I could work with it. After all, there were things that Emerald wouldn't know to ask. I might as well start there.

"I think it's better if I use Crimson to talk to you, at least for now," I said, as if Emerald was the one choosing the words. Should I try to talk like him? No, that wouldn't make sense, if I'd been prancing around as Simone for years speaking in Emerald's voice, people would have found that unsettling. I'd just speak like me, but as if Emerald was doing the talking.

I resigned myself to grunting quite a lot.

"Simpler, is it?" Humble asked, stabbing the eyes out of a sprouting spud.

"I've been trying to figure out the best way to do it. Nobody else has worked out what Crimson—or rather, Vagabond—is, and I thought it would look suspicious if anyone found us colluding."

Humble choked on a laugh. "Colluding? I see you're still as dramatic as ever."

Emerald? Dramatic? I considered that. He was always calling *me* dramatic, but I supposed I had come by it honestly. "You must admit," I said, "this whole situation is rather cloak-and-dagger. Why don't you tell me what you've learned?"

Humble drew a deep breath and sized me up. "Why don't *you* tell *me* what you've learned?"

I crossed my arms and lifted my chin. "How about we trade? One for one. A clue for a clue. I'll ask a question, and you answer it if you can. Deal?"

"Deal." Humble picked up the paring knife and stabbed it point-first into the wood. "I'll go first."

Naturally, she'd want me to reveal my hand. I couldn't think of any reason to withhold what I knew about the Brotherhood... We were on the same side, after all.

"Very well," I told her. "Ask away."

"That box that Allure carries to the ceremonies," she said. "What's in it?"

"Ashes," I replied at once.

Humble wrinkled her nose in disgust. "Ashes? Why?"

"They're sacred, supposedly." I shrugged one shoulder. "She showed me, but I have no idea what they're from or what they do."

"Interesting." Humble pressed the pad of her thumb to her lips, and her blue eyes unfocused. Her beauty was striking enough, but in that moment, she looked as tired as Emerald ever did. "Is that all you can tell me about them?"

"About the ashes, yes. The box they're stored in is one that we had in our old room growing up."

"Really?" Humble wrinkled her brow. "I don't remember."

That wasn't surprising, but I didn't remark on it. Instead, I told her, "My turn. When was the last time you saw Brother Reticent?"

Humble's lips parted, and that vague, confused expression that I had seen on Emerald's face so often in the last few months stole over her features. She frowned at nothing for a few moments, then shook her head. "I don't... I don't remember." She slumped forward to rest her elbows on the table and massaged her temples as she tried to think. "Oh, that's frustrating. I swear, I've been forgetting things so often. It's *infuriating.*"

"That's because someone is using mental *Aidea* on you," I told her.

Her eyes snapped back into focus. "What?"

"I don't know who, but I suspect Brother Harmony. I think he did it when we were younger." There was, I supposed, some small risk that Humble would let this slip to her old mentor, but judging by her indignation, she had neither realized this nor approved of it.

"Well, that certainly explains some things," Humble muttered, more to herself than to me. "When I spoke to Allure, neither of us could remember the other's *Aidea*."

I nearly trembled with excitement. "But you know now?"

"We reminded one another." Humble placed one hand to her chest. "I'm a Vulcanist, and Allure is a Shade. Or at least she was—evidently, her magic dried up after we left."

I very nearly rocked back on my heels. All this time spent trying to puzzle out who could do what, and I had my answer. *Allure is a Shade!* The word fit some knowledge rattling around in Emerald's brain. Not a Shadowweaver. A Shade. I had suspected it ever since the night when I'd faced the shadow-beast on the roof above the library, but now that Humble had confirmed it, the horror of that truth sank in. Allure, with all her power, had made that awful creature, and she had used it to...

To...

What exactly *was* she telling it to do? Lurk in children's bedrooms? Hide in the ceiling? To what possible end?

"My turn," Humble said, interrupting the flurry of my thoughts.

"No, it isn't," I replied, holding up one finger. "I've answered two of your questions, and you've only answered one of mine."

"Fine." Humble drummed her fingers on the table. "Go on, then."

"Have you worked out what exactly Allure is doing during her ceremonies?"

Humble scoffed. "Are you serious? That's the whole point on this investigation! If I had, I'd have reported it back to Finch by now." She fell silent for a moment, and a bit of her spite drained away. "I'll tell you what, Steadfast, I've *never* seen magic like that before. Not even in the prisons beneath Venta Bulgarum. Allure says that it isn't her, that she's just a conduit, and..." She shook her head, taking her time to choose the right words. "I didn't return to Guise any more than I expect you did, but after seeing that, I have to wonder."

"It's terrifying, isn't it?" I asked softly.

"It is." Humble twined her fingers together and stared down at her hands. I wondered if she had anything like a mind-cottage in *her* head, and if so, what memories she was revisiting there. "I've seen her do it dozens of times now, and it never gets any less disturbing. She isn't our Allure when she does that. You remember what she was like growing up? Soft. Nervous. Self-conscious. I know she grew into herself, but... this is different."

We were both silent for a moment. I wondered what Emerald would say, if he could be here now. I knew how he'd felt about Allure, but I also knew he'd disliked Humble back in the day.

"How long have you been back?" I asked, to fill the silence as much as anything else.

"Ever since Finch sent for me. It's been, what, a couple of months now?" Humble shrugged. "Give or take."

"And how long has this been going on?" I was ahead when it came to asking questions, but Humble didn't seem to have noticed.

"I do know this," she said, brightening a little. "Allure told me about the first time she found the box. She remembered, because it was one of the high holy days, on the solstice."

I stumbled back a pace. "The *spring* solstice?"

Allure nodded. "I always hated the holiday. They made us sit through all those awful services, don't you remember?"

I did not, in fact, remember, and I couldn't think of a single thing to say, neither to Humble nor to Emerald when he reached out through our link.

[I finally *got away. Have you learned anything useful, Crim?*]

I had indeed learned something useful, although it shook me to my core. The day that Allure had first used the reliquary was the same day that Emerald had stood on the bridge above the Bounder and tossed himself into its rushing waters.

The same day he'd nearly died before washing up in the Cronemire.

The next time he'd summoned me was the first day I became truly myself. My birthday, so to speak.

And now I had reason to suspect that I shared that birthday with the shadow-beast.

CHAPTER

TWENTY

Explaining what I'd learned from Humble was an exercise in frustration, since Emerald couldn't keep the facts in his mind for more than a moment or two at a time.

"So let me get this straight," he said when I snuck off to his room that evening to discuss the subject with him. "Allure can do shadow magic, which you think is a significant clue, because...?"

"Because it proves that she's the one who made the shadow-beast," I explained for what felt like the hundredth time. The outfit I had unconsciously arranged for myself that evening was even more grandiose and mismatched than the last. The heeled boots that stopped at the ankle were quite suited to my tight-fitting hose and garters, but the upper half of my attire was decidedly more feminine in its cut. The whole ensemble was stitched through with seed pearls and stag embroidery. If I'd seen myself on the street a month ago, I would have wept at my own unlikely fashion choices, but now it felt like the only thing I could control. It would have driven Modest wild to see me dressed this way, which only underscored my pleasure of being free to choose something for myself. Guise's acolytes would hate this outfit; ergo, it suited me.

"Right, right, the shadow-beast." Emerald rubbed his forehead as he sank onto the edge of his undersized cot. "I'm sure you've explained this before, but it won't stick."

"I couldn't have guessed," I said drily.

"But her being a Shade doesn't explain what she does in the tent," Emerald mused. "Shadow magic doesn't nullify *Aidea*. So correct me if I'm wrong, but we still haven't figured out what's happening."

You haven't figured much of anything out, I thought peevishly, but I refrained from saying the words aloud. Emerald had been about as useful during this investigation as he had been in Upper Bound, but this time, it was not his fault. He'd been doing his best, reliving the worst memories from his childhood, and he had yet to so much as glance longingly at a bottle of wine. True, there was no wine on hand to tempt him here, but no doubt he could have gotten his hands on some if he really put his mind to it.

"You're right," was all I told him. "I'm not sure how these things connect, except that Allure is in the middle of it all."

Emerald sighed deeply and leaned back. He made a halfhearted attempt to get comfortable in the little bed. "And Humble couldn't tell you anything about Reticent?"

I shook my head.

My friend rolled onto his back and stared up at the ceiling. Out of habit, I checked, but no new cracks had appeared.

"I hate this," Emerald muttered. "I hate not knowing what I've missed. I hate not being able to tell what's slipped past me. You have no idea, Crimson."

It was possible that I had a tiny idea. In the real world, I had never encountered a wall I couldn't simply walk through, but at that moment, I felt nearly as trapped as I had the time Emerald dismissed me to the mind-cottage. No matter how I approached the problem, I couldn't figure out what to do next. I felt very much as though we were going down two parallel tracks, and I could not for the life of me work out how they overlapped.

"Maybe I'll think of something in the morning," Emerald said. He laid one arm across his face, blocking the light of the lamp at his bedside. "I'm done for the night."

"Fair enough." I could feel his exhaustion as if it was my own, and I saw no use in pressing the issue any further that night. "I'm sure one of us will think of something." *Or I'll be torn apart in the night by my shadow-twin, and you'll be none the wiser.* "Just be sure to keep the light on, won't you?"

Emerald shifted his arm enough so that he could fix one bright-green eye on me. "Why?"

Oh, for Aster's sake. "Just trust me," I said, and rearranged myself for the journey back to my room.

I traveled quickly, just in case the shadow-beast was prowling the halls. I wasn't sure what Allure would ask of it, but during my chat with Emerald, it had struck me that the beast might not rely on Allure's direction any more than I relied on Emerald's. Perhaps it did as it pleased in the off-hours. For all I knew, it saw me as a threat, just as I saw it—which hardly seemed fair, given that I had done nothing to offend it, while *it* lurked in odd corners and attacked innocent people for no discernable reason.

In fact, Allure might not even know that she had created the beast. If she despised her use of the *Aidea* as much as she claimed to, maybe she was unaware of the monster she'd made—

I passed through the door of the dormitory, where I was met with a sight so shocking that all thoughts of Allure's Shadowweaving were subsequently banished from my mind.

Svelte and Blare were standing on my bed, shoulder to shoulder, supporting Quell as the lambkin jammed his stubby fingers into the hole in the plaster.

"Almost there," he said. "Almost there, almost... *got it!*"

"Vagabond!" Svelte yelped. "Where did you come—*oof!*"

She had turned to look at me, and in the process, she lost her footing. Her grip on Quell faltered. In the scramble that followed, the little humanoid pyramid collapsed, and all three of them ended up in a heap on my mattress. Fortunately, Quell landed on the pillows, and aside from where Svelte's shin hit the bedframe, none of them suffered any ill effects from their tumble.

"What are you doing?" I demanded, doing my best to hide my

dismay. I had been certain that all three of them were sound asleep when I left to speak with Emerald.

"What were *you* doing?" Svelte retorted, rubbing her injured shin. "I woke up, and you weren't here. We thought the shadow man might have taken you."

We did not, Blare corrected with a roll of his eyes. She *did.*

"But I said that you were off hunting the shadow-beast!" Quell exclaimed, popping up from the now disarrayed pillows. "And I was right, wasn't I? Your *Aidea* makes it easy for you to sneak around and follow it places other people can't go!"

"Er..." I turned this explanation over in my mind, and saw no reason to deny it. "That's right. I'm trying to figure out how to make it leave us alone." That wasn't a lie by any means. If I could find some way to get the beast to leave my friends alone, I would do so gladly.

"And we're helping!" Quell lifted a triumphant hand above his head, revealing a small bag clutched in his fist. "This morning, when we played Find the Bones, it got me thinking. And then Svelte had her episode..."

"I thought we agreed not to talk about that!" Svelte protested.

"We're not really *talking* about it," Quell said. "It just got me thinking that the bones might be good for something, you know? Like how people use talismans and loci for their *Aidea?* And then I thought, well, we found those bones in the floor. What if there were more in other places?" He pointed upward to the ceiling and waved his fist again. "And I was right!"

Blare held a warning finger to his lips before signing, *Keep it down. You'll wake the brothers.*

"Wait." I pointed at Quell. "You found *bones* in my ceiling?"

He made a show of adjusting his glasses, which had been knocked slightly askew by his fall. "Technically, it's our *collective* ceiling," he said. "But yes."

His discovery electrified me, and I hurried over to see what he'd found. Sure enough, a little collection of bones lay inside the bag.

Emerald has to keep his necklace on him at all times while summoning me, I thought. *But Coirpre was able to summon me using the same gem. Allure has shadow* Aidea, *but we don't know about Reticent. Maybe the bones* do *act as a locus for the shadow-beast using a different kind of magic? Or maybe Reticent* also *deals in shadows...*

Or maybe he did something else altogether. Something that can give Aidea a life of its own.

"Reticent might be a cast-off," I muttered, not realizing that I was doing so aloud.

"Who's Reticent?" Svelte asked.

Before I could answer, Quell butted in. "He was one of the old students," he explained.

"You know about Reticent?" I asked.

Quell wiggled one hand back and forth. "Only a little. He carved his name into one of the bedposts. That's how I knew Brother Steadfast was one of the old students, too. They left little reminders everywhere." His eyes lit up. "Say, do you think Brother Steadfast is one of the people who hid treasures under the floorboards?"

"Maybe," I hedged.

"I bet he was," Quell went on. "Maybe I can find a way to ask Brother Harmony, although I don't want him to get mad and take everything away—"

Focus, Blare cut in. *We were talking about the shadow-beast, and how Vagabond is trying to get rid of it.*

"Right, right." Quell turned to me and swung his little legs over the edge of the bed. "Have you learned anything useful?"

"We want to help," Svelte added.

Blare nodded resolutely. *We might not be able to walk through walls, but we have other talents that could be handy.*

They did indeed have other talents, not all of which were magical. They could do things that I simply could not do.

Things like, for example, opening the cover of a book.

If Emerald was discovered poking around in Modest's office, our investigation might end right then and there. But if four children were caught...

Well, then Humble would have a lot of extra hands to help her peel potatoes for a day or two.

"Actually," I said, "there is something."

All three of my newfound siblings leaned, their eyes gleaming in the lamplight. "Tell us," Svelte said.

So I did.

I WILL CONFESS that I gave no thought at all to the matter of picking locks. Locks were not part of my everyday life. I never had to worry about them, since they didn't hinder my passage in the slightest.

It was different for the children, who stood dressed in their pajamas in the dark and apparently chilly hallway outside Modest's office, huddled around a single lamp that cast just enough light to keep the shadow-beast at bay.

"I didn't think he'd lock it," Quell hissed.

Don't talk, Blare said. *Sign instead. I know you know how.*

"How am I supposed to sign when I'm the one holding the lamp!"

The boys appeared to be on the brink of squabbling when Svelte shooed them aside and knelt in front of the door. She fished a small item out of her pocket and teased it into the lock beneath the knob.

"You know how to pick locks?" Quell asked, clearly in awe of this unexpected talent.

Svelte shushed him and squinted at the keyhole. A moment later, the lock clicked.

"Teach me that!" Quell stage whispered as Svelte pushed the door open.

"Only if you don't get us caught!" she returned.

All four of us hastened through the doorway, and Svelte shut it carefully behind us so that it wouldn't slam. When it was closed, she locked it again, and all three of them let out a relieved sigh. I could almost *feel* the pounding of their hearts in the quiet room.

"What are we looking for?" Svelte asked.

"That book, just there." I pointed at the tome.

Quell set the lamp on the far edge of the desk before trotting over to reach for the book I'd indicated. He was much too short to see the cover from his height, so he dragged the nearest chair a few steps closer. Its wooden feet scraped across the floor and let out a piercing squeak. Svelte, Blare and I all shushed him in unison.

"Sorry!" Quell said, still in that overly-loud stage whisper. His stubby legs flailed as he clambered up onto the seat of the chair, finally setting him a head taller than the rest of us.

Svelte and I exchanged a knowing and exasperated look.

"That's what we get," she whispered under her breath, "for bringing a Sonicist on a secret mission."

"I'm being quiet!" Quell insisted, finally dropping his voice to a more reasonable volume.

"Sure you are." Svelte, who was tall enough to reach the book with no trouble at all, spun it around to face her. "Now, what are we looking for?"

"I want to see if we can find an entry on someone named Brother Reticent. He would have been a student here about, um, twenty years ago? At the same time as Allure and Emerald, and I think they graduated around that time."

Quell tipped his head to one side. "Emerald?" he asked.

"Brother Steadfast," I hastily amended, cursing myself for a fool. A slip-up like that around the adults could land both of us in dire trouble. If Humble could work out that we were, in fact, a pair of relatively well-known Conjury investigators, then surely other people would be able to do the same.

Svelte only nodded, utterly unbothered by my slip of the tongue, and began to leaf through the pages of the book, with Quell fussing over her shoulder all the while. Blare, for his part, wandered over to Modest's bookshelf and began to study the spines. One at the top of the shelf caught his eye, and he turned back to wink at me before making a complicated gesture with one hand: not a sign in the language he used with his friends, but the sort of gesture I'd seen other *Aidea*-workers use when controlling their magic. The heavy book slid out of the shelf, wobbled precariously, and then floated down into Blare's hand. The boy sank to the floor and crossed his legs, settling the huge book in his lap as he leafed through the pages, squinting in the dimly lit room.

"Well, we found Allure," Svelte said.

I returned my attention to the register. One of her fingers rested below a line where someone had marked out her name in blunt, bold penmanship. A few sparse notes filled the rest of her line, noting the relevant details of her arrival—*Father: Kairon of the Road (jotunn), deceased; Mother: Parnella of the Leechless Swamp (swamper elf), deceased; taken in at age five years and two months, orphaned. Shade & Shadowweaver.*

That answered one of my lingering questions. Allure had been old enough to remember her family when she arrived at the Brotherhood. No wonder she had clung so tightly to the bracelet her mother had gifted her.

"It should be earlier," I told them. "She was the youngest in her group."

"Like me!" Quell cried delightedly. The rest of us shushed him again.

Svelte, who was holding the book, didn't turn the page right away. "Do we think," she asked in halting tones, "that Sister Allure made the shadow-beast?"

Quell's eyes popped impossibly wide, magnified by his glasses. "Oh. *Oooh!* Do you think she's trying to steal our *Aidea* in our sleep?"

"If she wanted to, she could have done that by now," Svelte pointed out.

"Unless..." Quell finally dropped his voice to a true whisper, jabbing one finger at Blare's back as he did so. "Unless that's what she was trying to do the other night...?"

Svelte bit her lip, and the three of us turned to Blare. He was seated with his back to us, fully engrossed in his book once more.

"You might be right," Svelte admitted.

"But we have no proof of anything," I told them. "And I still need to know what Brother Reticent could do."

We flipped back farther, passing Sister Humble—who had been almost four when she was deposited with the brothers—and finally found the entry for Steadfast. The few words on the page were enough to break my heart.

Father: Ikeno of the Road (jotunn); Mother: Clarion of Kinmore (human); taken in during infancy, unwanted. Another hand had later offered the addendum, *Lightweaver.*

I stared down at the names. As I did so, I experienced a sensation that I had never known until that moment. There were people I detested, people who drove me to distraction, people I could utterly condemn. But the only time that I had ever hated anyone as fiercely as I hated those two strangers had been when I was swept up in the summoning of the Crone back on Kovin Isle. The dead goddess had every reason to hate the Fenguards, but I only had one reason to despite Clarion and Ikeno so utterly. *Unwanted.* These two people had created my dearest friend, and then they'd thrown him away like so much rubbish.

Unwanted.

If I had ever doubted the wisdom of bringing the children into this, that was the moment that proved I'd made the right choice. Harmony had told Emerald as much, but seeing the words written down might well have broken his heart.

They were dangerously close to breaking mine. Did he even know their names?

"Vagabond?" Svelte asked, probably not for the first time.

"Sorry." I pulled myself from my stupor. "What were you saying?"

"I was asking if I should look earlier." Svelte was giving me a funny look, but I had no way to reassure her. Despite my usual obsession with my appearance, I had no idea what sort of expression I'd been making when I stared down at Emerald's entry.

"Oh, I... yes, probably." I folded my hands behind my back and tried to look attentive.

Svelte flipped back another page, and moved to flip back again, but I stopped her.

"What's going on there?" I asked, nodding to the entry near the bottom of the page.

"Where?" she asked.

I pointed to one that appeared to be inked out. The whole line was blurry, as if someone had smudged it before the ink dried.

"I don't know what you mean," she said. She pointed to the line above it. "This one's for Sister Mindful, and just below it..." Her finger dropped two lines. "This one says Brother Cumbersome."

"What about the one between them?"

Quell leaned over at a precarious angle that threatened to send him toppling to the floor. "I can't read it."

Svelte squinted at the page. "That's funny... it's like I can't see it when I'm not looking right at it."

"Did someone use *Aidea* on a book?" I asked.

"Maybe." Quell reached out to drag one finger across the page, right below the line that none of us could quite make out. "I didn't see it, either, until you mentioned it."

I wasn't sure I'd have noticed it if I wasn't watching for anything out of place. When I skimmed the entries at random, my eyes passed right over that line, as if it wasn't there at all.

"It's like someone erased him," I muttered to myself.

Svelte shivered. "That's scary. Who would want to do something like that?"

Quell voiced my next thought before it was fully formed. "Who would be able to? I'm not sure what kind of *Aidea* it would take to work a charm like that, but I doubt there are many people who know how, especially not *here*. Do you think it was Modest?"

"Why would Brother Modest do this to a line in one of his own books?" Svelte asked.

Why, indeed? My young friends had the makings of capable investigators, but once again, I'd encountered a dead end. What was I supposed to do now?

Blare made a noise at the back of his throat and waved us over. Quell and I went, but Svelte stayed put, leafing through the pages of the register.

"What did you find?" Quell asked.

Blare pointed to an entry in the book. It was much older than the register, bound in a crumbling leather cover, with paper so brittle that it threatened to crack beneath his fingers.

Look at this, he signed.

The page he'd opened to included the heading, *An Enchantement for thee Nullification of Ye Aidea.*

"This is old," Quell said in wonder.

Blare was more interested in the contents of the book that the pages themselves. *Do you think this is what Sister Allure is doing to people?*

I gasped and leaned over him. "What does it say?"

It's a long entry, he told me. *And the spelling's funny. Some of the words aren't right, either.*

Quell bit his lip and rocked on his hooves before turning to me. "Would this help you?" he asked.

"It might," I admitted. "It seems more useful than anything we learned from the register."

"We could take it back to the room," Quell said.

My eyebrows show up. "Is that a good idea?"

"Even if Modest notices that it's missing, he won't know that it was us that took it," Quell pointed out. "We could hide it under the floorboards. With the treasure trove."

It was a daring move, but out of everything I'd scrounged up, Blare's random searching had produced the most interesting clue yet. Perhaps this dusty old tome could offer more insight into Allure's ritual. I felt the excitement that I'd experienced on a few previous occasions, when the threads of a mystery began to weave together.

"Bring it," I told them.

The boys got to their feet and began debating the merits of how to transport the book, while I turned back to Svelte. She was still looking at the register, and I suspected that she was making the same face I had when I read Emerald's entry.

"Svelte?" I asked.

She slammed the book shut and placed it back on Modest's desk, spinning it back into its original position. "We should get going," she said. She seemed desperate not to have to meet my eyes.

Blare ended up with the stolen book stuffed under his shirt, while Quell carried the lantern again. We locked the door from the inside before closing it once more, and set off down the hall in a little cluster.

"What were you looking at?" I asked Svelte as we trailed behind.

She walked heavily, with her arms crossed over her chest and a miserable expression plastered to her face. "I wanted to see what they put for Blare," she whispered. "I shouldn't have done it, but Brother Steadfast's entry made me a really sad, and I already knew what *mine* would say."

I nodded, recalling her earlier episode, and Modest's subsequent disdain. I did not ask about Blare's entry. I wasn't sure how he'd feel if he knew that Svelte had looked, but I was pretty sure I had no business knowing.

"I shouldn't have," she repeated. "It's just been a really long day."

We were halfway back to the room, and the boys had pulled well ahead of us by the time she spoke again.

"How can they say that?" she whispered. "*Unwanted.* Just because the horrible people who happened to be his parents don't want him doesn't mean that none of the rest of us do. He's my best friend. Before you and Quell came, it was only the two of us for ages."

The lamp was too far ahead of us, and the shadows warped and twisted around us, coming to life.

"We both know better than that book," I told her. "Now, come on. We should catch up."

We both broke into a run. My feet didn't so much as whisper against the floorboards, but I was less concerned about being caught mid-heist than I was about the shadows that nipped at my heels, just in case any of them were alive.

CHAPTER
TWENTY-ONE

[*You should see the book we found,*] I told Emerald over breakfast.

[*Oh?*] He settled next to me with the tray Humble had passed him from the kitchen. I had caught the significant look that she'd given him when they crossed paths, the subtle shake of his head, the pinch of disappointment on her pursed lips. As much as anything else, she probably wanted an explanation for why I'd gone so quiet the day before.

[*Quell found a book with a spell in it that can nullify peoples' Aidea.*]

With his spoon halfway to his mouth, Emerald choked on empty air. He thumped his fist against his chest with such force that Brother Harmony glanced up in alarm.

"Are you quite all right?" he asked.

"Went down the wrong pipe," Emerald wheezed.

Harmony's eyes flicked from Emerald's face to the spoon where the first bite of his meal still lingered. "Careful," he said, and went back to his meal.

[*I was surprised, too,*] I told Emerald. [*I wonder if it used to be in the library...*]

[If what did?] Emerald asked.

I resisted the urge to sigh extravagantly. *[The book I was telling you about, with the Aidea nullification spell! Maybe Allure found it in the library, but Modest took it away?]*

Emerald was about to put the spoon in his mouth at last, but he stopped short and dropped his arm to the table with a heavy thump. *[Crimson, did you break into Modest's office?]*

[That's not the point,] I told him. *[The point is, it might be able to tell us what Allure is doing during her ceremonies...]*

"Is everything all right?" Harmony asked Emerald.

Em offered an off-kilter smile. "I'm just a bit tired this morning."

"Mm." Harmony glanced around the table. Emerald was not the only one doing poorly that morning. Svelte yawned between every other bite, and Quell seemed to be in danger of falling asleep face-first in his porridge. Blare sat with his gaze unfocused, staring off into the middle distance.

When his eyes landed on me, I let out something in between a yawn and a burp, which was the best I could do on short notice.

"We had a trying day yesterday," he said at last. "I think we will cancel lessons for the afternoon. We'll reconvene for lunch as usual, and then the rest of you will return to your rooms."

Blare blinked himself back to the present. *No lessons?* he signed.

"I expect you to use this time to recuperate," Harmony said magnanimously. "I want you all recovered and attentive during the ceremony tomorrow."

"The ceremony?" I asked.

"Yes, Vagabond." Harmony's voice was polite but clipped. "You missed the last one, but every week our beloved Sister Allure removes the stain of *Aidea* from one supplicant. After yesterday's... events, I think it best if we are all on our best behavior." He nodded meaningfully to Svelte, who sunk down on the bench.

Are you worried that Modest is going to punish Svelte? Blare asked.

Harmony's stony expression softened ever so slightly. "No, I will see to it that nothing of that nature happens tonight. You have my word."

And oddly enough, I believed him. When it came to the children, I suspected he would do whatever he thought was right.

Trouble was, I didn't trust his code of ethics when it came to other matters.

[How convenient,] I thought to Emerald. *[We'll have plenty of time to read the book before the ceremony tomorrow.]*

Emerald finally got his spoon to his mouth. *[What book?]*

[Are you quite serious? I've already told you! The book we found in Modest's office! The one with the—]

The one with the nullification spell. Our biggest clue to date. How could Emerald have forgotten so quickly?

Probably for the same reasons he kept forgetting the shadow-beast.

THE INSTANT we were left alone in our dormitory, the four of us scrambled over to the loose board and retrieved the ancient book from where it lay atop the treasure trove. The board was put back in place, and we piled onto my bed, beneath the crack in the ceiling.

"Let me read it," Quell begged.

"You little book-wyvern," Svelte said fondly, "of course you want to be the one to read it. Go on, then."

Quell flipped open the book. It was much too big for his lap, so he sat directly beside Blare. That way, not only could the back cover rest on Blare's knee, but he could read the pages for himself as Quell spoke aloud to Svelte and me.

"All right, blah blah, a bunch of stuff we already know," Quell said as he skipped through the lengthy entry. "There's all the usual stuff, all the reasons people would want to get rid of their *Aidea...* although, this is interesting. I don't think this book is one of Guise's."

"What do you mean?" I asked.

Quell's index finger skimmed over the pages. "It doesn't talk about conforming and all that. It's just got the practical stuff. You know, how Lightweavers go blind if they use their skills too much, or Mentalists can start to forget things if they mess with other people's memories too often."

I thought back to Harmony's collection of gifts, the offerings from former students. They could be more than mementos. To him, they might be a test... if he started to forget things, he would know when his wall of bric-a-brac stopped being familiar. "That makes sense," I said.

"Arcticians start running fevers, or get frostbite even in summer." Quell skipped a few lines as he went in search of something. "Stone-feathers can get so light they'll blow away in a high breeze, or their bones can snap under their own weight... Oof, that's awful, Blare, don't do that. And Sonicists..." Quell, who had been reading each item off of his list with a mixture of delight and horror, fell suddenly silent.

"Oh, we know that one," Svelte said. "You can go deaf if you use your gift too much. I'm telling you, that's why you always need to be so loud about things. In a year or two, you're going to need one of those ear horns." She hunched her shoulders, held up an invisible trumpet to one ear, curled the other as if holding a cane, and dropped her voice to a quavering and comical imitation of an elderly man. "Hello, you young whippersnappers, what did you say? Speak up!"

Blare chuckled at Svelte's antics, but Quell's eyes were still glued to the page.

"Not just you," he murmured.

Svelte cocked her head.

"Not just you," he repeated, dazed. "It can affect the people around you." Quell shuddered, then turned to Blare, signing frantically as he spoke. "What if I made your hearing worse? You're in the bed right next to mine, and we spend a lot of time together..."

Blare rested one hand over Quell's until the lambkin quieted. *My hearing wasn't much better when I arrived. If anything, it's a blessing for our friendship, because you have to work that much harder to annoy me.* He was smiling, but Quell wasn't.

"Keep reading," Svelte urged.

Quell gulped and turned back to the book. "R-right. Um, so there's all that. And—"

"Does it say anything about Shades?" I asked. "What happens to them?"

"Uh." Quell's eyes flicked around the page until he found what he was looking for. "There it is, Shades. Says they start to fade out of existence."

"Ugh, this all sounds awful." Svelte crossed her legs and let her elbows rest on her knees. "I don't like it when the brothers get all weird about the *Aidea*, but maybe they do have a point about parts of it. None of these things sound good."

Skip to the ceremony, Blare signed. *This is depressing.*

Quell turned the page, moving gingerly so as not to break the brittle old paper. "Okay, here we go," he said. "It looks like you need a group of people with complimentary *Aidea*, whatever that means. And then those people... *fit in a ringe?* Oh, got it, *sit in a ring,* and then..." He narrowed his eyes and squinted down at the page. "Um."

"What?" Svelte bent forward.

"I'm not sure. It's hard to read." Quell shook his head. "I don't think it's even Osmarian. Maybe really, really old Osmarian. There are a couple of charts, but I don't know what they're trying to show."

"Is the whole rest of it like that?" she asked.

See for yourself. Blare spun the book around for us to read.

Svelte sighed. "Too bad," she said. "We stole this whole book for nothing."

I disagreed. As the other children turned through the next few pages, exclaiming over a familiar word here or a turn of phrase there, I held my silence.

They couldn't read the language in that book, but Emerald could, and by extension, so could I.

The nuance of the spell was lost on me, but I understood the charts well enough. At least four participants were required, and through a set of steps, they would activate their *Aidea*—and subsequently banish it.

One of the final images was particularly arresting. It lacked the detail of modern illuminated manuscripts, but the artist had managed to capture the intensity of the ceremony, with each of the participants seated in a circle, hands clasped, backs bowed and mouths opened as their *Aidea* joined together in the center of the ring they'd formed.

It looked uncannily like what I'd seen on our first night at the monastery, except that in that case, there had been only one person controlling the *Aidea:* Sister Allure.

QUELL SPENT the rest of the morning poring over the old book. Svelte, Blare, and I spoke in hushed whispers so that, should one of the brothers happen to be passing through the hall, they wouldn't overhear us.

"What does any of this have to do with the shadow man?" Svelte asked me.

I had been lost in a daydream of what it would look like to have four *Aideas* activated at once. I had no idea how powerful Brigane had been, relatively speaking, but she'd managed to cause a great deal of chaos during her ceremony. What would it be like to have all four of them going together? A Vulcanist, a Shade, a Lightweaver, and... whatever the hells Reticent was?

Unless he's the one with the ability to control memories, I thought suddenly. *I was so sure it was Brother Harmony! But then again, if they tried the ceremony, it didn't work. Emerald and Humble still have their powers, and presumably Allure does, too.* I was missing something important, and the only person who could answer it was one person I hadn't identified. Harmony was still here. Allure had never left. Humble had returned only a few months ago, and Emerald—

I jumped. "Tell me again when you started seeing the shadow," I said. "It was a blob at first, right?"

"That's right." Svelte nodded. "It was just a weird smudge on the walls."

"When did this start?" I asked. "In the spring, you said. Around the solstice?"

Blare shrugged. *Maybe. It was right around the same time Allure's ceremonies started. It was kind of hard to see back then, so I didn't worry about it at first.*

"Did it get sharper right away? Like it was feeding on whatever Allure is doing?"

Svelte paled, and the ruddy scatter of her freckles stood out sharp against her cheeks. "I don't think so. Oh, Guise's toes, can you imagine?"

It took months and months for it to get sharper, Blare said. *And then it happened all at once.*

"When?"

Two months, maybe?

Two months. That was when Humble had returned. I popped up out of bed and folded my hands behind my back, pacing the room the way Emerald always did when he was thinking hard. It had become my habit, too, although it probably looked a bit silly, given that I was currently two feet shorter and much more baby-faced than usual.

"And you didn't see it properly until after I arrived?" Or rather, after Emerald returned.

Not walking around like that, Blare confirmed. *It stayed on the walls until then.*

"What does that all mean?" Svelte asked.

I stopped short and turned to face them, lifting my pointed chin. "I'm not sure," I admitted. "I think I have an idea of how it was made, but I have no idea how to get rid of it."

Blare's mouth dropped open. *Really? Just from what we told you?*

"I've been... paying attention," I said. *I've been investigating this matter along with my companion and creator* would have been more accurate, but I couldn't tell them the full truth. Not because I didn't trust them, precisely. On one hand, they were very young, and on the other, they owed a great deal to the brotherhood. It would have been too easy for one of them to let information slip to the wrong people, either through accident, coercion, or confession.

"Are you going to tell us?" Svelte asked. "We want to help."

You don't have to, Blare signed.

"What?" Svelte socked him in the shoulder so hard he nearly rolled off the bed. "Come on, I picked a lock for them! We stole a book! The least they can do is tell us the truth."

I don't think they can, Blare signed, before rubbing his shoulder and blowing a raspberry at her.

"Why not?" Svelte demanded.

"Because they're not who they say they are." Quell looked up from his book, and for once, he spoke in a proper whisper.

"I—what?" I backed away a step. Svelte seemed as confused as I was, but Blare nodded in agreement.

"Think about it." Quell closed the book and slipped it under his pillow. "Have you *ever* seen Vagabond touch anything? They don't snore, they always wait until we're going out so that they won't have to touch the door themselves, and they've never woken up in the night to use the privy. Not *once*. I can always hear you two when you do."

"Er," I said, stalling ineffectually for time.

You're right. Blare's eyes lit up. *I never noticed! I thought it was weird that they never cried about their family, or got so mad they broke something. Most kids can't stop doing one of those two things, at least for the first week or two. When my parents left me here, I could barely get out of bed for meals.*

"That, too," Quell agreed.

"What!?" Svelte threw her hands in the air. "I never noticed anythi—" She gasped and swiveled her head toward me. "Your breath! You came into the frozen room the other day, and your breath didn't cloud! Your *Aidea* wouldn't explain that."

"Oh, dear." I drooped, unable to come up with a suitable explanation that would excuse all of my many missteps. I had thought myself so clever, but there were an abundance of details which I had entirely forgotten, or never known in the first place. Besides, how was I supposed to make enough noise going to and from the privy to wake a sleeping boy? I couldn't even turn the latch.

"So what are you?" Quell asked me. "I assumed you were a ghost, but I didn't want to be rude about it."

A ghost? Blare wrinkled his nose. *I thought maybe they were some sort of spirit sent by Guise to prove that Allure's been lying about her abilities. But then they kept dragging Guise's name through the mud, so I wasn't sure...*

Svelte shook her head. "No way. Not after how nice they were to me yesterday."

All of them turned to me, waiting for me to tell them who and what I was.

"Well..." I said slowly. "I'm not a ghost, that's for sure. And I'm *not* an emissary of Guise, either." *Perish the thought.* "I really am a cast-off, more or less. I don't know *what* I am. My father couldn't tell me."

All true, even if this confession required some elision of the facts.

"What about your mother?" Svelte asked, her voice laden with sympathy.

I thought briefly of Tincrown. "Haven't got one," I told her.

This elicited a round of sympathetic nods from the other children.

"So you're weird," Svelte said. "Like us."

"And you're *sure* you're not a ghost?" Quell asked. "Because you might not know if you were."

"I am quite confident that I'm not," I assured him. A near-death had gone into the making of me, but that was not the same thing.

"Then the rest of it doesn't matter." Svelte sat back and looked down her nose at me. "You're one of us. Isn't that right, boys?"

Both of them nodded.

And nobody looks out for us but us, Blare signed.

AFTER LUNCH, Quell didn't return with us to the room. Emerald had been particularly distracted during the meal, and when I asked him about it, he merely put me off. Both of them reappeared at dinner, Quell looking more solemn than I had ever seen him, and Emerald in higher spirits than he'd been in some time.

It was not until the children had gone to bed that I was able to flit through the halls of the Brotherhood and question him properly.

"You could have just explained what's going on," I scolded him once I'd rearranged myself back into human form.

"You won't tell me what you've been up to," he replied. "Besides, you'll see why I decided to go alone." Before I could ask where he'd gone, he indicated my appearance. "How are you doing that?"

I turned to the mirror, not sure what I would find, and stopped in my tracks. My attire was plain enough, positively drab by my standards, but my face was what he had remarked on.

Previously, I had only ever managed to appear as Simon or Simone, who could have easily passed for twins. My appearance as Simon could be altered within certain parameters, as could the appearance of Simone: clothes, hairstyle, makeup, and the like could be exchanged with hardly a thought, but the rest was fixed.

I did not recognize the person staring back at me from Emerald's dingy little mirror, but I knew them well. I was somewhere in between my two usual faces, with Simon's square jaw, Simone's full lips, her shallower brow, and his dusting of stubble.

"I don't know," I said, delighted, "but I like it."

My self-examination was interrupted by a furtive knock at the door, and I jumped back against the wall.

[I'll go,] I thought, and prepared to rearrange into my moth-self.

"It's me," hissed a woman's voice from the far side of the door.

I widened my eyes, and Emerald winked before opening the door just wide enough to let Humble slip through the crack.

She took one look around the cramped room and wrinkled her nose. "Gods above," she muttered, "it stinks like wet wool. Was that a lambkin's bed?"

"Sister Subtle's, apparently," Emerald agreed.

Humble made a disgusted noise. "I remember her. She was *awful.* She was with that group that used to bully Allure. What happened to her? Did they finally decide that she was too petty for even the Brotherhood and send her away?"

Emerald cleared his throat delicately. "She was a lambkin, Humble."

"That's what I just said!"

"And we left to join the Conjury nearly two decades ago."

"So?" Humble crossed her arms. Then a look of understanding passed over her face. "Oh, goodness. Speaking ill of the dead, am I?"

Emerald nodded.

"Well, too bad. She was still awful." Humble rolled her eyes as she dropped onto the edge of the bed. "So, you wanted to talk?" She didn't so much as glance at me.

"Yes," Emerald said, in the tone of one who would *really* rather not. In her presence, his good mood had abated. "I apologize for not speaking to you earlier."

Humble exhaled in a joyless laugh. "I know you don't like me, Steady. But once again, we need to work together. I've told you most of what I know."

Emerald lifted an eyebrow. "Summarize."

"Oh, in the name of Pulchradune—"

"You follow Pulchradune?" Emerald asked.

"I do now," Humble snapped. "Why?"

[Who's Pulchradune?] I asked.

"The god of fairness in all its forms, Pulchradune the Ideal." Emerald snorted. "I suppose that's a natural choice for you."

"Who do you follow?" Humble shot back. "Wait, let me guess. Odologys? Cydnei?"

[Is she insulting you by making rude guesses about what gods you follow?] Humble was certainly interesting. In another course of events, I might have liked her, but I could hardly take her side when she was antagonizing my friend, and not in a fond sort of way.

"Doesn't matter," Emerald said. "Not that there's anything wrong with Odologys, and I *do* approve of the Odological method. We're managing just fine on our own, so if you want our help, *summarize.*"

"You don't have to pretend that thing's real," Humble said. "Not with me, Steady."

Emerald looked askance at me.

[For the sake of this investigation, this one *time, you may pretend that I am a magical dummy.]*

Emerald's lip twitched. *[You're always a magical dummy, Crimson. Never doubt yourself.]*

Humble, meanwhile, had given in. "Fine. I've mostly talked with Allure, who seems to genuinely believe that she's working on Guise's behalf. Whoever messed with our memories seems to have messed with hers as well. There are gaps we can't fill in."

"You *asked* her?" Emerald curled his lip. "Not exactly top-notch sleuthing, Hum."

"Oh, shove it." Humble made a rude gesture. "The 'top-notch sleuth' the Conjury *really* wanted couldn't be found. They'd been looking for you for ages by the time they reached out to me, and this isn't what I'm trained for."

"What *are* you trained for?" he asked in disgust.

A sudden flush rose in Humble's cheeks. "Important Conjury work."

"*Deskwork.*" Emerald sniffed. It was hard to imagine the children I was living with sniping at each other in this manner, but I had already gotten the impression that Emerald and Allure hadn't fit in seamlessly with their more conventionally attractive siblings.

"Because what you do is *soooo* impressive. Whatever. Yes, I spoke to Allure, and I've watched loads of her ceremonies, and it's obviously *working.* I'm not sure if it's her doing or if it's coming from that box she carries around or what, but it's real. I'm not even sure what's *in* the box."

Emerald frowned, and his lips moved slightly.

[Ashes,] I told him. *[It's ashes.]*

"It's ashes," he said aloud.

"Oh, that's right. You told me that, didn't you?" Humble rubbed one temple, using her other hand to prop her upright against the bedframe where she said. "I hate this."

"So do I," Emerald agreed, and although his tone was causal, the full force of his distress swept through our connection like a tidal wave.

"That's all I've worked out, anyway," she said. "Or at least, that's all I can hold on to. What about you?"

[I need to ask her something,] I told Em.

[That's what you're here for.]

[I need you to ask her... word for word, mind you, since you can't seem to hold the thought in your head for more than two

seconds. Ask her if she's ever heard of a book with an** Aidea **nullification spell?]

"Have you ever," Emerald asked, "heard of a book with an *Aidea* nullification spell?"

There was just a moment in which I was sure that Humble knew. Something in her eyes, perhaps—a momentary clarity, followed by a widening of her pupils and confused twitch of her lips. She had gotten close to something, closer than Emerald had, but then it was gone.

I couldn't see the magic that peeled the thought out of her mind again, not the way I'd seen Allure's power draped around her like a veil, but its effects were obvious enough. There had been a time when Humble could have answered my question. Now she could only shake her head. "What did you say?" she asked.

"I... don't know." Emerald rubbed his hands over his face. "Blast it, that must mean we're close."

[Ask her something else for me,] I urged.

"Humble." Emerald dropped his hands, repeating my next question aloud. "If you were going to do a ritual, a *secret* ritual, here in the compound, where would you hold it?"

"In a tent with hundreds of witnesses," she deadpanned.

Emerald glared.

Humble whistled and slapped one hand across her thigh. "Tough crowd, geesh. If I was going to do something big, something powerful, something that would get me in a lot of trouble with Brother Harmony..."

"It would have to be somewhere private," Emerald said.

"Mm. Somewhere that nobody else would go." Humble squinted down at her toes. "Someplace where sound wouldn't carry."

I had to fight down the urge to slap my own forehead. There was one place that I had been eager to see since the day we arrived, and which Emerald kept casually avoiding. We'd always had a good reason not to go, or a distraction to keep us busy... but that was how the enchantment on Emerald's memory worked, after all. It was subtle enough that even I hadn't noticed until that very moment.

[The catacombs,] I told Emerald.

"The catacombs," Emerald repeated. When he slapped his palm to his own forehead, my own itch was satisfied.

"Of course! The catacombs!" Humble cried. "There'd be nobody around to bother me. Nobody alive, at least. It's quiet down there. Creepy. It's the one place nobody ever goes."

"*We* should go," Emerald said without prompting. "Tomorrow night, after the ceremony, when everyone's asleep."

"Fine with me." Humble got to her feet. "I would say that it's been lovely chatting, Steady, but I'm not a liar."

"Which might make you the only honest person in Venta Bulgarum," Emerald replied.

Humble laughed, and then she seemed annoyed with herself for having done so. She slipped back out of the room, leaving the two of us alone once more. Emerald locked the door after she was gone.

"I take it you learned something after all?" he asked me.

"I did." I moved for the first time since Humble entered the room. "Talking about it does no good, though. But I might be able to show you, in the mind-cottage."

Emerald sat down on the bed, in the spot Humble had just vacated, and a few moments later, we were standing in the mind-cottage, facing the wall where Emerald's door usually appeared.

"I need you to try and remember a book," I told him. "There's a spell in it, one that I think you did... or tried to do. A nullification spell."

"Like the one Allure does?"

I nodded.

Emerald stared at the wall, his face pinching in concentration. We had to repeat the exercise several times, since he kept forgetting what he was looking for, but at last, a door appeared.

My relief was short lived. No matter how many times we reached for the handle, regardless of how hard I threw myself against the wood, the door wouldn't budge. I finally succeeded in summoning a metal bar, which I used as a wedge between the door and its frame, pulling until the muscles in my arms screamed with an unfamiliar pain. At long last, I managed to pry the door off its hinges, which succeeded in impressing Emerald.

That was the only success. Behind the door was nothing but the wall. Whatever Emerald had once known about the spell was now so thoroughly buried that, even in a world of my own creation, I could not recover it.

"At least that means you're onto something," Emerald said in his approximation of comfort.

I was not soothed. Above me, the crack in the ceiling of the mind-cottage yawned, a vivid reminder that the haven of my mind offered no safety from the malignant darkness that saturated every shadow in the compound.

"Can you remember anything about Allure's shadow *Aidea*?" I asked.

Emerald wrinkled his nose before reaching for the doorknob again. This time, it turned easily. "It seems I can," he said. "Let's see what's in there."

I hoped for some clue about the origins of the shadow-beast, but what I found instead was infinitely more heartbreaking. I stopped just outside the doorway, still safely in my own memory. On the far side, Steadfast lay in his bed next to a smiling Allure. They were young, perhaps seven and five respectively. Allure must have been new to the compound. Steadfast held the green marble above his head, using it to project a light show onto the ceiling. He was telling her a story, which appeared to feature four children whose brilliant figures stood out brightly against the plaster. The words he spoke seemed to come from underwater, and I could not make them out from this side of the door. Allure giggled and held up one hand, opening and closing it like a mouth. On the ceiling above them, a shadowy dragon swooped into the picture, and the little figures readied themselves for battle.

"On second thought," I said, "perhaps I don't need to see this one."

There were some things that a fellow should be able to keep private, even from his imaginary friends. I closed the door instead, leaving this one happy memory untouched.

TWENTY-TWO

Quell was absent again after breakfast, and when Svelte checked, the book was missing from its place under the floorboards. It wasn't under Quell's pillow, either.

"Do you think he told Modest about it?" I fretted.

"And sell us all out to him? No way." Svelte leaned back against her pillow. "I bet he came up with some clever plan to get it back where it belongs without getting in trouble. He's smart, and everyone thinks he's so innocent, being a lambkin and all."

I huffed. "I thought we'd just go back into Modest's office and float it back up onto the shelf where it came from."

Doesn't work like that, Blare signed. *I can make things light, and I can do little things to manipulate density, but I can't make things float.* Just to prove his point, he reached into the cavity beneath the floorboards and pulled out Emerald's old green marble. When he tossed it into the air, it hovered in place for a few seconds before wafting down into his palm. After dropping it back into the stash of old toys and trinkets, he added, *I'm not very good at it, either. There are people who can do really interesting stuff with their powers, but nobody will teach me.*

"And by interesting, I'm sure you mean evil in the eyes of Guise." Svelte snickered.

The two of them were in a reasonably good mood, and neither had made any allusion to what I'd told them about myself the day before. I felt more than a little guilty for hiding the truth from them. Svelte had been almost painfully honest with me about *her* circumstances, and the hints I'd gotten of the boys' pasts were painful enough. I wished I could come clean to them. It would have been a relief for someone else to know. Someone who wasn't a whole ocean away.

Oh, dear, I was missing Tincrown. Emerald's mooning was bad enough. We couldn't *both* pine after him.

Their good mood soured slightly when Quell was not at lunch, and he didn't attend our afternoon classes either.

Halfway through Harmony's lecture on the virtues of dressing in uniform, Svelte's hand shot up.

"Yes, Svelte?" Harmony asked in his I'm-trying-to-be-patient-but-you're-testing-me voice.

"Where's Quell?" she asked.

"Quell has other obligations today," Harmony said.

"*Obligations?*" Svelte echoed as she lowered her hand. "He's *two*."

"He is seeking religious guidance with the member of our order best equipped to offer it," Harmony said.

My head whipped toward Emerald. ***[Do you know what he's talking about?]***

Emerald's brows pinched together. ***[No. I did see Harmony talking with Quell yesterday afternoon, but he didn't tell me why.]***

My anxiety increased as the evening's ceremony approached. The shadow-beast hadn't made an appearance in the room since Quell pulled the bag of bones from the ceiling, but rather than allow me to relax, the absence only left me more nervous. It would return, I was sure of that, and in the meantime, someone would lose their *Aidea.*

At least it was by choice. The people who went to Allure didn't want their magic, so who was I to insist that they keep it?

The weather was somewhat better than it had been the week

before, and the mud beneath our feet had dried and hardened into packed earth. Last time, I'd been able to safely ride along on Emerald's shoulder. This time, I was forced to walk amid the shifting throng, all while trying to avoid people passing through me.

I was relieved when Svelte positioned herself on one side of me, and Blare wedged himself on the other. Together, they formed a protective barrier between me and the people milling around us. With Harmony and Emerald walking behind us, I was effectively surrounded.

"Thank you," I whispered, adding a hand sign for Blare's benefit.

We found seats near the front, close to the waiting fire. Now that I knew what to expect, perhaps I should have been calmer, but my nerves were frayed. After this ceremony, we would enter the catacombs at last, where we would hopefully find answers about Reticent, and the shadow-beast, and the origins of Allure's power.

I'm getting worried, Blare signed beside me. *Where's Quell? Why isn't he here?*

At least the two obnoxious gentlemen who'd been sitting behind Emerald last week were conspicuously absent. I craned my neck to look for them, but they were nowhere to be found.

Perhaps their stolen buttons paid for their way out of Kinmore, I mused bitterly. Instead of them, I found Brigane on the far side of the crowd, wan but smiling. Happy, it seemed, to be freed from her burden.

I was still studying her when Svelte let out a horrified little cry and clapped her hands over her mouth. Two figures had entered the tent, padding barefoot along the aisle. One was dressed in white, her dark skin luminous in the firelight, her expression bordering on the beatific. Allure's earlier self-assurance had been restored.

The other was Quell.

"No no no no *nononono...*" Svelte breathed. She rocked toward Blare, who reached for her hand.

[Emerald?] I asked.

[I didn't know,] he replied at once.

I couldn't make sense of it. Quell's attitude gave no indication that he'd been made to participate against his will. He walked with his back straight and his rounded chin held high. And yet, only a week ago on our first meeting, he'd told me that he would never consider getting rid of his *Aidea.*

Why? Blare signed.

"It was that book," Svelte murmured into the suddenly still room. "It was that *horrible book.*"

Allure and Quell reached the center of the room, flanking the fire. Allure carried the box of ashes in one arm. She set it down before addressing the room, which once again had fallen still as they watched her.

"Brothers and sisters," she said. Her voice carried through the space, reaching every eager ear. "Tonight, you will witness something special. One of Guise's own, one of his *chosen* children, offers up his burden as a sacrifice." She turned to Quell, bending toward him with a kindly smile. "Tell them, little brother. Tell them why you're here."

Quell was trembling. His little hands were balled into tight fists. When he spoke, his voice cracked and quavered, but it was even louder than Sister Allure's.

"I know that *Aidea* comes with some risk. It can hurt its, um, its *host.* But yesterday I learned that my *Aidea* might be hurting my... my family." His large eyes glistened with unshed tears. "And nothing's more important to me than my family."

At the far end of our bench, Brother Modest coughed disapprovingly. No doubt he thought that Quell should put his love of Guise first.

I really didn't care what he thought.

The pieces fell into place, much to my dismay. Quell had been the one to answer Emerald's questions about the history of the Brotherhood and their hatred of the *Aidea.* When he'd read that his abilities might be harming Blare...

"I don't want it anymore," Quell told Allure. "I don't want to make things worse."

"Oh, little brother." Allure knelt before him, so that the two of them were eye to eye. She took his hands in hers and clasped them tightly. Even with an enormous audience, the scene they made was sweet and tender. And terrible, beneath the surface.

I thought of all those carved wooden faces in the ceiling of the prayer hall, scowling down on the present wards of the compound. Year after year, generation after generation, they passed their pain on to their successors with both hands, just as Allure was doing now, all cloaked under the guise of love.

"You are not making things worse," Allure assured Quell. "Your life has been hard, but it has molded you into something beautiful. Someone kind. It has made you selfless and gentle, and you deserve to have this great weight lifted from your shoulders." A smile crept onto her lips. "They are very small shoulders, but they have been sturdy enough to carry a burden that should never have been yours. Let me take it from you."

Svelte was still shaking her head and clinging to Blare, but Quell never once turned his head to see what his family thought of this idea. Instead, he held onto Allure.

"Show me what you can do, little brother," Allure whispered. "Let me hear."

It began as a gentle thrum, like the sound of a bird's wings. People around me jumped, looking down at the benches which rattled beneath them. Quell's lips parted, but I couldn't tell if the noise began within him or was coming from all around us.

Gradually, the note rose in pitch, until it became a hum, then a cry. It was so piercing that it cut through me. Svelte covered her ears with both hands and squeezed her eyes shut. On the benches around us, others did the same.

Only Blare left his hands resting slack in his lap. His eyes remained fixed on Quell as the sound around us rose to a roar, as if some great storm were raging inside the tent, so powerful that it made the poles rattle. Members of the congregation began screaming in pain, curling in upon themselves at the deafening noise.

I didn't bother. Covering my ears would do no good, after all, and I didn't have the anatomy required to feel pain. Quell's note was loud enough to drown out my thoughts, until it was so loud that I couldn't imagine the world without it.

Besides me, Emerald panted in pain and stuffed his fingers in his ears. He tried to think something to me, but I couldn't understand. There was no room in my head for anything but the crescendo of Quell's *Aidea*.

Blare shivered. Behind Allure, the fire flared white-hot, and once again, she seemed to grow as her shadow danced against the flames. She was a giantess, a minor goddess, the only star in a dark and terrible sky—

And then she was herself again, and the sound died away.

I was left sitting upright two spots away from Blare, who had never looked away. Svelte had her head in his lap and was bawling against her palms. The groans and whimpers of the audience rose up to fill the sudden silence.

Quell swayed on his hooves before collapsing into Allure's arms. She hugged him to her chest, cradling his head to her shoulder.

"It's all right, little brother," she said. Compared to the awful bluster of Quell's *Aidea*, her voice was a balm. "You're all right. You're safe now. It's over."

Over. Quell was now an ordinary lambkin. He no longer had *Aidea.*

He was no longer one of us.

Harmony had to all but carry Svelte back to our dormitory. She was inconsolable. Blare walked as though he were a puppet operated by a novice. Even Harmony, who I had expected to gloat about the whole affair, was somber.

"Why?" Svelte demanded when she was finally deposited on the edge of her bed.

"It was his choice," Harmony said softly. He pulled away from her and folded his hands in front of him. "This is what he wanted, Svelte."

"It isn't," she spat. "It's what you *told* him to want."

Harmony clicked his tongue. "Sister—"

She rolled away from him, taking the blanket with her. Once she was safely cocooned inside of it, she began to tremble.

Harmony sighed, and the lines around his mouth deepened. "Please don't freeze the room again," he said wearily.

[Crimson?] Emerald asked. ***[You're awfully quiet.]***

I lifted one shoulder and dropped it again. What was there to say? Quell's choice had been made, and his magic was gone. I couldn't say whether someone had altered his mind to force him into the decision, or whether he'd made it freely, but it was done all the same. It was over.

And I felt like an utter failure.

A faint rapping from the door caught all of our attention. Harmony opened it to reveal Allure and Quell standing on the other side.

"Good evening, brothers and sisters. And siblings," Allure added with a small smile in my direction. "You'll forgive me, but I'm exhausted. Brother Quell, we'll talk more tomorrow. Sleep well tonight." She dropped a kiss on his forehead before sweeping away down the hall.

Quell kept his eyes downcast. From where I sat, he looked sweaty and pale, almost gray.

"Are you all right, Quell?" Emerald asked.

The lambkin shook his head, then nodded. "Yes, sorry. I'm just tired. I've never used my *Aidea* like that before." He chuckled weakly. "And I suppose I never will again."

"You were very brave." Harmony approached him and patted his shoulder kindly. "I'm proud of you, Brother Quell. I know that it isn't easy to accept when change is required of us, but you did well. Very well indeed. Your reasons may not have been holy, but they were sincere."

"Thank you," Quell said.

"We need rest," Harmony told the group. He clapped his hands in front of him and summoned a smile that seemed halfhearted at best. "Good night, everyone. We can celebrate tomorrow."

What a sorry celebration *that* would be. Blare's eyes were blank, and Svelte had yet to reemerge from her blanket cocoon. Emerald and I held our tongues. I couldn't make sense of my friend's emotions any more than I could make sense of my own. Besides, our investigation of the catacombs loomed before us. We had larger concerns than the well-being of a single lambkin who had chosen his own fate.

Larger, but not more important. I had simply come to terms with the fact that what was done was done, and until we knew more, our hands were tied.

After another few moments of hemming and hawing, Emerald and Harmony withdrew. Quell was still standing near the door, where Allure had left him.

Blare was the first one to address him. *How do you feel?* he asked.

"A bit off," Quell admitted. "But like I said, I think it's just from using my *Aidea* so much—"

"*How could you!*" Svelte shot upright in the bed, shucking her blanket off. Her eyes were bloodshot, and the color was high in her cheeks. Her bottom lip wobbled as she threw one leg over the edge of the bed. "How could you do that to us?"

"Us?" Quell repeated.

"Yes!" She pointed one finger at Blare. "You think this is what he wanted? You think this was what any of us wanted?"

Svelte, please. Blare winced. *This isn't helping.*

"Nothing will help, after what he did, the fluffy little idiot! I thought you were smarter than this, Quell, I really did."

The lambkin's pallor was quickly giving way to a deep blush. He glared at his sister. I was tempted to intervene, but although I'd been deemed one of them, I didn't think it was my place to do so.

"It was my power," Quell snarled, with more ferocity than I could have imagined from a fellow of his size. "*I* was the one who gave it up. *I* was the one who didn't want it anymore! What does that have to do with you?"

"Don't you get it?" Tears streaked down Svelte's face. She made no effort to wipe them away. "You don't have magic anymore. You're not one of us. They're going to move you to another group, and it'll be just like Visage said. You'll be normal. You won't be one of us anymore." She choked on a sob. "They're going to take you away, and we'll lose you, just like we've lost everyone else."

Quell's stricken expression would have been comically dramatic on the stage, but even without a link to him like I had with Emerald, I knew that he was not acting. Svelte had hit him where it would hurt them most.

"That's not what I... I didn't..."

"You did," Svelte told him. "Like it or not, you did." She turned her back on him and pulled the pillows over her head to block out the sound of our voices.

"That's not what I wanted." Quell's voice was soft now. Svelte's words had sapped his anger as thoroughly as Allure's ceremony had sapped his *Aidea*. "I was just worried about all of you. I didn't want to hurt you any more than I already had."

Blare's hands lay still in his lap. He wouldn't look at Quell, but he wouldn't look at Svelte, either.

"I didn't want to hurt *anyone*," Quell whined. He, too, climbed into his bed and pulled the sheets up, shrouding himself and his misery in his own little bubble.

In the lamplight, Blare's signing threw long shadows across the wall, shadows that seemed to come alive when his fingers moved. *You didn't need to change yourself,* he said. *Not for me.*

I sat there in the miserable dark and waited for them to fall asleep. The sooner we could go to the crypt, the better. Anything was better than this.

[Are you ready, Crimson?] Emerald asked through our connection.

Svelte was still sniffling, and the sheets tucked around Quell trembled. Blare had yet to close his eyes.

They'd worked out more than I intended already, so what was the point of pretending anymore.

[I'm on my way,] I said.

To Blare, I signed, *I have to go. I'm sorry. I'll be back.*

He didn't question me or accuse me of abandonment. All he responded with was, *Good luck.*

TWENTY-THREE

Humble was waiting for us by the doors to the crypt when we arrived.

"Are you actually going to insist on bringing your *assistant*?" she asked. "Waste of energy, if you ask me."

I had decided to remain Vagabond for the time being, in part so that if we were caught, I would be able to explain my presence more simply. I wasn't thrilled by the idea of arranging myself into a bland version of either Simon or Simone, either.

"It might be useful," Emerald told me.

I glared daggers at his back. *['It?']*

[Magical dummy,] he reminded me.

Of course he *would* remember that. How come he only seemed to remember the things that annoyed me, rather than anything useful?

"If you say so," Humble muttered, and turned to the doors.

Neither of us had entered the crypt since our arrival at the compound, and I had no idea what to expect. The stairs leading down to the lower level were wide enough for all three of us to walk side by side, and we did so, with Humble's lantern and Emerald's handful of enchanted chartreuse fire lighting the way.

"This place gives me the creeps," Humble hissed.

"Is that my fault?" Emerald asked. "We agreed to work together, Hum. You can go back if you want."

Humble made an irritated noise deep in her throat. "I didn't say I wanted to go back, did I? I can dislike something and still acknowledge that it needs to be done."

"Your sacrifices are noted," Emerald drawled.

"Oh, shut *up*. I was only making conversation."

"Complaints do not a conversation make."

Humble huffed and fell back a pace. "I'm sorry that my conversations aren't up to your *intellectually superior standards.*"

They were fully preoccupied with their bickering, but my attention was on the thick-cut stone slabs leading down into the earth. The *plink!* of dripping water echoed from somewhere far below, and the light threw strange reflections off the floor and the walls. Moisture, probably, but the sheen was thick and dark as oil, and it made the walls seem like the glistening gullet of some living thing that was swallowing us deeper with every step.

Humble was right. It *was* creepy. Even if Emerald didn't agree, I most heartily did.

I didn't think to count how many steps we'd descended until we'd lost sight of the doors through which we'd come. Something moved on the ceiling above me, and I nearly shrieked before realizing that it was only a spider scuttling between the heavy beams that supported the ceiling.

"Your poppet's getting jumpy," Humble noted, craning her neck forward so that she could see around Emerald and observe me.

"It's been acting up lately," Emerald said.

"I think it's your subconscious. I think *you're* jumpy, but you don't want to admit it, so it's coming out in your illusion." Humble smirked up at him.

Their endless needling wasn't helping with my nerves, and I was relieved when we finally reached the bottom of the steps and emerged into the main crypt. Down there, the ceiling was made of stone, supported with pillars that stood between the raised caskets. Stone tombs and faceless statues lined the floor in rows. Alternating capstones in the floor were inscribed with names and dates as well.

More of the brothers must be buried there, planted upright in little oubliettes designed to house their bones into eternity.

There was no sign of anything amiss, but panic gripped me. Fear that the dead would somehow return to life, cast the lids of their mausoleums aside, and clamber free, descending upon us in a furious horde, jealous of the lives we had that they did not.

Am I even alive? I might not be, I reminded myself. Still, the terror did not leave me. It took too long for me to realize that the fear wasn't mine, but Emerald's. I would never have guessed it from his impassive face, but *he* was the one who was afraid of being swarmed by the dead.

Funny, he'd never worried about anything like that when we were in Dyrne. Was this fear a new one, born of our misadventures in the Cronemire? Or an old one, leftover from childhood, which he thought he'd put behind him?

"What exactly are we looking for?" Humble asked. She was shivering, and her pale skin was prickled with gooseflesh. One arm was wrapped around her chest, but she needed the other to hold the lamp.

"Clues," Emerald grunted. He stepped deeper into the crypt, careful not to step on the engraved stones. To another eye, it might have looked like reverence, but I knew it was out of superstition that the dead brother might take offense and seek retribution for the sleight.

"*Clues.* Brilliant! I couldn't have worked that out for myself." Humble's sarcasm echoed through the cavernous room. "Pulchradune's useless nips, you're *exhausting.* It's a wonder you managed to keep any friends at all. Or have people given up on you by now, like I almost did?"

"Oh, please." Emerald snorted and shook his head. He shone his torch behind one of the moldering crypts. "You always thought you were better than us. You and Reticent both. We were never friends."

Humble began to laugh. It was an eerie sound, refracted by the damp walls and cold monuments, and it seemed to be coming at us from every direction. "We were *children,* Steady. We were trying to survive. We were told that we had one thing that made us valuable, *one thing.* Our ancestry. Our looks. Yes, I was an ass. But are you really going to hold a grudge after all this time? You, of all people?"

Emerald froze. "What do you mean, *me of all people?*"

"You got out!" Humble's voice cracked, and she let the hand holding her lantern fall. It illuminated her face from below, smoothing away the wear of years and transforming her, if only momentarily, into the semblance of the child she had been. "What favor do you think my ancestry got me? You think that I'm thriving in Venta Bulgarum? You truly believe that I'm serving alongside the Castcadesmen and the greatest powers in the land? I thought you were supposed to be *clever.*"

I recognized the bitterness in her voice, but I did not understand its source. Every memory that Emerald had shared with me made it clear that the tension between them had always existed, and that appearance and lineage had been at the heart of their mutual dislike. Sister Humble had mocked Steadfast for what he was, and even in adulthood, Emerald envied her.

"What do you mean?" I asked, when it became clear that Emerald was too stunned to do so.

"I'm a Vulcanist," she told him, presumably clinging to her theory that I was just an extension of Emerald's subconscious. "I control heat. Fire. But I don't have power. I'm talented enough to keep a kettle of tea hot, to warm a chafing dish, to light a cookfire. That's all. I can't make anything. I can't even destroy anything—and let's be honest, that's what the Conjury is best at. I'm nothing more than a glorified tea light. A pretty one, though." She bared her teeth in a sickly ruination of a smile. "A pretty girl with no power, raised by men who told me that the only thing that made me special was the very same thing that others would try to take from me."

Emerald was as weary as I'd ever seen him. "Humble..."

She shrank back from him, shaking her head, pain etched deep in the lines of her face. "You think you were the only one who ever hurt yourself, Steady?"

Emerald raised one eyebrow. "I don't see any scars."

"No," Humble growled. "You see what everyone else sees. You're supposed to be the one who looks past the surface of things. The greatest investigator in the land!" She threw her hands in the air. "That's what all the songs say!"

"How difficult it must be, to be liked for your looks, rather than hated on sight," Emerald growled. "I don't—"

[Em,] I said suddenly. *[Stop.]*

"Why?" he snapped, forgetting himself.

"Because Harmony told me to!" Humble screamed. She thumped her fists against her slender thighs. "Because he told me time and time and *time again that it was the only thing that mattered about me!*"

"What in every hell are you talking about?" Emerald demanded.

I knew, though. I had seen the thing that Emerald willfully ignored. I had seen Emerald avert his eyes when Harmony scolded Svelte for eating too much, for wanting too much. For *being* too much.

"I did exactly what I was told to do," Humble went on, "and I became what they promised I would be. Pretty, but worthless. Slim. Beautiful." When she lifted her head, her eyes burned in the darkness. "They hate you on sight, but they *want* me." Her voice rose in a sing-song lilt. "*Don't eat too much, Humble. Watch your figure, Humble. Too much dessert and they won't want to put their hands all over you when you're not looking, Humble, so you'd better put it back. A girl like you is only good for one thing. Better to be disposable than undesirable.*"

"Hum." Emerald blinked at her. "Hum, wait."

She shook her head. "You. Got. Out. Don't you think that I would trade my looks for yours in a *heartbeat* if it meant I could have your freedom? Your power? Do you think I wouldn't pay money for those power-hungry bastards in Venta Bulgarum to avert their eyes, if it meant keeping their hands off me? They put me to work in the *kitchen.* Harmony spent my whole childhood reminding me that I was only useful if I was pretty and slim, and when I came back, they *put me to work in the kitchen.* I'm so tired of the tests. I'm tired of thinking about every bite of food that passes between my lips, of watching my figure in the mirror to make sure I'm still the *right* kind of pretty. And when that's all said and done, when I'm exactly the thing they want me to be, I'm *still* supposed to hate myself for it."

Silence fell in the catacombs, apart from the distant trinkle of water eating away the mortar, and the hush of something small and unseen dragging its belly across the stones. A rat, perhaps. It seemed the perfect place for rats, and cockroaches, and all manner of despised beasts.

Emerald had created me so that I might speak on his behalf, but it was not my place. Humble knew what I was, even though I was more than a splintered fragment of my friend's mind, I was still made from him. My understanding of the world came from him, and when he was fundamentally wrong about its working order, I too would be wrong. I had taken it for granted that he knew Humble's story and believed that his version of events was correct.

I still believed that, but I was beginning to see that it was not the *only* correct version.

"I didn't know," Emerald murmured. "I didn't even think about it. I'm sorry, Hum."

She scoffed. "For what part? It has nothing to do with you, *Emerald Flame*. It only strikes me as a bit sad that a man of your reputation would still harbor such resentment toward a child. Sister Humble no longer exists. She hasn't existed for years. She's as dead as the monks in this miserable crypt. And for the record, just because my scars don't look the same as yours doesn't mean I don't have them."

She strode past him, her torch held above her head, lighting the way as she made her way deeper into the yawning maw of the catacombs. A few paces on, however, she paused to turn back.

"I'll forgive your ignorance," she said, "if you can forgive mine. For what it's worth, I'm sorry, too."

Humble plunged forward into the darkness, winding her way between memorials built to commemorate long-dead disciples of a god that had failed them both at every turn. Not for the first time, I pitied someone whose life was not as easy as Emerald assumed. I didn't believe that Humble was weak, or that her lack of control over the *Aidea* made her less valuable than my friend, only less lucky.

I pitied her because she was alone in the world. No one had thought to tell her that she mattered.

And more than ever, I hated what this place had done to the people it was supposed to protect.

The soles of Emerald's boots squealed against the damp pavers as he followed her. It was a long time before he spoke again. "You said she was dead."

Humble emitted the most put-upon sigh I had ever heard a person muster. "Who's dead, Steady?"

"Humble. You use a different name now, I suppose. What do you go by?"

She sucked her teeth for a moment before answering. "Calla," she said at last.

"Mm. Like the flower?"

She nodded.

"Pretty," Emerald said. "Suits you."

"Oh, piss off."

"I mean it. I like plants. Thought about naming myself Moss at one point, before I got the prominence title." Emerald dragged the fingers of one hand along the edge of a tomb. The lid depicted a man, carved from stone, lying in repose with his hands crossed over his chest. Like the statues of Guise, he had no face.

"Did you really?" Humble's—*Calla's*—voice had softened. "I would have thought you'd name yourself after a mushroom. Not the common name, either."

"Mycelius?" he suggested.

Calla stuck her finger in her mouth and gagged at a joke whose punchline evaded me, but I was glad that they'd arrived at something resembling peace.

"You asked what we're looking for," Emerald said. "The thing is, I don't have an answer. I'm sure there's something down here that will help, but I don't know what it is, because I can't remember long enough to work that out. I'm hoping that we'll know it when we see it."

During their squabble, I had been focused on the two of them, and since nothing had been asked of me, all I had to do was trail after them, silent as the ghost that Quell had assumed me to be. As their search continued, however, I spent more time looking around. I wasn't sure what I could offer, and like Emerald, I was waiting for something to jump out at me.

Metaphorically. I hoped. Emerald might be mindful of the dead lying entombed in the shadows, but I was more worried about the shadows themselves.

It was Calla who found our clue, if it could be called that. Emerald was examining one of the walls when she cried out.

"What are you doing here?" she exclaimed.

Emerald froze for a moment, but I hurried toward Calla's light, and within seconds, his boots were pounding against the wet stones.

When we found her, Calla was standing a few paces away from a figure dressed entirely in white.

"Allure?" Emerald asked. He, too, held back from her. "What are you—?"

She was barefoot, and the hem of her white robes were damp from where they'd dragged upon the stones. She stood with her hands at her sides, her eyes unfocused, swaying back and forth.

"Allure?" Calla repeated. She shuffled half a step closer, but no more.

Allure whispered to herself, so softly that her lips barely moved. I couldn't make out what she was saying, but it seemed as if she was saying one word, over and over.

"Is she sleepwalking?" Calla asked.

"I never knew her to," Emerald said. "Should we wake her up?"

"I don't think you're supposed to." Calla nudged him with her elbow. "Can we at least agree that *this* is creepy?"

"Gods, yes," Emerald said, without missing a beat.

Their words didn't disturb Allure, who was still swaying, staring at the wall ahead of her.

Emerald frowned and held his light closer to the wall itself. "What is that?" he asked.

"What's what?" Calla held her lantern up.

It was difficult to tell in the poor lighting, but there was a mark on the wall. A blotch, marked only by some dark residue.

"Oh, no," Calla moaned suddenly. "No, no, no."

"What—?" Emerald began, but then he choked into silence.

"Allure, honey, we've got to go." Calla wrapped her one arm around Allure's shoulders.

[What is it?] I asked Emerald.

He didn't speak, but his hands were shaking, and two fat tears spilled over his cheeks. He shook his head, but his voice wouldn't come, not from his lips or through our thoughts.

I bent closer, squinting at the shape, ignoring Calla's pleas to an unheeding Allure. I still couldn't tell what I was looking at, only that the discoloration looked as though it had been left by fire.

Scorch marks.

"Oh, gods," I breathed.

That was when I realized what Allure was whispering over and over to herself. One word, the question I'd been asking for days, and which nobody had been able to answer.

Reticent.

Reticent.

Reticent.

Where was Reticent? Emerald didn't remember. Calla didn't remember. Even the books had forgotten, but I'd been told the answer days ago and ignored it. In amongst the heartless warnings and vicious parables, I'd ignored the one warning I should have listened to.

That kid who got burned up, Visage had said in the courtyard. *He tried to do an evil spell, and got set on fire. They say that the only thing left of him was ashes and an outline on the wall from where he burned alive.*

"Emerald?" I squeaked. I reached for his arm.

The instant I touched him, I saw the whole thing. Every bitter detail.

For the first time in almost twenty years, Allure's second family was reunited at last.

CHAPTER

TWENTY-FOUR

"It'll work," Reticent said, pointing down the book in his lap. "I'm sure it will."

Steadfast scratched his head. "But what does it mean by 'complementary Aideas?' Does it mean all sorts of different ones, or all the same type?"

"I don't know," Reticent said. "But think about it. We're complementary, aren't we? You deal in light, Allure works in shadow, Humble uses heat. And heat's the opposite of entropy, don't you think?"

Humble, sitting next to Reticent on the bed, blushed. "Are you saying that we complement each other, Ret?"

The scene reminded me of the little enclave my generation had formed the morning when we read through that very same book. The children were older, perhaps in their mid-teens. Judging by what I'd seen of the other groups, they were nearing the age when the Brotherhood would send them off into the world.

"That means Steady and I complement each other!" Allure exclaimed. She bounced on the bed, ever the baby of the group. "I think we do, don't you?"

"I don't know." Steadfast was still eying the book with naked skepticism. "There's too much guesswork involved."

"You're the one who translated it," Humble pointed out. "Are you saying that we shouldn't trust your linguistic talents?"

"Not the point, Hum," Steadfast told her. "What happens if this goes wrong? Someone could get hurt."

Allure clasped her hands under her chin. "Oh, please, Steady, let's try it. If we do, then none of you will have to be sent off to train as Castcadesmen! We can get a house in Kinmore and stay together and just be... normal. Like Brother Harmony says!"

"I'm not living in a house with you," Humble said. "Steadfast smells like an old sock half the time, and you whine too much." Her eyes slid toward Reticent, and her cheeks darkened another shade. "Maybe we could find neighboring tenements instead?"

If Reticent noticed Humble's obvious interest, he didn't let on. He remained focused on the task at hand. "Come on, Steadfast, do you really want to work for the Conjury? You know how they'll treat someone like you."

"A jotunn, you mean?" Steadfast asked. The word dripped off of his lips like a poisoned curse.

"Someone as talented as you? They'll use you up and throw you away. And me... you know what they'll make me do." He shuddered. "I might not be as skilled as you are, but I'm at least as powerful."

"You could be more skilled, if you practiced," Steadfast pointed out.

"Practiced?" Reticent snapped. "On what? On who?"

Steadfast shrank away from him. "You don't have to kill anyone, Reticent. There are other ways to use your power that don't—"

"—result in something's insides getting scrambled like an egg? Sure, I could learn to control it more, but what do you think the Conjury's going to ask me to do? You saw what happened to that mouse I caught last week." Reticent held his head in his hands, not meeting anyone's eyes.

"Reticent..." Humble reached for him.

He slipped away before she could. "Don't!" he exclaimed.

She pulled back at once, cradling her hand in her lap. "Sorry," she said. "I'm sorry."

"None of you get it," Reticent told them. "You've all grown up being told that your Aidea is bad because it might hurt you, or because Guise is a *picky bastard, or because your families didn't want you, so why would anyone else."*

Allure squeaked.

"Oh, gods, we know.*" Humble glared at her. "Your family wanted you, but they're dead. Boo hoo. It doesn't make you as special as you think it does."*

"That's not what I was thinking." Allure chewed on her thumbnail. "He's right about the Conjury. They'd see him as a weapon, wouldn't they?"

Steadfast's shoulders went slack, and he closed his eyes. "So the choice is this," he said. "Either I agree to risk my life and surrender my Aidea, the one thing I actually like *about myself, or we get separated and Reticent gets turned into a tool of a government that none of us trust, full of people who are going to use us and our powers for their own ends?"*

"Always so dramatic," Humble said. "What's the worst that could happen?"

"We could die," Steadfast told her.

"What!?" Allure shrieked.

"I don't know that it's likely," Steadfast added hastily. "But that's generally the worst thing that could happen when Aidea is involved."

"So what?" Humble demanded. She gestured toward her arms. "It's not like you haven't thought about it."

"Humble." Allure balled her hands into fists. "Don't."

"Yeah, Hum," Reticent agreed. "Back off."

"Why?" Humble looked around at all of them. "I'm tired of tiptoeing around everything. Steadfast was in the infirmary twice with injuries he gave himself. Ret has to live in a bubble just in case he vaporizes anyone by accident."

Reticent tried to interrupt her. "Hum—"

"That's why you haven't kissed me, isn't it?" she asked.

"Um." The tip of Reticent's ears turned pink.

Steadfast gawked at them. "Hold on. The two of you...?"

Allure swatted him. "Really, Steady? All of the details you obsess over, and you miss this?"

It was Steadfast's turn for a blush to rise in his cheeks. "I never thought about it."

"That's because you're dense when it comes to feelings," Humble told him. "You probably haven't even noticed that Brother Assertive makes moon eyes at you every time you walk by."

Steadfast's eye twitched. "He does?"

Humble held up both hands. "It doesn't matter. This isn't just about me and Ret. It's about Ret forever. He wants to get rid of his power, I want to get out of this hellshole, Allure wants us to be able to stay together after we age out, and Steadfast—the only one who's worried that we might get hurt in the process—has already proven that he's not afraid of dying. So what are we waiting for?"

All three of them swiveled their heads toward Steadfast, who sat still as a statue as he considered their offer.

I already knew what he would say, but even in the aftermath of what was destined to happen next, I prayed to whatever god would listen that he would give another answer. Aster. Rilus. The Middling Godlet. Ardus. Even Guise. Please, gods, let this end another way. Let these young people avoid the inevitable. Let the story end the way it should have, rather than the way it did.

But in the end, Steadfast uttered the words he could never take back, the ones that had brought us to where we were, the ones that could not be avoided once they'd been spoken.

"Fine, then. Let's try."

THEY AGREED that the crypt was their best option. Very little was needed for the spell.

"Should we have brought candles?" Humble asked as they snuck deeper into the catacombs. "This seems like the sort of thing that requires lots and lots of candles."

"We're doing a spell, Hum, not trying to match some sort of aesthetic out of your novels," Steadfast shot back. "It doesn't call for candles, and besides, you're a Vulcanist. Doesn't it seem dangerous to set your power loose in a room full of lit wicks?"

"Guise's balls, fine." Humble rolled her eyes and groaned. "I'm just asking. It would be nice if we could see better. This place gives me the creeps."

"We don't need candles, though. Do we, Steady?" Reticent's voice was clear, even though his face was shadowed in darkness.

"No." Emerald held out his hands, palm up, and produced a fistful of green fire. "We'll be able to see just fine."

"Unless the spell works," Humble muttered to herself. "Then we'll be stuck down here, with no light at all."

Reticent laughed. He sounded younger than before, as if he already anticipated the burden of his Aidea being lifted from him. "Then we'll all hold hands and find our way back together."

Humble stopped complaining after that.

"I think we should go back there." Allure pointed to a far corner of the room. "It's far away from the stairs. More private."

"Perfect." Reticent steered the group toward where she had pointed.

He'd been carrying the book, but when the time came, he passed it to Steadfast. The boy who would become my father, mentor, and friend opened it to the appropriate page and pointed to Humble. "All right, you sit there. Reticent, you sit in the spot beside her, near the wall. Allure, you'll go next, and I'll sit in between you."

"Girl, boy, girl, boy," Allure said, plopping down into a cross-legged position on the damp stone. "Complementary!"

"I was more concerned about how our Aideas would interact," Steadfast told her.

"That, too!" she chirped.

Steadfast and the others joined her on the floor. "Just checking the notes before we get started," he said. "Do you all have your focuses?"

Reticent held up a familiar little pouch, no doubt filled with animal bones. Humble pulled the leather cord around her neck, which revealed a glittering black stone strung through like a pendant. Allure nodded, although she didn't offer anything up.

Steadfast produced a broken sliver of green glass from his pocket and set it on the floor in front of him; the marble he'd used when he was younger was safely tucked away under the floorboards in their room. "Put them somewhere easy to reach. The general idea is that we'll activate our magic, and then pour all of it into our focuses. Our Aideas will overlap and mix a little, but according to this, they'll sort of... cancel each other *out." He tapped his finger against the paper. "Our Aidea will have nowhere to go except where we tell it."*

"What happens to our focuses?" Allure asked nervously.

"They'll hold our magic," Steadfast explained. "They might be destroyed in the process, though."

Allure bit her lip. "So I won't have a shadow anymore?"

"I don't know," Steadfast admitted. "Because we're working from a book that's written in an ancient language, in a compound where everybody hates magic, and there's nobody to tell us how this works—"

"We get it," Humble interrupted.

Allure fidgeted for a moment before lifting her chin. "It doesn't matter," she said. "I'll do without a shadow, if I have to. As long as we get to stay together, I don't care."

"All right, then." Steadfast closed the book with a snap and set it behind him on top of a crypt. "So we're going to activate our Aidea, and then we'll channel it into our focuses. Don't let it get away from you. Just put everything you have into the focus."

"Easy," Humble said. "I barely have any magic, anyway." She closed her eyes, rested her hands on her knees, and took a deep breath.

Steadfast closed his eyes, too. "Ready," he said. "Three. Two. One..."

I wasn't used to feeling sensations, even in Emerald's memories, but that was all he had of the next few moments, and they were so powerful that even I could experience them.

Beyond his eyelids came a growing light, enough to stain his vision red. From his left, where Humble sat, came heat—an unnatural warmth, but not too much of it. The sensation from his right was more confusing, a sort of numb negation. Steadfast was satisfied. He'd chosen the order of their circle well.

Amidst everything else, he was sad. Sad, but hopeful. The future could be different than he'd imagined. He'd lose his Aidea, but he'd gain a family. A family that wanted him.

Even Humble was better than nothing.

With the patient precision that I had come to know, he gathered his power and prepared to direct it into the broken base of the bottle he'd used as his focus for the green fire.

The next thing he knew, someone was screaming.

"Reticent!" Allure wailed.

"No, no, no, no..." That was Humble's voice.

Steadfast opened his eyes, taking all of his magic back, and was met with a scene even I, knowing what I knew, had not anticipated.

Reticent had been flung backward, his arms spread wide and his eyes rolling back in his head until only the whites showed. His spine pressed to the stone wall behind him, and his limbs twitched and spasmed uncontrollably.

"Reticent." Allure was sobbing, crouching on her hands and knees before him. Behind her, on the wall, a magnified version of her did the same, but instead of using its arms to hold itself up, it reached for her friend, her brother, the boy who was about to die.

"No, no, no, no." Humble scrambled toward him across the stones. There was blood on Reticent's lips, bruises blooming deep purple beneath his eyes. His skin sagged around him, as if he no longer held organs and bones, only water. Only something wet and shapeless, vibrating at a frequency so high that it whined in Steadfast's ears.

His bloodshot eyes rolled toward Humble, and his lips moved. I could not tell what he said. His tongue was black between his lips, decaying into the palate of his lower jaw. I had never seen anything so horrible.

I no longer had to wonder what had happened to the mouse.

Humble's hand stretched out, and for a fraction of a second, their fingers met.

And then there were only flames, and a writhing mass of light and shadow as Reticent was set ablaze.

THERE WERE ONLY SNATCHES after that, confused images and sensations that blurred together.

Stumbling up the stairs to the main floor.

Upending the box of treasures under the floorboards.

Allure and Humble, still screaming as Steadfast scooped ashes into the box. To what end? To hide this? They could never hide it. They had killed Reticent. Killed their brother. Steadfast was to blame as much as Allure, who had insisted. As much as Humble, who had lit the blaze. More blame lay with him, in fact, because he had known they shouldn't do this, he had known, and yet he had let it happen anyway.

He should have pretended he couldn't read the damn book. He should have put his foot down. Now, his brother's ashes were streaming through his fingers like so much sand, clumping against the wet stones, clinging to his palms. When he'd done the best he could, he wiped his hands on the thighs of his trousers, leaving handprints in what remained of Reticent when he did.

He was a murderer.

They were all murderers.

And Reticent was gone.

TWENTY-FIVE

Emerald's memory ended where the present began: with Calla crying, "No, no, no..." and Allure repeating Reticent's name. She slumped in Calla's arms, clinging to her sister as she sobbed.

"Emerald?" I pulled my hand away from my friend's arm.

"We did it," Emerald murmured. "We killed him. And we *forgot*."

"I think we should go," I said.

The power that had been draped around Allure's shoulders was shivering to life, glistening like mother-of-pearl in the near dark. It peeled away from her, coiling against the stones, feral and desperate.

I didn't know enough about *Aidea* and ancient spells to know what exactly had gone wrong all those years past. I didn't even understand exactly what Entropy, as a form of magic, could do. That bit of information was missing from Emerald's memory, hidden within his altered mind.

What I did know was that their powers had blended at the seams. Humble had lit the fire, but Allure's shadow had reached for Reticent in those last moments. Her focus hadn't been destroyed. It had become its own thing—a creeping, crawling, snarling beast.

Emerald staggered back against the catacomb where he had once rested the old spell book. "Gods," he panted. "The shadow-beast. Is this what you've been asking about?"

I nodded dumbly as Calla yelped and recoiled from the monster, dragging Allure with her. "What is that?" she shrieked.

The beast had been terrifying enough on the roof of the Brotherhood, or when it prowled from Blare's bed toward mine. This was worse... *much* worse, because it was so large, and so solid. Its eyes blazed as its long muzzle opened, and a few drops of black liquid dribbled between its teeth. It sizzled when it hit the stones and turned to steam.

"Stay back," I warned, even as I slid back a pace. Emerald did the same, and his hip struck the nearest tomb. No wonder this place awakened all of his long-buried fears of the dead. He had killed Reticent, and he feared comeuppance, even if he usually didn't remember why.

The shadow-beast did not listen. It prowled forward, its shoulder blades shifting beneath its thin and leathery skin. Beneath the pelt of shadow, it was all bone and shriveled sinew. Its rotten tongue licked the parched lips, and I shuddered.

It could touch me if it wanted. What would that tongue feel like against my skin? Would those decaying teeth break off when it bit me?

I admit, I was in no great rush to find out.

Calla clung to Allure, pulling her away from the beast and the outline of Reticent on the wall. She looked sick to her stomach, and her eyes never wavered from the beast. The look on her face reminded me of Blare, who had watched his brother surrender his *Aidea* as if exacting penance. She blamed herself for Reticent's death, just as Emerald did. Allure squirmed in her grip, reaching for the shadow, still clinging to the life she'd wanted, to the family she'd adored. Either she couldn't see what Reticent had become, or she didn't care.

I suspected the latter, and I was sorry I'd ever doubted her. She wasn't doing this on purpose. She was as innocent as the others, even if her *Aidea* had created this thing. To my knowledge, it hadn't hurt anyone, at least not badly.

Not yet.

I dug in my heels and lifted my hands in surrender. The shadow-beast had raked at me and menaced me for days, but it had done me no real harm. Perhaps it could be reasoned with. At the very least, I ought to try. Reticent deserved that.

"They didn't mean to hurt you," I told the shadow-beast.

"Crimson?" Emerald's voice was hoarse. "What are you doing?"

I ignored him and took a hesitant step toward the shadow-beast. I would have felt much more confident if I didn't have to look like Vagabond, since I was *very* small compared to the creature that had once been my... uncle? Was that the right accounting? Either way, Reticent was family, and he'd died young. Perhaps I could convince him to be patient with me.

"They're sorry, Reticent," I cooed, trying to muster some affection for the horror that prowled before me. "They're so sorry. You have no idea. Trust me, I can feel it. It was an accident. They would never have done it on purpose."

The beast's small and brilliant eyes blinked once. Twice. It tilted its bony head to one side, then the other. When it opened its mouth again, it let out a dry cough, and then a lower version of the *kek-kek-kek-kek* I'd heard before. It took a long moment for me to process that the phlegmy rattle was meant to be a laugh. It swayed as it chuckled, then lifted its head sharply. Its eyes met mine.

[I am not Reticent.]

I had known that the shadow-beast could hear the thoughts that passed between me and Emerald, but until that moment, I had never heard its voice in my mind. It was worse than when my creator and I spoke. For all his surliness and posturing, Emerald was, by and large, affectionate. Hearing his voice in my mind was like receiving a soft nudge, the way Svelte bumped Blare with her shoulder when she knew he needed a boost of confidence. The shadow-beast's voice, however, clawed at me. It rent me open from the inside.

It was worse than being slit open with its claws. It was a violation, and I hated it.

[I am not Reticent,] it repeated. *[Reticent is* dead.*]*

It lunged forward, not toward me, but toward Emerald. My

friend's eyes widened, and he rolled backward over the lid of the stone tomb behind him. The shadow-beast followed, clearing the casket in a single smooth leap at odds with its usual jerky movements.

Emerald hit the ground with a thump, and the shadow-beast tackled him. He raised both arms over his head to protect himself. I scrambled after them, passing right through the stone of the crypt, and the dusty remains of the corpse within.

"Emerald!" Calla screamed.

Emerald tried to ward off the shadow, but he couldn't get a grip on it. The beast's claws slipped through his fingers and his robes, only to slice through his skin. Blood welled on the fabric, and Emerald gasped in pain. As it prepared to launch a second attack, a fistful of fire burst to life in Emerald's palm. He flung it at the monster, which skittered back, shaking its head and shielding its eyes.

Before, light had been enough to dispel the beast, but apparently that was no longer the case. It hissed and snarled at Emerald, falling back to the edge of the ring of firelight but no further.

"It was an accident," I repeated. "And we're here to help. Stay away from him."

The beast's desiccated lips curled back from its canines. *[I don't follow orders from you, Crimson Smoke. I only do what I must to protect her.]*

"Allure?" I asked.

"She's back there," Emerald said. He clambered to his feet, still gripping the illusion of fire.

"I know," I told him irritably. "I was talking to—"

I pointed to where the beast had been standing, but it was gone. I whirled in a circle, searching desperately for it. I was just barely tall enough to see over the top of the stone catacomb—why, oh *why*, had I made Vagabond so short?—but I had no trouble hearing the wet sizzle of a wick tipping against a wet floor. The lamplight died. An instant later, Calla screamed.

"Hum!" Emerald swung around the end of the monument, and I gave chase. Calla screamed again. Allure's voice joined with hers, and when we came back into view, I found the supposed mouthpiece of Guise on all fours, reaching for her sister. Calla lay on her back, her hair splayed against the pavers, doing everything she could to hold the beast at bay. Its teeth nipped at her throat.

[They are hurting her, and they must stop!] it thought.

"They aren't!" I insisted.

[You don't understand—of course you wouldn't. Their very presence hurts her, because it makes her remember. None of them are good for her, only I can help her. They must be stopped.]

Emerald rushed toward his sisters and fell to his knees beside Calla. The beast retreated from the firelight, but as before, it did not go far. Emerald threw a protective arm around the half-elf's shoulder.

"Are you hurt?" he asked her.

"Hit my head," she panted, struggling upright. "What the hells is that thing?"

"I dunno, but..." Emerald swallowed hard. "I think we made it."

[You made nothing, Emerald Flame.] The beast retreated to Allure's side, standing guard over her. She yelped and tried to crawl away, but it followed, keeping pace with her. When she reached Emerald and Calla, the latter pulled her close. The beast waited, stalking them at the edge of darkness. *[I was made to protect her. She wanted a family. She wanted love. And none of you could give that to her. You wreck everything you touch, you broke her heart by leaving. She is mine now. Only I can help her. She is better with me. Stronger. I help her, I obey her, I remained when no one else stayed by her side...]*

"Judging by the way she's trying to escape you," I snapped, "she doesn't *want* your help."

"Um, Steady?" Calla gulped. "I think your poppet is talking to that thing."

"So it would seem," Emerald agreed. He knelt beside the two women, his green eyes following the shadow-beast. In the light of his enchanted fire, his eyes seemed glassy, like the marble he'd used as a focus when he was a boy.

[You can't hear it?] I asked him.

[No...]

[Of course he can't,] the beast replied. *[He is not like us, Crimson Smoke.]*

"I'm not like you, either." I turned to glower at the monster. "Just let us leave. We can talk to Allure. Sort this out." I turned back to the white-clad sister. "Can you dispel it?"

Allure shook her head. She gripped Calla's arm so tightly that the Vulcanist winced. "I didn't summon it," she said in a faint voice. "I haven't had shadow magic since the day Reticent died."

[I cannot let them go,] the beast told me. *[They want to hurt her. To spy on her. They only care about her when it suits them. They will try to take me away from her. That is why they're here, is it not?]*

I frowned. People had consistently referred to Allure as the mouthpiece of Guise, but it seemed she'd played host to something else entirely. If the shadow-beast truly wasn't Reticent, it was at least something made of magic. Allure had wondered what would become of her focus if they tried the nullification spell. Apparently, it had been repurposed as the focus for another sort of *Aidea* entirely.

[You begin to understand.] The beast nodded. *[I am indeed like you. I am my own being. They were all the instruments of my emergence. But I will always be hers first.]*

"Then how come—" I began. I meant to ask, *How come you only recently came to life?* My own siblings had made it quite clear that the shadow-beast was a new addition to their lives. It had only begun appearing months ago.

On the spring solstice, the same day I was born. The first day Emerald summoned me after nearly drowning in the Cronemire.

Maybe we had more in common than I'd like to admit.

None of this was relevant at the moment, and my musing was cut short as the shadow-beast rose up on its hind legs. As it did so, it expanded, losing its shape as it expanded to fill the room.

[I was hers first,] the beast said, almost regretfully. *[I would do anything to protect her. You must understand.]*

I did. I, too, would do anything to protect my friend. Not because he'd made me. Not because I was compelled to.

Because I was the only person who could, and I loved him.

A force like wind howled around us, and to my horror, Emerald's illusory fire guttered in his palm. I wasn't sure if shadow magic by nature had the ability to affect lightweavings, or if the shadow-beast had been born from the confluence of all their magics, but either way, it could snuff out his fire with the same ease that it had scratched me open. They would be left alone in the darkness at its mercy.

Confluence. Sister Aster had used that word when she described the Middling Godlet to me. According to her, the Middling Godlet was the ruler of the in-between places and had one foot in every realm. If the shadow-beast and I *were* made of the same stuff, then I was the one best equipped to fight it. I was its equal and opposite.

And if I was going to fight it, I would be wise to do so in the place where my power was strongest.

As Emerald's fire threatened to blow out, I plunged into the midst of the darkness, wrapping my small arms around the beast's skeletal body. My arms slipped between its ribs, finding purchase on its spine. Just as I had suspect, its body was real in the same way *I* was real. In a world full of objects that I found intangible, the beast and I could touch.

[Let go,] it snarled at me, but I was never very good at following orders. Instead, I dug my fingertips into the spongy discs between its vertebrae and tipped sideway, carrying the beast with me.

We hit the floor of the mind-cottage with a bone-shaking thump. The beast landed on top of me, howling its indignation as it fell. I grunted as my back hit the floor and rolled out of its reach, coming to rest against one wall.

[What is this place?] it demanded.

"The one place I can fight you." I flinched when I sat up; I'd fallen hard enough to bruise, in a place where I *could* bruise.

The shadow-beast was no less terrifying than it had been in the catacombs, but at least here, I could see it properly. I controlled the lighting, although it occurred to me for the first time that there were no lamps on lanterns in that familiar room. The light radiated from nowhere in particular. The shadow-beast screeched and clawed at its eyes, gathering its darkness close, like a bird nursing a broken wing. It flung itself at the walls, desperate to escape the glow, its attack on my person forgotten.

In addition to the light, I had two more things in my favor. First, I was in my own territory, in the place I could control with little more than thought. Less importantly, but still of note, I had shifted during the retreat. I was no longer Vagabond, and neither Simon nor Simone. I was only Crimson, as I had appeared that night when we faced off on the roof of the compound. It wasn't helpful in the practical sense, but I certainly felt more confident than I had before.

It was time for a rematch, and I was more than ready.

I got to my feet and cracked the knuckles of my right hand, then the left. "You might as well admit that I've trapped you," I said. "Are you ready to talk nicely now?"

The shadow-beast had withdrawn to a corner and was scrabbling at the floor. Now that we were in my realm, I could smell it— the stinking, mildewed rot mixed with the hot tang of moldering flesh. It was enough to turn my stomach, which implied that I *had* a stomach here. It would all have been very interesting if I'd had the time to puzzle over these new revelations.

Alas, I did not. My voice drew the beast's attention. Apparently, it decided that its efforts to escape were in vain, and that its energy would be better spent on harming me. It lunged forward, growing to fill the space. The hot stench of its breath gusted against my face. I only just managed to dodge its blow as I feinted beneath it and rolled to the far corner of the room.

"Why did you try to hurt Blare?" I demanded—in *my* voice, not the childish shrill of Vagabond.

[I didn't. I was drawn to him, to the possibility of death. And he is so like her.] The beast shook its head, as if to dislodge an old thought. It was a gesture I knew well from watching Calla and Emerald.

"You get confused, don't you?" I asked. I stood upright and tried to catch a full breath without making it obvious that I was winded. I had no experience with such things, but I was learning on the fly. "About Allure, for example. I'm not your enemy, you know. I don't want to hurt her."

[It doesn't matter!] my opponent shrieked. *[You hurt her anyway, no matter what you do! I was by her side forever, I was the only one who was with her when her father died... when her mother died... I dogged her steps all her life. I was the only one she could rely on.]*

I sighed. "Nobody looks out for us but us," I quoted.

[Nobody but me.*]*

It lunged again, but I was ready this time. I could conjure anything I needed, after all. Before the beast reached me, I pulled a sword out of nowhere, swinging it above my head. The blade rippled with Emerald's verdant fire, and the shadow-beast shrieked when the blade struck home.

"You forget where you are," I said coldly. "This is *my* world."

The beast slunk back, laughing its chittering laugh. *[Maybe,]* it corrected. *[But you don't control everything.]*

It had not occurred to me that, if the two of us were indeed of a kind, then it would have some power here, too. Before my eyes, the shadow-beast rearranged itself in the same manner I often did into a massive, coiling serpent with jet-black scales, the same iridescent hue of the black stone young Humble had used as her focus.

"Oh, *Driaweep's blistered co—*" I began.

The serpent struck. Not with fangs, as I had expected, but with *fire.*

It should have occurred to me that the beast was more than shadow. It was, in fact, fashioned haphazardly from four *Aidea*s. Fire, shadow, light, and... whatever the hells entropy was. All I knew about Reticent's power was that it was very, very dangerous, and I didn't want to end up as a fashionably-dressed sack of boneless skin and melted organs.

The beast could change its shape here, but so far, I was the only one who could control the world. As a blast of heat filled the room, I adjusted the world around us, closing my eyes as I did so to better focus my energy.

Instead of a gout of flame, I was instantly doused in warm water. Uncomfortably warm, to be sure, but it was better than being scorched alive—which was something that I might very well be able to experience here. I had been hurt by the shadow before, and the mind-cottage was the place where I was the most *real,* at least in the traditional sense. Who was to say what would happen if it killed me here?

When I opened my eyes, I was crouched in murky water. There was no sign of the beast.

I rose to my feet. As I did so, my head broke the surface. I was in the shallow waters of the Cronemire, standing just beside the shores of the Black Hollow. The sword I'd been holding still flickered in my hand. The water had no impact on its glow.

From the grassy banks, a strange figure watched me: a giant bird with black feathers and a single brilliant red eye. It was clear to me that this was the Crone, although I'd only ever seen her skull. A few weeks ago, she'd used my magic to exact her revenge on her murderers.

"Is this real?" I asked.

The enormous bird tilted her head to one side. She blinked once.

A ripple in the waters around me made me turn. The shadow-beast was just behind me, its scaled body undulating across the surface of the bog. That answered my question: we were still in the mind-cottage, which meant that I had conjured the Crone. But why?

My subconscious had an annoying habit of showing me what I needed to see, but not explaining it properly.

"I could use some *real help*!" I snapped.

The shadow-beast reared up on its long tail. When it opened its mouth again, I tipped away.

When I regained my balance, I was standing in the tower where Aindreas had been imprisoned as punishment. While the trappings of this room were the same as they'd been when I was here before, the place was conspicuously empty.

Of course—Aindreas was invisible. But even if he wasn't, the *real* Aindreas wasn't here. This was my mind, and the only thing that I didn't control was the shadowy monster that was currently trying to kill me.

"Oh-*kay*!" I bellowed. "I get it, I've solved two other mysteries before. Not exactly helpful!" I wasn't clear if I was yelling at myself, or the Middling Godlet, or the mind-cottage in general. "If you're trying to give me hints, these are *lousy clues!*"

A shadow shifted beside the bookshelf, and I turned just as a familiar outline coalesced along the wall. It looked alarmingly like the beast that was chasing me, except that instead of a snout and four legs, it walked upright like a person.

A person dressed in dark velvet, with leathery gray skin and a sweep of coal-black hair topping their cadaverous features. They advanced a pace and leered at me.

"Is that supposed to be *me?*" I asked.

The shadow leered. *[I already told you. We're alike.]*

"Oh, go to hells," I snapped, and then I charged.

As I did so, the shadow produced a blade of its own, one that rippled with darkness. They met without a sound, but the impact traveled up my arm and left a thrill of pain in my shoulder.

I fell back a pace to regroup myself, and the shadow-me laughed. *[All style, and no substance. All bark, and no bite. You can't win this, Crimson Smoke.]*

I bared my teeth in a feral smile ill-suited to my otherwise soft appearance. "Watch me."

I spun, keeping my body low, leading with my fist instead of my blade. I had no practice with fighting, but I *imagined* that I would be a dab hand at it given the chance, and that seemed to be good enough for the mind-cottage. My first sank into its belly, and the shadow screeched. Its legs swung beneath mine, and I went down.

Limbs, it turned out, were a damned inconvenience.

This time, the shadow met me with both hands open, grappling with me instead of attacking. We rolled, and as we did, the world changed once more.

We were in the hall of records inside Dyrne's church, where Emerald had first compelled me against my will. The shadow's back hit the stones, and it drove its knee up into my gut. When we rolled again, we found ourselves beside a riverbend where peat-reddened water met the brine of the sea. The smooth stones were entirely too familiar, and the broken wine bottles lying by the shore told me exactly where this memory had come from.

Emerald's pockets had once been filled with these very same stones.

I paused for a moment as understanding slammed into me. In the Cronemire, I'd possessed a god. In the tower, I'd attacked Aindreas. In each of these places, I'd utilized some unique power particular to me. Perhaps—

The shadow drove its elbow into my back, right above the spot where some delicate organ was housed. Stars burst in my vision, and I collapsed forward as the shadow struck me again and pinned me down.

[See?] they asked. [Even you know that you are nothing without him. You are nothing at all.]

I clawed at the pebbles and tried to buck the shadow off, but it did no good. Their fingers tangled with my hair. Claws dug into my scalp.

Then came the *push*. Not a physical one, but something in my head. The shadow was attempting to do the same thing to me that I'd done to Emerald. It was trying to possess me, to compel me, to control me.

Come on, stupid, I told myself. *There's got to be a way to do this. This is my world, and they're an interloper. There must be a way to do this, and according to my useless, unhelpful, smug little subconscious, I already know how to solve this problem. How am I supposed to get rid of something that can hurt me from inside my own head?*

How indeed?

[Give up, Crimson Smoke,] the shadow wheedled. [You can't get rid of me. You can't wish me away.]

No, I couldn't, any more than Emerald could wish away the memories of what he'd done to his brother.

"Oh!" I exclaimed. My sword had been knocked aside in the fray, but I didn't need it. I'd been using the wrong tactics.

I lashed out one elbow, driving it into the shadow's ribs. They grunted and toppled sideways, and I took the opportunity to scramble to my feet. As I did so, I grabbed the shadow by the throat.

"I told you," I snarled, "this is my world."

The shadow clawed at me. Even in my shape, their fingers ended in wicked claws. They bucked and hissed, snapping their deterio-rating teeth beneath my chin. *[You won't. You can't. You're not strong enough. Only the Emerald Flame cares about you, and he will leave you too, if he gets the chance. He wants to be rid of you...]*

I tightened my grip and closed my eyes. Other than Emerald, I had never compelled a person before. Then again, the shadow wasn't a person. It was a being made of *Aidea*, like the Crone.

This was my world, and I could shape it however I wanted. I reached into the shadow the same way the Crone had reached into me, twisting and pulling until it fit *my* purposes.

The shadow contorted, doing its best to fight back, but it could no more fight back than I could fight Emerald when he dispelled me. It only had as much power here as I gave it. So I gave it none at all.

This time, when I changed our location, I changed the shadow as well.

The riverbank was gone, along with our useless weapons, and I was kneeling on the floor, holding a small velvet bag. Inside, I could feel the brittle texture of tiny bones.

[What are you doing?] the shadow demanded. *[I am not yours to control. I am stronger than you. I am more real than you. I have drained the* Aidea *of more conduits than you can count, you frivolous, shallow, pigheaded wretch.]* In my hands, the bag jerked and shuddered, as if the bones were trying to rearrange themselves.

I wouldn't be able to keep the shadow-beast contained forever. I had no doubt it would find a way to change into something else deadly and menace me again if left to its own devices.

I could do something it couldn't do, however. So far, the shadow hadn't managed to make any changes to my mindscape. I had seen inside Emerald's head. I knew that it was possible to lock up some things so tightly that nobody could reach them.

"Quiet," I commanded. "I might not be able to kill you, but I can damn well make sure you don't get out. And don't bother insulting me. That kind of nonsense works on other people, but you'll never convince me that I'm anything but a wonder."

I lifted my hand toward the ceiling, and when I did so, the stars bent down to reach me. The crack in the plaster widened as the ceiling warped toward my palm. The moment it was in reach, I stuffed the little bag inside.

As soon as my fingers parted from the drawstring, the shadow burst free of its velvet prison. Even as it did so, I ran my fingers over the hole.

The blue ceiling immediately healed over, and the star in the middle was restored. Harmony had offered to plaster over the hole, but here, I didn't need anyone's help to seal the fissure myself. The last thing I saw before the break closed up was a single eye pressed to the hole.

And then I was alone.

I stood there, breathing hard, painfully aware of all my various bumps and bruises. I waited for the stars to tremble, or for the plaster to collapse, but no such thing occurred.

"Is that what I was supposed to do?" I asked.

The room stood empty except for the dummy of Emerald. Its only answer was a lopsided grin.

"I'll take that as a yes?" I hazarded.

There came a faint scratching, like mice in the walls. *[Where have you put me?]*

I gulped and crossed my arms over my aching chest. "Away."

[WHERE HAVE YOU PUT ME?]

"Someplace safe, until you can decide to be reasonable."

[Let me out, let me OUT. I must go to her. She needs me.]

I shook my head. "I don't think she does," I said. "If you're what I think you are, then you don't help her. Not like I help Em. If I'm guessing right, you only make her feel more alone."

A keening broke out, and the scratch of claws circled the room, looking for a way in. I wasn't sure what existed outside of the mind-cottage. Surely not joists and studs, or even straw stuffing, as one would find in the walls of a normal building. When the beast's snuffling and wails even traversed the floor below me, I shifted my feet to avoid crossing its path.

[You think you are clever, Crimson Smoke?] the shadow asked. *[You think you have bested me? I am in your kingdom now. I am in your terri-*

tory, and someday, I will find a way to escape. On that day, I swear to you, I will make you pay for what you've done to me—]

"I look forward to it," I sighed.

The shadow kept up its ranting, but I was done listening. For the moment, I'd won, and my friend was waiting for me.

I left the mind-cottage, with its new prisoner, and returned to Emerald's side.

THERE WERE four people in the crypt when I returned. A new lantern had been produced, along with a new enchanted fire. Brother Harmony knelt on the floor beside Allure, cradling her head in her hands.

"It's all right," he murmured. "You're all right."

Allure shook her head, grabbing at Harmony's wrist. "We killed him, Brother. We killed him..."

The moment I appeared, Emerald spun toward me. *[Where have you been? What happened?]*

[Sorry.] In the form of Sibling Vagabond, I offered him a weak smile. *[I was dealing with the shadow-beast.]*

[...the what?]

Allure's weeping quieted, and Brother Harmony released her. When he turned away, his eyes found mine.

"Ah, Sibling Vagabond," he said coolly. "I wondered where you were."

"You... did?" I shifted from foot to foot and lifted my eyebrows.

"We have had a most unfortunate accident," he said. "It seems that the great Emerald Flame and Calla of Venta Bulgarum were here to investigate the matter of Guise's presence. Alas, it appears to have been a misunderstanding."

"It was?" Allure wiped her eyes.

"Indeed." Brother Harmony gestured to a dark object on the floor beside them. It was the old toybox, now turned on its side. Ash spilled out of it, clumping on the wet stones. "I am not quite sure of *all* the details, of course, but it seems that your time as the mouth-piece of Guise has run its course."

Allure lifted one hand to her lips. "Really? Oh, Brother Harmony, I didn't mean it. I didn't *mean* to lie."

"It wasn't a lie, child." Harmony got to his feet and lifted her, too. "It was only a misunderstanding. And who's to say that Guise himself wasn't responsible for all of this, in a roundabout way? His methods are mysterious, even to his most ardent followers."

"I don't understand," Emerald murmured.

I crossed my arms and glared at Brother Harmony. "I can't say I do, either."

Harmony's eyes, usually dark, glinted golden in the dim light, the way Yoyoh's had done back in Upper Bound. "No one acted with the intent to deceive, or to do harm. Did they, Sibling Vagabond?"

I scowled up at Brother Harmony, searching his face for some clue as to his intentions. He was lying, that much was obvious, and I was certain that he was indeed the person who'd tampered with everyone's memories. He stared back, his mouth set in an impassive line.

After a long moment, I nodded, albeit with reluctance. "I think that explanation will do for now."

"Will it?" Emerald scratched his ear.

"What we all need is some rest," Brother Harmony said. He lifted Allure in his arms as if she was still a child. "Come along. You, too, Vagabond. I'm sure the details will fall into place tomorrow."

I wasn't sure what to think about the way he spoke to me, but I decided to treat this statement as a promise. When he headed back toward the stairs, I followed, and Calla fell in line behind.

Emerald lingered for a moment, examining the outline burned into the old stone. His lips twitched, and his eyes narrowed.

[Come on, Em,] I said.

He shook himself and turned away, trailing after us as he tried to make sense of his own thoughts. By the time he reached the foot of the stairs, however, I could tell that he'd already put the matter out of his mind.

For once, it didn't annoy me. If forgetting was the only thing that could protect him, so be it. I would carry that burden for both of us.

CHAPTER

TWENTY-SIX

"How can we have solved a mystery," Emerald complained, "if I don't remember doing it?"

"Your memory has been faulty the entire time we've been here," I reminded him. "Rest assured, we've solved it."

Emerald dropped down onto the edge of the out-of-use fountain. It was an overcast morning, and the children were all indoors at this hour. The Brotherhood was still asleep. Only a few songbirds were present, and Emerald's store of passive knowledge told me that they'd soon be flying south for the winter. Autumn was ending, and it was taking with it a part of Emerald's history that had lain dormant more than half his life.

"We did?" he asked, clearly not convinced.

"We did," I agreed. "Guise wasn't responsible for the magic after all. It was Reticent."

"*Reticent?*" Emerald's voice rose so high it nearly cracked. "How? We haven't seen him since we came back."

"We confronted him last night," I told him. "He confessed to everything, and he agreed to leave for good."

"Oh." Emerald massaged the muscle between his eyebrows. "And we just let him go?"

"We did. He was afraid of being sent away to work for the Conjury, and all he really wanted was to live in peace." I twiddled my thumbs, finding any excuse I could to avoid Emerald's eyes.

I had decided on this version of the story while Emerald was still sleeping. He would have little choice but to believe whatever I told him, and this seemed like the safest thing I could say.

Allure had truly believed in what she was doing, and while I worried what would become of her, I knew that handing her over to the Conjury was the wrong choice. She was a victim of these events, as were the rest of them. She had never meant to do anyone harm, as Brother Harmony had said.

Things were so much simpler when there was someone at fault, someone who could be blamed. Fenguard and Aindreas had done terrible things to protect the people they loved, but twenty years ago, three children had done something horrible *to* someone they loved, which was so much worse. The shadow-beast had been trying to protect Allure, but she had lost control of it. In its absence, I would do what I could to ensure she came to no harm. It seemed only fitting.

Without her focus, and without Reticent's ashes, she wouldn't be able to complete the ritual. In the end, the childrens' magic *had* worked, but it had taken the *Aidea* of strangers instead of their own. In a way, they'd managed something more impressive than what they'd originally set out to do. But, oh, at what a terrible cost.

"And we're quite confident that he won't go around stealing people's *Aidea* in the future?" Emerald asked.

"Mm." I thought of that poor boy and his last horrific moments. "We're positive."

I could feel Emerald's eyes on me, but I pretended not to notice. As Vagabond, I looked surpassingly innocent, and I could only hope that my childish charms would sway him into believing me, despite whatever suspicions he harbored.

"Very well," he said at last. "I trust you."

Could he have found any words that would have wounded me more deeply? I hated having to lie to him, but I couldn't tell him the truth. Quite literally. It would fly out of his head as soon as I uttered it, and for the few seconds he *could* understand, it would only cause him pain.

"We'll need a better story than that for Finch, though," Emerald said.

"It's not a bad story," I retorted. "It's more or less what you did in Dyrne."

One side of Emerald's mouth rose in a smile. "Yes, it's very like me to tell an untruth here and there, if it means protecting the people I care about."

I looked up at the clouds and pretended to find them very interesting.

"That wasn't what I meant, though," he went on. "If we're going to cover for Reticent, then we'll need a story Finch will swallow. Something that she'll believe."

"And we'll need to make sure that Calla tells her the same thing," I added. "Independently."

"Calla?" Emerald paused. I wondered if the whole conversation he'd had with her would be locked away with all of his memories of the night before. That would be a shame, given the progress they'd made.

But Emerald snapped his fingers after a moment. "Humble," he said. "That's right." He dipped his head and offered me a commiserating smile. "See, I'm not so useless that I forget *everything*."

"You're not useless at all." I got up from the lip of the fountain. "And you're going to be even *less* useless when you figure out what we can tell Finch to keep her satisfied."

"That won't be hard. All I have to do is tell her what the Conjury wants to hear. Where are *you* off to?"

"I have someone I need to talk to," I told him.

Emerald hummed. "I knew it," he said.

I turned back to him, surprised by the smug look on his face. "You do?"

"Of course." He grinned at me, cocksure in the way he only was when it came to solving riddles. "Reticent didn't *really* leave the Brotherhood, did he?"

He hadn't, and he never would. All that remained of him was ash, and a stain on the wall, and whatever parts of him had been pulled into the shadow-beast, which now lived in my head rent-free.

"Don't answer," Emerald said, before I could think of a suitable lie. He waved one massive hand at me. "I'm sure you have your reasons."

The sky was turning gold above us. For once, the changing light brought me no comfort.

I no longer felt kinship with it, given all the darkness that I now contained.

I FOUND Harmony in the infirmary, sitting in a chair beside Allure's bed. She was sitting up, her bare feet dangling just above the floor. Without the wreath of power that I'd grown accustomed to, it was easier to see the child she'd been. She was diminished.

"My shadow's gone," she said. "I don't remember what happened last night, Harmony. *Again.* After the ceremony, I think I did something... terrible."

"Oh, child." Harmony leaned forward, and I ducked behind the doorframe. I was not supposed to overhear this, that was obvious, but I couldn't contain my curiosity. I still had questions, and nobody else knew enough to ask them.

Allure's mentor took one of her hands in his and reached the other toward her face, as if brushing away a tear. There was something intimate about the gesture, but not predatory. He let his fingertips rest against her cheekbone.

"You did nothing wrong," he told her. "Out of every child I've cared for over the years, your heart is the kindest, the most open. You have always given everything you have to help others, and you've asked so little for yourself."

Allure choked and grabbed his wrist, holding on to him as tightly as she'd held Calla the night before. "But I'm greedy, too. I want. I want so *badly.* I want a family, I want people who care about me. I want to be loved, and not just by Guise. I know it's wrong to want so much, but I can't help it."

I bristled at her words. So much? To me, it seemed that she

wanted very little. If Harmony told her that she didn't deserve even that, I would be tempted to release the shadow-beast from its prison and let it have its way with him.

"Oh, child." The wrinkles around Harmony's eyes deepened. "You are loved, never doubt that. You aren't greedy for wanting the same thing everyone craves. But such things aren't meant for people like us. We must take kindness where we can get it."

"Because of Guise's will?"

"No," Harmony said, so abruptly that it startled me. "Because we will always end up hurting the people we love. *Always.* No matter how hard we try. We're safer if we let them go. Although this may not be true of you anymore, after last night."

Allure shuddered. "Last night...?"

"Last night, you were sick," Harmony told her. "You did what you were meant to do, and Guise took pity on you."

Allure sat back and stared at Harmony in wonder. "It isn't just my shadow, you mean?"

"No, my dear. Guise granted your prayers. He made you as you were meant to be."

Allure pitched forward into his arms, crying out with delight and relief. "My *Aidea* is gone!" she crowed. "Praise be to the Unifier."

Harmony patted her back and closed his eyes. "You earned his blessings, Allure. Your gift is gone, and your burden with it. You're free to live as you see fit."

I had seen parallels between Emerald and Harmony before. It was unsettling, though, to note the ways in which we, too, were alike. Harmony was reassuring Allure in the best way he knew how, reshaping her memories of the past to keep her safe. Wasn't that essentially what I'd done to Em earlier?

I moved a bit farther into the doorway, and Harmony spotted me. He let go of Allure and pulled back.

"I have someone else I must talk to," he said. "Will you be all right?"

"All right?" she repeated. "I've never been better, Brother."

Harmony got up and approached me, shooing me out the door with a flick of his fingers. "We'll talk in my office," he said.

I wasn't sure how to explain my presence from the previous night, or what little lies to tell him that would explain my involvement in the whole affair.

In the end, none of it was necessary, because the moment the door of his office closed behind us, Harmony said, "So, you really *are* a lightweaving."

"I... what?" I gawked at him. "How did you...?"

"I recognize my students' handiwork." Harmony strolled past me toward his chair. "I suspected, right from the moment you showed up. You don't work the way you ought to, though."

I had counted on Crimson Smoke's reputation to offer me one last line of defense, as it had with Calla, but my story was unraveling faster than I could catch the strands.

He dropped into his chair and studied me. "I was confused at first. I meant to trap Steadfast in the lie when I separated you that first morning. He was with me in my office, and he couldn't hear the conversation in your room. And yet, according to the children, you were quite capable of carrying on a conversation on your own."

I slid toward the empty chair. On one hand, I was pleased that we'd foiled his attempts to prove that I was, as Calla had put it, a poppet. On the other, his cleverness made our situation all the more precarious.

"Having seen Allure's shadow-work," Harmony concluded, "I can only assume that you came into your own as a result of the failed spell all those years ago."

I was in the process of sitting down in the chair, but his words startled me so badly that I forgot to stop, and I fell all the way through the seat.

"What?" I popped up again, standing right in the middle of the chair, half of me above the seat and half below. It was an embarrassing position, to be sure, but since Harmony already knew what I was, there was no point in hiding. "That's not right at all!" I had been born in the Cronemire, in the in-between places watched over by the Middling Godlet. Reticent's death had nothing to do with it.

No? Then how could the shadow-beast hear your thoughts? Why could it speak to you and follow you into the mind-cottage?

I had no way to prove how I'd come to be, but Sister Aster's explanation had seemed like the most probable one I'd received. Had she been wrong? Or half-wrong? Of course, that would imply there was a strict right answer, which the Godlet didn't have much taste for, apparently.

Maybe it was all just wishful thinking. The thought of being a god's gift to Emerald, or some magical homunculus sprouted from the mind of a tortured genius, or even the chewed up and spat out remnants of an unfortunate child's Aidea... I had my obvious favorite option, but all of them no doubt made me unique.

Special.

Perhaps, as Emerald had warned me against during our first mystery together, I was seeing patterns where there were none just to confirm my own biases.

But I was sick of trying to find reasons for things to exist, especially after my time in the Brotherhood, and if I was going to have an existential crisis, I was at least resolved not to do so in front of this particular man. I hopped back up onto the chair and crossed my arms.

"What are you going to do about it?" I demanded.

Harmony laughed. "Nothing."

I stared at him.

"Who would I tell?" he asked. "The Conjury? I'm sure they would like to know, but I've only been allowed to do the work I do because nobody knows what I am."

"A Mentalist," I said.

He nodded. "They tried to use me once. I *refuse* to return to that life. Turning you in would mean handing over the one person who had the information that they would need to find me again. The one person whose memories I cannot hide away."

For him to know what I was, and still call me a person, left me unaccountably giddy. "So we're at an impasse?" I asked.

"So it would seem." Harmony smoothed back a stray strand of hair at his temple. "Believe it or not, I don't need to use my *Aidea* much. Mostly, I use it to protect children from harmful memories of their old lives. It soothes them, but it doesn't change them. This... this is not what I wanted. But you see why I had to act."

"To protect them?" I asked.

He nodded. "Steadfast's mind often strayed to dark thoughts even before Reticent's death. Allure has a gentle soul, easily bruised. And Humble blamed herself when I found them that night. She was... unwell. I feared that her condition would become permanent had I not interceded as I did."

I didn't care much for Harmony. I didn't like what he believed, or how he spoke to the children in his care. If he hadn't spent so many years telling his wards that they were cursed with *Aidea*, then they might never have attempted to rid themselves of it.

And then what? Reticent would have been sent to work for the Conjury, where he would have killed other people, rather than dying as he did. Perhaps he, too, would have wound up traveling the land for the Conjury, alone, drowning his guilt in drink and viewing himself as unworthy of this world for reasons he could not control. There was no easy solution, no clear moral high ground, just as there were no clear villains in this sorry affair.

"I understand," I agreed at last.

"You'll take care of him, won't you?" Harmony bent toward me. "He's always needed looking after, that boy."

"Emerald?" I asked, surprised, forgetting to use his Brotherhood name.

"Emerald, Steadfast." Harmony bobbed his head. "Whatever you choose to call him, he was always one of my favorites. I know I shouldn't differentiate, but Guise knows I'm not perfect."

"I do my best to keep him out of trouble," I said.

Harmony snorted, and the sound was familiar. It was the same sound Emerald made whenever he was amused by something foolish I'd said. "Then perhaps you should try harder," he said.

EMERALD AND CALLA sat in Modest's office, where the head of the Brotherhood sat, glaring at the pair of them.

"Leaving together?" he said. "I expect that the pair of you mean to run off together. Incestouous, I call it. *Disgusting.*"

Emerald and Calla exchanged a silent look before Calla burst out laughing. Emerald joined in a moment later.

"Gods, no." Calla had to speak between peals of laughter. "No offense, Steady, but can you imagine."

"No," Emerald chuckled. "You're not my type at all."

From my vantage point on Emerald's shoulder, I was quite sure I was about to see steam pouring out of Brother Modest's ears. I got the impression that people didn't often laugh in his presence, much less *at* him.

Calla wiped a tear from her eyes as she kept giggling. "Goodness me. No, Brother Modest, that's not the case at all. I'm simply tired of being treated like mud on the heel of someone's boot."

"And I'm tired of telling children that your god hates them just for existing," Emerald added.

Modest's face was so bright red that it nearly matched my hair. "How dare you," he spat. "We gave you everything!"

Calla, who had just managed to get herself under control, let out another howl of laughter.

"And we're incredibly grateful," Emerald deadpanned. "But we're still leaving."

On the way out of Brother Modest's office, still riding in Emerald's collar, I snuck a peek at the shelf from which Blare had nicked the spell book. Its place was empty, with only a scrape through the fine layer of dust to show that it had ever been there. Had Harmony destroyed it? Or was it back in the library now?

"I've wanted to do that for literally years," Calla said, thumping Emerald's bicep with her much smaller fist. "I suppose it'll come back to bite us if we ever need to come here in the future, but I can't say I care."

"I'm *never* coming back," Emerald said.

"I'd rather be a glorified tea light in Venta Bulgarum than a prop here," she agreed.

Emerald sobered. "Calla, about what you told me last night..."

She groaned and shoved him away. "Pulchradune's puckered

arse, *never* bring that up again. Unless I bring it up first. *Which I won't.*"

"I'm just saying, if you ever need someone to talk to…"

She scoffed. "You'd be the last person I'd go to, trust me."

"Calla?" A soft voice from down the hall made both of them pivot.

Allure's robes were gone, replaced with a soft tunic and loose trousers tucked into plain leather boots. She was spinning her mother's bracelet on her wrist in a way that made me think she didn't realize she was doing it.

"Al." Calla circled back to her, and Emerald followed, keeping his distance. "Where have you been? I was looking for you earlier, but nobody seemed to know where you'd gone."

"I was thinking," she said. "Now that my *Aidea* is gone, I get to make some of my own choices for once. I thought… I was thinking that maybe I should go somewhere new. I hope that isn't ungrateful, after all the brothers have done for me."

"It isn't," Calla said firmly.

"And I was wondering… if you wouldn't mind…" Allure shuffled her feet. "That is, I grew up in Kinmore, and there are too many memories here, but I would still like to…"

"Come to Venta Bulgarum with me?" Calla finished for her. "That's what you mean to ask, isn't it?"

Allure nodded. "I've always wanted to see the city."

"What's the point of having a sister if you can't stay with her when your cult falls apart?" Calla asked.

Allure's eyes widened. "Cult? Oh, Calla…"

"Only joking," Calla said, although it was quite plain she wasn't. She wrapped one arm around Allure's shoulder. "I'm not exactly living the Dregandresalian dream, but I've got a bed and connections, and I know all the good taverns."

Allure beamed at her. "Thank you. Steady, will you come with us?"

"He's not invited," Calla said at once.

Allure elbowed her in the ribs. "Don't be rude, of course he is. You're his sister, too."

"I can't," Emerald told them.

"Damn right he can't," Calla grumbled. "He's half the size of my tenement."

"He could live next door," Allure said.

I saw the wish there, shining in her eyes, just as bright as it had been all those years ago when Humble first suggested it. She wanted a place to live, with her siblings on either side, where they would share the good times and the bad ones equitably, where they would always have someone to turn to when nightmares woke them at the witching hour, where they would share meals and holy days and argue about what plays to attend.

I felt the wish, too, spilling through my link with Emerald. I wanted him to agree.

But just as his acquiescence in the past had been inevitable, so too was this refusal. "I can't, Al. I have other obligations."

Her face fell. "Maybe you can visit sometime?"

"Maybe," he agreed.

"I'd let you *visit*," Calla agreed. "But you'll have to rent your own room if you do. Come on, Al, let's get you packed up. I've got a report to write."

"A report?" Allure asked as her sister led her down the hallway.

"Long story," Calla said. "I'll tell you on the way."

Emerald went the other direction, but instead of heading straight to his room, he made his way to the prayer hall.

[You could have hugged her goodbye,] I scolded him.

[Before we leave, maybe,] he said. *[Once I know where we're headed next, and I can't change my mind.]*

[Aren't we going back to Kovin Isle?] I'd assumed the first thing he'd want to do would be to return Tincrown.

[It's complicated.]

Emerald sat down on a bench in the empty prayer hall, across from the faceless god he'd long since turned his back on.

I scanned the room, making sure that we were alone, before fluttering up out of his collar and transforming back from an innocuous little beetle to a slightly less innocuous but still fairly plain little orphan child.

"What's complicated?" I asked.

"I don't want to talk to you about this," he growled. "That's like talking to an annoying little sister and myself all rolled into one."

"I would think that's what would make you *more willing* to discuss it with me." I folded my legs up under me, shifting closer to him on the bench. "Because either way, I'm going to make fun of you, and I'll still love you when it's over."

Emerald snorted as he stared up at the statue of Guise the Unifier. The late afternoon sunlight filtering through the windows, drenching it in gold, adding to the air of holiness that surrounded it.

It was a large statue, to be sure, but there was no beauty in it.

"All my life," he murmured, "they told me that I was the problem. That there was danger in being myself, Crim." He swallowed hard, and the knot in his throat bobbed. "And I *believed* them. Because of my father. Like my blood was tainted with what he *was* and what he *did*, and I would be the same. I hated that. I hated *me*."

"Em—"

"Let me finish." He dashed the back of his hand across one cheek, almost angrily. "I hated the story they told me so much that it almost killed me. I didn't want to *exist*. And I ended up drawn to the wrong sorts of people, people I could never be *with*, but who I wanted to be."

I smiled without meaning to. "Like Coirpre?"

Emerald choked on a laugh. "Like Coirpre. And then I met..." He stopped to draw another deep breath. "I met *him*. Tincrown. I never wanted to be him, Crim, because then I wouldn't have gotten to be *with* him, and that would have been a damn shame. Not just because of how I feel about him, but because I loved who I was when I was with him. For the first time in my life, I didn't want to be anyone else." He held out his hands so that the sleeves of his shirt pulled down, revealing the first of those pin-straight scars. "For the first time in my life, I was happy to be the Emerald Flame."

I reached out to touch him, and stopped just shy of doing so. "I didn't get to see that part of you. The happy part. You sent me away for all of that."

He let out a pained noise and turned to me. "I'm sorry."

I shook my head, and a lock of my scarlet hair tumbled over my shoulder. "I know why you did it. I just... I wish I'd gotten to be there, so that I could have been part of it, too. But I don't see how I could have been, all things considered. Go on, I didn't mean to interrupt."

His lips pressed into a taut line as he lifted his eyes to the statue again. "Everything that I was told growing up made me afraid of myself. The story they told me back then nearly killed me. The person I am with him is the person I want to be."

I pulled away and twisted my hands together in my lap. "I realize that this is a bit ironic, coming from me, but I don't like the idea of you needing someone else to define you, or... or *change* you."

The sorrowful expression lifted, and a bemused smile took its place. "That's what I'm trying to tell you. He didn't change me. He never tried to change anything about me. Everyone here, even Brother Harmony, told me that affection comes with *conditions*, and that I had to kill off parts of myself to be worthy of it, until I believed that it was impossible to earn anything more than their indifference. Tincrown never asked me to change. Never once." He leaned back against the stone wall behind us and let his eyes flutter closed. "But we can't go back yet. For one thing, the Conjury will be keeping an eye on me now. For another, I want to find a way to keep my promise to you, to help you get free of me. And when that's done, I want to go back to Kovin Isle and find a way to stay."

I sat back, too. "Really? You mean it? The part about helping me, I mean."

"I'm hardly going to chain you to me," he said. "And I'm not saying that you couldn't come, too, but... you wouldn't *have* to." His nose wrinkled. "Of course, if he won't have me back, I'll be on my own then, but I think I could manage that now."

I rolled my eyes extravagantly. "Idiot."

Emerald shot me a quelling look. "I was in Dyrne for six months. He has no idea if I'll come back. It's a reasonable concern."

"Do you really need a reminder?" I asked. "Hold out your hand."

He did as I asked, and I lowered my hand to his again, taking special care not to intrude on his thoughts. Instead, I let all the feelings that Tincrown had given me on our last day in Dyrne spill through me.

"You told me to remind you how he feels about you, if you ever forgot," I said. "Well, here it is. I don't think there's any reason for you to worry."

His hand twitched beneath my illusory palm. "Fair enough. But we can't go just yet, anyway. The Conjury has their eyes on me now, so I might as well play the good dog for a bit. Fetch when they say fetch, bark when they say bark, and all that. Besides, if we're going to find a way to free you, we might as well stay in Kinmore. There are masses of *Aidea*-users here, and people come and go through the port all the time. It's a good place to start. Plus, this way we can make sure that everything settles down at the Brotherhood. And if Reticent comes back, we'll be here to intercept him."

"Hm," I said, which he could take as an agreement if he pleased. "Very well."

Emerald pulled his hands away and got to his feet. "We should get packed up, too."

I didn't have anything to pack, but I hadn't yet told the other children that I would be leaving. I wasn't looking forward to telling Svelte that I would leave. If we were going to stay in Kinmore, perhaps I could visit.

Or perhaps...

"Emerald?" I asked.

He glanced down at me.

"If we're going to stick around a while, we'll need someplace to stay," I said. "Maybe the Lute and Goose?"

"Might as well," Emerald agreed. "I'm sure Yerik will be happy to have us. Oh, dear. What's that face?"

"This face?" I pointed to my nose and batted my eyes innocently. "It's my normal one."

"You're *scheming*," he accused.

"Only a little." I dropped my hand. "This place, the Brotherhood. It's an orphanage, right? The children are only here until they age out, or are adopted?"

"Hardly anyone gets adopted," Emerald told me. "Most of them get sent to work for the Conjury."

"But someone could adopt them, if they wanted to?" I pressed.

Emerald saw where I was going. "No," he said. "Absolutely not. We're investigators, Crimson. We live on the road. We're *not* taking in three strays. We're not. Stop pouting. I don't care how many times you ask, the answer's still going to be no."

His words were firm as stone, but his heart had longed for a family his whole life, and it was saying something else entirely.

CHAPTER

TWENTY-SEVEN

Commander Finch looked up from Emerald's handwritten report.

"So let me make sure that I *fully* understand this," she growled. "You discovered an enchanted artifact at the Brotherhood that was being used to nullify people's *Aidea*. And you destroyed it?"

"Not on purpose," Emerald told her. He sat back in the chair. "The Brotherhood was dosing its followers with sand from Tide Island that was still generating Aidea Nulda. In our attempts to recover their stash as proof, it was damaged."

Finch's feline brows rose. "How did they manage to keep it from degrading in transit? Small particles like that don't travel well."

Emerald shook his head. "Enchanted box," he said.

[That's not going to be good enough for her,] I thought.

Finch squinted at Emerald. I had the impression that the two of them were engaged in a stare-down, and that whoever looked away first would lose.

[I think she'll accept that answer,] Emerald replied.

To my surprise, his theory proved correct when the Commander sat back. "Eating sand? Gods, what a miserable notion." Finch rested her chin on her fist as she eyed the report once more. "I

292

suppose they thought it was proof that their god was helping them?"

Emerald nodded.

Finch pushed the report aside. "Well, if the faithful want to eat sand, let them eat sand. Nothing illegal about that. We'll see if any of their powers come back with time. The Conjury tried that at one point, but once the sand passed through their system, as it were, their powers returned."

It shouldn't have surprised me that the Conjury would already have thought up that particular punishment.

The leonhite commander found it easy to dismiss Guise's hand in the matter, but ever since Harmony theorized that Reticent's death had a hand in my creation, I'd been turning the matter over and over in my mind. I believed in the Middling Godlet, Emerald believed in Aster, and we had tangible proof of the Crone. If I believed in one god, why shouldn't I believe in all of them? Perhaps Visage had been right, and Reticent was burned up as a punishment from the Unifier. Or perhaps Guise had been the one to guide Allure to the long-hidden reliquary. No one could tell me how she'd come to find it again. Might that have been Guise's doing?

One thing was clear to me: just because a god may or may not exist didn't mean that I was obligated to revere him. I would stick with the Middling Godlet, thank you very much. Guise and the Brotherhood deserved one another.

"I take it you'll be leaving Kinmore now?" Finch asked.

"Nah." Emerald sat back and crossed his arms over his belly. "We've decided to stick around. I have a few leads on some private jobs in the area that pay better than my Conjury salary."

"And yet you keep drawing Conjury salary even when it takes us months to track you down," Finch said drily.

Emerald's green eyes flicked toward me. "I can only be one place at a time," he said.

I had resumed my usual appearance as Simon for this interview. Now that I was able to shift my shape a little more freely, I'd begun dressing a bit more conventionally again. I still looked forward to experimenting with my appearance in the future, but doing so at that moment, when so many people had already worked out what I was, did not seem prudent. Besides, ever since I'd taken in the shadow-beast, I hadn't been in the mood to celebrate.

Finch drummed her clawed fingers on the desk. "Will we be seeing more of you while you're in town, then?"

"If you have work for me," Emerald said.

"I'm sure I can think of something. Where can I reach you?"

"The Lute and Goose," he told her. "Just outside of town."

"Leave the address with the secretary. I could use a little more support around here. You'll be hearing from me, Emerald Flame."

And just like that, our interview was concluded, and Finch moved on with her day. Emerald and I were left to show ourselves out.

"Do you really have leads on a case?" I asked as we made our way through the village on the edge of Kinmore.

"There's always work to be done," Emerald assured me, shuffling sideways to avoid stepping on a small flock of errant hens that had meandered into the road. "You can't begin to imagine the sort of trouble rich people get themselves into on the mainland."

I could, in fact, begin to imagine. Marsha of Midtown had learned how to manage a criminal underbelly during her time in this city. Kovin Isle was small and remote, and we'd uncovered all sorts of clandestine goings-on in our time there.

"And what about breaking my tether?" I asked. Emerald had expressed interest in getting me a body of my own, and I had yet to admit that I was of two minds on that front. When it came to my independence, however, my desires were clear cut.

"There's loads of magic to be learned in Kinmore, too," he said. "And if we can't learn anything here, I have a few contacts in other cities."

I wasn't looking forward to trying out another mystery ritual, but I promised myself that anything we attempted this time would be tried and tested before we made a go of it ourselves.

The Lute and Goose was mostly empty at that early hour. Yerik had already put his three temporary residents to work. Svelte was wiping down the counter beneath the smiling portrait of Coirpre, Blare was sweeping, and Quell stood beneath the largest table with a scraper clutched in one hand.

"What is this?" he asked, jabbing one finger into a tacky substance jammed against the wood.

"Sapgum," Yerik said without bothering to check. "There's a lot of it, isn't there?"

Quell wrinkled his nose and yanked his hand away. "This was in someone's *mouth*?"

Svelte looked up from her work and bounced on her toes when she saw us. "Vagabond's back!" she cried.

It was strange, being with my siblings while also looking a great deal older than them. I had been worried about being Simon or Simone in front of them, worried that it might shape their perception of me, but all three of them had taken it in stride. To them, I was still Vagabond, and I was more than content with that.

"How did it go?" Yerik asked.

Did you tell the Conjury representative about us? Blare signed.

"It went well." Emerald signed back as he spoke. "And no, I didn't tell them. No point in that. It's not like they'll come after you to conscript you, and technically speaking, I'm your legal guardian, at least for the time being."

I wasn't sure what Emerald had said to Brother Harmony in order to convince him of this arrangement, but given the upheaval at the Brotherhood, it was certainly in the children's best interest. The flock of the faithful hadn't been thrilled to learn that Guise's so-called mouthpiece was no longer taking away peoples' *Aidea*, and the once-worshipful encampment had taken on the feel of a siege. Anti-*Aidea* sentiment ran high there, and Brother Modest seemed to suspect that Harmony had a hand in Allure's "retirement."

"For the time being?" Svelte asked. "You're not going to send us back, are you?"

Emerald snorted. "Hardly. We'll find places for you. Until then, Yerik has extended his hospitality to us."

Yerik nodded. "Speaking of, we've got a little time before people turn up for lunch. I thought we could all eat together before things got hectic."

Blare sighed contentedly. *Yerik's food is so much better than what they served in the dining hall.*

"Plus, he doesn't mind when we eat until we're full," Svelte added.

"Indeed, I take it as the highest compliment." Yerik ushered them all to the large table just as Quell emerged from beneath it. "Wash your hands, and I'll bring everything out."

The children hurried off to the kitchen to wash up, and Emerald took a seat. Yerik grinned at me. "Will you be joining us, Crimson Smoke?"

I shook my head. "I'm not hungry. Besides, I have something I need to do."

Emerald arched an eyebrow at me. *[Keeping secrets now, are you?]* he asked.

Truly, he had no idea.

I left them to their meal and withdrew up the stairs, to the room that Emerald and I shared. The children had their own room next door.

There was no one to perform for on the second-story landing, so I simply slid through the door, sat down in the faded brocade-patterned armchair in the corner of the room, and closed my eyes.

The crack in the ceiling of the mind-cottage was still mended, much to my relief. I sat down on the chair Emerald had once summoned there and peered around the room. The walls held firm.

"Are you still in there?" I asked.

For a few seconds, there was only silence. Then the growling began, deep and low, so loud that the wall shuddered beneath my palms.

[I am here,] the shadow told me. *[I am here, and I am waiting, and the moment you forget to cage me, I will make you pay for what you've done.]*

I squeezed my eyes shut. So far, Emerald had given no indication that he could hear the shadow-beast, but it was still there. My burden to carry. My curse. If I let it out, it would try to hurt the people I loved. If I kept it in, I was sure that I would be driven to the brink of madness by its presence.

"That won't happen," I told it. "You're staying right where you are."

[For now, Crimson Smoke. For now. I will walk where you walk, see what you see. And one day, the walls won't hold me.]

I pulled away from the wall. The beast needed a name—I could not share my head with a stranger. It was not Reticent any more than it was Allure, or any more than I was Emerald. It was its own thing, a living creature. I decided then that I would name it as the brothers did, not after what it already was, but in the hopes of what it might one day become.

"Until then, Innocent," I said. "I'm leaving you here. Good luck."

Innocent howled as I withdrew, returning to my chair. I sat there with the shade drawn for a long time, enjoying some small measure of peace.

I was old enough by then to know that it would not last long.

~

K.C. and I truly hope you enjoyed this Heavenfall novel. We love Crimson and Emerald as much as we hope you do.

Interested to read more in this world? Sign up for our newsletter at: rileyrookhouse.com/subscribe

We have a novella that takes place between this book and book four of the Crimson Smoke and the Emerald Flame series called the Tale of Humble Bead. Find a link to it and many other Heavenfall titles on RileyRookhouse.com

Acknowledgments

From K.C. Norton: Writing this series always means dredging up a bunch of emotional debris I'm not quite ready to look at, mudlark style. My sincere appreciation to everyone who's helped me sift through the mud in search of the good stuff.

In addition to the usual suspects, I want to give special thanks to John Andrew Quale, better known as Prince Poppycock. My appreciation, in fact, to everyone whose gender identity (or gender expression) can best be described as "Yes, And..." Especially for younger people, I know it can be hard to see what's going on in the world right now. You're not alone. We're in this together, with our powdered wigs, makeup, and 17th-century silk high-heeled shoes.

From Riley Rookhouse: I'd like to give thanks to all the usual suspects: Amy and Ami for our long bouts of plotting—I owe them so much; Diane Callahan, Story Garden's lead editor; and the Zanesville crew who inspired Heavenfall in the first place.

We have an amazing team over here at Story Garden. I couldn't ask for a more creative and reliable writer than K. C. Norton, who turned an idea I had decades ago into reality, creating characters with such depth that they have become living, breathing people in my mind. I often say that K.C. opened up an emotional vein and bled this story onto the page. You can see it in every word she crafted and every wound she exposed to make these characters more than the sum of their parts.

We're grateful for Angela Traficante's thorough copy editing. Our compliments also go out to the book cover illustrator Hannah Elizabeth who can finally add this cover to her portfolio. As well as letterer James T. Egan of Bookfly Design for his assistance on the cover.

We can't wait to share the rest of the stories in the Crimson Smoke and the Emerald Flame series. And thank you, dear reader, for reading until the very last line.